Silk & Steel:
A Queer Speculative
Adventure Anthology

Edited by Janine A. Southard

Produced by Jennifer Mace, Janine A. Southard,
and Django Wexler

Silk & Steel: A Queer Speculative Adventure Anthology

Published November 2020 by Cantina Publishing.

Cover Art by Alexis Moore
Cover Design by James, GoOnWrite.com
Copy Edited by Adrienne Smith
Interior Art by Kerin Cunningham

ebook ISBN: 978-1-63327-025-1
Print ISBN: 978-1-63327-026-8

ASIN: B088C49VMD

Contents

Editor's Introduction

You never know how you'll get involved with a book project. For me, it was a rare, sunny Seattle day when Django Wexler (an author with a story in this volume and who contributed to another anthology of mine years ago) asked for one of those "brain picking" meetings.

You know the kind—where you're familiar with something the other person wishes they were an expert in, and after they've gotten all your knowledge, they'll go their own way. Well, I met with Django, who introduced me to Jennifer "Macey" Mace (an author and Hugo-nominated podcaster who also has a story in this volume). He explained that Macey had a brilliant anthology idea and a bunch of authors already signed up, but knew nothing about funding, or editing, or any of those time-consuming production things.

I happily explained all that I could... and then found myself signed up to actually *do* them all. This wasn't a "brain pick" so much as a stealth job interview!

Of course, I was thrilled to be involved because Macey's idea truly was brilliant. It was also another perfect example of how people fall into things. You see, she'd re-posted a beautiful piece of art (by digital artist Al Norton) on Twitter with a wistful caption about how she'd love to read (and write!) a story that matched it.

Other authors jumped on her post like iron filings on a magnet. "I'd write that!", they chorused. "Please let me be in your anthology!", they begged.

And the readers, too, emerged, writing about how they wanted to read all these stories. Suddenly, Macey had an anthology on her hands—full of authors, with a built-in audience, and dear to her heart—and no way to move forward.

Well, Macey, I hope I've done your vision justice with this volume of stories.

That original image (not reprinted here for obvious legal reasons) had a princess and a swordswoman facing danger. It was full of adventure and romantic potential, and elegantly captured two particular styles of femininity—the high femme and the weapon wielder.

Those styles have been prevalent through cultures and literatures for eons, of course. We can list off the femme archetype easily—princess, courtesan, "squishy" magic user, dainty musician, scholar, fashion editor. For the sword wielder, we quickly think of pirate queens, Amazons, and hiking expedition leaders.

While men traditionally take the warrior roles in media, they're not the only option, and this iconic artwork only made that clearer. Almost seventy years after the first lesbian pulp novel (*Spring Fire*, 1952), there's still space for new adventurous ladies who love other ladies.

Of course, this being a Django-Janine-Macey project (in alphabetical order, not by greatness), it had to be speculative, as well. Every story here has an element of science fiction or fantasy, in addition to adventure and romance.

Herein you will find a historical wonder tale of magical encounters, a space opera of aliens and wars, a modern quarantine race (you knew there had to be *one* quarantine story in a 2020 anthology), and everything in between. Our heroines are bodyguards and duelists, scholars and princesses, cis and trans, and exceedingly loveable.

Because when it comes to stories of daring and romance, love—its emotional resonance—really is all you need.

Janine A. Southard
19 June 2020
Seattle, WA

Introduction from the Woman Who Started It All

There are a few familiar ways to be a strong female character in science fiction and fantasy.

You can be a Xena or a Buffy or, more recently, an Arya or a Rey—a warrior who fights evil with laser swords or wooden stakes or daggers. Or you can follow the model of Chrisjen Avasarala, and turn to words, forward planning, and a deadly eye for the intricacies of societal maneuvering to save the day.

But sometimes, you don't want to choose. Sometimes, as a reader, you want both.

In July 2019, artist Al Norton posted a digital painting of two characters from Ryohgo Narita's *Baccano!* light novels. A young lady in military epaulettes holds another girl in a pink gown prisoner, sword placed intimately across her throat. They're staring into each other's eyes—one skittish, the other smug. "#wlw" read the caption—women loving women.

It lit a spark.

Now here we are, more than a year later. In many ways, the world is a different place. But as a queer woman, I maintain that there is something vital and triumphant in bringing an anthology like this—one that celebrates the diverse ways to be a strong, queer woman and still fight for what is right—into being.

It is not frivolous to take joy in being queer, in loving who we love. There is no one right way to be strong. In many ways, queer joy is a transgression, even today. Prominent creators think nothing of spouting transphobic views in public; Villanelle and Anne Lister may front popular television series, but mainstream comic book movies such as *Wonder Woman* still determinedly erase their characters' canonical bisexuality. Fourteen years after Tara Maclay's violent death as a queer woman on Buffy, CW's *The 100* merrily killed off its main character's love interest Lexa shortly after a reconciliation, in an eerie echo of Whedon's storyline.

The message is hard not to absorb: we are not safe. We, queer women, are at best distractions for the heroine, and at worst... well. At worst, we are the evil that tempts innocent mermaid girls into giving up their legs. We are the corruption.

I refuse to allow that message to take root in my heart. The only way to fight such stories is with more stories— different stories, from different perspectives, showing myriad ways to be women, and incandescent, and triumphant, and alive.

Inside these pages, you will find tales of humor and tales of romance, stories of smugglers and stories of dancers—you will find women wielding swords and magic and books and nothing but the power of their voice.

Above all, we hope to leave you with a joyful celebration that goes beyond the clichés of what it means to be strong while female, and while queer. Stories that allow those who choose not to wield weapons to be just as powerful, just as respected, as those who do.

Sometimes, the grumpy one can be soft for the sunshine one—sometimes, the warrior falls for the gentlewoman. And we think that's wonderful.

Jennifer Mace
7 August 2020
Seattle, WA

SILK AND STEEL

Margo Lai's Guide
to Dueling Unprepared
by Alison Tam

Margo Lai woke to the unpleasant news that she was engaged to fight a wizard's duel for Miss Philippa Sastrowardoyo's hand.

Sometime between the hours of eight o'clock and noon, when Margo and all other right-thinking individuals had been asleep, the letter of challenge made its way through the humid streets of Oum and onto the pile of correspondence next to Margo's breakfast plate, assaulting her with its accusatory gilt script before she could even finish her morning jook. It took a moment for her brain to remember how to read English, too, instead of just Chinese, but once she got the language bit sorted she almost ripped the paper in her dawning horror.

There were three problems with the letter. The first was that she didn't recognize the name of the man she was supposed to be fighting, and didn't remember anything about the challenge. The second was that she was not and had never been romantically involved with Miss Sastrowardoyo. The third, and perhaps the most important, was that she was not a wizard.

Margo barely even remembered to sling her sword over her hip as she rushed out of the house, tugging her coat on over her nightgown and clutching the letter in one shaking hand. It was a fine day, and too cursedly bright. The attempt to move into a light jog sent Margo's insides reeling, and so her long walk to Miss Sastrowardoyo's house was conducted in a sullen, seething trudge.

She took the spare key from the little hollow in the persimmon tree, stomped right up to Miss Sastrowardoyo's boudoir, and slammed the door open, brandishing the letter.

"Pippa! Pips! What in the seven depths of hell is this supposed to be?"

There was no response, then a faint groan came from a lump on the settee. Upon closer inspection, Margo realized that the lump was in fact the lady herself, hidden under a tangled mound of blankets.

"Oh, please not so loud, Madge," said the lump in a thin, reedy voice. There was a damp towel over her eyes, her hand pressed to her forehead in the very picture of elegant distress. Margo ruthlessly snatched the towel away and brandished the letter again with renewed force.

Groaning in protest, the lump opened her eyes. The beauty of Miss Philippa Sastrowardoyo, known to most as Pippa and only to Margo as Pips, was in Margo's opinion marred only slightly by the grease and grime from the previous night, which had still not been washed from Pippa's deep brown skin. Even her squinting against the daylight only drew attention to the long sweep of eyelashes against her soot-dark eyes, the endearing little furrow between her brows.

"I'm very angry at you," Margo said, as much to remind herself as anything else. "I went along with all of your wretched schemes all throughout primary school… And secondary school, and I'll admit I have been very cooperative so far throughout university, but now you've finally gone too far! I'm done with it, Pips! I'm at the very crust-end of my patience! What in the devil's toes have you gotten me into this time?"

"I think you got yourself into this one, actually," said Pippa.

Margo felt the blaze of her righteous anger crumble into a very sheepish ash. "Did I?"

"Oh, yes. You shook your sword at this, er… Mr. Frakes, told him you'd face him in any kind of duel he liked, and then when you tried to slap his face with a glove, you sort of…"

Pippa couldn't speak. She was making little snorting sounds, a *hh-hh-hh* she barely attempted to muffle, and though she tried to keep her face serene, she couldn't hide the way the corners of her lips kept twitching upwards.

"It's not funny," Margo protested.

"You tripped and f-fell face-first into the duck pond!"

It was too late. Pippa collapsed into giggles, and wherever Pippa went, it was hard for Margo not to follow. She was beginning to see the humor in it, as much as she didn't want to, the story as Pippa would inevitably tell it unspooling itself in her mind. Pippa would brandish a knife in place of Margo's sword, relive Margo's fall into the pond complete with the splash of her tripping into three feet of water and the startled quacks of the ducks.

"Maybe it is a little bit funny," Margo conceded, "but it won't be once that Frakes fellow burns me to a crisp with a single snap of his fingers. I could die, Pips. Who'll grease the doorsteps of your enemies with you then?"

"Don't be dramatic, Madge," said Pippa, brushing her (perfect, luscious, admittedly slightly matted from sleep) hair back from her forehead. "Have you forgotten that your best friend's father is a legal genius? Papa's gotten his clients out of worse than a duel. He'll help us, and this'll all be nothing more than a funny story we'll tell over tea next Tuesday."

The elder Sastrowardoyo's laughter was neither as charming nor as infectious as his daughter's. Margo stood stone-faced in his study as he struggled to his feet, still wheezing with laughter, to give her a hearty slap on the back.

Usually, it was quite nice that Mr. Sastrowardoyo treated Margo very much like one of the family. He was forever telling her stories about the wild world of taxation law and ruffling her hair, and there was always an extra plate set for her at dinnertime, should she choose to drop in. Margo had the run of the house as she pleased, could rifle through the pantry and let herself in through the side door in the dead of night. Today, however, Margo heartily wished that he'd show a little more consideration towards society's rules of polite communication for those not technically kin.

"Oh, I could help you, Madge, I absolutely could. It would be very easy for me."

He paused theatrically, his beard waggling on his chin. Pippa refused to take the bait, glaring up at her father with more dignity than could usually be summoned by someone whose breath still smelt like stale wine and last night's sausage rolls. Margo was not so strong.

"But?"

"But I will not, because I would very much like to see you attempt to fight a wizard. Did you know that Mr. Frakes is one of the most accomplished magicians of our decade?"

Mr. Sastrowardoyo's dramatic, courtroom-trained manner was not dimmed one bit by his disapproving audience of two. He had the precise, inventive diction of someone who had learned all his English from books, and the waver of his accent only grew stronger with emotion. He stabbed the air with a finger, raised his voice to its signature boom.

"When a sailor cut the queue for lemon ices in front of him, he spelled his name in cursed boils upon their forehead. When the Sage of Seven Forests became a wolf to snap him up in her jaws, he made himself into a mosquito and stung her till she cried forfeit! He's the reason Josiah Lim spent three months as a stoat, and in his last duel, he—"

"Papa! You're making Margo sick!"

"I'm all right," Margo managed, though it felt a little like the room was spinning around her. Chastened, Mr. Sastrowardoyo patted her on the shoulder with considerably less force than before, and Pippa helped her into the velvet-upholstered armchair her father kept for only the most important guests.

"Don't fret. Legally, he can't inflict any permanent damage," said Mr. Sastrowardoyo.

"My parents are both cultivators. They can fly, and I can barely even hop sideways! Mr. Frakes is going to humiliate my whole family, and, worse, I'm going to be a laughingstock! I think that's rather permanent enough!"

Margo put her head in her hands, hunched over in absolute misery and despair. Pippa braced protectively over her and began to rub her back a little, which only further cemented Margo's determination to never cheer up.

"If it's that bad, I'm surprised the two of you haven't used the easiest way out yet. Since you're dueling for Pippa's hand, all it would take is for her to claim a prior attachment and render the challenge moot. And since she already—"

"No!"

Pippa's cry of protest was loud enough that Margo was certain it could be heard on the street, but by the time she looked up Pippa had already regained her usual unruffled poise, as prim and dainty as a rose.

"I don't have any current romantic attachments, thank you," she said. "Now, if you'll excuse us, Papa..." Pippa tugged an unresisting Margo away. They ensconced themselves back in her bedroom, where Pippa had attached a rug to the window with clothespins to block out the light.

"Are you sure you don't have anyone?" asked Margo tentatively, fixing her eyes on the wall so she wouldn't have to see Pippa's expression, whatever it was. "Not even a flirtation, or a one-sided yearning, or a tiny little pash? I know you said as much, but your father was there, and you've always been damned secretive about your paramours..."

"There's no one," Pippa said, her mouth pressed into a thin line. She drew a blanket back over herself, and the slight cotton barrier felt as impregnable as the old city's siege walls.

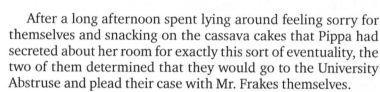

After a long afternoon spent lying around feeling sorry for themselves and snacking on the cassava cakes that Pippa had secreted about her room for exactly this sort of eventuality, the two of them determined that they would go to the University Abstruse and plead their case with Mr. Frakes themselves.

Ordinarily, one had to answer three riddles, navigate a maze of mirrors, and whisper their deepest secret into the trunk of an elephant to access the university, but Pippa and Margo entered through the back way with the launderers instead. They did have to do an arcane ritual for Mr. Frakes's room number, but Margo had begged the instructions and a stick of camphor off her second brother years ago for a prank.

"Do you think we did it right?" Pippa asked, tilting one of the glowing glyphs upside down to get a better look. "Only it doesn't seem—"

A plume of smoke erupted from the center of the room, little fizzing sparks dancing in spirals through the air. A cloak of the darkest shadow blotted out the fading light of sunset, and guttural, demonic laughter emanated from the floor. When it all cleared, Margo saw a blond man lounging on a floating cushion. His sumptuous wizard's robes, the exact shade and texture of a waterfall, were long enough to brush the floor.

"Hullo," he said. "I suppose you're here about the duel."

"Yes! I wanted to explain that it was all a massive misunderstanding, and there's no need for a duel at all. Very funny, really. You see, the thing is... the reason why... It's..."

They'd planned a script for Margo to say in advance, but faced with a man who was even now spinning little balls of lightning in between his hands, all their prepared words rushed out of Margo's mind like sand through a sieve. She wouldn't have been surprised if Mr. Frakes had already cursed her into a state of magical panic, but unfortunately the sensation was familiar enough for her to realize that the blank nothing in her mind was entirely her own.

"You don't want to marry Pippa," Margo said, the words emerging fully formed onto her tongue with little to no input from the conscious centers of her mind. "And that's because... It's because she's disgusting."

"Madge!"

"I find that quite hard to believe," said Mr. Frakes, giving Pippa what Margo supposed was his version of a charming smile. Margo glanced over at Pippa, who had cleaned up for their visit and was looking quite neat and fresh in her teal-green day gown. This was going to be a more difficult argument than she'd thought.

Margo had forgotten that when other people looked at Pippa, all they saw was a pretty, graceful young lady with a charming smile and elegantly turned-out ankles. They hadn't seen, like Margo had, Pippa creeping to the kitchens in the middle of the night to pour jam down her throat straight from the jar. If they knew her as Margo did, they'd know that Pippa was not a thing to be won. She could only be followed, and listened to, and sometimes, very occasionally, coaxed.

"She leaves all her clothes on the ground," Margo blurted. "They're everywhere. And if she can't tell if something's from the dirty or clean pile, she'll just wear it again anyway."

"I do not!" Pippa yelped, completely undermining Margo's argument. Margo gave her a significant look, which Pippa somehow failed to psychically understand, then gave up and dragged her off to the side for a whispered conference.

"I'm trying to keep him from wanting to duel me, if you haven't noticed!"

Pippa crossed her eyes at her. Margo frowned back. Then, as unstoppable and ominous as an oncoming train, a smile of pure mischief crossed Pippa's face. Margo had seen that look before, usually immediately preceding ideas that had gotten them both banned from establishments of ill repute all across the city. She reached out, but it was too late. Pippa, the very picture of demure elegance, had already glided back to Mr. Frakes.

"My friend has neglected to mention the most important reason you ought to cancel the duel, which is that it would be beneath you. You see, Margo doesn't have any magic at all, and what's more, she's very stupid."

"Am not!"

"She may look strong, but all that muscular development has hindered the growth of her brain. Did you know she once asked me if an oligarchy was a type of cheese?"

Pippa glanced at Margo with that little sally, her smug smirk calling to mind a very specific and lurid fantasy of Margo tackling her bodily onto the carpet, and wiping that taunting smile off her face by, er. Wrestling, Margo supposed. At that point the fantasy dissolved into hazy images that Margo did not like to dwell on in public.

"Yes, well, you drink your coffee by pouring it into the sugar bowl until it becomes a sort of brownish sludge, which is a far more compelling reason—"

"What's more, Margo is a coward, as evidenced by her debilitating fear of ballerinas—"

"The way they move is legitimately disconcerting! And what about your—you pranked me last month by putting crushed chilies in my open mouth as I slept, and I ought to warn Mr. Frakes that that's what he could be waking up to every morning!"

"Well, you deserved that one, especially after—"

Abruptly, Pippa fell silent, her hands flying to her throat in alarm. When Margo tried to ask her what was wrong, she found herself unable to speak, either. As one, they turned towards Mr. Frakes lying indolently upon his cushion, his lips crackling with the telltale sparks of a curse.

"One by one, please," he drawled, letting one of his little lightning bolts strike the ceiling. Even though it came nowhere near her, Margo couldn't help but flinch. He pointed at Pippa first.

"While I may have indulged in certain youthful japes, I must assure you that I am quite respectable, and what's more, Margo—"

Mr. Frakes silenced her with a gesture. Apparently, it was Margo's turn to speak.

"I'm not a coward," Margo said. "And as a matter of fact, my family's cultivation is stronger than any sort of Western mystical mumbling, so I'll thank you not to underestimate—"

"Well, then," said Mr. Frakes, the hem of his robe beginning to evaporate into mist. "If Miss Sastrowardoyo is a lady and Miss Lai is a worthy opponent, then I don't see either of your objections. Besides, I like to duel."

With alarm, Margo realized that his legs had started to fade as well, and the cushion was quick to follow. Before either of them could protest, his chest disappeared, then his head, then finally his stupid floppy hair.

"I hate wizards," Pippa said, and Margo could only heartily concur.

The university had rearranged itself around them so that they had to take the long way back out. Margo and Pippa walked through hallways that had them floating up to the ceilings if they stepped on the wrong floor tile and past a bubbling moat of greenish, sour-smelling slime. Pippa was unusually quiet throughout the walk. The only sound she made was the whisper of her dress against the floor.

"You don't really see me that way, right?" she asked suddenly. "Disgusting, I mean. I know all those things you said were true, but—"

"Uh," said Margo. In front of her, right there on the path, was a jeweled ring. Something in the facet of the gem mesmerized her, a promise of love and glory insinuating itself into her mind. Margo kicked it into the moat.

"A little bit, maybe? I do think the way you take your coffee is utterly nauseating, but"—and here she hastened to stave off Pippa's offense, or worse, her hurt—"I like that part of you. It might be my favorite. Don't get me wrong, I'm dead impressed by how good you are with words and clothes and things, but I wouldn't like you half as much as I do if you were Pippa the Perfect all the time."

The next corridor had eschewed a floor entirely in favor of a path made of massive, floating stones. Pippa skipped merrily onto the first and offered a gallant hand to Margo to help her over. Even after they were safely on the path, she didn't let go.

"I like who I am with you," she said, squeezing Margo's hand. "It's nice acting perfect, sometimes, or at least it's nice knowing that I can be convincing enough, but I'd much rather have fun."

"That's why we're best friends, isn't it?" said Margo. She squeezed back. Pippa's hand was only very slightly larger than hers, close enough in size that they could press them fingertip to fingertip, palm to palm. "Though if you tell me that your favorite thing about me is that I'm so stupid, I'm going to salt your tea."

The next morning, Pippa arrived at Margo's house with a little basket of mangosteens for her parents and a plan.

"We're going to have to fight Mr. Frakes on his own level," she said, bouncing with unrestrained energy. "Magic runs in your family. Your father has one of the best scroll collections outside of Suzhou. I don't know why we hadn't thought of this before."

"Possibly because I've never been able to understand my father's magic. It's all so…" Margo waved her hand in the air in a sort of whooshy way. Her father had tried several times to impart the family knowledge to her, but the lessons were always so philosophical, and Margo never understood the convoluted metaphors.

"Oh, we're not going to make you the magician," said Pippa. She paused, striking a subtle yet dramatic pose on

Margo's doorjamb. Just like her father sometimes, with his same love of playing to an audience.

"Get on with it!"

"I've been reading through the Duelists' Code, and found quite the loophole," said Pippa. "You might not be able to use magic at all, but I can, and the arena will let me. All we need is to convince your father to teach me magic."

It fell upon Margo to carry out the delicate task of asking her father for the favor without letting slip any of the other aspects of the situation and landing herself in a heap of trouble, but it all seemed to go well.

"Of course I will," he said, his ink-stained hands ponderously stroking his scholar's beard. "These spells are secret only to our household, but Pippa, my dear, I have always eagerly awaited the day my daughter invited you to join our family."

The blood in Margo's veins turned to ice. She went still, like a rabbit feeling the gaze of the fox. She couldn't look at Pippa. No, she had to. No, she couldn't!

"Don't say that," she managed, barely remembering to switch into Chinese so the conversation couldn't embarrass her any further. "I haven't. We aren't!"

"A man of integrity must always speak the truth," said her father, which was honestly so typical.

"I'm going to go train," Margo said, in English this time, and avoided Pippa's gaze the entire way out. She didn't want to know if Pippa was embarrassed, or disgusted, or worse, half-laughing at her with the glint in her eyes that usually seemed so inviting. What she did want was to go hit things with her sword.

She'd never minded Pippa laughing at her. They wouldn't have met otherwise. In primary school, the children usually grouped together based on heritage, Chinese and Malay and Anglo and Igbo. Margo had always been too shy to speak to anyone she didn't already know from her neighborhood. Then one day she was fumbling through a presentation she was entirely unprepared for, and Pippa had laughed.

At any other time, with any other two people, that would have been a humiliating incident of schoolyard bullying, but Margo had been grateful to hear something other than the sound of her own floundering voice. She saw Pippa mortified with her hands over her mouth, and wanted to make her laugh again. Her next sentence had been something about how the Tang Dynasty was named so for their groundbreaking invention of soup. By the time Teacher Liu finally forced Margo to sit back down, Pippa was clutching her stomach with laughter and Margo knew that they would be the best of friends.

It wasn't like she didn't sometimes wonder what it would be like to kiss Pippa, or occasionally imagine living together in some far-off, nebulous version of the future. She would make jokes about the way Pippa cooked breakfast and would fall asleep in a bed where Pippa's side was always heaped up with extra blankets. They'd argue about the laundry, and Margo would trade dish duty for organizing their closet as she pleased.

But if Pippa wanted that, she would've said, wouldn't she? She had never shied away from saying exactly what she wanted, not to Margo. There would've been a sign, some admiring look or casual brush of her hand. Margo spent enough of her time looking at Pippa that she ought to have noticed.

She didn't like thinking about it. Margo picked up a wooden sword and headed into the garden where the training posts were, but her mother was already there.

"There you are. Come! We never finished our lesson."

Another lesson where her mother talked at her with allusions to classical Chinese literature. It sounded only slightly better than thinking about Pippa, but Margo walked over and got into stance anyway. Her mother looked her over with a proud nod, as if already assuming Margo's success despite the many previous lessons' worth of evidence to the contrary.

"Feel the energy moving through your body, the way it's connected to the energy around you. Chi means breath, and the breath in your body wants to be air. Let it, like so."

Her mother leaped into the air, as if pulled upwards by invisible wire, and landed gracefully upon the rooftop. Margo tried the same, and landed gracefully in the flowerbed about a foot away.

"No, Margo! Think about the clouds, the way they drift in the air..."

There with the metaphors again, and Margo was feeling incredibly sorry for herself. She hoped Pippa was having more luck with her father. She hoped Pippa....

Pippa was watching her from the study window. If there had ever been a moment for a sign, that was it.

Margo pretended she hadn't noticed Pippa at all. She unbuttoned her outer shirt, casually, and flexed her shoulders. She had good shoulders, didn't she? She certainly spent enough time training them that she felt rather impressive, sometimes. She stretched, though she couldn't quite get the right angle to see Pippa's reaction without giving herself away, and took off running.

Halfway across the garden was almost enough. Margo leaped—*be air, be air*—and curled herself into a single weightless flip before crashing back down. Had Pippa seen? Was she looking, even now?

"Margo! Are you showing off?"

The laughter in Pippa's voice made Margo's ears turn red. She checked to see if her parents were watching and made a covert rude gesture in Pippa's general direction. What a fool she was, to have expected admiration or perhaps uncontrollable lust. All she could do was amuse Pippa, and she ought not ever hope for more.

"Aren't you supposed to be learning my ancient family spells?" she snapped.

"Already have," said Pippa, holding up a calligraphic talisman that looked much neater than Margo's usual wobbly, blotchy attempts. Margo was not feeling especially charitable, so she only grunted in reply. Pippa leaned out the window, hands resting on the sill, as pretty as a painting that had decided to come out of its frame.

"Margo? I didn't mean it that way," she said, looking rather contrite. "It was quite astounding, you know. All that raw physical skill and everything. I was very impressed."

"No, you weren't," said Margo. "You just want me to compliment you on your talisman. Which, all right, you have beautiful handwriting and it looks like the work of a natural talent."

"I didn't want to say it myself, but..." Pippa said, and turned her nose up in the air like a conceited cat. Margo laughed, and took her arm so she could haul her over the windowsill and onto the garden path.

"Come on, oh wise and powerful sage," she said. "I'll walk you home."

Margo didn't remember what they talked about on the way back. It was one of those glorious conversations where she was barely aware of what she said at all, where the words arrived into her mouth without her stopping to think. They took the long way to Pippa's house, stopping to buy aiyu jelly and roti prata and eat their spoils under the banyan at the center of Pippa's neighborhood.

"You seriously only learned a talisman that causes rainfall?" she asked. "We're in the tropics! It rains every other week!"

"I didn't know how to ask your father to learn something more dangerous," Pippa protested. "I couldn't very well tell him you were going to a duel tomorrow, could I? Though I do think the consequences wouldn't be as bad as you think. They only took your sword for a week after we got caught putting soap-suds in the school fountain."

"Yes, but I'm still feeling their guilt trip! Every time anyone says 'sacrifice' I'm right back in the dean's office, listening to their lecture."

"You suffer so much," said Pippa. "Here, have some roti."

Pippa yanked it away from Margo's hand, because of course she did, but it was still in range. Margo leaned over, stealing the roti with her teeth faster than Pippa could react, but then their faces were very close, enough for Margo to smell the hibiscus oil in her hair. Pippa let her hand fall, eyes very wide. Margo chewed.

"Why did I challenge Mr. Frakes to a duel, anyway?" she asked, mouth still half-full. "You seem to remember the night far better than I."

"He was flirting very badly," Pippa said. "Nothing too horrible, just that he'd quite like to take me shopping sometime. Something about my being too girlish to wear the clothing of an old maid. I was about to pretend that I didn't feel terribly insulted, when you went over with your hair all askew, shaking your sword. It was… It was quite gallant, actually."

They were still very close. Margo could see each individual eyelash, the pores that Pippa obsessed over in the mirror and Margo usually didn't notice. Her eyes were dark, almost fathomless, a brown only a single shade removed from black. Pippa leaned in, or Margo leaned in, or both. She couldn't tell, she didn't remember, because they were kissing and Pippa was so soft and so, so close.

For a second Margo was worried that she would not rise to the occasion. She had forgotten everything except pure instinct, and she had no way to tell if her lips were moving too slowly, or whether Pippa liked that Margo had put her hands around her waist or wanted her to move them. She was also worried that she might have gotten roti stuck to her teeth, because what if Pippa put her tongue in her mouth and then came back out again with a bit of unchewed dough?

Then Pippa tugged at the end of Margo's braid, just once and very lightly, and Margo knew that this was still her Pippa, and anything she did would make her smile. She breathed in the heady scent of hibiscus and then she was aware of barely anything at all.

Eventually, one of them had to have pulled away, because Margo was staring at Pippa unmoving in her arms. Her mind was blank again. The smell of hibiscus lingered. Was this where she was supposed to prostrate herself and confess her love like in a wuxia novel? Were they supposed to pretend they were only sharing a casual moment's touch, like in those artistic French books that Pippa liked to read? Pippa's lips were right there and Margo knew exactly how they felt. She had to speak. Anything was better than that expectant silence.

"What?" said Margo, which was exactly the worst thing to say. Pippa pulled away (no!) and wiped her mouth off with her sleeve (why!) and then she was Perfect Pippa again, but a worse version, because her smooth, unruffled mask was based on the Pippa that Margo knew.

"Just for luck," she said, "since you're so worried about Mr. Frakes turning you into a baboon tomorrow. Who knows if anyone'll kiss you then!" She laughed, a sort of tinkling, musical gurgle. It sounded extremely fake. Then she sprang up from the bench, curtsied for reasons that Margo knew not, and ran away. She didn't even take the rest of the jelly.

Margo leaned against the banyan, her mind spinning. Why had Pippa kissed her? What did it mean? What did she want from her? Where had Pippa learned how to kiss so urgently and so sweetly, and why hadn't Margo been involved?

She still had to fight a duel tomorrow. Margo picked up the aiyu jelly that Pippa had abandoned so heartlessly and began the long walk home.

She arrived at the dueling ground the next day unslept and unnerved but looking very, very sharp. She'd had to ask her older brother for help, but her bangs fell in careless, tousled waves, her braid pinned up into a crown around her head. She wore a cultivator's loose robes in the blue and silver of her family sect, her Western-style boots spit-polished to perfection.

Mr. Frakes was already waiting in the arena, his robes shining with every shade of the sunset. If she looked at them for long enough, she could see them changing as the sun stitched on his back traveled from his collar down to his ankles. It was the clothing of a man who didn't expect to break a sweat.

The umpire called them to inspect weaponry. Mr. Frakes presented him with his staff, made of a moonbeam with studded, inset circles of silver starlight. Margo handed him hers.

"That's not a wizard's staff! That's a sword you've stuck a crystal on!"

Mr. Frakes's voice was not so indolent anymore. It was fascinating how his accent changed with alarm, rougher and deeper vowels suggesting that, at one point, he might have actually held a job. He looked like he was only then realizing that the duel would be quite different from any he'd fought before.

"I think you'll find, Honored Judge, that Margo's weapon meets all the stated requirements in the Duelists' Code."

A high, sweet voice made the objection from the front row. Margo didn't have to turn around to see that it was Pippa, but she did. It was the first time she had seen Pippa look like such a frump outside the home. Her hair frizzed, and she had buttoned her dress slightly wrong so one extra buttonhole flopped awkwardly above her collar. She looked beautiful. Her eyes met Margo's like they were sharing something significant, though Margo didn't know precisely what.

The umpire called paces, and Margo spent five of the ten steps away from Mr. Frakes thinking about that look and the other five about her imminent humiliation. At the sound of the whistle, Mr. Frakes turned and immediately flung a bolt of lightning, which Margo dodged by diving onto the ground and rolling away.

He had spells aplenty, glowing glyphs and purple bolts of pure magic that he threw out faster than Margo could even inhale, but that didn't matter as long as he couldn't hit her. He called vines up from the floor to tangle around her ankles and she cut them in a single swing. The floor itself rumbled and split beneath her, but Margo jumped and skidded back onto solid ground.

She had to close the distance, and she was. He was throwing everything he could at her, but she was relentless, each dodge and duck bringing her a step closer. If she could only move forward, until she was a sword's length away....

Mr. Frakes launched an armory's worth of magical knives at waistheight, packed so close that there was nowhere for Margo to sidestep, and Margo dived underneath them and rolled, somersaulting like she and Pippa had learned together in primary school. She had perhaps a few more paces to go. She sprang up into a crouch, tensing the muscles in her calves.

Mr. Frakes smiled, and only after she had begun to leap did the floor in front of Margo burst into a wall of flame. She managed to throw herself sideways at the last second, landing awkwardly on her hip, but there were flames behind her and to the right, and they were only getting closer.

This was it. She had fought, but she had lost. Margo squeezed her eyes shut and raised her hand to forfeit, feeling a tear run down her... forehead?

She opened her eyes again. Rain was falling indoors, the storm clouds gathering in the arena's eaves, a gentle pattering rhythm against the stone floor. Her painstakingly arranged curls flopped into her eyes, and through them Margo saw Pippa standing with the talisman gleaming in her hand.

"Now, see here," said Mr. Frakes, frustration creeping into his voice. "I was just about to defeat Miss Lai! No outside interference!"

"The Duelists' Code states, in exact language, that none may cast spells upon the arena except for the parties involved," said Pippa primly. "As the person whose hand is being fought over, I am quite definitely a party involved."

The umpire consulted his rules, while Mr. Frakes muttered exasperated imprecations against interfering females and Margo lay exhausted on the floor. She watched as the umpire conferred with a colleague, then his book again.

"I'll allow it," he said. Pippa looked panicked for a second, then the mask descended and she was perfect again, as indolent and commanding as Mr. Frakes himself.

"No," she said.

"What? But you just argued—"

"I actually prepared a rather longer argument, and I'd like the chance to give it, if only to establish legal precedent," she said, very convincingly grave. She snuck a glance at Margo, though, and when their eyes met and Margo saw that familiar mischievous gleam, Margo knew. Pippa was giving her time to catch her breath.

The whole crowd, and Mr. Frakes, watched, mesmerized, as Pippa held forth upon the nature of dueling, marriage, womanhood, and magic itself. Margo eased herself upright, and slunk along the side of the arena, behind the massive stone pillars that Mr. Frakes had been so kind to raise for her. The only one who noticed her move was Mr. Sastrowardoyo, in his promised front-row seat, but he had just enough mercy in him to beam with silent glee and wave her along.

From experience, Margo knew that Pippa could speak extemporaneously for hours on end, but the umpire had none of Margo's patience. He cut her off after a minute, and Mr. Frakes sighed in relief, then gasped in alarm.

"Wait, where did she—"

Margo leapt at him, sword extended. Faced with eighty centimeters of cold steel inches from his face, Mr. Frakes defaulted to instinct and turned himself into a jaguar, then a komodo dragon, then a great white bear. Unfortunately for him, Margo's mother had taken her into the wilderness for training several times, and all those animals were susceptible to being stabbed.

"Forfeit! I forfeit!" cried the great white bear that was Mr. Frakes, Margo's swordpoint at the vulnerable underside of his belly. He reverted to his human form and raked his hair back with his hand, dropping his staff to the floor. "Damn it all to Bristol, you win! You can have Miss Philippa's hand!"

Margo felt the entire arena audience focus its attention on her, Pippa not excluded. She blushed, again. Lowered her sword. She could still hear Pippa asking her if she was showing off. She could still feel her kiss.

"Right, er," she said. "I'm giving it back to you, Pippa. I suppose."

Pippa was very silent and still for a second, then she mimed catching something and grinned, to the general laughter of the arena. Mr. Frakes picked his staff up again and leaned against it, looking harried.

"Hang on a second, so you didn't even want her hand in the first place? I don't— but why— If you're not getting anything, I still have to give you a forfeit," he said. "It's only fair, and that was the most exciting duel I've had in a year."

"You have to fund the celebration party," Margo said, feeling abruptly like she had fought a thousand duels instead of just one. "And tell me how you do your hair."

Mr. Frakes had thrown possibly the most extravagant party Margo had ever been to, but she couldn't bring herself to enjoy it. Not the dancing candy figurines on the table, or the life-size ski jump that launched partiers into a bed of soft, fluffy clouds. Even the wizards in the crowd trying to best each other at casting marvelous illusions couldn't put a smile on her face.

Pippa was enjoying herself immensely, dancing with the ten illusionary simulacrums of herself Mr. Frakes had summoned from thin air, but Margo needed nothing more than some quiet and fresh air. She left Pippa's house through the side entrance, carefully avoiding Mr. Sastrowardoyo recounting the story of her duel to some legal colleagues in the foyer, and walked towards the banyan.

She was going over the events of the past few days in her mind, and trying to think about what she could've changed to make everything go right instead. She had frozen up, like she always did, even after Pippa had given her chance upon chance. When her mind went blank she worked on instinct, and every single one of her instincts was wrong. She wanted to be someone else, someone who knew things like how people felt and what to say to them.

She didn't want to be Margo Lai anymore. Even all the— all the breath in her body wanted to be air.

She felt like she was floating already before she even leapt, and then the sky dipped down to meet her until she landed among the branches of the banyan. The city seemed so small from up there, or, well, at least the neighborhood did. She could see the lights of Pippa's house shining through the dark, multi-colored fireworks exploding from a window. She even thought she could see Pippa herself, or maybe just a corner of her scarlet gown.

The moon was large in the sky, and Margo felt that if she only leapt again she could perhaps brush her hand against its surface. Years and years of trying to learn magic, months of the same lesson from her mother, and she had finally mastered flight the... what? Thousandth time? She'd lost count.

There had been nothing special about the leap she'd made, no epiphany or perfect metaphor. All she'd had to do was try one thousand times, and then try again.

She squinted at Pippa's house and saw that it really was her, walking down the cobbled path with her practical shoes clicking against the ground. Margo shouted and waved, rustling the roots, until Pippa looked up.

"How did you get up there?"

"I finally learned how to jump," Margo said. "Like my mother's been trying to teach me. I could take you up here, if you like."

"I think I'll wait till you get some more practice in, thank you," said Pippa, face taking on an exaggeratedexpression of concern. Margo could make a joke back, fall into their practiced rhythm, and Pippa would let her. They would never have to talk about the kiss again, if she didn't want to. If there was bad news, Margo would never have to know.

"Pippa, I..."

She didn't know what to say. Her heart was pounding, blood roaring in her ears. Margo tried again.

"I think... I loo... After, everything I mean, the roti..."

She was fumbling again, trying out words and then discarding them just as quickly. Margo could hear nothing but the sound of her own voice, not even the party only two streets away. Then Pippa laughed, a small, quiet, fond sound, and Margo laughed, too.

"You can have my hand, you know," Margo said, rediscovering the ability to form sentences with each word. "In marriage, and whatnot."

"Yes!" Pippa said before Margo could even finish saying "whatnot." "I—It's been eons, you know? That's how long I've wanted you to say... Well, not that, precisely, but something. Anything. And you can't say I was the one who kept us waiting so long, because I did try. I kissed you! First!"

"But you couldn't tell me what it meant," said Margo, grinning. "So I think I should really get the credit."

"You—Come down here so I can argue with you properly!"

"Not a chance," said Margo. She rustled the roots of the banyan a little more so that they brushed against Pippa, making her shriek with laughter and shake her fist up at her.

"Come down here so I can kiss you again," Pippa said, and Margo did.

It was a perfect night. Moonlight making Pippa's brown skin gleam, faint music from the party, and a distant shout when someone knocked over a vase. The scent of gardenias, because Pippa had changed her shampoo. For a while, it felt as though they were the only two people in the world, and yet also part of the world, their hearts beatingin the same rhythm as all the lovers who had ever loved before.

Then, nestled in Margo's arms, Pippa asked:

"We're not going to get married just yet, though, right?"

"Spirits, no," said Margo, with feeling. "I think—I feel much too young. Don't you feel too young?"

"By decades," Pippa said. "Though for a while there I thought about pretending that I wanted to get married next week, just to really give you a scare."

"You're horrible," said Margo, and Pippa giggled and tugged her braid, then kissed her again. Being perfectly in love was all right, but she liked Pippa laughing at her even more.

Princess, Shieldmaiden, Witch, and Wolf
by Neon Yang

My liege is the most beautiful woman in all the land. No one knows this better than I, her shieldmaiden, who has watched over her since memory has been memory. Her beauty grows with each exchange of sunrise for sunset, and today her shining hair catches the afternoon light and she is as bright as the summer around us. Nothing compares to her: not the net of jewels dancing across the river, nor the smell of honeysuckle on the breeze. At the water's wild edge she pulls off her tunic and trousers and beckons, hair loose around her shoulders.

"Come, my dearest." She holds her hand out as she wades in, calf-deep, free of every care in the world. Light plays upon her glowing skin. "Join me."

It's a hot day, and the water is inviting, but fear grips me. We're meant to be at sword practice, except the allure of bird-song drew my liege, giggling, to the ribbon of water lacing the woods around the castle. I cling to the cotton shield of my clothes.

"I can't."

"Why not?"

The glitter of the brook gets in my eyes. "I don't want to." Then, a lie: "I have to protect you." I heft the blade fastened at my waist.

My liege is the one person I can't lie to. She sighs. "You're afraid of me seeing you."

"I'm not," I mumble, wishing my body were smaller, wishing it prickled less with heat.

"My love." She comes to me, up and out of the river. Water drips and runs down her ankles. "I won't force you if you don't want to. But you should. The water's lovely. I've seen all there is to see, anyway."

She holds my wrist for a heartbeat, then lets it go, slipping back into the water. The shape of her is breathtaking, and I watch her swim against the river's current like it's nothing. I can't be like her. I'm only good for doing what I'm told. So I watch her, one hand on my sword and one hand over my heart, which aches like a loose tooth.

Father is the one who finds us, the captain of the guard. He's livid; he and his men have spent the last hour combing the castle and its surrounds looking for us. His width takes up most of the space between two trees as he comes at me, spittle flying.

"Why, I'll be damned! Never in my life—"

I flinch at memories of his palm landing hot against my cheek. But my princess saves me, surging out of the water barefoot and bare-skinned.

"Sir Errol! The fault is mine. I demanded that we come here, and my... protector had no choice but to comply."

Father stares at her, dripping and golden, and recalibrates his composure.

"Your Highness," he chides. "It's hardly seemly for the crown prince to shirk his duties for a spot of midday swimming."

My liege wrings water from her hair. "Yet the summer's day is as beautiful as it is rare. Could you not begrudge me one childish fancy, while we are still children?"

Father frowns, but says nothing. My liege finishes dressing, still river-damp, and we head up the path that leads to the castle. Father falls in step with me, taking up the rear, and hisses all cat-like: "Did you forget, boy? Your duty is to guide your king. If you cannot steer him on the right path and away from harm, then you have failed him. Do you understand?"

I nod, even though his statement lacks logic and sense. Father needs someplace to put his anger, and since he cannot lay it upon my liege he has directed it towards me. He pinches my upper arm, twisting hard enough it will purple for a few days. As a reminder. Of my duty.

My liege has arithmancy next; the tutor is waiting in the castle depths. We break from my father's side and hurry down echoing stone corridors. The princess walks with a broad stride and fists clenched, and I know she has heard—and guessed— what Father did.

"It's nothing," I say, but her face only tightens further in displeasure.

All of a sudden she brightens and grabs my hand. "Come. There's something I want to show you."

"But your lessons—"

"I don't care about lessons."

I cannot refuse her. She pulls me to the highest parts of the castle, to its most private regions. Dodging servants, we climb stairs into airy light and slip unnoticed into the queen's chambers. My liege runs across the wide marble floors and flings a closet open.

"A merchant from over the southern seas came by yesterday. He brought Mother all these. Look!"

Inside is a riot of color and fabric. Silks and feathers and furs spill to the ground. Perfume scents the air. There are a dozen dresses packed jowl to jowl, and my liege pulls them loose one after another and tosses them upon the bed. I stroke the puffy sleeves and sequins in wonder, entranced. Embroidered dragons dance over ruby-red silks and gold threads gleam in the pistils of floral embellishments; there are delicate lace collars and fur trims so fine they are cool to the touch. I run my fingers over this field of decadence and sigh in astonishment. I had no idea such beautiful things could exist.

Laughter breaks me from my reverie; I look up from the queen's gathered treasures to find my liege wreathed in a dress of the brightest red. Despite being half-grown she already fits her mother's wardrobe, and as she twirls in the crimson confection the world slows and becomes treacly around me. I have to remember to breathe.

She notices me watching, and pushes me with a laugh. "Go on, you've got to pick one, too."

I hide my wince; my arm is still sore where Father pinched it. I pretend my liege hasn't seen my reaction and busy myself hesitating over the dresses. She tries to help.

"What about this one? Oh, the gold on that would match your eyes. How's this?"

In the end I settle on a sheer drape of peacock blue so delicate the light passes through it. Bells and gold coins dangle from its hems.

"Here, allow me—" the princess says, and then her warm hands are undressing me, trading the scratch of cotton and linen for the cool whisper of silk. She fastens the robe's dozen ribbons around my waist. "There. Wait—no." She ducks and picks my discarded sword belt from the ground. "You need this."

I put the weapon on and lean into its comforting weight. My liege glows with delight. "It's perfect for you. Come, you must see."

She takes my hand and leads me across the floor of her mother's room. The queen's mirror—taller than I am and twice as wide—shows two girls with hands clasped, flushed with excitement and gorgeously wrapped in color. I hardly recognize myself; the shieldmaiden in the mirror is an avatar of possibility, someone I could be, but am not allowed to.

"Look at us," my liege says. She twirls, and the red dress flares around her like a ring of petals. I grab her hands and we dance the way we used to as children, clumsy and stumbling. The bells on my hem sing in a dozen voices. She's laughing and I'm laughing, and the peacock silk is honey against my skin, and I feel I might float into the air at any moment. My weight means nothing, and in this unmooring I loosen my jaw and let spill careless words with a smile.

"My beloved, my liege, you are the most beautiful princess in all the land."

She shrieks, half in embarrassment, half in delight, and pushes me over onto the bed. We land in the nest of dresses, and she looms over me, golden hair spilling into my face. Breathless.

"And you are the most loyal, the most noble protector a princess could hope to have."

For long seasons we have carried longing in our chests like bird eggs, too timid to handle them, afraid of what might hatch. But this brilliant moment shines with audacity and I, emboldened by its brassiness, lean up to kiss her.

She freezes. I freeze—I've been too bold. I've crossed a line. Then I realize her terror is not directed at me, but at a more distant source. I turn.

Standing in the doorway, tall and broad and draped in furs, is her father the king.

My liege pushes off the bed—leaps away, really—but the damage is done. The king marches towards us, a column of fury. He who is the Cetus King, savior of men, uniter of the land, and vanquisher of the Blood Witch, bears down on us with all the rage he has. The world crumbles like clay, light and hope splintering into gray dust.

"Father, I—"

"That's enough." The king's anger is familiar enough to lance me through with fear. I should be jumping to my liege's defense, the way she jumped to mine earlier, but I am frozen, a coward. My liege stands square-shouldered, still fearless, as her father stares her down, twice her size, ruddy at the sorry mess around us. "You are a disgrace to your lineage," he growls. "To think that I could have raised a son like this—"

"It was only a bit of play," my liege says, defiant to the last. Thinking to lie her way out of trouble.

"Only a bit of—" The king seizes her by the collar, ruched and elaborate as a pair of lips. Something tears, a seam yielding to the roughness of his fingers. I can't stand it anymore.

"Forgive me, Your Majesty. It was my idea. My liege had nothing to do with it."

The king drops his burden and turns on me as my liege mouths my name in horror: my birth name, the name I told her never to call me.

"You," he says. "I should have known."

I steel myself for a blow that never comes. Someone like me isn't worth the king's effort to punish.

"Of course I should have known," he says. "A degenerate like you... the nature of your birth... Of course you would only poison my son with your filth. But I gave you a chance. More chances than you deserved. My son loved you. You were his best friend. I was a fool. That foolishness will now be rectified."

"Father, please," my liege says, tugging at his sleeve. Still trying to protect me. But she is no longer a child, and her damp eyes no longer have the same pull on her father as they once did.

"You," he says. "To your chambers. And stay there. I will think of how to deal with you later."

Mother comes to my cell that night, a warm, dark presence in the guttering lamplight. The guard lets her past the bars without a word. She must have bribed him. Or perhaps they're friends. Father does not allow me to see her, but she comes to see me anyway, every now and then. She still smells like the kitchen at this hour; I reckon the scent never leaves you. They say I look like her, with my skin and my hair. Too much like her, probably, the way people glance sideways at me. Mother knows about the ways of the world, both the seen and the unseen. Some of the guards call her a witch, but she's just Mother to me. She was the first one I told. About being a girl.

She hugs me. "My dear child," she says. "My girl. You have to leave this place. It's no longer safe for you."

I nod; my throat is raw and mucus-clogged still. She wipes at my face, then says: "Here, I've brought some things for your journey."

Mother isn't the sentimental kind—she was never good with words. She's brought a rough hemp dress in my size, neatly folded. A traveling cloak to match. A bagful of supplies—preserved fruit, dried meats, biscuit, a square of hard cheese. A pouch of coins with a range of patinas betraying their ages.

"What journey?"

"Listen," Mother says, pressing my palms together. "And listen carefully. There is a witch who lives in the forest to the west, at the foot of Crow Mountain. Do you know the place? Where the poplar bends just so, at the fork in the road? You used to accompany the young master there for training..."

"Young mistress," I correct her.

Mother smiles and rubs my cheek fondly. I realize she is saying goodbye to me, as well, and my throat swells up again. She pulls something from her pocket, a muslin pouch with a sharp, earthy smell. Inside: strange herbs, glittering stones, other things I cannot name.

"Take this to the witch in the forest, and she will grant you your fondest desire."

"My fondest desire..." I shake my head. "What I ask for is impossible."

"Not for her." She squeezes my bruised arms, and the sadness in her eyes could fell fortresses. "Go. Be swift and silent. Become who you were always meant to be."

But I am a fool who cannot leave well enough alone, and I had to see her one last time. With the dark as my cover I flit upwards to my liege's chambers and slip inside unnoticed. They have trained me well. My liege wakes with a soft confusion that turns instantly sharp and needy when she recognizes me.

"My love! Did they hurt you?"

"No," I say, as she buries her face in my neck. My chest aches. We have loved each other since before we knew our names, yet in retrospect all that time seems like nothing. Why couldn't we have had one more day? One more week? One more summer? I have so many things I have yet to say to her.

"I'm coming with you," she says. This after I tell her where I'm going, and why. She's already climbing out of bed, lighting a candle, everything else forgotten.

"But your duties," I say.

"Fuck my duties," she says. "My duties can drown in the bottom of a well."

"But your father—"

She turns, and the candle outlines the knit of her brow, the twist of her jaw. "My father can drown in a well, too."

From a chest under her bed she pulls out a dress the soapy color of bluebells. Too coarse for her station, but too fine for a commoner's everyday wear.

"I stole it from a serving-girl's cupboard," she admits. "I suppose it was precious to her. Perhaps. I left some coin for her. She could just get a new one from the market, couldn't she?"

It takes her no time at all to assemble supplies for a long journey. Food, medicines, a dagger she fastens around her waist. A pouchful of money, more than my mother could have saved in a lifetime. She moves with practiced ease, as though running a routine she has envisioned a thousand times in her mind.

"How long ago did you decide on this?" I ask.

She frowns. "I decided nothing. These preparations were made just in case."

Before we leave we sneak into the armory and steal weapons. My liege takes a bow and quiver, which she prefers to the blade. To me she hands an iron sword and leather shield. Not the best, but useful, and light enough for travel. Something that might not be missed. Something that will not stand out.

We flee the castle under the auspices of a velvet sky peppered with stars. The moon hangs high and waxy and cold, casting road and rough in gleaming blue. I turn back to look at the place I once thought of as home, but its bulk is impossible to make out in the dark. My liege tugs at my hand and we vanish into the night.

By the time a pink bite of dawn shows on the horizon, the next hamlet over is a foggy smear in our sights. We have run through the night, making quick time, but we have also run ourselves ragged. We have not slept, and the ache in my flesh penetrates my marrow. My liege and I have an argument about what to do. I think we should rest in the woods, hidden from sight. She wants to go into the town and spend the day in a bed, a real bed. I argue that this is foolish and risky, but she wins the argument. Although we are no longer princess and shieldmaiden, in so many ways we are still princess and shieldmaiden. It takes another hour to reach the hamlet, by which time I can no longer feel my feet. I was barely fed while imprisoned, but my liege does not know this.

The hamlet has one inn, which slants in the yellow morning light. To me its facade looks like a leering face. Despite my misgivings we go in. There's a wide-hipped woman there, cleaning last night's spills off the tables. She straightens up too fast when she sees us.

"My lady! How may I serve your needs?"

My liege seems startled. "I would like a bed for the night, if you have any."

"But the night is fresh over... well, I suppose it matters not." She wipes her hands on her skirts. "What of your servant? Will she share your bed? There's space yet in the stables..."

My liege freezes, stiffens, then gestures to me. "Let's go. I've changed my mind."

It was the shoes that gave her away. Thick-soled, made of fine leather, lacking the wear of a wandering adventurer. That, or her cloak, forest-green and sturdy and never patched. The news that the heir to the throne has gone missing will not percolate here until later today, or perhaps even tomorrow, but the memory of a noble lady and her servant will stick in the innkeeper's mind.

"You were right," my liege says. "I'm sorry."

I think of sleeping in the stables, but as I do so the stable boy walks past us, and the leer on his face is the same as the leer on the building, and I change my mind. The world is full of dangers for two young women, particularly two young women like us, and I have a duty to protect my liege.

In the end we rest in the woods like I'd originally suggested, nesting in the moss between two oaks. Nothing will harm us in the wild; nothing ever has. I am my liege's lucky charm, they used to say. But the truth is the dappled green holds more peace than the hard edges of life in the royal court. Life here is softer and brighter and borderless.

So we travel to the witch's forest this way, resting in daylight and traveling by moonlight. We ration the supplies we have, hunt for fresh meat, and harvest fruit and mushrooms where we find them. It comes to us without thought, we who have spent so much of our young lives living off the land. As insurance. To toughen us up. They thought to train us for war as men, but they were really training us to live in the world as women. Sometimes we stop to dip our feet in the cold clear of streams. I braid my liege's hair in ways we have never been allowed. We talk about the names we want to use.

"If the witch would grant us each a new body," she says, "what kind of body would you like? Me, I think I would like to be tall, still. Perhaps with longer hair. What do you think?"

"You can always grow out your hair, you know." I brush silken strands from her face, contemplative. The sunlight is warm and slow and sleepiness is overcoming me. The ache of being away from everything I have ever known fades with each day. "I think I would like to be more like my mother."

"It sounds lovely," she says, eyelids fluttering into sleep.

By the time we reach the witch's forest, weeks later, the bruises left by my father have completely faded.

An old woman suns herself on a stone under the crooked poplar, her belongings resting in a grey pile by her side. Legs outstretched, entirely carefree, she offers us a gummy smile as we come up to her. It is late afternoon and my liege and I are exhausted: we sacrificed rest to cover the last ten miles of our journey.

"Why, my dear girls," she says, "the day is too pleasant to be going about in such a big hurry. Whereabouts are you headed?"

"Grandmother," I say, with all the respect my mother has taught me, "we are looking for the witch who lives in this forest. Do you know where we might find her?"

"A witch? Ha! Ha! What do you want an old witch for, anyway?"

"To grant us our hearts' desires," says my liege.

The old woman scans us up and down with her dark eyes, so deeply hooded and canny. "And what may your hearts' desires be?"

"Only the freedom to be who we truly are," I say.

The old woman squints at us, and I feel as though I am made of glass, and she can peer through me like a window, all the way to the depths of my beating heart.

"Hmph," she says. "Girls these days are so easy to please. In the old days they would ask for a husband or untold riches. Gewgaws and a soft life! But freedom, eh? What a thing to ask for." She gestures to the thick woods behind her. "Well, the witch's house lies in the heart of that there forest. See the path yonder, between the oak and the myrtle? Follow it and you will find what you seek. A house with red shingles and yellow ivy over the door. Can't miss it." She cackles. "But beware! For those woods are indeed a witch's wood, and you may find dangers and strange obstacles in your way. Go boldly and go truly, and maybe they'll leave you alone."

"Thank you, grandmother," I say.

"Thank me? Ha! Ha! No need. You have provided me entertainment this day, and that is enough."

"What a strange character," says my liege as we walk away. But I don't think the old woman's strange at all. She seemed purposeful, as if she talked to us for a reason.

When I turn back to look, the rock under the crooked poplar is cool and empty, as if the woman has simply evaporated. The fields around us wave placidly in the breeze. We are—and perhaps have been—entirely alone. Was the old woman an illusion? Or was she sent to wait for us?

"We should be careful," I say. I think of all the stories my mother has told me about witches, and what should be done around them. Witches have to be respected. They demand it.

Dimness awaits us in the forest. The trees here seem older, more self-assured, their crowns twisted together and sparing with the light. Moss curls around our feet as we walk in the silence. My liege takes my hand.

"How peaceful it is," she whispers. "How beautiful. Cool. Not too light, not too dark. Don't you think?"

"It is peaceful," I agree. But not because of the light or the breathless air. Here, the whole world feels like it knows what it is doing. Like everything is just right.

We sit for a while and eat the last of our supplies. My liege puts her head in my lap and drinks in the filtered gold descending softly to earth. She smiles at me.

I say: "I could stay here forever. I've always liked the forest better than the royal court."

She shuts her eyes. "A misfortune of birth. Duty and family—if I could, I would shed them like old skin."

"Are we not here to do that?"

She opens her eyes, blinking into the sunlight. A slight frown crosses her face and she gets up. "We should keep going."

So we do. We follow the scrubby, winding path through the forest, which is larger than it looked on the outside, because we walk for hours and there is yet more forest waiting for us.

"Are we lost?" wonders my liege.

"I don't think so. There hasn't yet been a fork in the path."

"I wonder what these woods have in store for us," she says. But it isn't wonder that fills her voice. She sounds tired.

The light grows yellower before it shades into dusk. Soon it will be too dark to travel; the trees are too thickly woven to let in moonlight. Worry creeps into my heart, not because I fear the forest around us, but because I fear we have failed a test, somehow. Something has gone wrong.

My liege asks again: "Are we lost?"

"I don't know."

"Perhaps we should turn back."

For the first time I hear uncertainty in her voice. I do not want to turn back. "We should be there soon."

"If there's a house ahead, we should see lights," she says. "I do not see lights. Do you?"

"It's too early for that. Come on." Stubbornly, I take the lead, and she falls into step behind me. I pray to the spirits of the air and water that I am not wrong. That something good is coming. We cannot—I will not—turn back.

We are being followed. I first become aware of it as a series of soft sounds, ferns rustling, hot breath that isn't mine or hers. A low growl like the voice of an angry father.

"We are being followed," says my liege. "Who's there? Show yourself."

A sound; we turn. A black shadow steps out of the brush, winding slyly between the twisted trunks of oak. Wolf-shaped, but not a wolf: a creature the size of a bear, with eyes that glow like a winter's fire. A smile that belongs on the face of no natural creature.

"Hello, little girls," it says. "Have you come to feed your uncle wolf?"

I draw my blade. "You are no uncle of ours. Stay back, lest I paint the ground of this forest with your blood."

"Tsk. How you repay my courtesy with threats of violence! The men who raised you have trained you well, I see."

"You threatened to eat us," says my liege.

"Ah!" The wolf laughs. "I never said such a thing! Why would I eat you, little scrapling? The flesh of humans is so unappetizing. Dry and stringy and tasteless. Your desires, on the other hand, are nectar and honey to me. How juicy they are, sweeter than the brightest summer fruit. Give me your wants, little girls. I will eat them from you. They will fill my hungry belly."

A trickster. Mother has told me about them.

"We'll do nothing like that," I spit, before grabbing my liege's wrist with my free hand. We flee up the path, away from the wolf-not-wolf. My shield bounces upon my back. "Don't listen to anything it says!"

My legs are burning, but not as badly as my chest. Air hurts my lungs, which can never have enough. My liege stumbles, exhausted, and I pull her forward. I drop my shield. We run some more. Thank the spirits our waterskins are empty and our bags have been lightened. More weight that we do not need. Soon, soon—we just have to reach the witch's house before our pursuer does—

The wolf lopes beside us, tongue lolling. "Come, now," it says. "These desires weigh so heavily upon you. Give them to me, and they will trouble you no more."

"Leave us alone," I gasp. "We will give you nothing."

"Are you not tired of running?" the wolf asks. Grinning its sharp-toothed grin. "Your natures are ill-suited to the lives you were born into. Let me take them from you. Do you not wish to live life unburdened?"

Its voice is sweet. It says things so close to the sentiments we have whispered to one another for years, sleeping in the wild under the canopy of stars. To live life unburdened. To be free.

"Give me your desires," the wolf says. "I will eat them and release your hearts from their weight."

My liege drags upon my wrist as she slows, footsteps losing speed. She is exhausted from so much running. A lifetime of running.

"Don't you want to go home?" asks the wolf.

Her wrist breaks from my grip as she stumbles to a stop at last. I turn in alarm to see her doubling over, chest heaving with effort. I grab her again and she pulls away.

"I can't. I'm tired."

"Please," I say.

She shakes her head. "It's too much. Maybe he's right."

In the dimness I see that wolf has her already. Its smoky tendrils twine over her calves and ankles and its jaws are locked on her forearm. Am I too late? My liege looks at me, her eyes shining.

"I'm sorry."

"Aurora," I say. The name she said she wanted.

"Go on," she says. "Leave me. Find the witch and claim your heart's desire."

Leave her to be eaten. To be picked apart, consumed, and the remains put back together by the wolf. To stand up once again the young prince, child of the Cetus King, heir to the throne of the country. To go home the prodigal son and forget all she has dreamed, to give in to the upbringing that shaped her, to accept the fate placed upon her by duty, family, obligation. To fill the space she was assigned to when she was born.

"No," I say. "Never." For a heart can desire many things, and my heart desires most of all to be with her: two women who chose themselves and chose one another. I dart forward and strike, plunging my blade between the wolf's eyes. I claim my heart's desire.

The wolf laughs, a rumble through my bones that lightens into evening birdsong and the gossip of leaves in the wind. The shadow dissolves into smoke, and then nothingness. My liege folds in half and crumples as though her strings were cut.

"Aurora," I whisper, gathering her into my arms. "Aurora?"

She breathes still, pale and delicate. I look up the path and see lamplight peeking from between the trees. The witch's house. It has been there all along.

I shed everything: sword, bag, all I'd brought. The herb pouch my mother gave me is mysteriously missing. When did I lose it? Could it have been earlier? I carry my liege up the path towards the witch's house.

The trees part before me and open into a large clearing in which a low-slung cottage waits. Red tiles on the roof, yellow ivy over the door. It looks unbearably pleasant, even in the fast-fading light. An herb garden, a vegetable plot, a pond with cat-rushes and lilies. The door to the cottage is open, and I carry my beloved over its threshold.

"Hello?"

The house is empty, although the hearth is stoked. Bread and fruit sit in a basket on the table. A bundle of herbs hang over each window, and the air is sweetly spiced. A breath of welcome—the cottage has been waiting for us. Already my bones feel lighter. More at ease. Perfectly shaped.

Somehow, none of this surprises me. Somehow, this is exactly what I expected.

I lay my beloved upon the bed, made up with white sheets, large enough for two.

"Rest, my darling," I say. "We are finally home."

In the morning I am woken by the yellow sun that slants in through the window. My love is already outside, exploring, exclaiming with delight and wonder. I stretch, and saunter to join her. We have all the time in the world.

"Come look," she says, pointing at the golden surface of the pond. The light catches her hair like it's full of stars. I go over and look where she points and there, reflected upon the calm surface, are the two of us. The witch and her beloved, the most beautiful woman in all the land.

Elinor Jones vs.
the Ruritanian Multiverse
by Freya Marske

D*ear Sami,*
Well, I did it. Contract signed, deposit paid, leaving on Friday.

My genetic material turned up a plum match for my preferences. This particular universe's Ruritania has gender essentialism and heteronormativity at zero—thank *fuck*, and can I smuggle some back through on the way home?—and a moderately high Narrative Causality Index, which means events should play out more or less predictably, but with plenty of room for improvisation on my part.

Danger level: moderate.

"When you say *moderate*," I said, as they were giving me the sales pitch, "do you mean, do a refresher first-aid course, or do you mean, update my will?"

"Maybe a duel-happy courtier, or revolutionary elements. Less effective anaesthesia, if you slip and break your leg." The saleswoman fixed me with a look that said, *the contract doesn't hold us legally liable for any of this, but I'll pretend to care until you've paid a deposit.* "It's adventure tourism. Far more people die canyoning in New Zealand, Miss Jones."

Then they showed me the list of all the things that Crown Princess Elinor, in disguise as Normal Hot Mess Elinor, is and is not allowed to do to my life while I'm absent from it. Did you know that our world has quite a high NCI? The Agency has had trouble with several Ruritanians falling in love and not wanting to go home again. They asked if I had any attractive single neighbors, or perhaps a close friend who may have always secretly loved me.

(Pause for you to laugh uncontrollably for thirty seconds.)

"And finally," she said, "it's worth considering that some of our clients have trouble with the lack of connectivity and social media."

I was dearly tempted to say:

Actually, I just "resigned from" my job because my dickhead boss told me to put something on his Twitter feed, and I told him it was a bad idea, and he told me that HE was the senator, not me, and so I did it and surprise!! there was a PR shitstorm!! And I took a severance payoff and Senator Dickhead announced it was an unfortunate independent act by a staffer who had since resigned. So now half the country thinks I'm a bigot, and half of my friends think I'm a moral coward for taking the money to be shoved under the bus, and honestly, who cares about the danger rating—at this point I would escape to the fucking MOON if that was an option. A holiday in a parallel universe seems like the next best thing.

What I actually said was, "Going offline won't be a problem."

Wish me luck and relaxation and not too many duels, I guess,

El

D*ear Sami,*
I'd been in Ruritania all of four hours before someone tried to kill me.

Let's back up.

The real Crown Princess Elinor will be formally crowned in two weeks' time, which is apparently a trigger for her to be gifted with an entire coterie of attendants-of-the-bedchamber and personal guards. Most of whom she's exchanged barely two sentences with in her entire life, but all of whom are young relatives or friends of someone on the Privy Council. Or someone who's bribed a member of said council.

It's uncannily like my first week on the senator's staff, when the people who'd been with him on the campaign treated those of us who'd merely answered a job advertisement with narrow-eyed suspicion. Politics! Multiverse notwithstanding: same shit, different plumbing.

I missed half the names because I was too busy admiring the sheer number of clothing layers, and the embroidery, and the jewels, and the embossed leather sheaths for swords and daggers—Sami, it's *hedonistic*, it's like someone regurgitated the Royal Shakespeare's costume-storage facility.

The other half of the names, recorded for posterity and assistance with recall:

- Honor: gives the impression of being flower-crowned even with no flowers present, probably about to drop a folk-pop album
- Anton: nine hundred feet tall, might have an inappropriate relationship with his sword?
- Luisa: sweet and awkward, absolutely stunning blue dress
- Moritz: prominent nose, would be striking and attractive if he weren't so self-aware about it
- Dominica: looks like a classical statue and frowns like my second-year poli-sci lecturer, more on her later
- Jonty

Imagine you're in an Evelyn Waugh novel and someone turns around from the billiards table, cue in one hand and glass of port in the other, and is introduced as *Jonty*. Yes. There. That's exactly what Jonty looks like.

I mention him because he's on the Agency payroll, and therefore the only one who knows who I really am. I'm meant to make him my favorite so he has an excuse to stay close, but I get a depressingly creepy vibe from him. You know. In the Waugh novel there's a smirky, classist remark daubed on his lips at all times. In our world he's probably about to monologue the plot of his screenplay directly at your breasts.

Barely enough time for imperious nods and being laced into my own outfit before I was bundled off for a court dinner, featuring lots of people whose names I'd at least had a chance to learn from the briefing packet. Food very butter-heavy. My kingdom (hah!) for a nice, sharp salad.

And then there was a round of fancy wine, for toasts, and I'd barely taken my first sip from my cup when there was a gasp and someone *smashed* it out of my hand.

More gasps all around. I was too surprised to do anything. The same someone—it was Dominica, personal guard of the disapproving frown—picked up the spilled cup, stared at it, and then lunged at me and scrubbed at my mouth with a napkin. All I could think was that she was smearing my lipstick everywhere.

"*Excuse* me," I managed, through the napkin, and shoved her away.

"Poison, Your Highness." She tilted the cup to show me. Green pearlescence clung to the rim. "It's subtle, but it leaves a surface residue. It caught the light. How do you feel?"

The word *poison* by this stage had spread halfway across the room. I felt—odd. My chest was tight and the room was dark at the edges. In retrospect I think that part was just shock.

"My lips are tingling," I admitted; they were.

That was the end of the party. I was bundled back to my rooms in a knot of guards, a doctor was summoned and did nothing but proclaim me healthy and inform me darkly that he'd been waiting for something like this to happen, everyone *knew* that there were religious sects who favored poisons and didn't want me on the throne, blah blah, get some rest, Your Highness.

Dominica was still hovering by my side like she'd been glued there. Jonty gave her a black look and me what was probably meant to be an encouraging nod, before he left with the rest of the attendants.

"Thank you, Dominica," I said.

The woman's face twitched and then she actually *knelt*, and took my hand. I'd already logged the basics: bone structure by Bernini, hair mahogany brown and tied sleekly back. In that moment I discovered she also had short fingernails and eyes like topaz: dark gold and faceted and very clear.

"No harm will come to Your Highness while I am at your side," she said, and it was very stiff and formal but her voice still sounded like the first sip of coffee on a cold morning, and I'll tell you what, that was when I really *got* the whole Ruritanian fantasy thing. Some bizarre feudalistic bunch of lizard-nerves woke up and sang like a fucking motet choir at *that*.

I think I went bright pink under my face powder. She was dignified enough not to comment.

One now wonders what *high* danger levels look like: imminent plague? Palace built on the edge of an active volcano?

Yours, still in possession of functioning internal organs (and also a brand new wank fantasy, if I'm honest),

El

D*ear Sami,*
Unexpected side effect of monarchy: I've got *peasants*.

Imagine that said in either the tones of "I've got pubic lice"or "I've got a firethrower." The way people speak about them to me is usually one of the two. Unfortunate nuisance, or useful resource!

And look, it wasn't *un*expected, it's just that what with all the fancy dresses and the terrifyingly beautiful women kneeling and swearing their loyalty, I'd forgotten that this country runs as every country has ever run: on someone's sweat. They took me on a pre-coronation grand tour of the surrounding villages and farmland today, and there was the kind of nodding-and-smiling you get when shoving a phone camera in someone's face as they exit a polling booth: I'll pretend that this isn't an annoying interruption to my day, because I don't know how much power you have over me.

Only here they *do* know.

It all put me in a foul mood, which I took into an afternoon of party planning. Sorry, *coronation logistics*. Dominica was clearly bored to tears by the entire thing and nearly glared a hole in a saucer when I, foolishly, asked her to help me choose between two near-identical tea services.

"The green pigment of Hurst porcelain is a byproduct of dangerous mining practices and is toxic to the children who do most of the detail work," she said, with far more repressive and princessy hauteur than I'd managed so far.

The Keeper of the Plate (I wish I was kidding) looked as if someone had farted.

"What?" I said. "Children?"

"Dominica," said Jonty. "I'm sure it's understood that Her Highness is not to be bothered with such things until after the coronation."

Rental property to be left in the condition you found it, in other words, and directed at me.

But... child labor and toxic paint. Come on. I chose the gilt-edged pink plates instead and asked for a report on Hurst porcelain to be prepared by the next morning, and we moved on to menu planning.

At dinner tonight Dominica did her usual iron-faced act, but she also interrupted to usher me away for a Very Important Thing when the Baron Wilhelm spent ten minutes going down the list of his sons and daughters in the clear hope that I might like the sound of one of them and agree to be betrothed on the spot. He was very patronizing and very drunk. Dominica put her hand deliciously in the small of my back as she steered me to my Very Important Thing, which turned out to be complimenting the kitchen staff who'd constructed the enormous chocolate swan. I was handed a small silver axe and asked to decapitate it, which is more violence than I'm accustomed to in my desserts.

Then I took the head away on a plate and prodded it with a tiny fork, trying to convince myself it wasn't looking at me accusingly. I kept thinking about the children in the fields, and children with paintbrushes. The chocolate was cloying on my tongue.

"Dominica," I said, because we were alone. "Do you know..."

She stared at me as if I were another gilded saucer, and I heroically managed not to whimper *please step on me.*

"Do you know why people want to kill me?"

Another long stare. It's safest for her to think I'm some sort of deeply sheltered sugared-rose-petal of an idiot, who's simply never thought to ask about whether people might be dying in her mines or suffering to make her pretty tea service.

"Was that a serious question, Your Highness?"

I nodded.

Dominica said, "You're different from what I expected."

Which wasn't an answer to my question, and at that point I was swarmed by Jonty and Moritz and Luisa clamoring for me to come and dance, so we didn't finish the conversation. But I haven't forgotten it.

Yours,

El

Dear Sami,
I'm ninety percent sure someone is reading this, or at least trying to. Remember in high school when I proved my parents were reading my diary? Same tricks apply. And same method of making it a useless endeavor for whoever's snooping; raise a glass to Nanny Tilda, the one tolerable member of my godawful family, and her work as a secretary in the days when shorthand was a useful skill.

I still remember you learning it from me in two days flat—I was *thrilled*—and the look on Mr. Dunn's face when he intercepted a note and tried to read it aloud.

I'm *all the way* sure that something is going on with Jonty. He keeps changing around my other attendants' schedules at the last minute and vanishing during meals, and now he's come down with a sudden attack of piety and begged leave to attend midnight service at the palace chapel, which Honor says is unusual for him.

I got Jonty alone and asked him outright if something was wrong, if the Agency was having issues—if maybe Princess Elinor had fucked up something about my life, and they were trying to keep it from me? But he just put on his most placid and smirky face and told me that I had nothing to worry about.

He's going to chapel tonight.

I'm going to follow him. (Don't look at me like that, it's a *mystery*, I can't help it.)

Jonty's also done a complete about-face on the subject of Dominica, which I find even more suspicious. He still treats her as barely one step above a servant, but he's now providing more and more excuses for us to be alone together: acting all concerned about the *stress* of the upcoming coronation, and I look *peaky*, and wouldn't I like to rest quietly in my chambers? With my personal guard?

If he were a normal sort of attendant I'd think he's noticed my epic crush—frankly, it wouldn't be hard—and is tacitly encouraging the crown princess to have a hot fling before the inevitable political marriage looms.

During one of these The Princess Has A Headache interludes, Dominica was teaching me how to cheat at a card game that's popular among the guards, and we got onto the subject of how she came to *be* on my personal guard. She volunteered for it in her twin brother's place, after he died; they grew up very close, their mother never told them who their father was, and then the brother died last year in a skirmish which—reading between the lines—was the royal army bullying farmers in the northern towns when a blight meant they couldn't produce the usual crop yield.

"Sending a single unit up against desperate people with farm tools and nothing to lose," she said, very bitter, looking up to meet my gaze from the winning hand she'd just laid on the table. "Someone's bright idea."

I waited for the usual respectful addendum—*Forgive my outburst, Your Highness*—but she just kept her chin up, as if seeing if I could take it.

I wanted to say, *Neither of us are what we're supposed to be, are we?*

Instead I said, "My best friend died a few months ago."

"Oh?"

"I'd known her since we were—really young. I still feel completely lost when I remember she's gone."

Like the world is a different world. A shift for the worse in the multiverse. It hurts so much. I didn't know how to tell her how much it hurts; I was absolutely sure I didn't have to. She tilted her head and firelight reflected off the polished sweep of her hair, and her mouth was the softest and most careful I've seen it.

"I'm sorry," she said.

"I'm sorry about your brother."

...God help me, I think we might be *friends* now. She answers all my questions and bullies reports out of bureaucrats, and we're in the midst of a fragmented lecture series entitled Why People Might Want To Kill You. Some of the religious sects approach it from a woo-woo perspective—full of mutterings about bad omens and prophecies—but I'm rapidly coming to the conclusion that the revolutionaries, the ones involved in violent social protest, have a real fucking point. Frankly, Ruritania is a *mess*. And what am I supposed to do when I hear about a local lord tyrannizing a village, or an entire edict slapping down the right of peaceable assembly, or a charity hospital in the city about to close for lack of funds?

Answer: write a letter to that lord under my personal seal, and flounce my way into the Privy Council chambers to repeal the edict—changed my mind, so sorry, *what* a flighty girl I am! I even sold some of the ugliest pieces in my vast jewelry collection to raise money for a personal donation to the hospital, which went into embarrassing royalist spasms and instantly renamed itself in my honor.

Jonty looks more constipated by the day. He can't exactly contradict me in public, though.

And maybe the Crown Princess Elinor will come back and reverse it all again, but maybe she won't bother, and at least I'll have left the rental property with a well-weeded garden and a more nicely arranged linen closet. *Better* than I found it.

I miss you,
El

D*ear Sami,*
Fuck. All right. *Fuck.*

I roped Dominica into the "go and see what Creepy Jonty is up to" plan, because I'm not a complete moron and there are, as established, plenty of people trying to kill me. Plus it's very difficult to *sneak*, as a princess, and I needed an ally.

The main chapel is a glorified wing of the palace, high-ceilinged and hushed. It was dense with candlelight as midnight service began. We were a long way from Jonty's heels, but saw him slip into a side chapel, and Dominica took hold of my arm when I went to follow him. She pointed at a narrow set of stairs tucked in a corner. I did have a *brief* moment of wondering if I was about to be thrown down from a height and turned into an exciting corpse in the middle of the mosaic floor.

But the stairs led to a middle gallery shrouded in wicker screens—a kind of service corridor—and when we crouched, we ended up with a reasonable view down into the chapel where Jonty stood. Alone. I'd assumed some sort of conspiratorial assignation. I'd even have settled for a *licentious* assignation, simply to know what was going on with him, though voyeurism in combination with desecration of a chapel is a bit heavy-handed on the kink even for me.

And then Jonty pulled a multiverse gate opener out of his pocket and fired it up.

Dominica's hand was still gripping my arm. I assume she didn't trust me to be quiet. When the gate opened, expanding from speck into perfect circle with a quiet *thwop* and a shimmer of that sickly yellow-green, her fingers went tight as a vise.

The person who stepped through the gate was me.

Dominica inhaled hard and I dug a warning elbow into her side. It was the Crown Princess Elinor, obviously, wearing my favorite pink skirt and a denim jacket I didn't recognize. It seemed unfair. Why did *she* get to come home for a visit?

Then I remembered all the jewelry-selling and edicts and other parts of Ruritania that I'd merrily been tampering with, and swallowed a great big mouthful of something that probably should have been guilt. Wasn't, though. I don't regret any of it.

"What is taking so long?" Princess Elinor demanded. "The revolutionaries have been slowly coming to the boil for months. We allowed that Ruys woman to infiltrate the guard, and the general assured me that the rest of them would be vanity placements—next to useless. Everything was poised for a successful attempt. Why isn't she dead?"

It actually took me a moment. The startled fascination of seeing someone with my face, in my clothes, was still sinking in. Dominica's fingers tightened even further before she snatched them abruptly away. When I looked at her, all I could see was the wide whites of her eyes. *Then* it hit.

She. She was me. *I* was meant to be dead.

"Dominica Ruys is the problem, Your Highness," Jonty was saying, beneath us. "I've given her plenty of openings for violence, but she hasn't taken any of them. I think she's become friendly with the replacement."

"*Friendly*." Spoken as if holding a dirty tissue at arm's length. "This is unacceptable, Jonathan."

Jonty bowed deeply. "There was always a risk of this, Your Highness. The Agency's contract did stipulate—"

"Oh, do shut up. How much could this *tourist* really have done in—" Princess Elinor cut herself off and rubbed at her forehead with two genteel fingertips. It was a gesture totally unfamiliar, totally unlike *me*, and somehow that eased my heartrate down from rabbit levels. "Very well," she said. "We move to the backup plan. Inform the general. It will take a bit more work, but he should be able to pin her death on the revolutionaries. Produce a convenient confession from someone defiant and idealistic. Then we proceed as planned. Use the excuse to round them all up for deplorable violence and high treason, produce me bruised and shaken but miraculously alive, and the threat is eliminated before the crown is even on my head."

Jonty closed the gate once the princess had stepped back through, and he left the chapel. My head was spinning and one of my feet was numb and tingling from my crouched position, but I didn't move. Couldn't.

The Agency.

What a good business model theirs is, after all, taking money from both sides. Fantasy holidays for young people estranged from their families and gone reckless with irritation and grief. And a useful service for Ruritanian royals all over the multiverse: could you use a doppelganger? No doubt some of them really are just looking for a two-week escape in another world before assuming their royal duties.

But some of the others....

What's the saying—if you're not the consumer, you're the product? Looks like it's possible to be both.

I braced my hands on the screen and managed to stand up. Neither Dominica nor I spoke as we scurried back to my chambers, but we exchanged looks that said: *once we're safely shut in the bedchamber, it's going to be a fucking race as to who gets to shout at the other one first.*

In the end Dominica won because she cheated by shoving me up against the door the moment it closed and getting her face *really* close to mine. My brain and my heart and my ladyparts all short-circuited at once in a combination of leftover fear and inappropriate lust. That gave her enough time to speak.

"You're not the real Princess Elinor?"

"My name *is* Elinor!" I protested, like an idiot. "And can we agree that I'm not the *worst* person that you've seen tonight wearing this particular face?"

"That's not what I..." She shook her head, looking frustrated. I'd no idea how much of what we'd seen she'd actually understood, but it turned out: most of it. Because she said, "This is our life, and it's all just a joke to you? A holiday?"

Solid hit. I swallowed. "It's not a joke."

Dominica's grip on my shoulders loosened. She was still frowning. Emboldened by her pause, I continued: "And don't think we're not going to talk about the fact that *you were going to kill me*."

"I was not!" she said. "Not after the first three days. My main job was to sound you out; none of us had been able to get close enough, before, and we thought it was good luck that I managed it." Sounding bitter. She was as much a dupe in this as I was. "We'd only ever judged you—the princess, I mean—on her actions and her speeches, and they were... troubling."

No doubt. Poisonous entitled little shit, my Ruritanian counterpart. Pity I'm not still working for the senator; she'd have fit in just fine on his staff.

"I was meant to find out if you were a completely lost cause. And if so... yes. I would have done what was necessary to protect Ruritania from your rule."

"You swore to protect *me*, on the first night," I said accusingly. "Before you knew me at all. You knelt down and everything. I remember, because it was unspeakably hot. Was there even any poison?"

Her face colored on *hot* and then colored some more. "Yes, but I added it to the cup *after* I'd knocked it away. And there was only a single drop on the napkin I used to wipe your mouth, so that your lips would tingle. It was a quick way to gain your trust."

"Revolutionary elements," I sighed. "I was warned, I suppose." I looked at her more closely. Unknown father. Brother dead under maybe-suspicious circumstances. "Dominica, are you sure *you're* not a princess? A secret heir? I don't think anything else could surprise me tonight."

"I am not *royalty*." She looked as offended as if I'd accused her of whipping puppies for fun. Which I kind of had, given the standard for royalty in this place.

"Narrative causality," I said, in apology. "It's—let me explain."

I rang for someone to fetch hot chocolate from the kitchens, and Dominica and I sat on my bed and drank and talked and planned, and I was pathetically excited by her bare feet when she deigned to relax so far as to remove her boots and socks. Her sword stayed within arm's reach even though there was another guard on duty outside; Dominica's only the daytime shift, usually, and sleeps when I sleep. Maybe she, too, had the words *vanity placements* still dancing uncomfortably in her mind.

She's asleep now, on a couch in the outer room. I should try to sleep myself, but my skin is still buzzing. Writing this instead. We have a terrible, foolhardy plan that's likely to increase the Narrative Causality Index of this universe all by itself, if we pull it off.

I'll take whatever luck you can send me,
El

Dear Sami,
I'm writing in a cabin in the mountain woods, with a thick blanket draped over my knees. There's a view through the small window down to the city, where the lights are dimmed and bells are calling mourning every hour. The Crown Princess Elinor is missing, presumed dead.

Sometimes you have to shove a stick into the trap and let it slam shut. Or in this case: if a real assassination attempt is on the horizon, sometimes you have to let a fake one happen first. Dominica got quick word to her revolutionary allies, and they staged a *very* dramatic scene with an explosion on a barge. Thank fuck for just enough years spent in Scouts that I learned how to swim in heavy clothes.

As expected, the general and everyone else in Princess Elinor's conspiratorial faction raised a great fuss and called for the arrest of all known revolutionaries, but given said revolutionaries were pre-warned, Dominica tells me they've all vanished into countryside retreats like this one by now. And it's nighttime, and winter. Nobody wants to be racing around in the dark when they think they've had victory handed to them unexpectedly.

Tomorrow, no doubt the crown princess will appear just in time for her coronation. Tomorrow, the *real* fireworks of this plan begin.

The only people in this cabin with me are Dominica and a middle-aged man who treats her with enough familiarity that I'm wondering—uncle? Neither of them has said. I haven't asked. I was too busy shivering in my drenched underthings until Dominica threw some towels at me and told me that the entire plan would be ruined if I went and died of a chill. Her already mediocre deference-to-royalty, which was clearly an act anyway, has dwindled to a scrap.

"Tell me you weren't lying about your brother," I said, when I was toweling my hair.

"No, I wasn't," said Dominica. "He was the best thing about me. He would have fought, like I'm fighting."

My throat was thick. "My best friend would have fought, too," I said. "She would probably have stormed out of the palace and led a rebellion herself rather than do anything involving a chocolate swan. She was much braver than me."

All right, I was fishing. Dominica didn't play along, but amusement looked good on her. The side of her mouth curved like the bend of a river.

"What would she say about all of this?"

I grinned. "She'd tell me to go ahead and raise hell."

You know you would, Sami,

El

Dear Sami,
Today has lasted at least five years and also I don't think I've taken a single conscious breath. No way to put this down except step by step.

There's an old-fashioned Ruritanian veil that covers the face—mostly worn by dowagers who want to spy on everyone from beneath them—and we disguised me with one of those. We sneaked into Jonty's chambers when the palace was near empty, just after everyone left for the coronation ceremony, and found his multiverse gate opener tucked into a chest full of cravats. I hid the opener down the front of the red dress I was wearing; it was one of the princess's own, smuggled out of the palace in the furor surrounding her "miraculous return."

Dominica still had her guard uniform, and she tucked her hair up under a felt cap and marched us to the front rows of the coronation hall as if escorting someone's grandmother who'd fallen ill and slept through breakfast.

Crown Princess Elinor made her grand, smug way to the front of the hall, to the sounds of trumpets. As soon as she was standing alone, I yanked the veil off and strode up onto the dias—between two very confused guards—to stand beside her.

It wasn't *subtle*, as plans go.

"*You*—" the princess hissed, and was clearly raising her hand to gesture for my capture, but I grabbed her wrist and forced it down.

"An *impostor!*" I yelled at the top of my lungs. "You shall not harm Ruritania!" I threw my other hand to my bosom in Shakespearean dismay, and retrieved the gate opener. We hadn't found Jonty's Agency directory, so I'd pre-set the opener to a random code on our way to the hall.

I pressed the button. A gate *thwopped* itself into existence and I dragged the princess through it, then closed the gate behind us before I could hear more than the beginnings of shouts and excitement. There'd been one princess, then two, then none.

Dominica would have killed to protect her country from a bad ruler. I hadn't entirely ruled that *out*, but I did have other options.

This place in the multiverse looked similar to the Ruritania we'd come from, but the scent of the air was completely different. The air was warmer and drier. We were halfway up a gentle hill carpeted with scrubby grass.

"Unhand me!" the princess shouted. I unhanded her. She jabbed her finger in my face. "Take me back there immediately!"

"No. I have another offer for you," I said. "Go back to my world. My life. You can have it." I supposed it was too much to ask that she might have fallen in love. My looks are completely wasted on someone with a personality that unpleasant.

She hesitated, and frowned. "There are certainly some interesting aspects to your world," she allowed. "But you have no position of influence, no significant wealth, and no friends. And an *extremely* rude and condescending person claiming to be your brother keeps trying to contact you. And the throne of Ruritania is *mine*. I have worked too hard for it to give it up now."

I wondered suddenly and unpleasantly about the hunting accident that resulted in the death of the late king.

"It might be yours, but you're ruining it!" I said. "You don't care about these people!"

"How *dare* you, you—you *tourist*! I was *born* to lead—"

"Hereditary monarchy is a stupid system!" I shouted, and kicked her legs out from under her.

She went down with a surprised yelp. For all her ruthlessness, she's lived a life with other people wielding swords on her behalf; I'm no expert fighter, but I did grow up with Brendan for an older brother, and at least I know how to lash out when cornered.

"And feudalism might have its sexy moments," I went on—I was angry—"but it's not much better. I take it that's a no to the offer?"

I dialed another code and stepped through the gate. Scent of faintly burning wood and salt on the furious wind. A city on the horizon that took up half the sky. My hair whipped around as Princess Elinor scrambled to her feet and came through after me; what choice did she have? The opener was her only way home.

I glanced at the NCI reading on the device and repeated the process through two more worlds—one green-clouded and actively raining, smelling of unfamiliar plants, the path active with people. One city that could nearly have been my home, except that the smells of metal and smoke were off-kilter, and the buildings too tall, their colors extravagant.

That one had a fairly high NCI.

"How do you feel now?" I asked hopefully.

"Go to hell," the princess spat. She tried to grab the opener from me but I danced away and dialed another number, and we raced through a couple more nodes of the multiverse. My hope was that in a very high NCI world, the essential romance narrative would grab at her and she'd agree to the switch.

A light on the opener flashed rapid orange. I was forcing a lot out of it and its charge was running low. And the adrenaline holding my bones was beginning to crack, leaving me shaky.

The princess must have noticed. She was breathing hard herself, and kept eyeing the opener and myself with equal venom.

"You can't keep this up forever. If you're going to knock me out and abandon me, stop messing around and *do it*."

Sami, you said something to me once. We were sitting side by side on your hospital bed and you were kicking my ass at some video game or other. You put down the handset and said, quite suddenly, not looking at me, "It fucking sucks that you don't realize how much you want to live until the worst possible moment."

You were right, as usual. I've been ambivalent on the subject of living for weeks. And then in the moment of deciding that even the Princess Elinor deserved to live, and not be knocked out and abandoned in a world with a danger rating that could be *anything*, I realized—

Well, I realized I was finally looking forward to whatever came next. Even if it was going to be hard.

Back then I looked at you and you picked up the handset again and said, "Keep taking the chances you've got, El. Don't waste them. Promise."

And because I did promise, you'll be pleased to know I entered one more gate code and stepped through. Sunny skies, paved streets, glassy green buildings; we were in an alley between two of them.

I looked at the opener, nodded, and dropped it to the ground. It took two good hops with my entire body weight for the cracked screen to go blank. Glass and bits of shattered plastic skidded across the stones.

Princess Elinor gave a little shriek. "What have you done?"

"Ruritania doesn't need either of us, and the Agency doesn't know where we are," I told her. "This seems like a nice place with a high chance of indoor plumbing, and the NCI here is nearly a perfect ratio. Probability is shifted overwhelmingly towards a predictable and satisfying story. Which means you'll get what's coming to you, based on the role you choose to play. I advise you to make better choices from now on."

Pleased with that as a parting blow, I turned and began to walk towards the mouth of the alley. I did sneak a look over my shoulder; she'd leaned against the wall, as if to catch her breath.

I got a few yards before there was another *thwop* and a yellow-green gate opened in front of me. Dominica stepped through it, an intact gate opener in her hand.

I froze. Dominica saw me, and froze too. Her expression of blinding fury had a brief spat with one of equally blinding relief, before she glanced over my shoulder and lunged to grab me by the hand.

"You are such an *idiot*," she snapped, and pulled me through the gate before I could respond. There was another shriek of dismay from the princess, behind me, but the sound vanished into nothing. Dominica had closed the gate when I was barely through it, and we were standing in a small corridor with the familiar wall panels of the Ruritanian royal palace. The smell was right. We were back.

Dominica tossed her opener to the ground and skewered it with her sword. It made a sad little noise and began to spark.

"*What?*" I said.

"I told you I wouldn't let any harm come to you."

New, improved question: "*How?*"

"I threatened Jonty," Dominica said. "I thought he might have a way to contact the Agency and ask for someone to bring a new one of those little gate boxes, in case his own one stopped working, and I was right. And then I asked the woman who appeared if there was a way to cut *this* world out of the multiverse, to stop people coming here from anywhere else, and—well, she looked quite relieved at the idea, and said we weren't going to be any more use to them now anyway. And something about wiping the coordinates from the database," Dominica spoke the words gingerly, as if she didn't trust the syllables, "and payments not being refundable. And Jonty decided to go back through the gate with her, which was wise of him because otherwise I would have made him *very* sorry."

I stared at the smoking pile of ex-opener and didn't doubt it.

"And you were what, going to keep putting random numbers in until you found me?"

Dominica shrugged. "Yes."

"That could have taken years!"

"Well, it didn't."

I wondered what the probability was that she'd somehow managed to dial the right code on the first try. The odds must be infinitesimally small.

But *very* narratively satisfying.

"You can't go home, Elinor," Dominica said. "I'm sorry."

"I didn't want to. I didn't *intend* to," I said, weakly. "I was making a gesture!"

"A gesture? Sacrificing yourself for Ruritania like some kind of—of—" And then Dominica knelt at my feet like she had the first night we met, and the kiss she gave my hand was *savage*, like she wished it was a bite instead.

The kiss she swept me into when she stood up was more savage again. I'd wondered if maybe she was one of those revolutionary creatures who dedicated themselves to liberty and ignored the pleasures of the flesh, but her lips were lush and confident against my own. This was someone whose flesh had definitely been pleasured before. It was fucking *glorious*.

"Come on, Your Highness," Dominica said, when she'd released me and I'd shaken myself out of my kiss-glazed state. "We'd better get you crowned."

"About that," I said.

I gave her the feudalism-is-stupid speech. Dominica shouted at me for repeating her own talking points back to her. Then she kissed me again, and then settled into a contemplative frown when I suggested that the best course of action would be a gradual, peaceful transition to democratic government. After all, I'd already proved good at signing away my power, and I do know my way around political PR.

"I can be the last queen of Ruritania," I said. "Sounds impressive, don't you think?"

Dominica told me again that I was an idiot and not to be ridiculous, but her eyes were alight with fondness and I'm pretty sure only *half* of it was directed at liberty and democracy and all of those things; the other half was all for me. I can't wait to hear how much she shouts when I suggest she runs for office.

Maybe somewhere in this world is a version of you, Sami. You'd be different; you might hate classical music and love blue cheese. We'd have no history. It wouldn't be *you*. I'm not going to go looking. But it's a thought to cling to: somewhere in the infinite multiverse we do have infinite chances.

I'm not going to waste this one.

Yours, always,

El

Plan Z
by Django Wexler

The starship *Wild Ride* blasts away from Velinx Station at an acceleration that, were it not for the various esoteric fields pervading the interior, would reduce me and my girlfriend to a thin layer of comingled paste on the rear bulkheads. We're pursued by a desultory spatter of pulse-beams, fired by a Commonwealth weapons officer who knows he hasn't got a hope of stopping us but needs to be seen making an effort. A few moments later, a burst of blue-white light envelops the ship as it drops into the trackless depths of hyperspace, and we're safe.

"Well," Ahn says, leaning back in the battered pilot's chair and tossing the Skolig idly from one hand to another. "Chalk up another one for Plan Z?"

I'm working on my breathing, resting my head against the cracked cushion of the co-pilot's chair in the *Ride's* cockpit, looking out the forward viewport into the blue nothing of hyperspace. In and out, in and out. Keep breathing so you don't have the chance to scream. Not from fear at our narrow escape—say one thing for Ahn, it's that she's good at flying and blasting, and anyway if I screamed every time I'd nearly been shot, disintegrated, asphyxiated, devoured, torn to spaghetti by gravitational forces, and generally come within a whisker of having my corporeal existence prematurely terminated over the last few years, I wouldn't have time for anything else. Rather, it's Ahn who is on the verge of provoking me into hysterics, because under the circumstances she has the audacity to *fucking grin at me*.

Plan Z, in her parlance, means, *oh shit everything's gone wrong, time to blast our way out. Plan Z* means, *shoot first, run for it, and ask questions probably never. Plan Z* means burning away from *yet another station* at top speed, with nothing to show for our efforts but carbon scoring on the hull, the unwanted attention of the authorities, and an utterly priceless gemstone that is now so radioactively hot (in the stolen-goods sense) that no fence in the Commonwealth would lay a finger on it.

Ahn is extremely fond of Plan Z. To her credit, she's an amazing shot, and has a sixth sense about diving for cover. It makes her good to have on your side when things take a sudden lurch into the shit, and utterly fucking useless when it comes to little details like keeping the ship fueled and paying overdue docking fees.

She knows she's in trouble. I can tell by the way she's suddenly making shiny megakitten eyes at me, like she can get me to ignore what just happened by being unutterably adorable. It's a delicate moment for our relationship, and definitely requires a touch of diplomacy. Fortunately, diplomacy is my specialty.

"Fuck you," I tell her, "and fuck your *Plan Z*."

I turn around and stalk down the long central corridor of the *Wild Ride*—named by Ahn, of course, because my girlfriend's sense of humor apparently fossilized at age twelve—kicking aside a half-eaten box of jyck-buns and snatching a pair of stray underwear from where they inexplicably adorn a light fixture. Ahn, after hurriedly checking the autopilot, comes after me.

"Come on," she wheedles. "We made it, didn't we? And we've still got the thingie." She holds up the crystalline Skolig, which throws multi-colored sparkles from its many facets. "It's fine!"

I turn around, waving the dirty undergarment with such vigor that she takes a hasty step back.

"You *shot* a Commonwealth customs officer!" I growl. A thoroughly dirty one, but still. "In the face!" I still have evidence of this, in the form of bits and pieces and fluids that had once belonged to said customs officer, smeared and drying all over my dress and in my hair.

"He had a gun to your head!" Ahn says.

"We were *negotiating*."

"He was going to negotiate your brains across the wall."

"I could have talked him down."

"Forgive me if I wanted to *protect* you."

"*Protect* me by getting into a gunfight with half a company of marines." I let out a long sigh and use the underwear to mop a bit of customs officer off my forehead. "Who by now will have uploaded our descriptions, and that we were trying to sell the *thingie*"—I indicate the priceless Skolig Ahn is again casually juggling from hand to hand—"which has therefore gone from a billion-credit score to the galaxy's most fabulous paperweight."

Ahn frowns at the Skolig. "I told you this job was too complicated."

"It would have been fine if you could keep your blaster in your pants!"

She grins again. "I thought that was what you liked about me, Princess."

"*Don't* call me princess."

"It's still technically true, even if your father disowned you."

"He disowned me because I ran away with *you!*"

"I can't be held responsible for the effect my roguish charm has on a certain type of girl—"

I hit her in the face with the wadded-up underwear and stalk away to slam the button that opens the door to my cabin.

"Ilya, wait!" Ahn peels the panties off and frowns at them, then holds up the Skolig. "What are we going to do with the thingie?"

The suggestion I offer is anatomically improbable, or at least extremely uncomfortable. Before Ahn can think of an appropriate retort, I hammer the control panel with a fist and the door hisses closed behind me.

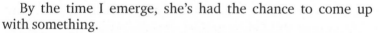

By the time I emerge, she's had the chance to come up with something.

"I thought about what you said," she says, turning the Skolig over in her fingers, "and, you know, with a little industrial-grade drive lubricant I might be able to—"

"If you can cease being puerile for one moment," I say, going for austere haughtiness, "I have something to show you."

"Do you need the thingie?" Ahn says innocently. "Or the drive lubricant?"

Fortunately, a few hours alone in my cabin, including an extended shower to rid me of the customs officer's lingering presence, have done wonders for my disposition and I'm able to respond to Ahn's "humor" with something approaching equanimity. I find it helps to think of her as a divinely appointed burden, assigned to me by the creator of the multiverse to make up for my sins. Which particular sins, I'm not sure, but they must have been fucking awful ones.

Ahn comes in and sits on my unmade bed, which takes up at least half the diminutive cabin. I ignore her and move to the console, tapping at the inputs.

"Do you remember my smuggler friend Kestra?"

Ahn frowns. "I remember *Kestra*, but I'm not sure about the *friend*. Didn't she try to kill you after Gaios?"

"If I cut off contact with people after they tried to kill me once or twice, I'd have a hard time filling out a dinner party. I got in touch with her, and she's willing to take the Skolig off our hands."

Charts flicker into being above the console, showing the Igan system and an object in a long, elliptical orbit. I rapidly plot a hyperspace course from where the *Wild Ride* is currently resting, somewhere above the third fractal harmonic.

"She hasn't heard about the Commonwealth alert yet?" Ahn says.

"I warned her myself. Less chance of a misunderstanding that way. But she's a smuggler, and she has a better chance than we do of selling the thing over the border somewhere. So she'll buy it, at a *significant* discount."

"Perfect!" Ahn bounces to her feet. "See, I told you it would work out."

"You did not, in fact." I press my hand to my forehead. "And it may still not 'work out.' Kestra can be... twitchy, and she might expect me to be angry about Gaios. So when we get there, *no Plan Z*, understand?"

"I mean, sure." Ahn grins. "Unless there's no other alternative, right?"

"Ahnika." I grab her shoulders. "Please. I need you to *trust* me. I will make this work, but I need you to stay calm. Can you do that for me?"

She blinks her irritatingly beautiful blue-green eyes. "Okay."

"Okay."

"Okay."

I let go of her, and she leans in to kiss me.

"Looks like we've got..." She taps the console, and the ship *thrums* as it starts executing the hyperspace transition. "Three point two five hours to kill." She arches one eyebrow.

My girlfriend, master of subtlety. But there's fuck-all else to do in hyperspace, I suppose.

Three point one hours later, Ahn is hurrying through her shower, while I finish getting dressed. I frown at my reflection, and reluctantly conclude that the crown with the spikes is perhaps a bit over the top.

Ahn emerges, naked and tracking wet footsteps across my bedroom floor. She gives a low whistle. I turn around, fast enough to make the cloak flare. No point in wearing the thing if you're not willing to go for effect.

"Wow," she says, toweling off. "Are we selling stolen goods or accepting the surrender of an enemy kingdom?"

"One never knows," I say coolly, "what the day may bring."

But I'm smiling, because the dress is a good one, red and black with little silver touches, clingy where it needs to be and swinging dramatically elsewhere. It's the kind of thing you *could* wear on the bridge of your battlecruiser to order the subjugation of a recalcitrant planet. My hair, long and red, gleams like it's been polished.

Ahn, of course, dresses in dark pants, a light shirt, and the same ratty synthleather vest she always wears, open at the front. Her hair, still damp from the shower, is short and brilliantly blue, contrasting with her soft brown skin. And, of course, there's the pair of blasters holstered low on her hips. She honestly wouldn't look dressed without them.

The ship's system *pings*, indicating imminent emergence into realspace. I turn the wall from a mirror into an exterior display. Labeled AH-1310, the small object we're approaching looks like a smallish asteroid. There are thousands like it scattered across the Commonwealth—played-out mines, abandoned military outposts, and so on. A typical smuggler meet.

It isn't, actually, *quite* typical. But if all goes well, that's not going to matter.

Kestra's ship, the *Alcie*, is already docked to one side of the rock. It's several times larger than the *Wild Ride*, with a crew of about a dozen and plenty of space for illicit cargo. Our security system reports they're scanning us, but politely, no targeting beams. I tell the ship to take us in, and the *Wild Ride* accelerates, leaving a wake of coronal blue particles dragged out of hyperspace.

"So what are we going to do?" I ask Ahn.

She frowns. "Sell the thingie to Kestra?"

"And?"

"Not shoot anybody."

"Right."

"Unless—"

"Ahn!"

"Right." She sighs, patting her blasters mournfully. "But what if—"

"Don't shoot *anybody* unless I tell you to, all right?"

She takes in my expression, which is thunderous, and grins. "All right."

I examine her for signs of insincerity and find nothing obvious, so I give a short nod. "Good. Let's go."

We dock on the opposite side of the rock from the *Alcie*, nestling against the bulbous surface of AH-1310. The *Wild Ride* attaches itself to the airlock, proclaims the environment safe, and opens her doors onto a corridor lit by intermittent glowpaint. It's native rock on all sides, bulgy and weird-looking, with only the floor smoothed. I step out gingerly, but gravity holds.

"You have the Skolig?" I ask Ahn.

"The what?"

"The *thingie*."

"Oh, yeah." She holds it up, spraying rainbows, and tosses it to me as though it weren't a priceless cultural treasure. "Here."

I catch it—not that it really matters, the thing is basically indestructible—and run my fingers over the sharp facets. It's surprisingly heavy, denser than lead. I tuck it into a hidden pocket—*of course* this dress has hidden pockets—and stride purposefully into the asteroid, with Ahn following cheerfully behind. It's a good dress for striding purposefully.

The tunnels are a maze, but that doesn't bother me. My ability to keep track of myself by dead reckoning is essentially perfect, courtesy of the genetic meddling of a long-ago ancestor who figured that would be a useful ability for the royal family of an orbital kingdom. A glance at the map before we left the *Ride* was all I needed to keep it straight.

I direct us through several junctions to a large central chamber, roughly equidistant from both ships. It's some sort of old command center, its walls lined with derelict equipment. A catwalk overhead supports more dead monitors and broken terminals.

Kestra's waiting in the middle of the room. She's a large, broad-shouldered woman, blonde hair buzzed short, her lower body swathed in a power suit. I recognize the man standing at her shoulder as Drav, her lieutenant, who has sleepy eyes and a ready smirk. But it's the third figure that really catches my attention. He's a Wrax—a humanoid lizard, basically, though that description would annoy any Wrax as human-chauvinist. He wears what looks like a gilded loincloth and a purple sash over hard gray-green scales, stippled with blue patches.

His presence is unusual not because the Wrax are unknown in Commonwealth space—quite the opposite, rather. For the last decade, the Wrax and the Commonwealth have been in a state of not-quite-war, fleets bristling along the shared border. Finding one of the lizards *here* is a bit of a surprise.

I can tell it unsettles Ahn, too, by the way her hands drop to her blasters. I quickly touch her shoulder, and she subsides. Kestra glares at us like we're a particularly unpleasant bit of septic discharge, and I give her my sweetest smile in return.

"Hello, Your Highness," she says.

It's mockery, but I accept with a nod. "The correct term of address would be 'Your Radiance', actually, but I appreciate the effort. Hello, Kestra."

"You're looking well."

"That must be very disappointing for you."

"A bit." She smiles, humorlessly. "But from failures come new opportunities, they say."

"So I hear." I glance at the Wrax. "Fascinating company you're keeping."

"This is Custodian Xythiss," Kestra says. "He was very interested in meeting you."

"Custodian?" Ahn says. "Like he cleans the toilets?"

"The translation is not exact." Xythiss takes a step forward and executes a deep bow with unexpected dexterity. His speech is surprisingly good, too, with only a trace of the hiss one usually hears from Wrax. "It means one who cares for the needs of his people. In your language, 'prince' might convey the meaning better." He straightens up, a forked tongue flicking past a muzzle full of needle teeth. "Greetings, Princess Ilya Fortuna Dobraev McDonaugh. Rumors of your beauty have, if anything, understated the case."

Bemused, I bow in return. "Greetings, Custodian Xythiss."

"Smooth-talking lizard," Ahn whispers, and I wave a hand to shush her.

"Before we get bogged down with chit-chat," Kestra says, "can we finish what we came here to do? I'd like to see the merchandise."

I turn my back on them for a moment and extract the Skolig, holding it up for inspection. Even in the dim light of the corridor, the gemstone throws fractured rainbow patterns into every corner.

"Drav?" Kestra says, her eyes fixed on the stone.

"It certainly looks right," he says. "Have to run a test to be sure, of course."

"Of course," I say. "We'll wait right here while you do that."

Kestra gives a nod, but Xythiss holds up a hand.

"Actually, I think that Princess Ilya would be much more comfortable aboard our ship. I would like to extend an... invitation." His tongue flickers again. "We have a great deal to discuss."

Kestra turns her glare on her companion, frowning. "That wasn't what we agreed. If you want to talk to her, you can talk here."

"Indeed," I put in. "I'm not going anywhere."

"I'm afraid I must... insissst." Some of Xythiss's hiss comes through.

Now, I've been doing this long enough to know that when someone says that, in that tone of voice, everything is about to go *rapidly* sideways. More to the point, so has Ahn, and so I get ready to throw myself flat in anticipation of the inevitable thunder of blaster fire. But it doesn't happen—there's a clank of metal and the rising *hum* of energy weapons overhead, but that's all.

The catwalk above us is suddenly ringed by two dozen armored shapes. Half are Wrax soldiers with long, ugly-looking rifles, while the others are spindly wardroids, skeletal things that look like they'd fold up into neat little cubes.

From the looks on Kestra and Drav, this development is as unexpected to them as it is to me. Even more unexpected, though, Ahn is standing still, perfectly calm, arms crossed and not going for her blasters. When I look at her incredulously, she raises her eyebrows, and I can practically read her mind.

No Plan Z, right? There's no gloating in her expression, nothing passive-aggressive, just simple faith. *You asked me to trust you.*

Which is, of course, what I wanted. I just wasn't anticipating running into a platoon of Wrax marines on top of Kestra's smuggler goons.

I force myself to take a deep breath and be calm. It's probably for the best that Ahn hasn't defaulted to shooting everyone. Twenty wardroids and lizard soldiers might be a bit much, even for her, and it's a long way back to the *Wild Ride*. Whatever Xythiss wants, there's still a chance of getting out of here without bloodshed.

"You fucking *snake*," Kestra snarls. She rounds on him, suit legs whirring. "What exactly do you think you're doing—"

Xythiss calmly draws a small pistol from behind his back and shoots her in the head. The crackling energy bolt sprays a mist of blood, brain, and bone against the wall behind her, incidentally painting Drav a mottled red in the process.

Okay. We can still get out of here without any of *my* blood getting shed, which is what really counts. Xythiss holsters his pistol as Kestra's body wobbles and topples over. Drav, looking up at the ring of weapons, raises his hands sheepishly.

"I hope that clarifies matters," Xythiss says. "Master Drav, in case you are pondering anything clever, the squad I left on your ship will have secured it by now. Princess, will you do us the honor of accompanying me to have a conversation in less... squalid surroundings?"

"Well," I manage calmly. "When you put it that way."

The Wrax soldiers descend from the catwalk while the wardroids keep us covered. They search me, not roughly, and to my surprise make no attempt to confiscate the Skolig. Whatever this is about, it doesn't appear to involve the most valuable gemstone in the sector.

Two lizards relieve Ahn of her gunbelt and take hold of her arms. She gives a yelp when one of their claws catches her, and I see a trickle of blood. I take a long step forward and glare at Xythiss.

"I don't know what you're planning," I tell him. "But if you don't tell your thugs to back off, I swear I won't rest until I put you out an airlock."

He blinks, nictitating membranes sliding into place, and hisses something in his own language. The two Wrax step away from Ahn.

"Escort Master Ahn somewhere she can... rest," he tells them. "Politely, please."

I catch Ahn's eye as they lead her away. There's no sign there that her faith in me has been shaken, which perversely shakes *me* in a way I can't really explain. The last I see of her, she's vanishing into one of the weirdly bulbous tunnels, flanked by armed Wrax.

Fuck.

Xythiss's soldiers provide a polite escort back to the *Alcie*. He dismisses most of them, and they take Drav away, while a couple follow us to the rear of the ship. The *Alcie* is older than the *Wild Ride,* but she's in good repair, with no discarded underwear strewn in her corridors. We end up in a passenger cabin—Kestra's smuggling business often includes people, especially those interested in staying clear of the authorities. It's furnished neatly but blandly with a simple bunk, storage unit, and wall console, while a few alien-looking pieces of machinery are presumably Xythiss's. I can't tell if they're navigational systems or kitchen equipment.

"Leave us," he says to the guards. "And do not bother me unless a Commonwealth battleship drops out of hyperspace."

They hiss in the affirmative, and the door slides closed behind us. Xythiss lets out a very human-sounding sigh.

"I apologize for the... unpleasantness," he says. "My research indicated that you and Kestra were not on the best of terms. I hope her demise was not unduly painful to witness."

"I'm used to it," I say. I walk slowly around the room, feeling wary. "It's going to make my business arrangements significantly more difficult, though."

"Selling the Skolig?" He extends a clawed hand. "May I?"

I hand it over with a shrug. He holds it up to the cabin light, watching rainbows swirl and re-form on the walls.

"Beautiful," he says. "But ultimately, of course, simply a gew-gaw." He hands it back to me. "I have a proposition for you, Princess. One I think you will find considerably more advantageous than disposing of stolen merchandise."

I toss the Skolig from hand to hand, feeling its weight. "I'm listening."

"How would you like to be queen?"

I nearly miss the next toss. Xythiss smirks at me, to the extent a lizard can smirk, and turns to a wall console. A few tapsbring up a map of the Commonwealth, with the Kingdom of Ventimosk highlighted. My father's kingdom. My home. Two dozen orbital habitats and half a hundred asteroids spread over three systems.

"You may not be caught up on current events," I say, finally. "My father disowned me and officially struck me from the line of succession. And even if he hadn't, I have two sisters, three brothers, and a great-grandfather in cryonic suspension who would ascend the throne before I could."

"I am aware," Xythiss says smoothly. "But as your father demonstrated, the legalities can be... amended."

He taps another key, and long, curving blue lines slice over the display, crossing the Commonwealth border from Wrax space and impaling it like a volley of arrows. One them goes straight through Ventimosk.

"You're planning an invasion." I keep my voice level, not quite successfully.

"The Commonwealth has grown weak," he says, staring at the plans with satisfaction. "Kingdoms like your own chafe under the rule of your obstreperous Senate. With the proper encouragement, we believe the people of Ventimosk would accept a new ruler. One with... more appropriate ideas."

"Proper encouragement meaning a Wrax war fleet, I assume."

He inclines his head. "Certainly it would be preferable to the alternative, in which your ships are broken and your stations taken by storm. A great deal of unnecessary resource expenditure, and unnecessary bloodshed for you. It could all be so much... simpler."

My heart is beating fast. I swallow, playing for time. "Why me? Why not my father or someone else in the family?"

"Your father and your siblings have a great deal invested in the current order," the lizard says. "You, on the other hand, are an outlaw. Hunted by your own people. Our analysts suspected you would be more open to persuasion."

On the surface, it's not a completely crazy idea. Well. The Wrax are crazy if they think they can defeat the Commonwealth, or that because the people of Ventimosk grumble about taxes and bureaucracy they'd be willing to knuckle under to a bunch of lizards. Clearly Xythiss has not read much of our history, which is about eighty percent doomed last stands against impossible odds. But given that he thinks he can pull that off, having a puppet monarch to put on the throne seems like a good way to go, and who better than the runaway princess playing at thief-with-a-heart-of-gold?

More importantly, by showing me this, Xythiss has made it clear that I'm not walking out of here a free woman. Either

I sign on to this scheme, or he'll have to dispose of me for knowing too much.

Fortunately, I have a plan, and it isn't Plan Z.

I hope Ahn is all right. They wouldn't hurt her before Xythiss gets what he wants from me, would they? I made it clear enough that I wouldn't cooperate if he did.

My fingers tighten around the Skolig.

"I'm sorry," I tell him, "this is just a lot to take in."

"I understand." His tongue flicks. "But you appreciate that our position here is precarious. I require an answer."

"You've got the defenses at Anaxomander Gap wrong, though." I step closer and point to the wall display. "There are three battle stations, not one, and they're closer to the edge of the system."

Xythiss blinks, then turns to examine the map more closely. "Impossible. Our plans are based on the latest intelligence—"

At which point I hit him very hard on the side of the head with a priceless gemstone.

Knocking out an alien is always tricky business, but the Wrax are humanoid enough that the procedure is similar. Xythiss stumbles sideways and sprawls on the floor with barely a squeak. I polish a little green blood off the Skolig and tuck it back in a pocket, then step to the console. A few moments later, a data crystal joins the gemstone, and I gesture the display off.

Time to think about getting out of here. I go to the door, tap the pad to open it a hand's breadth, and call to the guards outside.

"Custodian Xythiss requires the human prisoner Drav," I tell them.

There's a long silence. I picture them looking at one another.

"If I could speak to him—" one says.

"Custodian Xythiss is busy," I snap, with my best royal hauteur. "He ordered that he not be disturbed."

Another silence, then an affirmative hiss. One of the guards walks away.

I spend five minutes pacing back and forth, fretting about Ahn. I have the presence of mind to make sure Xythiss's unconscious body isn't visible from the doorway, though, so when the guards return with Drav, they don't see anything obviously amiss. I wave them away, and they leave the smuggler and shut the door behind him.

Drav has cleaned himself up, thankfully. He raises his eyebrows at me, and I beckon him closer, until he can see Xythiss stashed behind the bed. He gives a low whistle.

"I'm assuming," I say, "that you're not thrilled about working with a bunch of murderous lizards."

He looks at Xythiss for a moment, and my pulse slams in my throat. This is the most dangerous bit—if Drav has cut some kind of private deal with the Wrax, I am *fucked*. Last time I met him, he struck me as a run-of-the-mill scoundrel, but loyal to Kestra. But I've been wrong before.

"No," he says, with a slight spacer drawl. "I can't say that the prospect has me enthused."

"Then you wouldn't be averse to working together to get the fuck out of here?" I produce the Skolig and give it a twirl, spraying rainbows. "In exchange for, say, a share in the proceeds? Assuming you're privy to enough of Kestra's contacts to sell it on."

"I don't think I'd be averse to that at all," he says, smile widening.

"Good." I tuck the Skolig away. "If you can get us off the ship and back to the asteroid, I can get us to the *Wild Ride* and we can be in hyperspace before the lizard wakes up."

This is another gamble, but a safer one. If I know anything about smuggler ships, it's that they tend to be fitted with a bunch of extremely non-standard passages, tunnels, and crawl spaces, ideal for avoiding the attention of any snooping authorities. Sure enough, Drav gives a confident nod.

"I can manage that," he says.

"Then what are we waiting for?"

He grins. After taking a moment to claim Xythiss's hidden blaster pistol, he leads me into the cabin's small washroom, where a wall panel pops off with a few sharp raps. Behind it is a narrow corridor, sandwiched between the outer hull and the inner bulkheads. It's low enough we have to walk bent over, the murmur of the ship's systems washing over us.

"So how did Xythiss and his goons manage to get on board?" I ask quietly. "I thought Kestra was more careful than that."

"Times have been hard lately, and we needed a big score." Drav grimaces. "Xythiss and his entourage paid well. He said he was a merchant who needed escorting around Commonwealth space without official questions. When we heard from you, he acted very interested in that gemstone. Then once we get here, it turns out his big cargo container of 'merchandise' is full of battle armor and wardroids."

"Ouch," I sympathize.

"Fucking lizards." He holds up a hand. "Gotta be quiet for a bit. There's a hidden tunnel under the docking corridor, but if anyone's up there they'll hear us."

I nod and follow his lead. He kneels by a small opening at floor level, barely large enough to crawl through on hands and knees. After listening for a moment, he scoots into it. I follow, with only a slight sigh at the thought of the dust that's going to get all over my beautiful, swoopy dress. Can't look a proper space pirate with gray streaks messing up your black and red. But needs must.

At one point, Drav freezes as heavy footfalls pass directly over our heads. But no one notices our hushed breathing, and once they're past, we keep crawling, until Drav pushes loose another panel and we emerge at the other end of the *Alcie's* boarding tunnel. Drav wiggles out, pistol first. The rocky corridor is empty, the lock behind us closed and dark.

"I hope you know where to go from here," he says, "because I sure as fuck don't."

"I grabbed a map off Xythiss's console." I turn slightly, lining my memory up with the dead-reckoning sense in my head. "This way. Come on."

We hurry down the tunnels as quietly as we can, ducking into side junctions whenever we hear an approaching Wrax. Fortunately, Xythiss's soldiers think they're alone and make plenty of noise. Most are heading back to the *Alcie,* presumably wondering what's keeping their boss. Eventually, somebody is going to overcome their reticence and break into his cabin. We'd better be well away from here by then.

"Shh," Drav says, crouching by a tunnel entrance. "There's a guard."

We're back at the central cavern. All roads lead through here, unfortunately, which makes it a good place to post a watchman. I risk a quick glance and spot an armored Wrax, blaster rifle in hand, walking a slow circuit.

"Can you hit him from here?" I ask, nodding to the pistol.

Drav shakes his head. "With that armor, it'll take a head shot to be sure."

Ahn would have been able to make the shot. Ah well. "I'll get him closer then." I brush dust off my dress. "Be ready."

Before he can say anything, I step into the open. The Wrax hears me and turns, rifle coming up. Whatever he was expecting, though, it's not me in full imperious stride. I figured he wouldn't shoot, since he last saw me in the boss's company, but I can't deny my heart beats a little faster until he lowers the weapon.

"What... you... doing here?" His words are a choking hiss, with none of Xythiss's sophistication.

"I've come to collect you, of course," I tell him. "Custodian Xythiss wants to speak to everyone, now that we've come to an arrangement."

"You... prisoner!" He raises the rifle as I get closer. "Sssstay back!"

I hold up my hands and put on a demure smile. "Well, not a *prisoner*, but I'm certainly not going anywhere. Come on." I loop one arm around his and bat my eyes. Probably wasted effort, given that he's a lizard, but you hear stories. "Custodian Xythiss is waiting."

"Waiting?" He looks confused, but allows me to tug him forward a few steps. Then he shakes his head. "Musssst check in. Orders." He reaches for a control pad at his throat.

"He *did* say he was in a hurry," I manage, dragging the guard another step. "Just ask him yourself."

"No!" He pulls away from me, raising his rifle again. "You, hands up!"

The Wrax takes a couple of steps back, putting him well out of my reach. Fortunately, since I managed to turn him around, this also puts him within a meter of Drav's hiding place. The smuggler emerges, pistol raised, and I sidestep neatly to avoid being caught in the spray of lizard-bits. The headless guard sprawls on the floor, rifle clattering away.

"You," Drav says, "have got some serious guts, I have to admit." He shakes his head. "What would you have done if he'd started shooting?"

"Fucking died, obviously," I say. "But in this line of work you develop a sense for itchy trigger fingers." I let out a breath and point to another tunnel. "All right. That way."

Drav's eyes narrow, and he points another direction. "Your ship is that way. I saw it when you came in."

Damn. I was hoping not to have to explain. "It is, but Xythiss has got Ahn locked up over there. We need to grab her before we get out."

"You've gotta be kidding," he says. "There's a half-dozen wardroids with her, and they'll be on to us any minute now. We'll get slaughtered."

"I have a few ideas."

"I'll hear them once we're out of here," he says. "Besides, the fewer shares the better, right?"

"Ahn's my partner." For my sins.

"You can find a new partner." He grins. "Hell, we might do pretty well together, have you considered that?"

I give a tired sigh, because I can see exactly where this is going. "I'm not leaving without her."

"Really," he says. "What's she got that I don't?"

For starters, I think, as he turns the gun on me, I trust her. And she trusts me. No Plan Z, I'd told her, and she'd gone along quietly when a bunch of lizards marched her to a cell. Trust was important to me when I was a princess. Now that I'm a thief, it's a commodity more valuable than even the Skolig.

Plus, of course, she's a hell of a lot better looking than Drav. I shrug.

"Fair enough." Drav aims the blaster at my chest. "I'll take the gem and be on my way, then."

"How unexpected." I raise my hands. "It's in my pocket."

"Slowly," he says.

I extract the Skolig, and he points to the floor. With another sigh, I set the gemstone down and back away. He shuffles forward, snatches it up, and backs off again.

"I guess this is where we say goodbye, then," he says. "Unless you want to change your mind."

"Aiming a gun at me is not helping your argument," I tell him.

"Nothing personal." He reaches the tunnel's mouth and salutes me with the weapon. "Another time, Princess. Good luck with the lizards."

Then he's gone, running toward the *Wild Ride*. His footsteps fade away, and I sigh for a third time.

I *really* didn't want to do this. My poor dress.

I pick up the guard's blaster rifle, make sure I know how to fire it, and go to the wall. Picking a section that bulges outward, I deliver a few hard kicks. It cracks open like an eggshell, revealing darkness beyond.

The thing about AH-1310 is that it's not really an asteroid. It's a waxworm nest.

It looks like an asteroid, which is the whole point, as far as the waxworms are concerned. Only if you did a really detailed subsurface scan would you notice the sinuous tunnels running everywhere, just below the larger spaces that long-ago humans sealed off and pumped full of air.

Waxworms are large, harmless creatures with a complicated life cycle, one segment of which involves a sort of space orgy. A writhing ball of worms, furiously mating in all directions, builds up a nest out of their waxy secretions. Where the stuff is exposed to vacuum, it goes hard as rock, leaving an asteroid-like object shot through with weird tunnels, perfect for unsuspecting guests to take over.

The worms have long since moved on (or, more accurately, metamorphosed into space-going moths coasting on diaphanous lightsails) but the nest is still here. Under the thin shell, it's a spaghetti-like mess of tunnels just about wide enough for a human to move through, if said human were willing to hold her breath and deal with the fact that the place is still half-full of worm secretions.

I thought this particular quirk of AH-1310 might come in handy, and so it has proved, but I really, really hoped I wouldn't have to use it, or at least would have the chance to change into a spacesuit first. The worm goo isn't toxic, but it smells *awful*, like rotting meat.

Once again, though, needs must.

I take a lungful of air and climb through the opening I've made, rifle first. It's like stepping into gelatin, not quite liquid but definitely not solid either, light enough that I can make reasonable progress with a sort of half-shuffle, half swim. The map in Xythiss's console helpfully indicated the old storeroom where they're holding Ahn, and combined with my inborn navigation talent—thanks again, great-to-the-whatever-grandma—it's not too difficult to worm (pun somewhat intended) my way there. By the time I arrive, my lungs are burning, but breathing in is too horrible to contemplate. I slam the butt of the rifle against the wall until the rocky shell breaks, letting me slide out with a gush of waxy, gray fluid, like some horrible mutant birth.

Ahn, sitting on a dusty crate, jumps to her feet in alarm, then rushes over as I clamber up onto my hands and knees, dripping slime.

"Ilya!"

"Please don't kiss me," I say, getting up, "I'm—"

She kisses me, then backs away, making a face.

"—covered in worm goo," I finish wearily. "Love you, too."

"Are you all right?" she says. "I've been really worried."

"Am I all right? I'm here to rescue you, aren't I?" I run my fingers through my hair and whip a handful of slime to the ground. "I have everything under control."

"I'll bet." She gives me her lopsided grin. "Have you still got the Skolig?"

"Not exactly. Drav took it when he ran off to steal the *Wild Ride*. But I've got something better." I pat my pocket, where the data crystal from Xythiss's room is still safe. "Wrax invasion plans, signed and sealed. I figure delivering these to Commonwealth intelligence should get them off our backs and score us a fat bounty in the bargain."

"Brilliant." She frowns. "But how are we getting out of here if Drav took the *Ride*?"

"The *Ride* will still be waiting. I didn't give Drav the trap code." Some time ago, we equipped the ship with a mechanism that floods the cockpit with a powerful neuroelectric stun field if the proper code isn't entered at startup, with exactly this sort of situation in mind. "So we can pick up the Skolig on the way out as well."

"Fucking *brilliant*." Ahn hugs me, in spite of the slime. "I knew you'd come up with something."

"You really did, didn't you?" I stare at her for a moment, then shake my head. What did I do to earn trust like that? Or to deserve it?

"Something wrong?"

"I'll tell you later."

I turn to the storeroom door. It's locked from the outside, but a blast from the rifle fixes that. Ahn's pistol belt is lying nearby, and I toss it to her. She buckles it on with a big smile, looking fully dressed again.

The wardroids have heard the shot, of course. I see lights flicker at the other end of the corridor as they clank toward us to investigate.

"Now what?" Ahn says, eagerly. "Time for Plan Z?"

I look at her, then down at my ruined dress and the blaster rifle in my hands. I can feel my own grin spreading.

"Yeah," I tell her. "*Definitely* time for Plan Z."

Little Birds
by Cara Patterson

All eyes followed the sultan's Little Birds as they marched towards the palace in twelve ranks of four abreast, indigo robes embroidered with the silver crescent moon and head-scarves patterned with silver wings.

Aiyla led the column through the gates, leaning on her staff to steady herself. For fourteen years, more than half her life, she had donned the indigo, and now she was the oldest. The youngest were scarcely beyond the first bloom of womanhood, following her guidance.

The life of a Little Bird was not a long one. There was no shame in returning a wounded warrior. Those who survived battle after battle and returned to the skies were respected, even revered. For each successful flight, they received a silver star. Aiyla's uniform was a constellation.

The chief eunuch greeted them inside the private palace courtyard. He was a plump man with a warm smile.

"The valide welcomes you," he said in his high, fluting voice. "Please follow me."

They had been summoned by the sultan's mother before, and they would be again. Not men, but not quite women, they were the only members of the sultan's military who could pass into the harem unquestioned. They were novelties to the ladies of the harem. Oddities to be appreciated and enjoyed.

At the foot of a staircase, Nuray reached out to Aiyla. They supported one another, the Little Birds, and offered a hand when one's feet were unsteady. Nuray winced in sympathy at Aiyla's labored steps, then drew back as soon as they were on even ground. The cohort paused there, unpinning their veils and shaking dust from their skirts.

The eunuch stared at Aiyla's face. "You were badly injured in battle?"

Aiyla half-wished she had remained at the barracks. "Only mildly." Silk stitches marred her cheeks, and an aching furrow carved across her calf. The physicians believed these would heal, but it would take time.

"Then we are doubly honored!"

She managed a thin smile, then raised a hand. The flurry of skirts sounded like the wings of pigeons as they fell in.

They didn't proceed to the valide's chambers, instead passing into a garden courtyard deeper in the palace, sun-washed kiosks spread around them. The valide was seated—accompanied by her own flock of ladies—in an open pavilion, her elegant hands resting in her lap.

Aiyla's gaze flicked along their faces and, to the far left, standing upright, she found the one she sought. Her heart leapt.

The valide smiled and Aiyla could not help recalling that a dancing monkey had received that very same smile. Behind her, the Birds fluttered.

"My son spoke of your bravery in the recent battle." With her fine clothing, soft voice, and refined manners, she made the Birds look coarse and common. Perhaps, Aiyla thought uncomfortably, there was a reason she considered them equal to dancing monkeys. "We wished to honor your courage and skill." The valide turned and nodded.

The woman at the far left bowed and withdrew. She returned a moment later, followed by more of the sultan's cariyes, each bearing a folded bundle of indigo. They approached the Little Birds, some staring, some flushing.

The leader came to Aiyla, as tall and slender as a willow, eyes as green as new leaves, hair the color of ripe wheat, skin as pale as milk. Why the sultan overlooked Zerren, Aiyla never understood. She had never seen anyone so beautiful in her life.

"Your face," Zerren murmured.

"It will heal," Aiyla breathed, lips barely moving to hide the extent of their conversation. She glanced down at the bundle in Zerren's hands and a smile escaped, straining her stitches. Aiyla reached out and, beneath the bundle, her fingers brushed Zerren's, the woman's skin as soft as feathers. "Thank you," she said. "They look very warm."

For each cariye carried a new uniform with quilted, layered fabric instead of thin silk. Only one person had heard her complain of the bitterness of the air when she flew and could have suggested new, warmer uniforms to the valide.

Zerren's cheeks flushed rose-pink and her eyes shone. She bobbed and retreated with her fellows.

Aiyla glanced along her flock, then barked the command. As one, they bowed to the valide, thanking her for her generous gift.

The valide seemed pleased and called for cushions and sherbet. Musicians emerged and the Little Birds broke ranks at Aiyla's nod, though most huddled together, careful and self-conscious. They had been here before. They remembered the stares and titters as they ate and drank like soldiers.

Aiyla sat—her leg ached too much not to—and set her new uniform in her lap, running her fingers along the collar. The texture caught her attention and she turned the fabric. Silver words shone, stitched into the lining. Aiyla's heart stuttered and she hastily pressed the cloth back down.

A rustle of skirts made her look up as Zerren descended on her, like a falcon to its master's glove. "Her Highness bid me bring you refreshments," she murmured, going to one knee, a golden goblet cradled in her hands. "And the cup, for your valor."

Aiyla curved her hands around Zerren's. "I thank her for her generosity." Her fingers drifted, tracing fine bones and smooth skin and she drank in those eyes, leaves in sunlight. "It pleases me to receive it." She held that green gaze as she put the cup—still warm from Zerren's touch—to her lips.

Zerren flushed, rising to join the other cariyes, and there were no further chances to exchange words. Too many eyes... and too many young Birds to watch over who knew nothing of palace etiquette. Every so often, a rap of her staff to the flag-stones reminded them of their place.

Once the valide had been sufficiently entertained, they were escorted out by the chief eunuch. Cariyes lined the hallway as they departed, and Aiyla caught a glimpse of green and gold and a smile before they returned to the world outside.

Only once they reached their barracks did the Birds break out in titters.

"New uniforms!" Yildiz squealed, delighted. "*Warm* uniforms!"

"I wonder who gave them that idea." Nuray looked knowingly at Aiyla.

Aiyla only smiled, holding the folded fabric close to her heart.

Despite her healing injuries, Aiyla was dispatched to the Polish border with nine other Birds only ten days after the visit. The army was marching in response to… Aiyla couldn't be sure. Another insult, battle, or dispute.

Inside their tent, Aiyla knelt by her bedroll. Each Little Bird respected the others' personal, pre-battle traditions. Now, they left her alone to pray.

Instead, she spread out her uniform. By flickering lamp-light, silver embroidery shone. She traced the letters with her fingertips, following the shape of the words, each one crafted by a most beloved hand.

It was a nonsense poem, playing on her name. Foolish and enough to make her blush. *Stay, the wheat whispered when the dawn came. Give me the silver of the moon, not the gold of the sun.*

Aiyla curled her fingers into the cloth. She should never have come to this, aching with longing.

The Birds could take no husband. From the moment they entered their barracks, their lives were the sultan's. Their names were taken and new ones given, as much an identity as the indigo. They were taught to fly, and when orders came, they took wing.

She buried her face in the fabric. No, it should never have come to this.

Without her wings and her stars, she would never have known Zerren existed. She would never have been invited—commanded—to demonstrate her skills for the valide those many months ago. She would never have requested "the tall one" help prepare her wings.

To her surprise, Zerren had not stared or giggled when she approached. She towered head and shoulders over Aiyla and took instruction readily, tilting the wing-frame so Aiyla could make final adjustments.

"Hm."

The doubtful sound caught Aiyla off-guard as she tightened her rods. "What?"

"It seems so fragile," the golden-haired woman said. "Are you not afraid?"

Aiyla almost lied—as she usually did—but the woman looked at her with such grave interest in her green eyes. "Every time," she admitted. She pulled one wing's fabric taut. "And every time I return, I weep for hours."

"Relief?" this golden angel asked quietly. "Or sorrow?"

Only another kind of bird in a different cage could understand.

When Aiyla bit down the treasonous reply, Zerren glanced at the pavilion wall and the ramp for Aiyla's run. Beyond, the city spread towards the Golden Horn and—across the water—the spike of Galata tower pricked the sky. Decades ago, a man had made the first wings and flown from that tower. Now, no men dared.

"How far will your wings take you today?" She tilted the other wing down.

Aiyla ducked beneath her arm, half-hidden by her flaxen hair—it smelled of rosewater and cedar wood—and pulled on the wings. "If the winds are with me, I will land on a flat roof-top. If not..." She had shuddered. "The water."

"I miss the water," Zerren said, strange sadness in her voice. "I used to swim."

Aiyla forgot all about the wings. "Swim?"

When Zerren smiled, it illuminated the world. "Like your flying," she murmured, "but in the water." Her brilliant green eyes sparkled with mirth. "I suppose I am a duck to your eagle."

Aiyla stared at her then. Oh, how she stared. It was as if she had stepped into sunlight for the first time and her words failed her.

Zerren's cheeks pinked. "Your wings." She cleared her throat. "They are ready?"

"Yes. Yes!" Aiyla nodded quickly. "All ready."

They stepped apart, both flushed and awkward. Aiyla donned her veil, and the demonstration went as planned, though she had to deal with the indignity of requesting passage from a family's roof.

That should have been the end, but days later a palace kira visited the barracks. The Birds occasionally did business with the kiras—Jewish women who could visit the city, buying and collecting on behalf of those confined by their positions. She brought paper and ink supposedly at Aiyla's request and—hidden among the unsolicited sheets—the first letter.

Zerren's beautiful writing brimmed with warmth and humor. For months, Aiyla found herself laughing into her hand, finding quiet corners where she could hoard her mirth and scribble responses. Their masters disapproved of any outside ties. Some had been beaten for flouting that particular rule. All too soon, she had to burn the precious pages.

The uniform, though....

Aiyla fingered the lettering stitched into the cloth frequently. Each Bird tended her own uniform, which Zerren knew— Aiyla had complained often enough while struggling with repairs. She had given a secret message, a portable token, a gesture of affection.

Tent canvas slapped and rattled.

"Aiyla?"

Aiyla pulled on the quilted jacket. "Come."

Nuray poked her head in. "The weather is turning. They want us on the hillside now."

Aiyla snatched up her helmet, plain dark leather with a chin-strap, and followed Nuray out to meet the other Birds. It was a heavy, sticky day and the new uniform felt too warm, but that was on the ground. In the air, it would be a different matter.

The hill's incline was shallow, but steep enough with help from the horses. Their enemies had grown wiser in the last two decades, seeking battlegrounds *not* edged by hillsides. No one wanted to be underneath the Turkish creatures who came from the mountains and rained fire from the sky.

Her groom nodded in greeting, and made a gesture she recognized as salutation. Despite her indigo veil, Tamraz always spotted her among her sisters and greeted her accordingly. He looked calm, which meant the ground was good, which in turn settled the nerves fluttering around her heart.

The squad master awaited them in a tent, a map spread out before him.

"Our spies report the enemy has gunpowder here, here, and here." He tapped three points with his stick. "Your main targets. If you cannot strike them, your job is fear and chaos."

Aiyla glanced around the table at her sisters, remembering the last battles. The rip of metal through her flesh, and the sound of her wings tearing. Pain.

"What of their weapons?" she asked. "Their guns—"

Five sharp raps on the map, pointing to colored flags. "Cannon. Muskets. Some new, upward-facing cannon. Catapults. Archers."

All made to target people in the air. Aiyla swallowed the hot, sick feeling in her throat. The master continued. Placements, munitions, secondary targets to weaken the enemy.

"Make ready," he snapped.

Nuray darted to Aiyla's side as they hurried towards the wings. "Upward-facing cannon," she murmured. When Aiyla shivered, Nuray caught her hand, squeezed. "We know where they are. We know how to avoid them."

The master's boys were readying the wings as they neared. They had a part in building the wings, yet not one of them was brave enough to fly, even before they grew too large.

"Fah," Nuray muttered under her breath. "The alignment is crooked again. Are they blind? Do they want me to fly in circles?"

Aiyla's veil hid her grin. "What do they know? All they see are sticks and cloth." She brushed Nuray's hand. "Go. Fix your wings. I'll sing today."

Mercifully, they were easy to divert. The sisters had a pact. If your wings were fine, you were the distraction, fretting loudy so the boys would fuss and speak over you and pay no heed to your sisters hastily fixing their own wings. Singing.

When she was still young enough to be foolish, Aiyla had raised her concerns directly and been told she didn't understand the technicalities of constructing wings. So she'd broken off a faulty piece and thrown it at them. She had been sorely beaten for it and learned to hold her tongue.

For Nuray's sake, she endured a long lecture about form and frame, as if she hadn't been flying for longer than the boys had been walking. Her veil was a mercy, hiding her yawns, as they fussed and arranged the ropes that would get her airbound. The leather loop suspended beneath the frame pressed into Aiyla's belly and she wrapped her hands around the grips above her head.

When the horn blew, they scattered.

Are you not afraid?

Every time.

Aiyla drew a shivering breath. A prayer should have been on her lips. Instead, she thought of green and gold. She glimpsed Tamraz's face in the torchlight, the flicker of his hands making the sign, and exhaled.

Aloft, the world was hers, but this moment, when the world tilted and she was ripped from the ground, never became easier. A torch waved and hooves thundered across the ground. Canvas snapped in the wind and one by one, with each dip of the torch, dark wings were pulled aloft. Smoothly, she hoped. Cleanly. There had been too many accidents.

The rope wrenched taut. She was torn from the hillside and flung skyward, the world dropping away and her heart left behind.

Feet up. Hold steady. Find the air current.

Cool wind whipped her face, her eyes stung, and she fumbled her feet onto the rear crossbar. And there, the current caught her, lifting her. Relief swooped in as she unhooked the rope and let it fall away. Her heart settled into a steadier rhythm. Below, trimmed in silver, she could see the camps.

Silver.

The moon was breaking through the clouds. No! Blades of pale light widened across the sky, picking out wings, turning the Birds into shadows against the brightness.

"Turn back!" she bellowed, but the wind tore her words away.

Gunfire rattled up from the camp below.

The Birds spread as much as the buffeting winds would allow. Some weaved between shafts of moonlight, hiding in the dark. Flames blossomed where their bombs fell, but nowhere near the targets. Chaos and survival were the only choice now.

Aiyla tilted, sweeping a curve out of the spreading moonlight. A shriek caught on the air as a Bird fell, punctured wings tumbling her over and over.

Low enough to be hit, but too high to survive.

Aiyla's hands shook and she swung in. She whistled a sharp, shrilling sound that cut through the air, then tilted and locked her grips in position. Her wings carried her in wide circles. Across the silvering sky, her sisters did the same.

With wind-chapped hands, she tore a bomb from her belt. The rasping wick sizzled to life and she aimed at the campfires' glow. *Let it rain.* They scattered bombs like burning chaff, sowing carnage, even as they ululated to the sky for their loss.

Tents burst into flames and people ran. Gunfire crackled and snapped. Above her, someone cried out in pain. The Bird broke formation, retreating to the Ottoman camp.

Good. Aiyla spun back into the swiping shadows. *Alive is better.*

Spreading fire illuminated the camp below, its scouring heat granting them a little more lift. *Enough.* Aiyla whistled sharply, the signal to withdraw.

A musket ball whistled past, making Aiyla twist and search for the enemy. There. Aiyla's heart leapt to her throat. Dozens of cannons, all aimed upward. Men scrambling over them, loading, filling, preparing....

So close, her Birds would be torn as easily as paper.

Aiyla took a shivering breath. She could not grant them speed, but where there were cannons, there would be gunpowder, and where there was gunpowder....

She angled her wings for increased velocity and smiled furiously behind her veil. No more sisters would fall tonight, not as long as she lived and breathed.

The enemy spotted her and she heard the shouts, the shrill of shots shredding the air. At least one hit her wings, taut fabric bursting open above her. Her every breath burned with the scorching updraft as she clung to the grips, trying to keep herself from spinning, falling, crashing.

Blinking the haze from her eyes, she snatched bombs from her belt, and as she descended, she dropped them towards powder barrels, delicate as Zerren scattering rose petals. Panic flooded the pale, upturned faces.

For a moment, there was nothing and then....

And then, the world was aflame.

Aiyla gazed at the ceiling, flickers of lamplight casting strange, blurred shadows along the beams. After the explosions on the battlefield, things were unclear. Pain, she remembered well, and hands on her. Darkness and shouts.

In the haze of lost days, she had been borne back to the city, with enough time passed for the burns on her hands and face to start healing. Her veil had been scoured away along with her lashes and eyebrows. The physicians said her eyes might never fully recover. Only the thickness of her uniform had protected her body, Zerren's gift the very thing that kept her alive.

Little of it had survived. Secret words burned to ash.

The muezzin's call from the mosque broke through the silence. *Dawn*, Aiyla thought, and struggled to sit.

Her chest tightened at once, a spasm of pain making her cough. Fresh blood spattered on her bandages. Ah. Yes. The worst of the damage. She'd drawn too many burning breaths, the physicians said. It might heal, it might not.

With trembling hands, she picked up a cup of cool, poppy-laced water. A sip seared enough to make her hazed eyes sting, but it took the taste of metal from her tongue and eased the pain a little. The cup felt unbearably heavy and all too soon, she had to lie down again.

What a ruin she was. A final star, no doubt. They could not—would not—let her fly again. No more wind against her face as she rose aloft. No more laughter with her sisters.

And in the secret, selfish part of her, she knew this meant no more green and gold smiles. No more letters slipped into the kira's hands. Too damaged and useless, she would be turned out as her sisters had been before her.

She would no longer be a Bird.

What did that make her?

Aiyla pressed her eyes shut. To weep would only hurt more, eyes and tattered throat. It would help no one. And yet the salt seared its way down her cheeks, dropping like rain on the covers.

Dawn became day and still she lay.

The physicians came, though they asked her nothing. She could not speak and even if she could, what could she say? They spoke over her as if she wasn't there, removing bandages and examining her hands. A slave was called in to dress her wounds. Rana, a one-time Bird hopeful. She was young, striking and dark, but had proved too frail to fly.

Rana gently smoothed salve on her cheeks. "Your sisters pray for your health," Rana whispered. Aiyla's eyes burned, but neither physician noticed Rana deftly dabbing tears. She took Aiyla's hands again, gently, and a folded parchment slid between bandages and flesh.

Aiyla's heart gave a strange leap.

"Enough," one physician snapped. Rana scurried out, and the physicians followed with stern words to rest and drink the poppy-juice. As soon as the door closed, Aiyla fumbled with the hidden parchment.

Her breath stabbed in her lungs to see Zerren's elegant hand. Unsteadily, she limped to the window, turning the page to the light.

My Eagle. They say you were wounded. Trust me and do not fear. You will not be cast out. I will make sure of it. I have the valide's ear.

Aiyla's face drew painfully tight as she fought the sob of relief. Zerren did not have much, but she had her influence and if she spoke truly....

With effort, she returned to her bed, clutching the parchment scrap to her breast. If. If she spoke truly. No, there was no place for doubt. Zerren would use her clever tongue and, like the impossible uniforms, she would see something done. Something that was not exile, cast out alone and stripped of position.

Anything was better than that.

Days crept by, one after another.

Aiyla's vision cleared and the pain in her throat eased, but her speech did not return. The physicians—speaking as if she was deaf as well as mute—decided it was unlikely. She would be fortunate if she was of use to anyone, they said. She tried not to listen.

Beyond their care, the medical room was deserted. They kept her sisters from her, not one of them permitted near her now she was no longer a Bird.

Only Rana could whisper news as she dressed Aiyla's wounds. Her final assault had detonated the enemy's powder-store and shattered several battalions. The Polish army had scattered and the sultan's troops had swept in, dealing with those who remained.

It was cold comfort when her hands shook and her breath tasted of iron.

When she woke in a cold sweat, fear still wrapped around her spine, she crept down to the courtyard and sat, watching the grooms with the horses. Their hands moved like dancers in silent communication, all of them forcibly muted for security's sake. Deciphering the gestures was a distraction, keeping away darker thoughts and nightmares that haunted her sleep.

She watched and she learned, but only Tamraz would exchange words with her. To the servants, she was an anomaly. To the grooms, she was no longer relevant.

To Zerren....

If Zerren were here, in this medical room, she'd smile and brighten the narrow places with her nonsense tales and jokes.

When the master finally came, Aiyla only looked at him when he rapped his staff upon the floor, fear knitted about her heart. "You are to be retired from the Birds." For once, his voice was gentle. Retired. Not dismissed. "Your deeds and sacrifices in the sultan's name have pleased him greatly. In honor of your service, you are to be freed and rewarded with an estate worthy of your actions."

Aiyla's world swirled.

Freed.

Once, she had been a small child with a family. A long time ago. Many hundreds of miles away. They were gone now, and she was... she was a woman again. A free woman. What could a free woman do without a family? Without a friend? Without her sisters?

Unexpectedly, her eyes brimmed over, hot tears spilling down her face.

The master chose not to notice. "When you are recovered," he continued, as if she wasn't shaking with grief and confusion, "we will arrange for you to be transported to your new residence."

Freed and granted a new home and funds, honored by the sultan! Yet the barracks were all she had known for half her life; beyond those walls, there was only one face she wanted to—and would never—see again.

This was all Zerren's doing. She had vowed to protect Aiyla and had spoken softly and whispered a home and a new life into existence for her.

Aiyla tugged the master's sleeve to get his departing attention, then made a sign of writing.

His bushy brows furrowed. "You wish to write? To whom?"

Helplessly, she waved in the direction of the palace.

The master's broad face widened in a smile. "Ah. To thank the padishah for his generosity?"

She inclined her head, clutching both hands to her heart. He could have named anyone in the palace. She would not have cared as long as she was given paper and ink.

The next time a kira was called to the barracks, she left burdened with a tight curl of parchment. Aiyla's letter for Zerren was brief. *Gentlest of ducks. You have done much for me. Would that I could repay you. Would that I could fly to you. Thank you, thank you, thank you. I hope one day you will swim again.*

It was not enough, not by far. If only she could have offered Zerren a way out of her cage, too, somewhere safe and free and provided for. If only... if only Zerren could come with her. But the sultan's generosity only stretched so far. To be granted a home and freedom were rare enough. To demand one of his women? He would never allow it.

Three days passed before the kira returned. "I have the salve you asked for to soothe your burns." She offered a small jar, and—as their hands met—parchment brushed Aiyla's fingertips.

Aiyla bowed in gratitude. Courtesy dictated she offer the woman refreshment, and the kira feigned fascination with a plate of honey cakes while Aiyla turned her back and unknotted her precious message, heart drumming.

Would that this duck could fly from these heights and seek a new nest.

Aiyla's throat ached. With a fingertip, she traced each letter. *Would that this duck could fly.* Ah, if they could both fly, far, far away, where none could follow them. But she would be free soon and Zerren closed behind the high walls of the palace, far above....

Far above the city. High enough for someone with wings to fly. To *escape.*

To fly if one had wings.

Aiyla smiled and scrambled to write her reply. Dangerous and reckless and full of possibilities.

"For the valide?" the kira asked mildly, a gentle reminder that a message required a cause.

It was an hour before she departed, carrying a grateful letter for the valide and something else entirely for Zerren. If that scrap of parchment fell into the wrong hands, the *bostancıs* would tighten silk cords around their throats and consign them to the bottom of the Bosphorus.

And yet, better to risk flying through the flames to come out the other side.

The choice lay with Zerren now.

No word came from the palace.

Until she knew Zerren's decision, Aiyla could not allow the masters to send her away. So she coughed and wheezed and took to her bed and waited.

The burns to her hands were almost healed, but Rana still came to apply salve and change linens. She worked slowly to outlast the physicians each day.

"The masters had an unexpected visitor today," she whispered, smoothing salve onto swollen fingers. "The valide intends to decorate the palace to celebrate the sultan's victory."

Aiyla's heart fluttered.

The sultan's victory. Aiyla's victory.

"They requested the..." Rana flapped a hand. "The... drawings of a pair of wings. They wish to make a pretty model to display in the gardens so the padishah's guests will remember how he defeated his enemies."

Aiyla had to bite the inside of her lip to keep from smiling. Someone had planted the seed of an idea for a pair of wings inside the palace walls. A duck, she thought with a rush of joy, who longed to fly.

The plan was in motion.

If the palace built wings, they would be simple—decorative, above all else—but if they were based on the standard design, they should still be functional.

"They will remember your victory well," Rana whispered. "Even if the sultan will not give it your name." She tied fresh linens in place and very gently squeezed Aiyla's hands. "The Birds will never be forgotten."

Aiyla bowed over their clasped hands gratefully, then rose and hurried down the corridors to the sand-strewn yard. Mercifully, the grooms had long since stopped questioning her presence.

Wings were built for a small, light passenger, she thought. All Birds were of a similar height and build. Zerren was both taller and had a... a fuller shape. Not as tall as a man, though, and Hezârfen Ahmed Çelebi had built and flown the first wings across the Bosphorus. If he could do it....

Aiyla frowned, sketching in the sand with a stick. The original wings were larger. She etched her own wings and then Çelebi's above them. Yes, larger, but not by much.

With only an estimate of Zerren's weight, she tried to work out the distribution ratio to a fully armed Bird. The trouble was that while the palace nested high, the city spread beneath it. Zerren had to get as far across the waters of the Golden Horn as possible, close enough to reach the other side where Aiyla waited without being spotted. Guards could not be aware of what had happened until it was too late. That was key.

The sun was sinking by the time she hurried back into her room. She hastily sketched her calculations with ink and hidden parchment ribbons, then sent another note to the master, pleading for the kira's medicinal balms.

Like finding and riding a current, the lift and dip, not certain when the next turn would come, parchment flew back and forth between the palace and the barracks. Little by little, an impossible plan took shape.

Finally, when Aiyla's eyes no longer burned and the pain in her lungs was almost faded, a single line was delivered in a small box of throat-soothing sweets.

I will look on the moon's face two days hence.

Two days. Aiyla's chest tightened sharply. The full moon. Dangerous, for its bright silver, but generous that Zerren could see.

Two days.

She made farewells as best she could as each squad passed through, exchanging a last embrace with Nuray, who— she was proud to see—had been elevated as the new commander. They would still be a flock though her own wings had been clipped.

No. She would be a different kind of bird; that was all. New walls, her own walls. It was a wondrous and terrifying thought, to be beholden to no master.

The masters agreed at once that she could depart on the night of the full moon. A good choice, they said. The Birds always traveled at night to limit curious stares.

"We can spare a groom," her master said. "He will see you safely delivered."

She tapped on the master's table, then traced a name on the wood with her fingertip.

"Tamraz?" The master arched an eyebrow.

She nodded firmly. He had been a steady hand when she took the wing and a good friend to her through her recovery. Now, it was only fair he was the one to see her on her way. And, if everything went to plan, she needed someone she could trust.

The following day and night were unbearable, like the moment before the rope pulled taut and she was flung aloft. A thousand and one fears assailed her, just as they did before she took to the air. Was everything prepared? Were the wings stable? Would they have enough lift? Would Zerren be able to balance them?

Sleep was a forgotten friend as she paced and fretted, spending hours gazing out over the sprawl of the city towards the palace.

More than once, she penned a note to Zerren, insisting it was too dangerous. And as many times, she watched the words burn to cinders.

Zerren wanted to escape her cage and would risk the unknown to do so. It would dishonor her to shy back out of fear.

When the second night came, Aiyla was sick with dread as she gathered her meager belongings and descended the stairs for the last time. The few Birds present flocked to embrace her and press small tokens into her hands. Some wept, but Aiyla's eyes were as dry as her mouth.

Tamraz waited in the courtyard beside the wagon. Its lamps glowed purple in the growing darkness, the only sign it would contain someone remarkable. He grinned, crooked-toothed, as he opened the shuttered door for her, then closed it on the world she knew.

Aiyla curled up on the seat amidst blankets and cushions. The carriage rattled out of the yard, and she tugged her dagger from her belt and wedged it into the shutters, cracking one open enough to see the city as it whisked by.

She had implored the masters to allow her to see the palace one more time, even from across the water. It would be a final farewell to the padishah. So instead of turning north, the carriage went south, winding its way behind Galata tower and down to the bristling docks that clung to the Golden Horn.

The city made a shadowy shape of silver-tipped minarets, domes, and towers. Lights flickered and glowed against the darkness, speckled like starlight. Vessels bobbed in the water-way, a rolling labyrinth she hadn't even considered.

When they drew parallel to the palace, Aiyla pounded her shaking hand against the wagon's ceiling. The carriage rocked, and Tamraz clambered down to open the door for her. He made a grand, sweeping gesture towards the palace, feigning awe. Behind her veil, Aiyla almost smiled.

The breeze off the water whipped at her skirts. If nothing else, they had a good wind.

She walked forward, gazing up, watching, waiting, a prayer catching in her throat. The lanterns spread mottled pools of purple light across the cobbles, and she heard the laughter and chatter of men smoking down by the water's edge.

The moon hung high and pale, brilliantly white in an otherwise empty sky. Had she read Zerren's message incorrectly? Was it the right night?

A startled yell from the men on the dockside made her jump. Their voices rose in a cacophony and she caught a word, turned, and there, hanging in the heavens, broad and dark, were wings. Aiyla ran forward.

Not enough speed, she could see at once. Not enough lift. The front tipped down sharply and—like a gull trying to ride out a gale—the wings tilted wildly from side to side. Her heart jumped to her throat.

Aiyla raised her hands to shield her eyes from the moonlight, trying to pick out Zerren in the shadows stretching beneath the wings. Yes, yes, there was someone beneath it, struggling, clearly fighting against the tossing wind. A long body dangled below the broad span of the wings, clinging to the hand grips, the harness flapping uselessly—broken.

Her legs weren't up, Aiyla thought wildly. She hadn't swung her legs up. Her weight was pulling the front down and she was dropping far too fast. There were boats below, too many for her to avoid, and someone screamed when the wings gave way. The figure fell, plummeting towards the moon-lapped water.

A strangled cry caught in Aiyla's throat as Zerren hit the waves, sending up a surge of spray. The wings spiraled down above her, crashing and catching on the current, whirling away. Zerren's arms flailed out of the water in the moonlight, then she went under, lost between the boats.

The men on the docks launched small skiffs, but the wings were already out of sight. If the current was powerful enough to sweep such a structure away, then a body would be— was— could have been—

Grief welled, sharp and sudden, almost enough to knock her to her knees. The men's shouts, the splash of their oars faded to nothing. She searched the water for any sign of movement, of a golden head, bobbing up, but only saw a trail of cloth—a veil? Something else?—swirling away.

Her fault, her doing. She had suggested this, she had designed it, and now, Zerren had ended —as so many who betrayed the sultan did—lost to the Bosphorus.

A touch on her shoulder made her turn, dagger drawn. Tamraz held up a hand defensively and she blinked at him. Of course. They had stopped. They had seen the palace. Now, they should be on their way to a strange place with no familiar faces.

Then she saw what he held in his other hand. A blanket from the carriage.

She stared at it, then at him, confused. She didn't need one, not on such a balmy night.

He grinned and tapped the corner of his eye, then tilted his finger just a little. *Upstream.*

Aiyla turned to follow his direction, away from the men rushing down the bank. The docks' far end had been abandoned in the haste to see what had happened, and there, peeping out between the hulls of two boats, still neck-deep in the water, was a pale, round face.

Tamraz offered the blanket again, and she grabbed it before running along the bank. Zerren clung to a dock post, trembling and grey, but she was there, alive, and Aiyla's world rolled, finding a new current, a new course.

Dropping to her knees, she reached down, but the other woman was shaking so hard that her hand slipped through Aiyla's and she almost went under again.

No! Aiyla lunged, grabbing a single wrist. They had come so far; they would not fail now. A Bird had many skills, including strength in their steering arms. She braced her heels against the dock and pulled with all she had.

Her muscles burned and ached, but she lifted Zerren high enough to get her chest onto the planks. Working together in the shadow of the boats, they dragged Zerren out of the water to collapse against Aiyla. She took ragged, gulping breaths, then rolled away and vomited over the side.

Aiyla quickly bundled the blanket over Zerren's shaking body, hiding her waterlogged hair and clothes, hoping no one had noticed them. With effort, Zerren got to her feet. Tamraz beckoned urgently; he pointed to the palace, to torches along the walls.

Half-carrying, half-dragging, Aiyla tipped them both into the carriage. At once, Tamraz slammed the door and cracked his whip. The wagon rumbled away, light slicing through the broken shutters.

No one would stop them. No one would question a carriage of the Little Birds.

Zerren still shivered, and Aiyla quickly stripped off the soaked clothes, wrapping her in another blanket, rubbing hands along Zerren's arms and back. "Safe," Aiyla rasped, though it felt like swallowing ground glass. "Safe now."

Zerren gave a frail laugh that turned into a sob. Her arms closed around Aiyla, fingers digging into her back. Aiyla crawled into her lap, bringing them as close as they could be, holding her as tightly, her own eyes burning hotly.

"My brave duck," she whispered.

That turned the sob back into a laugh. Pale fingers of moonlight crept over her, turning green and gold to silver and blue. Even pale and terrified, she was still the most beautiful person Aiyla had ever seen. She touched Zerren's cheek with gentle scarred fingers, and her eyes welled over when Zerren reached up and tugged away her veil.

The last battle had left its mark. Never a great beauty, her brown skin was waxen in places, as if held too close to a flame. She averted her gaze.

"No," Zerren said, her voice roughened and exhausted. "No, look at me. Please."

Aiyla swallowed hard, and her chest pulled tight for another reason altogether. "Zerren…"

"No." Zerren pressed her palm to Aiyla's cheek, staring at her as if she was beautiful. "Not Zerren. My name is Liliana."

No longer the golden bird in her golden cage.

Aiyla held Liliana's hand against her cheek, remembering a life and a place before she had wings and masters. "Rania," she whispered. "My name."

"Rania," Liliana breathed it like a prayer. She swayed close, tears like diamonds on her cheek, and pressed their brows together. "Rania."

And under the moonlight's gentle touch, they curled together as they left their old world behind them.

Positively Medieval
by Kaitlyn Zivanovich

Grynid understood that Asbjorn Haugen's guidebook on Humans was outdated, but it was the only reference book she had. It had led her to believe there would be more pitch-forks. She hadn't seen any on the flight from Norway to Ronald Reagan Washington International Airport, though, nor a hint of one at baggage claim. She saw Humans pushing luggage trolleys, drinking decorative coffees, and consoling their jet-lagged children. Not a pitchfork in sight. Humans, it seemed, were entirely modern and civilized.

Mother was wrong. A delightful thought.

Now it was up to Grynid to show Humans that Trolls were also modern and civilized. She took small, non-tromping steps through the U.S. Customs line. Instead of hefting, she plucked her book sack from the conveyor belt like a dandelion. She smiled with minimal tusk when she was mistakenly called an Ogre. Twice. Because of their quarantine, few Americans had ever met a real Troll. They still believed offensive medieval stereotypes set forth by Human authors. Grynid must make a good impression. Challenge their assumptions. She must be the model Troll.

Difficult, because these goggles made her want to tear a tree in half.

They perched ridiculously across her broad gray nose, cover-ing most—but not all—of both eyes. Pop-ups flared in the corner of her vision. *Another loser in the Stocks! Join the Roast!* a cartoon pig invited. A grainy gif of a unicorn licking a mermaid's fins: *WET and HORNY fairy-tale babes in your area!!* A reminder that with an upgrade she could opt out of advertisements.

She upgraded.

Outside there were no carriages or carts. Grynid sniffed for the ocean to orient herself. Industrial smells muddied her sense of direction.

"Excuse me? Is there a map? I'm trying to get to—"

"Use the app." The Human flicked a finger, tossing a link to Grynid's goggles: GetTHare! maps, free download!

A pink rabbit bounced across the empty street, a question mark over its cartoon head. Grynid looked at the address on her college-acceptance envelope and blinked. The rabbit's question mark popped into an exclamation point. "3700 O St NW! Follow me!"

"No, a map. Show me the route."

The rabbit hopped. "Follow me!"

Grynid toggled through the app menu. There was no map/route view option. Her lips twisted. She would defer to Human culture and customs in many ways. She'd eat lobster. She'd live inside a concrete dormitory with *carpet*.She'd even create a profile for this tech, linking all of her personal data, just to integrate into Human society! But a Troll is her own navigator. She always knows where she is. A lost Troll is a dead Troll. Grynid would not blindly follow a preposterously hued bunny who might lead her anywhere. Mother would die laughing.

How was she supposed to get to law school?

Flustered, Grynid ducked into a damp alleyway. It was dark, narrow, and smelled of mildew: cozy. Like her home cave. She removed her goggles and pinched the bridge of her nose. She wasn't lost. And she could not panic in public, it would scare the Humans. Worse, it would validate Mother.

Grynid tossed her sack to the ground with a heavy *whumph*. She rifled one-handed through her books: law, caselaw, rules of evidence. Strunk & White. Asbjorn Haugen's *Humans: How to Avoid Them and What to Do if You Can't*, 1st ed. Trollskog Press, 1590. An envelope brushed her fingertips. She slid her nail under the seal. A return ticket to Trollskog, dated for the solstice. Mother's handwriting on the back: *For when you come to your senses*.

Her guts were loam, sandy and rough. She snorted and flared her nostrils at Mother's smug confidence. Grynid would not be crawling back home. Not before the solstice or after.

She couldn't. She didn't have a map.

Tires squealed and acrid burnt rubber wrinkled Grynid's nose. A yellow headlight flashed into her eyes. There was a yelp, a screech of brakes, and a scooter bounced off Grynid's hip. She rubbed at the sting. The bike sputtered on its side; its solar-pack sparked. A Human woman stared at Grynid with goggle-less eyes. The tech had knocked free in the crash; it rocked askew on the asphalt. The woman jumped to her feet.

"You hurt?" Unlike every other Human, who glanced away as soon as they saw her, this woman traced peat-dark eyes down Grynid's form. She held her breath. Feeling seen made her blush.

"No." She winced. "My hips are sturdy."

The woman raised a pencil-thin eyebrow. "Lucky for me."

"Don't you mean lucky for me?"

"Here's hoping." A smile quirked her features then fell to a frown. "Hey, you okay?"

"What? I…" Grynid hastily banished a stray tear. Mother despised tears. "I'm fine."

The Human held up her hands. "I won't tell anyone. Hide as long as you like." She turned to her bike.

"How'd you know I was…"

Engines revved near the alley entrance. Whoops and cheers bit into the night air; headlights bounced against the building.

"Hide!" The Human knocked her shoulder into Grynid's still-smarting hip and pulled them both into shadow. Grynid pressed her back to the brick wall. Warm Human finger-tips pressed Grynid's lips. A Human shoulder nested into the crook of Grynid's elbow, her head on Grynid's pounding heart. Human hair tickled her bicep. Short hair, undercut at the nape. She smelled like cinnamon and woodsmoke.

The lights and sounds rushed down the street. The Human exhaled and slumped against Grynid.

"I see." Grynid bent her head to whisper into the woman's hair. "You're hiding, too."

The Human lifted her fingers. "Guilty. Those dudes've been after me for days."

Ah. Overly persistent suitors. Grynid understood. "Some men can't take a hint."

The woman whisper-laughed and looked up. She didn't move from the wall or the shadows, and Grynid felt her face heating like a hot spring. The guidebook hadn't mentioned how warm their skin was to the touch.

"Never met a Troll before," the woman said.

The burden of making a good impression doused her like ice water. "Don't worry." Grynid held out empty hands. "I promise I won't eat you."

The Human tilted her head. "Let's at least exchange names before we rule anything out."

Grynid extended a finger. "I'm Grynid. Law student."

"I'm Lupe. Night courier."

She blinked. Knight courier? Grynid had read all about knights!

"I'm freelance. Hence: no colors."

Grynid's goggles highlighted Lupe's form. A text bubble blipped: *No Affiliation.*

"Freelance, yes. Knight Errant. A Hedge Knight!" Grynid's relief almost knocked her flat. She wasn't lost! She was with a knight!

Lupe left the wall and inspected her bike; toggling switches and tightening attachments. "I can get you anything you need, any time of night. That's my guarantee."

"Like… a map? No—not GetTHare!" She warded away Lupe's attempt to swipe the app toward her. "A real map. With terrain features."

Lupe frowned. "You lost?"

"A troll is never lost. Also… I don't trust that rabbit. It seems… sinister."

"Fair enough. I got maps. Laminated. Terrain features, elevation lines, the works."

Grynid's heartbeat was thunder. "I will pay anything." The American dollar was so devalued compared with the Trollskog Crown, she could afford the expense. Grynid kicked herself. Despising pecuniary reward was part of a knight's code. She hoped Lupe wasn't offended.

"I got 'em stashed at my place across the bridge. Would you… want to come with me?" Lupe tossed her hair to one side and rubbed her arm. Nervous? She wiped her goggle lenses and fitted them over her ears. "We could—holy-cheese-and-crackers. You're a blank slate."

Grynid stepped back, edging against her book sack. "A what?"

Lupe's eyes and mouth were both wide. "A blank slate. You have perfect cred. No reviews."

Grynid fiddled with the new tech. "I only set up my profile this morning. Is that good or bad?"

"It means you're powerful. Dangerous."

Grynid didn't like those adjectives.

A swarm of engines roared. Grynid and Lupe whipped their heads towards the head of the alley. The dudes searching for Lupe were no longer searching. They'd found her.

"Holy shirtballs!" Lupe frantically mashed her goggle controls. "I forgot when these things hard reboot they default to broadcasting live location!" Lupe pulled at the scooter handlebars. "Can you lift this? If they touch it, the program lets them rate me. They'll ruin my cred."

"Why?" Grynid lifted the bike with one hand and set it on the iron fire escape above her head.

"It's how the software works. I can't afford to upgrade. They cannot touch my bike."

Motorcycle tires spun down the alley. Four more bikes zigged in formation. The goggles outlined them in blue. *Courier Affiliation: Pentagon.*

They were also Knight Couriers?

"Run, Grynid." Lupe tugged at her elbow.

"Run?" From suitors? That was not the way to deal with men. "I could help you."

The lead Pentagon dude toed his kickstand down and stepped off his bike. His fellows did the same.

"You'll… help me?" Lupe's voice was flat.

"Of course." Stern, direct logic would get through to them. "I'll take care of them. This sort of thing is my specialty."

"Luuuuuuupppeee…" the lead man called. "Bring out your wheels!"

"Hey, Craig." Lupe stepped from the shadows. "How're things?"

"You're not running? That's a first."

Craig's posse grunted and laughed. "The rat's cornered."

"Actually, you germy buttwipes." Lupe bounced with excitement. "*You're* cornered. You want me? You gotta go through *her!*"

Grynid lifted her sack of law books onto her shoulder. She tromped into the light. The Pentagon dudes cursed and shuffled.

"That's right! I'm not alone!" Lupe crossed her arms. "Grynid? They're all yours."

Grynid dropped her sack and straightened. Her tusks flashed in the headlights. She towered over the dudes, and spoke.

"Gentlemen, the lady does not reciprocate your affections and has no desire to continue courtship. Furthermore, trying to force her to accept *grenvalid* highlights a lack of character."

The men stood motionless.

Lupe punched her shoulder. "What are you doing?"

"I'm... explaining your position. What were you expecting me to do?"

Lupe waved at the book sack. "Club them! Dine on their flesh! Throw 'em in a stewpot!"

"I'm a Troll, not an animal!"

Craig leaned forward. "So... you're not going to do any of those things?"

Grynid huffed. "Violence is the refuge of the incompetent —hey!"

Craig whistled and the gang filed past Grynid with impunity. "It's up there!"

"You said you'd help me!" Lupe climbed a trash bin and leapt to the fire escape.

"I am! With logic and reason! Sir? Sir! Lupe has rebuffed your affections!"

"I'm not after her affections, Tolkien-spawn!"

The slur hit her like a slap.

"Boost me up, boys. Just need one touch!" Atop his crony's shoulders, Craig stretched his hand. Lupe lifted the scooter onto its back tire, almost out of reach. The dude's finger touched the rim. "Gotcha!" He dropped to the ground and touched his goggles. Five yellow stars appeared over his head. He blinked, and one by one the stars turned hollow. With a twitch of his jaw, the stars flew at Lupe.

Guadalupe DeSantos: Courier. Zero stars. Thank you for your review.

More dudes jumped to the fire escape. Lupe stomped on fingers poking through the grate. "Listen, Grynid." The Human woman scrambled at her bike, pulling wires and pressing buttons. She mule-kicked the next dude, but not before his palm slapped her handlebars. Five more hollow stars flew to Lupe. "Still want a map?"

"Yes?"

"Carry my scooter and I'll get you a map."

A third dude reached for her bike.

"In or out?"

Grynid heard Mother's judgment: *Two hours in America and you're running wild after some pretty face? So much for being serious about your studies!*

This was different though.

Lupe was a knight, and she had a map.

Craig had called her Tolkien-spawn.

"In."

"Get ready."

The dudes pulled down a rusty ladder and swarmed toward the bike like tree ants. Lupe pointed the solar-pack of her bike at their faces. "Eat this mother—wait, Grynid? Sunlight turns Trolls to stone?"

"No. That's a myth, popularized by *certain* Human writers. The truth is—"

"Close your eyes."

A puff of ozone; hot air dried Grynid's lips when the energy beam burst from the solar-pack. Veins of red and yellow spiderwebbed the insides of her eyelids. The dudes fell, clutching their overloaded goggles.

"Get my bike!" Lupe yelled from the roof of the building. She was already running.

Grynid gripped her book sack and the scooter's handlebars in her left hand and slung them over her shoulder.

Two quick pulls put her on the roof. She jogged after the knight.

"Do you often fight with fellow knights?"

"Other night couriers? That's *all* we do."

"Why were they giving you zero stars?"

"Today's the thirty-first." Lupe balked when Grynid shrugged. "Vassal & Lorde contract gets renewed on the first of the month. It goes to whichever courier has the highest rating at midnight on the thirty-first. As of right now, that's me."

"It's a lucrative contract?"

"Hecka lucrative. If I do well, a five-star review from V&L will set me up for years. I've been running nonstop to get my ratings up. Craig and his goons can't beat me so they're trying to trash my ratings. Just gotta keep them away from my bike until midnight."

"Why don't they just work harder to beat you fairly?"

"No one is faster than me." Her face pinched. "I've had lots of practice running."

The scooter bounced on Grynid's shoulder; its empty solar-pack sparked a weak death rattle. She was very resourceful, this knight. Half a dozen rival knights, and she bested them. She harnessed the power of the sun and crippled the monstrous hoard at the last moment—truly something from a ballad! Grynid's chest was light, she ran on her toes. *So naïve*, Mother's voice scoffed. *Daydreaming like a pebblekin.*

She cleared her throat. "Almost to the maps?"

"Soon." Lupe climbed a three-rung ladder to another roof. "Help me look, will ya? Purple suitcase with wheels."

Grynid set down the bike and her sack and caught her breath while Lupe tossed through cardboard boxes. There was little starlight to see by.

"Why'd you leave Trollskog?" Lupe said from the other side of the roof. "Aren't Trolls, like, isolationists?"

"True," Grynid said. When the Council of Legendary Creatures voted to reveal themselves to the Humans and fix climate change, the Trolls had been the only group to oppose. The Fae and Sprites were enthusiastic, of course— they loved to show off. But even when the Yokai and Baba Yaga and Bigfoot himself voted yes, still the Trolls said nay. "Historically, our peoples do not get along. Too many pitch-forks." And the representation in Human literature left much to be desired.

"Trolls to stone is a myth, huh?"

"Somewhat." It was a nuanced, spiritual issue. "If a Troll lives a great life, they often return to the earth in a big way, creating stone landmarks that they may always be remembered."

Lupe paused. "I wish I could go to Trollskog. Or anywhere else, really. But no one wants an American immigrant. Where's that suitcase? I stashed it here. If someone stole it, we'll be heading to the poop bank, and honestly I already pooped this morning. I don't know if I have any more in me."

Grynid had no time to process each increasingly ridiculous statement.

"Did you say *poop* bank?"

"No poop banks in Trollskog?" Lupe shrugged. "Folks here still live by quarantine rules, even though there hasn't been an outbreak in a decade. They stay inside and pay couriers to deliver things, so they don't risk infection. Since *we* live outside, we got, like, awesome bugs in our gut. Perfect for fecal transplants. Destroys c.diff. Poop banks saved the country, knocked out the SuperBug."

"The wealthy keep you outside, then harvest your feces to save their own lives?" That was barbaric. It was feudalism. "You're a serf," she realized.

"Surf? Not my thing. Aha!" Lupe lifted a maroon suitcase. "Found it."

"The maps?"

"The scrap. You want a map? Map is in my stash. Stash is across the bridge. Need the bike to get across the bridge, and we need solar to make the bike go. We're going to buy some solar."

A cold heaviness trickled to her belly. This was becoming complicated.

I told you so, sang Mother's voice.

Lupe waved. "Let's go to Target."

Welcome to Target! Expect More, Pay Less! Store currently under renovation. Order online!

Grynid blinked the ad away and faced a featureless, plastic Human. Dozens littered the second floor of the Target, in various poses and states of undress. A graveyard.

Lupe's "guy" had agreed to meet them on the second floor of the building with a red circle out front. That was what passed for landmarks in America. He had yet to arrive. The flickering fluorescent light bulbs did nothing for Grynid's apprehension.

The goggles chimed: person approaching. "Back here!" Lupe called. She leaned towards Grynid. "Don't make a big deal, but this guy is a burnout. Used to be freelance, like me. Bit of bad business two years ago, get it?"

"A burnout?" The goggles outlined Lupe's guy in striped red and gray.

"Bring it to the scale," the guy called. Lupe pulled the purple suitcase down the aisle.

"Burnout is destroyed credit. But it takes three neighborhood leaders working together to burn someone's cred, so it's super rare. But when they do? Worse than zero stars. Supernova. No one will work with a burnout."

Except Lupe, Grynid noticed. Her unease sharpened.

"Wait here."

Grynid stood by empty shelves declaring *Dollar Deals!* Lupe chattered at her guy. The guy grunted; hefted the suitcase. They haggled. Grynid sat on her sack of books and rolled the bike back and forth, actively ignoring Mother's laugher in her head. No. Lupe was a knight. Knights were trustworthy. She wasn't lost.

A pop-up obscured her vision. Would she like to rate Bobby Rowe: Scavenger? It was a push notification, as opposed to Lupe's rating system that required you to come in physical contact. Grynid scrolled through his profile. Every review was negative. Grynid shuffled her bare feet.

"How about we trade for solar?" Lupe needled. "Cut out the middleman."

"I'll give you cash, same as always."

"Come on! I'm giving you good stuff!"

"Where are you getting this stuff anyway?"

Lupe shrugged and said nothing. Grynid felt the hairs on her ears rise. Strange. It was the first time in two hours the

Human was at a loss for words. Knights were always supposed to speak the truth. Never deceive.

The guy rolled his eyes. "You want solar? Give me five stars, right here and now. Too chicken? You get cash." He waved a green stack of dollars under her nose.

Lupe stuffed the wad of bills in her fanny pack and stalked away. "Fine."

Grynid frowned. "I thought we were getting solar."

"Someone will be selling it this time of night." She tapped the air and blinked through her goggles, searching for such an establishment. "Grab the scooter."

Grynid looked at the guy and the purple suitcase. Her stomach churned. "What were you selling?"

"Scrap." Lupe zipped up her jacket. "Metal."

"Lupe, you said we were getting solar." She propped the bike on her left shoulder, her bag of books on the other.

Lupe sighed. "I can't rate a burnout, not tonight. It would drop my credit. Don't worry, next stop is solar, then your map."

Grynid glared at Lupe's back. I must be a model Troll, she reminded herself. No raging, no rudeness. I must politely resolve this situation. She blinked and twitched her nose. Five enormous stars appeared above her head. A flick of the wrist sent them to Bobby Rowe: Scavenger.

The red/gray line around him was replaced by a thick outline of gold. He glittered like a dragon's living room.

Lupe gasped. "Did you just—"

"A knight gives succor to the weak and defenseless," Grynid said. "Trolls can be chivalric too. Despite the stories, we are not Human-cooking oafs—"

Bobby Rowe dropped the purple suitcase. The zipper burst. Bullets flooded out.

Grynid whirled on Lupe. "You told me it was scrap!"

"It *is* scrap!" Lupe screeched back.

"It's arms dealing!"

Bobby Rowe sank to his knees. "You've… you're a clean slate. I've got… I've got perfect cred!"

Grynid dropped the scooter. "I want nothing to do with this. You are not a knight."

"Hey! My bike!" Lupe jumped on a shelf to bring her to Troll-eye level. She grabbed Grynid's collar with a tiny fist. "Who ever said I was a knight? What's your problem?"

Grynid would not escalate. She was a Troll. She was not a criminal. Or a barbarian. She would be civil but firm. "I do not approve of law breaking. You and I will part company. You're on your own."

Lupe froze as if slapped.

Grynid turned and tripped over Bobby Rowe, who was brandishing a pair of solar cells at her. "Take 'em, they're yours!" he cried. Grynid wobbled for balance. She flung an arm out to catch herself and grabbed the first thing she touched. The mannequin toppled; Grynid toppled. Her goggles flashed an alarm.

Lupe grabbed a mannequin arm and poked it at Grynid's torso. "Don't step on my bike!" she screamed. She pounced, and Grynid caught her in her arms. Her back hit a shelf. It fell into the shelf behind, and the shelf behind that. The alarm on the goggles grew brighter.

Her toe caught on the bike. She and Lupe tripped, spun, then bounced on the unmoving escalator and rolled downhill.

Grynid splayed on her back in the parking garage. Lupe's leg draped across her waist, her head on her shoulder.

"Ow…" they said together.

The goggles flashed. *Property Destruction. FINE. FINE.* It was not fine. Nothing was fine.

Lupe sat on her heels and rubbed her elbow. "You want to *part company*? You have no idea how to survive! You won't make it a week!"

"I shouldn't have followed you!" Grynid rolled to her feet. "I would've been better off with the rabbit!"

Lupe narrowed her eyes. Grynid bared her tusks. They both growled.

The scooter rolled down the escalator. Grynid's sack of books perched atop the seat, with two fresh solar-packs nestled inside. Bobby Rowe whistled. "Hey, Troll. I'm grateful as hell, but I gotta split before they get here."

"Before who gets here?"

Bobby blinked rapidly. "Everyone." He disappeared.

"No, no, no." Lupe lunged for Grynid's goggles. "Seriously? You're a clean slate, and you have your location set to public?"

"So?"

"You rated Bobby and tagged your location. Now everyone knows where you are. They'll swarm you and hold you hostage until you give them five stars. You *have* to customize your settings. Have you been living under a rock?"

"In a rock, actually."

"There. It's disabled."

Grynid replaced her goggles. *FINE. FINE*, they flashed. With GPS off the rabbit wouldn't pop up. "How am I supposed to get around now?"

Lupe glared. "I *said* I'd get you a map." She eyed the solar-packs in Grynid's sack. "Put those on my bike so we can escape them."

"You just want to protect your precious credit. All you do is run away!"

"And all you want is a map!"

Grynid glared. Lupe glared. Scooter tires screeched in the distance. With her keen night-vision Grynid saw a massive five-sided fortress in the distance: a castle! A storm of bikes spilled from its gates.

A mob. Coming for her.

Torches. Pitchforks.

Lupe stubbornly held out her hand. Grynid tossed her the solar-packs. She clipped them in. The bike sparked to life.

"Hold on," Lupe said. "I drive fast."

Grynid rested two fingers on the Human's hips. Lupe slammed her foot on the pedal.

Nothing happened.

Grynid flushed platinum. "I'm too heavy."

"You're perfect. I've carried industrial refrigerators on this thing, it's not you. It's... Oh." Her voice flattened. "We have a fine."

The goggle flashing intensified. Distant scooters became less distant.

"We busted up those shelves. Property damage."

"What do we do?" Grynid asked.

"Pay our debt to society. Money to the Pentagon authorities, or time in the stocks. The Pentagon offices aren't open until morning."

"The stocks?"

"We owe thirty minutes. We can do it while driving."

Grynid's shoulders hunched with each engine rev. "Yes. Let's choose that."

"Ever been in the stocks?"

"No?" It had to be better than the mob.

Lupe clicked 'Stocks.' The *Fine* alarm calmed and the scooter lurched forward. Lupe slammed on the pedal as a mob of blue-outlined scooters roared into view. The bike flew out of the garage; wind whipped Lupe's hair against Grynid's neck.

"We're near the border. Once we cross into Mall territory the dudes behind us will stop chasing!"

You've been naughty! A cartoon pig wagged a finger in the corner of the goggles. Absurd. Pigs had hooves. *Enjoy your time in the stocks!*

"Is this the fine?" Grynid asked.

"Keep your goggles on, no matter what!" Lupe shouted over her shoulder. "Turn them off, the scooter stops. Mute them, the scooter stops. You must listen."

"To what?"

"To every bored teenager and frustrated quarantine rat throwing insults and hatred your way."

Words? Only words? Branches and boulders might bruise my shoulders, as Mother would say. "Just thirty minutes?"

"Yeah." Lupe clipped her words. "Just thirty minutes."

The three-fingered pig pulled aside a curtain. Lupe gunned the scooter forward.

They zipped under a dark overpass and emerged on an empty forested road. Oaks and maples leaned toward them, heavy with their summer coats. Fir and spruce pointed toward the white moon. Grynid could barely see them through the wall of text flooding her goggles.

@cdiffsbatch: troll so fat look like it ate a whole village
@funkienloud: everyone hates you
@iwantfairytail: kill yourself kill yourself kill yourslef

Someone posted a link to a website. Instructions on how she might kill herself.

"This is the stocks?" she asked.

"Yeah. Hey, I have to turn mine to Audio since I'm driving."

"I'll do the same." She wanted to be able to see if Pentagoners or dudes of any variety were approaching. "Perhaps they will drown each other out."

"They won't." Lupe's words came through a clenched jaw.

"I've taken dumps better looking than you."

"you are the reason I don't go outside"

Grynid felt Lupe's shoulders tense. "It's not true," Grynid muttered. "They're just words. Clearly you're not unattractive, by Human standards." Or Troll standards, for that matter.

"If we talk too much they'll shut off the bike. Be quiet and listen."

Grynid tried to let her mind wander. Let the Humans hurl their insults. Trollphobic insults. Sexually violent insults. Increasingly sexual and increasingly violent insults. She checked the timer. They were only four minutes into their punishment.

A picture appeared to accompany the audio. It hit Grynid like an overripe tomato.

"look what I found! Ogre baby and Ogre mommy!"

"I just threw up in my mouth"

"kill me. I can't unsee that."

Where did they find her baby pictures? Oh that's right. She had to link her TuskBook account when she created her profile

"you see her mom's face???? here's my baby…anybody want to trade?"

Doctored photos flashed across her vision. They circled and zoomed in on her baby fat. They wrote obscene words across her nappies. No need to change Mother's expression, though. She always did look disappointed.

More photos appeared. Mother picking her teeth during Grynid's Acornclass graduation. Mother looking embarrassed at the Fire Circle Debate championship. A particularly unflattering picture of Grynid's debut into adult society. Mother was wincing there, too.

"Her own mama thinks she's trash!"

Laughter erupted. Did they have to broadcast the laughter? Grynid looked over Lupe's hunched shoulder.

"see the immigrant's pics? ALWAYS ALONE AND ALWAYS RUNNING"

"Hey guys, wait up! Wait up!"

"unwanted little sister"

Grynid frowned at the pictures flashing in the corners of her vision. Lupe was running in every single one. She'd been running the entire night.

"OMG she's applied to join the P-Gon couriers SEVEN TIMES!"

Lupe flicked a switch. The scooter sped up.

"And the Zoo couriers!"

"EVEN DUPONT REJECTED HER!"

"Spell desperate: L-U-P-E"

Lupe hunkered over the handlebars. "Almost to the bridge. That's Mall territory."

Grynid looked behind—no one was following. Lupe was speeding as if she could outrun the comments.

The trees on the sides of the road thinned. Lupe zoomed the bike onto a wide bridge. Wind whipped tears from under Grynid's goggles. A water feature, a landmark, and Grynid could not appreciate it.

"Go back to Norway, fugly monster!"

"Eat the Mexican for a snack on your way!"

She felt sick.

"Stop the bike," Grynid said. They were over the bridge. Lupe tapped the brakes.

Stone called to her. Grynid stumbled forward, climbing white stairs. She crawled into a cave built of columns and carvings. Lupe followed. The voices followed. She curled at the foot of a marble statue.

Twenty minutes left in the stocks.

Lupe clutched her own elbow and slumped against the far wall. She rolled into herself as if trying to turn to stone. Grynid knew that look. Lupe was lost. They both were.

Grynid reached out.

Troll and Human hands found each other in the dark. They sat shoulder to shoulder, hearing each other's insults, feeling each other's pain. The goggles streamed evidence after evidence they were losers. Failures. Forever alone. Forever disappointing.

Raindrops fell on stone. Grynid blinked through tears. The comments had stopped. The words and insults running through her mind were echoes. It was over.

They took off their goggles and listened to the rain. Lupe shifted. Grynid kept hold of her hand.

"How did they know?" she whispered into the silence.

"Crowdsourced bullying." Lupe sniffed. "They pinpoint your insecurities, then hammer away at them."

The Human took back her hand and wiped at her eyes. Grynid sat up.

"Hey," said Lupe. "Our debt to society is paid."

"Why would that be payment?"

Lupe shrugged. "People need an outlet. They do it to us, the consenting, and not to people who don't deserve it. It's a good system."

"It's a lemming-scat system. Lupe? Why are you always running?"

Lupe turned away and adjusted her jacket. "People can't hurt you if they can't catch you."

Grynid looked around the massive cave. A man of marble sat on a throne with words carved above him. IN THIS TEMPLE AS IN THE HEARTS OF THE PEOPLE...

"Who is Abraham Lincoln?"

Lupe glanced upward. "Old president?"

A smile tugged at Grynid's tusks. "I know little about American Trolls. It is good you Humans honor him so."

"I don't think he's a Troll."

"Half-troll. Troll-Human mix. It is the same."

"I think it's just a statue."

"Please, it speaks well of your land."

Lupe shrugged and smiled. Grynid smiled back. She didn't hide her tusks. Lupe didn't seem to mind.

"Lupe... I'm lost," Grynid admitted.

"That's your mom talking." Lupe put her fists on her hips. "You, Troll lady, are kicking butt."

Grynid blushed.

"Not literally, of course. You're very prim."

"Thank you."

Lupe tossed the hair out of her eyes. "Listen, those were shells. Expended rounds. Not bullets. A few miles south there's an old military base. They got piles of shells all over. I collected them for years. When I moved up here, I stashed them all over the city. Little bits of emergency funds I can always count on. Nothing illegal."

"Military base?" Grynid said in a small voice.

"That's where I got your maps too. Military types have a kink for navigating without tech. Grease pencils and laminated topographical maps. I found them all over the woods."

Some Humans appreciated traditional land navigation? Grynid had the sudden urge to strip a tree of bark and share it with Lupe.

"I'm sorry for accusing you," she said.

"Sorry I'm not a real knight."

Grynid scratched at her ear. She'd been so worried Humans would have the wrong impression of Trolls. She hadn't considered the need to temper her expectations of Humans.

Lupe waved her towards the stairs, and the scooter parked below. "Ready to get your map?"

Grynid took a final look at Lincoln. She'd chosen America for a reason. A half-Troll became president. Perhaps even she could succeed.

"Ready."

"Here it is. Home sweet home."

A red awning covering the entryway read, "The Prime Rib." The "i" was dotted with a star.

"Welcome to the steakhouse." Lupe nosed the door open with her front bike tire.

Inside, dark-paneled walls boasted intricate wainscoting. Button-tufted leather benches and chairs lay in piles. A glass-lidded grand piano tilted on a broken leg.

"This is a restaurant?"

"Was. Can you imagine? People coming from all over to eat, right next to each other? Food made in large batches by dozens of different germy cooks in a huge filthy kitchen? We were asking for an epidemic."

A ladder in the back led to the roof. They climbed in comfortable silence.

"Turn on your goggles. You'll see why this is the perfect location."

Bright-colored lines carved the rooftop into sections like a pie. Blue to the south, yellow-red and green to the north. Grayish-silver to the west. Borders of the different fiefdoms meeting at the steakhouse roof's center.

"Anytime I'm in trouble, I jump a few feet and I'm in a whole new world." Lupe pointed to each slice of territory. "That's the Mall, Pentagon, Dupont, and the Zoo. West is the Hoyas."

It was the perfect location if one planned to spend their entire life running and hiding. Grynid had an urge to again take Lupe's hand.

"Twenty minutes to midnight. The V&L contract is as good as mine. Tonight, we both win." Lupe threw back an olive-green tarp and popped the clasps on a black plastic trunk.

Maps spilled out. Handheld types. With—

"Elevation lines. Terrain features." Grynid's knees wobbled.

"See, there's the Potomac, that's—"

"The river we crossed." Grynid oriented the map. Everything was clear. Even the building layout followed the terrain to some extent. She could see!

A voice from street level cut through the night. "Come on down, Lupe!"

The color in Lupe's face drained. Grynid grabbed her goggles. "My live location is still off!"

"Mine, too!" Lupe's eyes popped wide. "The solar-packs! Bobby Rowe must've given everyone the tracking info, to get them off his back. Grab the bike. We'll jump into Dupont."

"Found ya!" A voice from Dupont territory.

Lupe turned left. "Fine, the Zoo."

A voice from the Zoo. Voices from the Mall. Shuffling and scraping: they were climbing the walls.

Lupe bounced on the balls of her feet. "We'll go to Hoyas' territory. Even though they're insufferable." She tugged at Grynid's arm.

"Lupe. Do we have to run?"

"They're after *you*, Grynid. They want your cred. They will never stop harassing you. You won't have a chance to kick butt in law school!"

Grynid's tusk twitched. Lupe wanted to protect her. Prevent the failure Grynid feared.

She believed in her.

Hands crested the roof. A torso. Legs.

"Go, Lupe. Twenty minutes to midnight, save your contract. I'm tired of running." Grynid hefted her bag of books. She was Grynid of Trollskog. She wouldn't fall to a bunch of dudes. "I have logic and reason on my side. I will take a stand."

Three other bodies summited and collected in the shadows. Grynid squared herself. She was a debate champion. She'd scored a 176 on the LSAT. She'd been accepted to one of the finest law schools in the world! She would not fail today, her first day away from home. She would teach them to respect the mind of a Troll.

A hand slipped inside hers. It shook.

"You're not running?"

"Knights don't run, right?" Lupe managed a smile.

Large Humans stepped into the light. The goggles highlighted them in various colors: leaders of separate courier factions. Their ratings were through the roof. Almost as high as Lupe's.

"Gentlemen, I look forward to a civilized discussion of your concerns," Grynid announced.

"You want her cred, you'll have to come through me!" Lupe called out. "And when you get through me, you'll have to deal with her!"

The Dupont Human snorted. "We're not after your pet, Lupe. We're here for you."

"Me?" Lupe said.

"*Pet*?" Grynid said. "Wait, her?"

Lupe looked at the faction leaders. They each held an invertedtripod, aslongastheyweretall. Onebyonetheyattached a device to one of the prongs. An icon flared on each of them: a matchstick. A torch.

This was a burnout.

"Waitwaitwaitwaitwait!" Lupe waved her hands.

"You cheat!" cried the Human from the Zoo territory. "You're too good for a freelancer!"

"I never cheat!" Lupe's hands clenched in fists.

"Where'd you get all that solar?" Dupont taunted.

"THE SUN!"

Grynid cleared her throat. "The solar-packs were obtained legally." She scanned them again. They were not law enforcement. They had no mandate to exact justice in this or any jurisdiction.

Craig, the Pentagon leader, spoke from behind. "You average an errand time of seven minutes. Our best guys, tricked out scooters, can't break nine."

"Because you keep to your districts! I can cross borders!"

"We don't know how you're doing it, but we know you're cheating."

"I'm not cheating! I'm just better!"

Of the forty-seven books in Grynid's sack, more than half were devoted to the legal principles that govern the proof of fact. "I-don't-know-how-you're-so-good" was not one of them. "You have no evidence?"

The Mall leader jerked a thumb at Grynid. "Shut your rancid mammoth up."

"*Rancid?*" Lupe said. "Are you blind? Can you not see her incredibly sturdy hips? She's, like, objectively by any standard, smoking hot."

"The Ogre's a pacifist," Craig said. "Don't worry on her."

The courier leaders relaxed and chuckled. They linked their burnout apps together, creating a web around Lupe. Then they clicked the tech on the tripods.

Pitchforks. They looked like pitchforks.

Grynid looked at the array of different colors. Heraldry from separate fiefdoms? A feudalist society complete with castles? Public humiliation as a punishment? For Grendel's sake, there was even a plague in this country!

Lupe closed her eyes and stood tall like a knight before battle. She didn't run.

Grynid snorted and flared her nostrils. This was unjust. They were angry because Lupe was—legally—better than they were. They were going to burn her?

At the steakhouse?

Grynid rubbed her tusk against her cheek. These villains were no different from the medieval mobs in Asbjorn Haugard's book. Lupe, standing brave, was no different from the medieval knights.

Screw it. Time for Grynid to be a medieval Troll.

"What the—!"

She swung her sack of law books in a perfect arc, slamming Craig and his tripod to the ground. Her second swing knocked Mall and Dupont into the Zoo Human. She swiped the tripods in her meaty palm, threw them in her jaw and chomped them in half. The Humans stared.

Grynid roared. It reverberated throughout the boroughs. She roared at this mob, at the Ogre-slurs, at Tolkien and the pink rabbit and her faithless *Mother* who never believed in her. She roared from the pit of her Troll belly.

With much limping, whining, and the acrid smell of urine, the witch-hunters vacated the roof. With each touch of the masticated tripods, pop-ups flared on Grynid's goggles. *Would you like to rate....*

"You all get zero stars!" Grynid swiped her claw at the air. Empty rows of stars flowed through the night. The Humans below cried out as if in physical pain. Grynid snorted past her tusks. She took two deep breaths.

Lupe stared with wide, frozen eyes.

Grynid pulled two law books out of the sack. "Technically, I did use logic and reason to defeat them."

Lupe climbed atop a box, closing the distance between them. Filling it with her warmth. Cinnamon. Woodsmoke. They stood on the roof, straddling every barrier and border, listening to night wind and the sound of the Potomac.

"You just saved my life," Lupe said. "Well, my cred."

"You stayed. To defend me. No one's ever stood up for me before."

Lupe flickered a frown. "You're really cool, Grynid. Like, above-average awesome. You're worth standing up for. Still. They were after me, not you. And you stayed."

Grynid shrugged, tried to swallow, found she couldn't look away from that absurdly beautiful tuskless mouth. "You got me a map."

Lupe reached out. Troll and Human hands found each other on the roof, as they had in Abraham Lincoln's cave. Cinnamon and woodsmoke and a warm hand in hers.

"Can I...?" Lupe timidly bit her lip, setting Grynid aflame.

"Oh, yes."

Grynid bent her neck, Lupe stretched on her tiptoes and two worlds built a bridge with a kiss. With a kiss, all else melted: time, the pink rabbit, Mother's voice. She was not lost. Not lost at all.

The goggles chimed midnight, anchoring them to reality. Lupe's outline blinked out, then flashed silver.

"Lupe." Grynid looked her over. "You won the contract! Vassal & Lorde!"

"Huh." Lupe turned her hand, examining her new colors. "Somehow it's only the second-best thing that's happened tonight."

Grynid felt her face flush pewter.

"You have your map." Lupe tucked her hair behind one ear. "Where will you go?"

"O Street. Georgetown Law."

"Wow, Georgetown? Impressive." She nodded her chin at her scooter. "Need a ride?"

"Escorted by a knight?" Grynid asked. "How could I refuse?"

They climbed down the ladder. Lupe switched out Bobby Rowe's solar-packs with a fresh pair from her stash. Grynid felt a bold impulse. Mother did not approve of impulses. Grynid no longer cared.

"Lupe." She cleared her throat. "So as to be clear. You are also, uh, smoking hot. Objectively. By any standard. And I really like you."

Lupe paused, goggles part-way to her eyes.

"I'm very focused on academics. But, when I pass the bar, join a firm—perhaps make partner—if you are still interested,

I would not be opposed to receiving romantic overtures. Perhaps even a *vakkerkart*."

Lupe held out her hand to Grynid. "Perfect. That'll give me time to figure out what a *vakkerkart* is. Until then we can just, like, kiss a lot, right?"

"Absolutely. Yes. A lot."

The bike started. Grynid held her map, her sack of books, and Lupe's waist. The sun rose behind them.

Book and Hammer, Blade and Bone
by Ann LeBlanc

I awaken in pain, knowing I am in the wrong underworld. I still feel the cold ache from the iron blade that slipped through my ribs and stilled my heart. My hands tremble; I hold myself tight as the adrenaline of my final struggle drains out of me in wracking sobs.

I should have been greeted by the sound of running water, the soft hands of the attendants of Cmlech, ready to accept me into death. I would share the news of the struggle above: of the strike and massacre at the quarry. Then I would enter anew into the service of the eternal insurrection of Cmlech, secret god of death.

Instead, I am dead and alone in a dry, stone room, surrounded by books.

I exit into an enormous chamber, high-ceilinged, with the muffled atmosphere of a holy place. I pass through rows of stone shelves filled with books.

At the center of the great hall, a woman sits behind a wide, cluttered desk. Her long, grey hair is bound by a silver and turquoise clasp; her gown is the color of a clear winter sky and looks like it took a year's labor to make.

My fellow dead wait in a line to see her. None will respond to my questions except to insist I be quiet. My feet tap an impatient dance, my hands open and close and I am close to screaming. Cmlech waits upon my news, and I am stuck in a queue.

Yet when I reach the front of the line and the woman looks up at me with eyes the color of wet soil, all my words flee.

"Library card?" she asks with hand held open.

"I... don't have one."

"It's the card you used to enter the library. Have you lost it already?"

She sighs and takes a closer look at me. Her eyes narrow, her back stiffens, and her hand darts below the desk to grasp something I cannot see. I step back, try to look smaller.

What must she think of me? A woman in ripped, sweat-and-blood-stained worker's clothes, my arms and shoulders wide and strong enough to earn the nickname "The Ox" at the quarry.

"Please. My name is Btta, I just died, and…" I grab the desk to stop my hands from shaking. "I don't know where I am, and I need help. My god needs me. Can you help me?"

She relaxes, having made some judgment of me. "Oh, you poor thing. You must be so disoriented. This is the local branch of the Great Library, serving the underworld of the Merciful Goat of Epnos. I'm Hillie, the head librarian. I'm sorry, but we don't do intake for the newly dead." She gestures to the great door behind her. "You must have wandered in from Epnos reception?"

I shake my head and point to a small door. "I died, and then I woke up in that room."

"Not possible. That's the book-return chamber." She looks me up and down, slowly. "And you, are not a book."

"I know I'm not a book!" Cmlech forbid. "I'm not supposed to be here at all. Not in a library, not with a goat! I'm in the wrong underworld; I'm supposed to be with… my god."

"And who is your god?" she asks, and my heart drops.

Why did she have to ask a question I cannot answer? "A god of death…"

Her face closes at my evasion. The patron behind me clears his throat, loudly and intentionally.

Hillie sighs, though I do not know if it is for me or the long line behind me.

"You're a fascinating mystery, but without a library card I cannot help you." She points to the line. "I have other clients to serve today."

"Wait! I'm not just another dead person. I have an urgent message for my god!"

Hillie looks behind me and says, "Next patron, please?"

My face flushes hot in embarrassment and I stifle the urge to grab Hillie by her expensive gown and shake until she aids me. I tried that once on an Iolan clerk and still bear scars from the lashes my anger earned me.

I storm out the enormous front door of the library and into the cave the library was carved from. At the other end of the cave is a narrow passageway—presumably leading to the underworld of Epnos's goat god—but it is blocked by a check-point. The goat-headed guards demand my paperwork and re-fuse entry when I explain why I have none. When I don't leave immediately, their hands move to their sword hilts.

I try to re-enter the library, but the doors won't open with-out a library card. I am trapped in this interstitial area, with no food or water, and nowhere to sleep but the hard, cold stone of a foreign underworld. I look up to the ceiling and wonder if any of my kin-workers survive miles above.

I should not have thought of them. My hands shake again. With nothing to occupy my mind, my thoughts return to the memory of my death.

It was snowing on the fifth day of the quarry-workers' strike. The sun rose dim behind pure white snow clouds as my kin-workers and I took turns guarding the quarry entrance.

Gray-eyed Myrna arrived with a hug and the news of our case. She'd been helping us navigate the Iolan's legal system, fighting the necromancers' legal claims to our quarry. We sang and drank and played games to pass the time while we waited for the Iolan magistrate to make his decision.

When the cloud-dimmed sun reached its zenith, and the snow was two fingers thick on the ground, the necromancers arrived in their bone-white robes and demanded we leave. Standing death-still behind them were fourteen animated skeletons, befouled with alchemical pitch and inscribed with gold and silver runes. How many of those skeletons were our own dead, turned against us?

Their leader approached us, sword in one hand, paperwork in another.

"Myrna! You should have taken our offer." He shook his head, mock-rueful. "It's too late now. The Iolan magistrate has confirmed our claim to this quarry. Your assembly here is now illegal."

Myrna walked toward him, her gray eyes wide and bright. "The magistrate doesn't own the quarry. He has never even seen this quarry, has never worked its stone. Why should he decide its fate?"

The necromancer stepped forward. "In one hand I have a verified title document. In the other is a blade. You decide which one is more persuasive."

"Do you really think the magistrate's paper is stronger than the bodies that work this quarry? What has your blade ever built?"

It was meant to be the opening of her argument, but the head necromancer responded with a swipe of his sword. The high curve of Myrna's neck blossomed with blood. I screamed as her body fell.

My world condensed down to my hammer and the crack of my enemies' bones. We fought with the anger of those who have had too much taken from them, and with the determination of those whose service to the god of revolutions will continue even after death.

The skeletons fought in silence, bound to their creators' greed. I brought two down with a roar and a lunge and a swing of my hammer and the rest surged upon me, separating me from the group. I was surrounded, but I did not yield. I pushed forward into the forest, hoping to draw enough skeletons away that my kin-workers could prevail.

We fought in the forest, the trees my allies, the skeletons untiring. The skeleton before me lacked half its skull yet it still loped along, sword in hand. I swung my hammer, unaware of the skeleton behind me. The back of my head burst black and white and I fell.

I awoke to the silence of the snowy forest, imprisoned by the iron-strong grip of two skeletons. Above me stood the necromancers' leader, his white robes stained red, his shaven head tattooed with the symbol of their order. His smile was triumphant, and his sword flashed silver-blue as it descended like the unfurling of a broken promise down into my chest.

I die, and the memory starts anew.

I cannot stop remembering. My breath comes fast and sharp and uncontrolled and I grip the stone beneath me, desperate for something to hold. I feel hunted without my hammer.

This is how the librarian finds me, crying on the steps of her library. I flinch at her hand on my shoulder. She helps me up, and I follow her inside and up the stairs to her living quarters. If she says words, I do not parse them. She places a mug of steaming beef broth in my hands, and I am brought back to my body.

I sit at her kitchen table and watch her cook dinner. She flows from one task to another, like a dancer who has practiced their moves five thousand times before.

It is hard not to admire her, to be grateful for her late-coming mercy. I want to stare at the way her wide hips move beneath the blue of her gown. But I must hold tight to my anger. I must not forget how she dismissed me. She is just like the Iolans, who prioritize their legalities over kin and compassion.

As she cooks, and the scope of the meal becomes apparent, I fear she hopes to trap me with a debt of hospitality. I have nothing to offer in return but myself, and I am bound by other obligations.

"Are you cooking all this for me?" I ask. "You don't have to do that." Secretly, I am joyous, my nose intoxicated with the scent of her food, my stomach desperate for sustenance after days of scant meals during the strike.

She turns and smiles and takes a taste of the sauce she is reducing. "Oh! I cook this much every night. What's the point of being dead if you can't enjoy yourself?"

I do enjoy myself. There are spices I have never tasted before; everything is smothered in peppers, though not all the dishes are spicy. After the meal, we drip honey on hollow fry bread. Cmlech have mercy on my stomach—I am stuffed, yet I cannot stop.

She watches me, eyes obscured by the steam rising from her mug. "So, my mysterious Btta. You appear in my library with no card, and no entry record. And there aren't any passages to the surfaces nearby, so I doubt you walked here still alive." She raises an eyebrow. "You have no idea how it happened?"

"No."

"And you follow a death god, but won't say which one." She grins. "You're going to make me guess, aren't you?"

"I would prefer if you didn't."

"Your clothes and your accent make me think you're from Iolas."

"Ytarra," I correct her reflexively with my island's true name.

"Does anyone still call it that? But if you're Iolan— sorry, Ytarran—and you worship a death god you won't talk about..." She taps her chin. "Cmlech!"

A hiss escapes my lips. "Keep that name out of your mouth. My god has enemies, and a bad death comes to those who don't keep their worship hidden."

Cmlech *is* a god of death, but not the death of the individual. The servants of Cmlech work for the death of empire, the death of the systems that press their boots on the necks of the powerless. This is why worship of our god must be done in secret.

She laughs with more sadness than mirth. "Dear, we are already dead. We get to leave all that behind us when we die." She takes my hand. Her pulse is warm beneath her soft skin. I cannot look up into her eyes. "Feel my hand. Look around you. You are safe here."

I pull my hand away, as my eyes blur with tears. How can I be safe with this woman who ferrets out my secrets, who tempts me with compassion I so badly want to accept? She is too much like the Iolans, usurper-lords of our island, who hold gold and paper in one hand and a whip in the other, who consort with necromancers that plot not just to steal our wealth but defile our dead.

I surge upward, knocking my chair backwards, and flee to her sitting room.

Unlike the Iolans, Librarian Hillie knows when to stop tugging a thread with pain on the end of it. She lets me be in her sitting room, and when she comes to apologize, she does so without touching or staring. She accepts my stone silence as response, not pressing me for forgiveness.

When she offers her bed, I refuse. In Ytarra, a bed is just a place to sleep—my kin-workers and I all share a bed—but

I have heard that foreigners conflate beds with couples and sex. I don't know what she means with her offer, or how to ask. I refuse her three times before she relents and makes up the couch.

Sleep takes me quickly, but so do dreams of my death. I awaken with a desperate scream, my body sweat-stained and sheet-tangled. Hillie rushes in and envelops me in a hug. She is so soft, and her scent reminds me of huddling beneath a warm quilt on a snowy day.

I want so badly to sink into her embrace; I hate my desire for this woman who is simultaneously enraging and compassionate. My skin is suddenly too hot. I roar and I curse her for invading my privacy. She flees the sitting room with an apology. My pillow is wet with tears before I fall asleep again.

In the morning, she serves fried eggs on a bed of spicy beans and rice. She does not mention the night before. Why should I be grateful for that small mercy? Instead, she explains the difficulties in getting me to Cmlech.

The underworld is a physical place, with real geography. It is full of gods who work against each other, and full of humans who bring their notions of borders and fear of foreigners.

Working out a route to Cmlech's domain—and acquiring the necessary paperwork for safe passage—will be a difficult and time-consuming task. Librarian Hillie tells me this with a grin, as if the challenge excites her.

In the meantime, I am trapped in the library, surrounded by books and indebted to a woman whose questions I do not wish to answer.

Hillie puts me to work: mopping floors, cleaning bathrooms, fighting the book-borer beetle infestation. She instructs me in the fire-prevention protocol, carefully demonstrating the emergency fire-suppression failsafe: a god-stone–powered device that will flood the library with an inert gas—suffocating the flames and anyone not wearing a breathing mask.

When I have learned the routine of the library, she asks me to help shelve books.

I tell her I cannot read, and she gasps like I murdered her goat. Then her face turns joyous. "I can teach you! We'll do daily lessons after closing time."

I cringe at the idea. "A kind offer, but no, thank you."

I try to change the subject, but she is so bewildered by my refusal to learn, so desperate to understand, that she hounds me to explain.

There is a reason Ytarrans keep their history orally. The Iolans weren't the first to invade our island; they won't be the last. Books can be burned or altered to suit the invader's narrative, but the words in our head are beyond their reach. Our children do not learn to read so they cannot be taught false words. We Ytarrans know our true history; we will always resist assimilation and extermination.

As I explain this, horror spreads across her face. She doesn't argue with me, but our conversations wither down to polite things like, "Would you pass the pepper flakes?" or, "Please tell the young couple in row thirteen to go have sex somewhere else?" Does my illiteracy offend her? Does she think I hate her because she is a librarian? She isn't Iolan; my unease around reading has nothing to do with her.

A part of me relishes the silence. Yet at night, my mind cannot help but dwell on the idea of Hillie and me on the couch, our thighs touching, her hand guiding mine as I trace out the letters on the book before us. I hate the way the thought slips into my head in the undefended moments before sleep. Yet it is preferable to the dreams of my death, of the falling sword, the silent grin of the skeletons, and the screams of my kin-workers.

When I awaken crying, Hillie does not come to me in her intricately embroidered nightgown. She does not surround me with the softness of a hug, wipe the tears from my eyes, and bring me a cup of something warm and soothing. Why do I even want that?

I must miss my kin-workers, whom I shared a large bed with. If I awoke in the night, it was to the soft sounds of sleep, knowing I was surrounded by love and mutual protection.

Now when I wake, I am utterly alone.

One morning, breaking the silence of breakfast, she says, "Would you mind if I asked how you died?"

"I was murdered. My kin-workers…" I struggle for words, for breath, for respite against the sudden pounding of my heart. She waits for me to say more, and while I still fear the memory of my death, the pressure of holding it in wears on me.

I tell her of the quarry, of Myrna and our legal struggles. When I mention the necromancers, she sucks her breath in.

I ask, "They're here too?" The back of my neck tingles. I feel the need to check that the door is locked.

Hillie nods. "The Order for the Utilization of the Spirit. I've had trouble with them." Hillie tenses, like she, too, fears they might walk through the door. "We have an original set of *The Eight Deaths of the Mantean Hetwoman*. I think we're the only branch that has all eight original volumes."

"Why do they want it?"

"I haven't read all eight volumes, but my understanding is that the Hetwoman's autobiography contradicts their accounts of the founding of their order—and contains several gorgeously illustrated schematics of their bone-rites. They claim it as their property, and want me to either hand it over or destroy it, along with our entire section on bone-lore."

"Will you?"

She looks like I slapped her. "Of course not! Joal preserve me. I moved the volumes to the restricted reading room. But they kept coming round, threatening me, and vandalizing the library. So I confiscated their library cards and escorted them out. They *won't* be coming back."

I don't share her confidence. The necromancers have been here, and I am sure they will return. They will come for the book; they will come for me.

I cannot be defenseless again. I flee downstairs to the supply closet. Surely in this mess of janitorial supplies and bookmaking tools there is a weapon?

I search through the bookbinder's knives; the blades are sharp but short, useless against a sword's reach. My hands shake and my grip is weak, but I can't stop to calm myself.

I grin when I see the book-backing hammers. I pick up the largest, an iron head and a nearly two-foot haft. Small compared with my rock-breaking hammer, but it feels achingly familiar in my hands.

When I show up for work, Hillie sees the hammer strapped to my belt. She catches herself before she asks me about it, and I have to hide my smile.

She does not protest when I take the hammer to bed with me. A day later she has—without comment—installed a bracket next to the bed for me to hang the hammer.

At dinner, I ask if she has made progress on a route to Cmlech. She frowns and says, "It would go faster if you could help me, if you learned to read."

I grunt and look away. It's good she doesn't know how tempted I am, how much I hate my own uselessness.

We explore other options.

Hillie asks, "Weren't you a quarry-worker? Why not tunnel upward, back to the surface and the world of the living? Like the legend of Boros Rock-Breaker."

I try not to laugh. Stone is my expertise—I explain in detail the difficulties involved in traversing a mile of bedrock with nowhere to put the removed stone. She smiles as I talk, basking in the breadth of my knowledge.

The next day, Hillie explains that when a person dies in the underworld, they will return to their god's domain, just like when they originally died.

She tells me this while making dinner, a knife in one hand and her eyebrow raised. I jump up from the table, eyes locked on the knife. She thinks she is being funny, but I still remember the feeling of the blade that killed me. I am not willing to die again to test her theory. I fear that whatever sent me to this wrong underworld—whether necromancer's magic or cosmic accident—still clings to me, and could return me somewhere worse.

Despite myself, I fall into a routine. After weeks of nightmares, I sleep through the night for the first time. Every corner of the library is familiar to me now. When did it begin to feel more like a home than a prison?

On the day we have cumin-crusted leg of lamb, Hillie places a large book on the kitchen table. The wooden cover bears an illustration of the Cloister of the Setting Sun, done in gold, silver, and coral. I stay silent; I don't pick it up. I won't rise to her bait.

I avoid looking at the book, not wanting to see her smile when I take an interest. Yet how can I resist? Ytarrans still tell stories of the glory of the art held within the Cloister, of the beauty of the building itself, of the way the sun would shine through the god-stone–veined marble. I have only ever known it in its present form: crumbling and blackened by the Iolans' burning-oil throwers.

I make it three days before I succumb to temptation. The book is full of illustrations of Ytarra the way it used to be. There are people who look like me, but wearing expensive and old-fashioned clothes. On the last page, there is a picture of a massive, marble tower rising from the hill where the Iolans' brick administrative palace now stands.

There are words, too, but not written in the Iolan script. For the first time in my life, I want to read.

The next morning, I confront Hillie. She must tell me what this book is, what it says. She smiles that damnable smile and I almost throw the book across the room. Instead, I clutch it to my heart. Yes, it is a book, but it contains something precious.

It happens like one of my daydreams. We sit on the couch together, her soft hips touching mine. I struggle between flinching away and pressing myself closer to her.

She guides my hand as I sound out the letters. Her perfume smells like the wind in the pine trees of home, and my heart thumps and my stomach drops. It is too much; I pull my hand away and hold myself tense.

Do I want her to kiss me? I don't even know how to ask. There are no pine trees here, and Hillie would not understand if I gifted her a sap-smeared branch. What I really want is to stop wanting her.

I can feel her looking at me. Time grinds slow as I stare at the floor until I cannot bear to look away. I bring my head up slowly, trembling at the effort. Our eyes meet and she is full of concern for me; her smile tentative.

"Btta," she says, then pauses. "You are so strong." One of her hands grips the muscles of my arm, the other she places on the space just below my neck. I cannot breathe; I quiver with the desire to leap away, but I fear what I will lose if I do.

She dips her head. "I thought that meant I couldn't hurt you, but..." She bites her lip, searching for words. "I want to know you. To know what you need..."

She moves her hand to my cheek, holds it gently, and pulls me toward her. Her kiss is soft and sweet and far too short. No! Why did she stop?

Hillie jumps up from the couch and stands before me, her face a page I cannot read.

She asks me, "Do you want this?"

I panic. Why did she have to fucking *ask*? Why is she always so full of questions I can't answer? I am pinned to the couch, shaking apart with the wanting of her, and with the hating of myself for the wanting. She waits patiently for my answer, no fear or judgment on her face.

I can't speak, but I nod and she takes my hand and pulls me up and leads me to the bed. She shoves me down onto the mattress and climbs over me and I cannot stop smiling. My tightly wound heart unfolds in the gentle heat of her embrace.

I awaken beside her the next day and I am still smiling. The quilt is warm, the mattress soft, and I am an unrippled pool of joy. She wakes and I look away until I feel her hands on me, her skin on my skin, her warmth to my warmth.

After we emerge from the quilt, I watch as she carefully chooses her outfit.

"Were you very rich before you died?" I ask from the bed, wondering how she could afford such an expensive wardrobe.

She turns, surprised, and I meet her eyes. "Have you never met a librarian before? I suppose not. I read that the last one we sent openly to your island was murdered as a spy."

"The last one you sent *openly*?"

"Joal—god of libraries—demands we collect all information everywhere. Even the most inhospitable places or people must be documented." She shivers at some uncomfortable memory.

"Even if they don't want to be? Neither my people nor my god want our secrets exposed on the pages of your books."

She throws her hands up, frustrated. "We aren't publishing your secrets! Do you really think you're the only people with a mystery cult? The library would have been burnt long ago if we revealed the secrets of other gods."

She comes to the bed, sits beside me, and holds my cheek. "We only write down what we see with our eyes."

She takes my hand in her own. "What we feel with our hands."

She brings my hand to her round belly. "What we taste with our mouths."

She draws a finger along my earlobe. "And what we hear with our ears. We only take what is freely given."

I open my mouth to argue, and she tries to quiet me with a kiss. I push her away. "No! Don't try to silence me."

"I just wanted… No. You're right, I'm sorry." She draws back, face marred by shame.

She reaches out for a hug, and I'm torn whether or not to accept. What do I do with this mess of contradictions? Her mercy and beauty and skill on one hand, and on the other hand her boundary-crossing obsession with learning and knowing things.

She sees my hesitation and turns away. I curse silently. Perhaps I can teach her, perhaps not, but for now, I need her and I want her and I care for her. I grab her hand and pull her close and in a moment we are whole again.

Over dinner that night, she says, "You asked if I was rich. No. Librarians swear an oath of poverty. I traveled the world studying textiles, yet I only ever wore the uniform of a librarian —or a cheap disguise. Now that I am dead… why not enjoy what I can?"

"Would you mind if I asked how you died?" Perhaps Hillie is rubbing off on me. I never would have asked such a personal question before meeting her.

"A book fell on me."

I laugh and she bats my shoulder.

"To be fair, the front-board was a lovely mosaic—so it was quite heavy. I was an old fool for trying to get it down by myself."

"How long has it been? Since you died?"

"A long time. Longer than I was alive. And I was older than you when I died." She pauses, and pulls away slightly. "Am I your first?"

First what? I don't know how to explain my relationship with my kin-workers. I never met a Ytarran anything like Hillie. I wonder what she sees in me, even as I am too afraid to ask.

Days pass and we believe we have found a route to Cmlech. Yet, our letters to the intervening gods return unopened, or with tersely worded rejections. I am not surprised, for Cmlech is a pariah god, working at the edges for the destruction of empires that provide other gods with followers and sacrifices.

We keep trying, but it is hard waiting for letters to work their way through the narrow and twisting caverns between underworlds. I am learning to read, and while it's unclear if I'm helping or hindering, at least I can pretend I am working towards my own departure.

Every night Hillie prepares a feast from one of her many cookbooks. I teach her a few Ytarran dishes, and try not to cringe when she writes them down.

We eat until we are near to bursting, then climb into bed, the frustrations of the day melting under the warmth of the quilt and the heat of our bodies. Perhaps Hillie is right: after a lifetime's work it is good to rest and enjoy the underworld.

And then I see the man who killed me.

He slips out of the book-return room. The book I am shelving falls from my hands. I freeze, doubting myself. Then I see the faint flash of his death-giving smile, and I am sure. I unstrap my hammer, hands clammy against the wood haft, and pursue him.

I dash across the great hall. He disappears into the stacks; I push myself faster. Hillie steps out in front of me—saying something I do not hear—and I almost tumble to the ground. By the time I catch myself and reach the stacks, he has disappeared.

I turn this way and that, searching for the flash of white robes in my periphery. Nothing. I rush back to Hillie.

"Come with me." I grab her hand and try to drag her towards our living quarters.

"But—" she says. I pull harder until she starts walking with me. She keeps speaking, not understanding my urgency. "Btta, I just received a letter from my god. They're going to personally escort you to Cm—to your god—in exchange for a story they've never heard before." She tries to pull away from me. "The contract is back on my desk."

My stomach lurches. I can't handle the thought of leaving right now.

When we reach the kitchen, I put my hands on her shoulders and say, "I just saw the man who killed me. He's inside the library."

She stiffens her back, head held high, and says, "I'll go kick him out."

"No!" My hands grip her shoulders, remembering Myrna's death at the tip of the necromancer's sword. "Hillie, this isn't an unruly patron. He killed my kin-workers. I'm not losing you, too!" I struggle not to shake her. "Stay up here, where it's safe. Lock the door. I'm going to get rid of him."

She protests at first, still thinking her routine more important than her safety. Yet she chooses to put her faith in my fear, and I hear the click of the lock as I head down the stairs.

I run to the great hall, but I am too late. Smoke occludes the stacks and library patrons flee through the entrance doors, which have been forced open from the inside. White-robed men with torches are burning the books. My killer must have let them in.

I slip into the stacks and bring the first one down with a wet crumpling sound, barely audible under the growing roar of the fire. Thinking the library undefended, they are armed only with torches. They don't expect me; so I kill or maim four before the rest know I am among them.

Then my killer finds me, his sword in hand. I roar when he sees me, but to him I am just an unknown woman who stands in his way.

He closes the distance between us, and I step back. His sword slices the smoky air and I shudder at the memory of its sharpness. He has reach-advantage on my hammer, and the narrow stacks leave little room to maneuver.

My only hope is to distract him enough to slip beneath his guard and land a crushing blow. "Why did you send me here? What happened to my kin-workers?"

He steps forward, sword held tip up, ready to fall upon me. "Ah, you're that Ytarran death-cultist." He steps forward again, driving me back. "I needed to test the targeted -death ritual before performing it on myself. You were a convenient sacrifice. The only thing I ever wanted of you is your death."

I fake a forward thrust, then turn and run. I weave left and right and lose him in the smoke.

I hide in the stacks, hoping for an opening. My killer and I see Hillie at the same time.

She strides through the smoke, kitchen-knife held aloft. I told her to stay upstairs!

The necromancer whirls and advances toward her. I scream and I run and I am almost upon him when he turns on me and the flashing sword slices jagged-red across my torso. I fall against a bookshelf, the stone burning my back.

The necromancer's death grin rises above me, but I won't give up while I still hold my hammer. He lazily blocks my one-handed swipe with the flat of his blade. I am going to die again, and then he is going to kill Hillie. I will never see her again.

"Why do you still struggle? You have nothing left to fight for. Your quarry is ours; its god-stone fuels our great work. Your friends are dead; your nameless god did not aid them."

I watch Hillie behind him; she puts on a mask and fiddles with something at her desk. Oh. Of course she would prioritize her books over her life. She is going to activate the emergency fire-suppression failsafe.

Wincing at the pain, I speak in an attempt to delay my death. "What 'great work' could justify this?"

My ears pop. Wind buffets the necromancer's robes. I close my mouth; hold my breath tight within me.

He smiles. "We work for your freedom, Ytarran. Neither the living nor the dead exist to serve the gods. The gods exist to serve us. We bound our god with god-stone chains, and now he enacts *our* will. If you had done the same, you would not be lying bloody on the floor, praying for help from a nameless god who will not answer."

His sword rises slowly to its apex. He blinks and sways and shakes his head. It is enough of an opening. I grab the haft of my hammer and bring it hard against his knee. He goes down and I rise up and press him against the floor with my bloody hammer.

"My god has a name, killer." He yelps as I grind the head of the hammer into his chest. "My god's name is the sound of the death of empires, the sound of the triumph of the weak against the strong." I lift my hammer. "My god's name is the sound of your skull breaking beneath the iron of my hammer."

He is dead.

My vision darkens. I should have kept my mouth shut, but it was worth it to say Cmlech's blessing at the moment of my triumph. At least I will die of suffocation instead of the blade. My body weakens and falls, and I plunge into the ocean of unconsciousness.

I awaken in pain, knowing I am in the right underworld.

My head throbs with the agony of my suffocation. I shudder at the trauma of my almost-death, then I look up into Hillie's eyes and all is well. She pulls the breathing mask from my face and leans down to kiss me.

She smells of ashes and the destruction of her library. Her tears track channels across her soot-stained cheeks and drip on my face.

"I'm sorry," I say, knowing words are not enough. I should have been faster, stronger, smarter. How many of her books did I fail to save?

She grips me tight, pulls me closer. "No. You have nothing to be sorry for. Without you, I'd be dead. Or—even if I survived—" She sighs, trying to express her feelings. "Yes, I mourn the lost books. But wisdom isn't just written down on paper or carved into clay. It lives in our heads and our hearts." She ruffles my hair, then places her hand on my chest. "People are books, too, and I never want to stop reading you."

Tears blur my eyes. I want to tell her how much she means to me, but the words don't come. What could I possibly say that would compare?

She shifts beside me. "I saved your transit-contract." She hands me the papers.

I stare sightlessly at them. She watches me, waiting.

This is my path to freedom. A long road to walk—alone—and then reunion with Myrna and my kin-workers. My desire to see them is an ache nestled hard against my heart, my duty to Cmlech a searing brand held an inch behind me. And yet.

"I can take you to the checkpoint now, if you like." She wipes her eyes. "I'll be… fine here."

I clutch her arm. "They might come back. I can't…" But that is a lie. I could leave, if I wanted to.

No.

Hillie is right. I have served my time in the world above and have earned my rest. Perhaps I don't need words to tell Hillie what she means to me.

I take the contract and begin to rip, but Hillie grabs my hands.

She smiles at me, understanding my intent. "I want to be with you, too." She puts the contract on the ground and kisses me. "But I don't need you bound to me. You should have the freedom to leave… or we can go together, or stay here and rebuild, or…" She throws her hands up. "Whatever happens, I want to be with you. Do you…?"

"Yes," I say. I take her hand and hold it as tight as I can, in the hope that we will never let go.

What Finds You in the Deep
by K.A. Doore

Lammeët's lips pursed with doubt as she pulled her lambskin hood back, spattering the ground with rain. "This is it?"

Tucked beneath a rocky overhang of what had once been a lake, the cave had been passed by for an entire town's memory until a few farmers came looking for stones. When they'd found the cave, they'd done the proper thing and alerted their council—after removing as many stones as they needed for their fences, of course.

The entrance was little more than a slice of darkness, barely wide enough to squeeze through. A pile of yellow-painted rocks was a recent addition from those same farmers, without which the entrance was invisible to passersby. Now the yellow glowed like a beacon despite the spitting rain on this early summer day, still chilled by its memories of spring.

"Some of the local kids got inside and found ancient tech," said Kuolma. "That means it could be a lost cultist refuge. The Council believes we'll find magic."

"The Council believes we'll find *bodies*," corrected Lammeët, but a tight excitement underlaid her words and she approached the entrance with sharp curiosity.

Just getting Lammeët here had been the work of months and countless favors and—yes—bribes. Officially, the fourteenth princess-elect of the Republic of Saavki had better things to do with her time than waste it exploring a cave. Magic, wherever it was found, was the sole purview of Kuolma and the other seven specialists, not any of the hundreds of elects.

But Lammeët was not just any of hundreds; she was Kuolma's elect, and Kuolma her guard. Even though now Lammeët's station required a rotating dozen of guards, Kuolma had been her first and closest. And, if Kuolma were being honest, they'd been more than mere elect and guard for a long time. While Kuolma no longer attended Lammeët as often as she once had—some state affairs weren't for the ears of a mere appointee—she still protected Lammeët. Stood by her side. Cared for her. Understood her. Knew what she needed.

And if there was one thing Lammeët needed more than anything else right now, it was an excuse to step away, if only for a few short hours, from her tightly controlled and constantly critiqued life in the castle, where the election for principal-elect was on the horizon and the expectation hovered over her every waking moment that she would not only run, but *win*.

Kuolma couldn't do anything about those expectations, but she could give Lammeët this: a trip into an unexplored cave, potentially rife with toxic magic and deadly animates, and a chance to temporarily shed her constant responsibilities and expectations.

It was a gift to herself, too: time alone with Lammeët, time enough to remember what had kept them together beyond their bond as guard and guarded, to rekindle the spark of what they'd had, once, to see if they could be more than occasional lovers. Lammeët loved danger and Kuolma loved Lammeët. This cave was what they both needed.

"Do you think the magic is old enough for animates?" asked Lammeët, the thinnest edge of hope in her voice.

"If this *was* a cultist site, then it's old enough to move stone."

The corners of Lammeët's lips twitched up. "Stone animates?"

"I can't make any promises—"

But Lammeët had already turned sideways and slipped through the crack as if it had been carved just for her. Kuolma shoved down the worry that flashed within her before it could catch and keep. There wasn't anything at the start; she'd already made sure of it.

She pushed her pack through first—*someone* had to carry provisions in case they got lost or stuck—but the stone tried to trap her when she slid in after, rocks sticking sharp into her chest and back. She sucked in a breath and squeezed and wiggled, the stone so close she wasn't sure she'd make it through this time, but then she passed the tightest point and the stone gradually opened back up again until she could slide and then shuffle and then, finally, walk free.

Kuolma pulled a torch from her pack and unraveled the wax cloth, but didn't light it yet. Ahead, Lammeët's steps clicked on stone. The princess-elect insisted on wearing boots fitted with spikes even in a cave, even in the yawning edge of spring, when there wasn't a sliver of ice in sight.

Only when Kuolma was far enough into the cave that she no longer felt the walls within reach did she strike a spark. The torch caught, flickered to life, and spilled warm yellow—*safe*—light on their surroundings.

"Oh." Lammeët's breath steamed as she turned in a slow circle, pupils huge enough to devour the entire cave. "It's bigger than I thought."

Having seen this cavern already, Kuolma drank in Lammeët instead. Even damp and sweaty from traveling, the princess-elect was a sight to behold: warm lips pursed tight, pale cheeks reddened from climbing the muddy hill outside, dark eyes sparking in the dim light. Before Lammeët could catch her staring, Kuolma glanced around the first of many connected caverns.

The ceiling curved away, out of easy reach, and extended far past the small circle of their torchlight. But what the light could touch gleamed. Metal and glass and plastic, all of it ancient, all of it preserved, all of it covered in dust. Shelves lined the walls, stacked with cans and boxes and books and supplies marked in a language that had shivers of familiarity while still not *quite* their own. There were chairs and desks, empty cups, broken plates, scattered children's toys, and even the withered tendrils of fibrous plants.

Most of it had been left as if awaiting an owner that would be back any moment. Chairs had been pushed away, turned as if someone had just stood up. Plates with a fork on their lip, as if they'd just been set down.

But there were hints of the troubles the people in the cave had endured in their final days: smashed glass, overturned tables, broken tech, and pieces of precious circuits and metal scattered across the floor. Whoever had once inhabited these caves, seeking shelter from the apocalypse they'd both feared and prayed for, they hadn't been the lucky few who'd emerged again. These caves were their tomb, but their tragedy could be the Republic's fortune.

Click. Lammeët had extended her cane, its metal tip meeting the floor. She approached a curving hulk of old technology, still intact. Its light was long gone, but hints of purpose remained: a smooth surface like a dark mirror; a series of raised buttons marked with their common alphabet, familiar in shape if not order; and a smaller piece of plastic attached by a long wire. She ran one gloved finger along the buttons, their soft clack like pebbles falling.

"I wonder if we can repurpose some of these. It's dry in here, preserved from the elements. I think…" Lammeët wiped off some of the grime. "There's no rust. We can use this to get another wind catcher running."

Kuolma smiled. Even with the promise of an adventure, Lammeët was still concerned about her people. One more wind catcher would make a difference for an entire town, but Kuolma wasn't here for tech. There were other specialists for *that*.

They didn't have the luxury of dawdling and dreaming of all the tech they could fix. Kuolma might be one of Lammeët's personal guards, but the Council guards waiting in the carriage had been ordered to return by nightfall and they wouldn't leave a princess-elect behind. Kuolma couldn't risk them coming into the cave and spoiling the surprises she had planned.

"Come on." Kuolma moved toward one of three dark hallways. "This isn't what we came here for."

Lammeët turned away from the tech, but her fingers trailed along the smooth plastic as if reluctant to let go. Then she straightened. "Right. You promised me magic, not old tech. So where do you think the bodies are?"

"They'll be farther below," said Kuolma. "Cultists went underground when threatened. If something happened here, they would have gone deep."

Lammeët grinned, all teeth and wolfish sharpness, a reflection of the stylized wolf that circled her neck in silver. "Then why are we dithering? If there are monsters, let's find them."

Lammeët reached for Kuolma's hand, then pulled her in for a possessive kiss. Before Kuolma could relax and explore beyond those lips, Lammeët had already broken contact. But she stayed breath-tasting close for another moment, gaze darkened by the conflict of her desire and duty, before straightening and clearing her throat.

"Lead the way, guard."

Kuolma was tempted to disobey for a heartbeat, to surprise Lammeët as the elect had surprised her, but the real surprise waited below. Hands tangled together, they left the old tech behind and ventured into the curving stone corridors in a steady rhythm of beating heart, clicking steps and cane, and the intermittent tap of her own fingers on the wood of her club. Kuolma had a knife, too, tucked into her belt *just in case*, but the real dangers would come from the magic they sought and the animates it created. A sharp blade was little match for opponents made of rock and bone.

A familiar chill seeped through her coat and gloves, finding skin, finding bone. Soon, their breaths became ghosts that lingered, twisting without a breeze. The walls clung close, narrowing and expanding at uneven intervals as if the cave itself were breathing. The warm torchlight reached only far enough to make them uncomfortable, but as long as the torch's flames stayed yellow and orange, they were safe.

Kuolma ignored the first few off-shoots from the main corridor; magic seeped through dirt and ice and stone, which meant the real treasures were farther down. Besides, she'd left marks on the wall to guide their way and knew just how far those treasures were.

But Lammeët couldn't tamp down her curiosity. Her soft glove slipped easily out of Kuolma's hand, and then the princess-elect was flitting down a side corridor, the torchlight just catching the soft brown highlights of her dark hair.

"Lammeët!" called Kuolma, but Lammeët ignored her.

With a sigh that was more acceptance than annoyance, Kuolma followed. The torchlight caught up to Lammeët and filled the room she'd found, spilling across a confusing jumble of shattered wood and scattered dirt. Glass glittered, catching the torchlight—still yellow.

Lammeët pinched something between her fingers, long like a rope but twisted and distorted. She rolled it between her fingertips, then tossed it back to the dirt.

"A garden."

Lammeët's words gave the chaos shape: the wood had been boxes that held the dirt; the thin ropes were withered stalks; the glass had been their light. In the far corner, crumpled wire must have once been a chicken coop. The knowledge that the cultists had cultivated and grown crops in this darkness turned Kuolma's own internal story about them on its head. She'd skipped these corridors her first time through, assuming these caves were just like ones they'd found before, where apocalypse cults had gone to die or to shelter for a few years with just enough canned food for both options. This one had meant to outlast the apocalypse.

"They had everything they needed." Lammeët hugged her arms close, looking around. "Why didn't they make it?"

Kuolma could guess—the shattered tech upstairs and the things she'd seen below made it clear that there'd been a struggle —but she didn't say. Instead, she held out her hand to Lammeët. "Leave that to the historians. We're here for the magic, remember?"

Far off, a stone clattered, its echo a whisper. But they both stiffened.

"Animate," breathed Lammeët.

"Maybe." Kuolma's hand went to the handle of her club. "It's too high up, though." She glanced at the torch, but its flames hadn't begun to purple; if it *was* an animate, it was still far away. "We should keep going."

Lammeët was already heading back to the main hallway, her steps quicker now. Even though Kuolma had used danger to entice the princess-elect here, doubt sluiced through her like a dam over-flowing. Already this trip was not going exactly to plan. Kuolma kept one eye on the torch and the other on the princess-elect as Lammeët's cleats and cane tapped out a faster rhythm.

The echoing scrape of rock against rock happened more frequently, coming from close and far away, from ahead and behind them. So Kuolma was already on edge when Lammeët suddenly stopped and pointed at the wall.

"What's that?"

Kuolma's heart leaped ahead at a gallop and she gripped her club, still attached to her belt. She scanned the stone, looking for what had startled Lammeët. The glitter of a rogue stalactite? Some other rock animate? But there was nothing.

Lammeët stepped forward until her finger met the wall, just below a scratch mark. "There."

Kuolma froze with a different kind of fear now. "I don't know."

"It's fresh." Lammeët dragged her finger and the tip came away clean, no sign of the dust and dirt that coated the rest of the walls. "Someone else has been here."

Fighting her suddenly dry mouth, Kuolma croaked out, "Kids got in here before. From the town. Remember?"

Lammeët peered closer at the mark. "I've seen a few of these. Like… they're marking our way or guiding us toward something."

"Hah," said Kuolma. "Maybe the kids found the magic first."

A troubled look crossed Lammeët's face. "Let's hope not. That would be very dangerous."

Reluctantly, Lammeët left the mark and continued on down the corridor. But instead of relieved, Kuolma was disquieted. She would have welcomed an animate over Lammeët's worry. Alleviating that worry, though, meant confessing: that those were her marks, that she had been here before, that she had fabricated more than just this excuse to explore a cave together. If she confessed that much, she knew she'd confess every-thing, down to the hope she'd stowed away below. The words remained unvoiced and Kuolma followed her princess-elect.

The distant scrapes had ceased, but Kuolma found herself willing them back again, if only to fill the silence. Lammeët usually talked enough for both of them, but she was just as on-edge as Kuolma, her hand going to her side again and again as if to reassure herself that she still had her sword.

So when they finally found the bodies, Kuolma was relieved.

The cave yawned into another cavern. This one was as cluttered as the first, but its debris was not ancient tech and furniture, nor dissolving books and forgotten dinners. Instead, this cavern was full of the dead.

"Oh," said Lammeët, both a sigh and an exclamation, and the single sound filled the space between the ancient bones.

The cultists' bodies clumped in groups of five or more, arms jumbled together as if they were still holding each other in death as in life. They'd been undisturbed for however many centuries. Hundreds of cultists—of *people*—who'd planned for their future, until that future had been so twisted and distorted that this had become their only option.

Lammeët stared at the nearest body, its skin in desiccated tatters. "What happened?"

"They lost hope," said Kuolma, her voice barely a whisper but loud enough in this tomb.

Lammeët tucked a stray hair behind one ear and turned slowly around. "But all of them? Like this?"

"The accounts from similar sites show that once the global communication networks went down, a lot of these communities fell prey to their own fears," said Kuolma. "Then all it took was a single charismatic leader to convince them the outside was too dangerous to return to, and. Well." Kuolma gestured at the dead.

"They just needed to listen to the local communications! Those stayed up."

"They would have smashed those first," said Kuolma.

"But *why*?"

Kuolma's smile was tight. "There was a lot of chaos and confusion in those early days. It would have been easy enough to convince their people that it was all lies, to tell them they couldn't trust what came from outside. They wanted to believe it was the end of the world; that's why they built these caves. They'd already given up."

"But they could've just opened the cave and gone out," said Lammeët. "They could've rebuilt the communicators. They could've talked to someone, *anyone*."

"Sometimes, it's easier to believe the worst." Beside Kuolma's foot was a bony hand, its fingers splayed wide as if it had just let go.

Silence spilled between them for a heartbeat, two, then Lammeët whispered, "Please."

Startled, Kuolma looked at the princess-elect instead of the bones. Lammeët's head was high and her lips pressed tight, but her eyes glittered with unshed tears. Kuolma's heart warmed, even as she flushed with guilt; while she might be inured to death, Lammeët was not.

Wordlessly, Kuolma took her hand and led her through the graveyard. As they wove between the bones, the calm magic pulsed gently under her feet; even though they'd died, at least they'd died on their own terms, and that affected everything they'd left behind.

Kuolma whispered a prayer, more for her own benefit than the cultists'. Their souls were gone now, taken up by the twelve gods while their raw energy went back to the earth, animating it, sustaining it, and becoming the magic that powered the Republic.

Kuolma and Lammeët exited the cavern and walked the following corridor in silence. Lammeët was clearly shaken by the experience, and Kuolma wished she'd found a way around instead. This trip was supposed to be filled with adventure that would lead to the kind of kisses they'd shared above, not disquieting tableaux of the dead.

The sound of stone scraping against stone resumed, louder than before. Maybe they *should* turn around and head back. But that would be abandoning the only thing that had given Kuolma hope in the past few months and by the time she had bribed enough officials and arranged enough schedules to bring Lammeët back down here, the election would be long over.

Then the edges of her torch sparked purple.

The cool color spread quickly: one moment the torch had blazed a warm yellow and orange, the next it was wholly purple. The transition was so abrupt that Lammeët noticed and stopped.

"I've never seen it turn so quickly," she breathed, pupils dilated in the dim light.

As if in answer, the walls themselves began to tremble.

"We need to move." Kuolma tightened her grip and pulled Lammeët along.

"But what's going on?"

"This magic isn't ready yet." Kuolma tried to keep the quiver from her own voice as she hurried Lammeët through the shaking passage. "It's still too tied to its deaths. Most of the magic has seeped farther below and calmed down. But there must have been a fight amongst the people in this area; this magic is still scared."

She could taste it in the air, thick and cloying like fear-tinged sweat. Then the walls began to close in on them.

"Run!" said Kuolma.

They ran. The scrape and groan of rocks smothered the sounds of their footsteps and breath. The torchlight was nearly black. Kuolma didn't dare touch the seeping walls, even with her thick gloves and thicker boots. Raw magic was invisible except in its effects, the way it animated the inanimate, the way it burned through flesh.

Lammeët's hand slipped from hers, and she heard a cry crushed between the stones. Kuolma spun, heart in throat, fear in chest, but Lammeët was still alive, still there. Her coat had been caught by the closing walls, trapping her.

Kuolma closed the distance, her dagger already in hand. She severed Lammeët's coat with a slice, freeing the princess-elect into her arms. Then they ran again, the walls closing behind them onto empty air.

Thankfully, stone was slower than flesh, and they outpaced the danger. The cave's groans continued, however, shuddering through Kuolma's chest so that she couldn't tell what was her own heartbeat and what was the movement of the cave.

Lammeët slowed, her hand reaching for the wall to steady herself. Kuolma interposed herself, letting Lammeët lean on her shoulder instead. Lammeët gasped out a breathy *thanks*.

After a few moments, Lammeët shifted her weight off Kuolma to her cane. "Well. That was exciting."

Kuolma glanced back the way they'd come, the corridor completely swallowed by darkness. The torch was still purple, if a few shades lighter.

"That wasn't supposed to happen," she said, more to herself. Then, pasting on a smile, she added, "But it explains the sounds we've been hearing. Guess we'll have more to report than I'd expected. Are you okay with continuing?"

Lammeët glanced pointedly into the darkness. "We can't really go back *that* way."

"There'll be another way out," said Kuolma. "Or the walls will re-open. Volatile raw magic doesn't usually stabilize. The cave will move again."

"That isn't as reassuring as you think."

But there was a bright edge to Lammeët's words and she was smiling. Kuolma couldn't help but smile, too: at the fact that they were alive, that they were together, at the absurdity of it all.

"Well," said Lammeët, her cane clicking as she navigated the uneven floor. "Let's find the next thing that's going to kill us."

She reached without looking and took Kuolma's hand. Even muted by their gloves, Kuolma could feel Lammeët's warmth, as reassuring as it was solid. Their lives had changed so much over the past year—Lammeët's increased status in the Council, her bid for the seat of principal-elect, Kuolma's elevation among the specialists—and they had been together through it all.

But the upcoming election meant that was no longer guaranteed.

"I'll still be at your side, you know," said Kuolma before she could stop herself. "Even when you become principal-elect."

Lammeët's grip loosened and, although she didn't pull away, she didn't look at Kuolma, either. "Yes. Well. We'll have to see about that."

Kuolma's stomach plummeted. "The principal-elect might be forbidden to marry, but they're not forbidden from taking a consort," she said quickly, hopelessly.

Lammeët looked at her, lips pursed tight. "You don't want to become a consort."

"I do. I would."

But Lammeët only shook her head, the slightest smile on her face. "You can do so much better than that." Then, before Kuolma could disagree again, Lammeët picked up her pace. "We haven't found the magic yet and we are running low on time. I expect you to keep your promise, guard."

Kuolma lagged until Lammeët was all but pulling her along. Her stomach churned with ice; Lammeët had been acting strange for months now. She'd recently disappeared for a few weeks, ostensibly on business for the Republic, but she'd been even more reluctant to share details than usual and hadn't taken any guards along. Then there were Lammeët's late nights outside the castle spent doing… *something* that she simply never talked about.

Of course, a princess-elect had many obligations and duties. And Kuolma had her own work to complete when she wasn't at Lammeët's side.

It was little wonder that they'd hardly seen each other, that they'd fallen out of the habit of conversations, let alone stolen moments and kisses. After all, wasn't that the reason Kuolma had concocted this plan? A few hours alone together, picking their way through bodies and scraping past murderous walls was just the thing for their relationship.

And now with the election looming, Kuolma had to choose: continue at Lammeët's side as a shadow instead of a real partner or let the princess-elect go unimpeded into the future she had built for herself.

Kuolma wasn't ready to consider that "or." Besides, Lammeët was right. At this moment, they were here in the cave together—at least until the Council guards determined their time was up and came to drag them back to the light and their responsibilities. The impending election might as well be another country away in time and space. Kuolma still had a promise to keep—and to give.

After a time both endless and short, the walls peeled away into another cavern. Kuolma held up her torch, its edges a persistent purple now that they were surrounded by ambient magic. Icy stalactites curved along the cavern's rim like so many jagged teeth. But despite the threat of those glittering teeth, the cavern was quiet. Content. Peaceful, even.

At its center was a pool. The water glowed with its own pale-gray light, its surface as smooth as glass. The pool was wide enough to step into and deep enough to fully submerge an adult. It was a water source that must have made this cave a choice location for an end-of-the-world cult.

But the water wasn't what caught Kuolma's eye. This cavern held more bodies, although these lay peacefully beside the water, hands carefully folded over their chests, swords placed beneath their hands. Someone had taken the time to arrange these bodies, either out of respect or as a warning.

What had these cultists worshipped? A single, distant god or all of the twelve? Kuolma knew some cults had worshipped no gods at all, but a single idea.

Whatever their beliefs, this had clearly been a sacred space. One important enough to merit a guard, even in death. Had they understood how magic worked? Kuolma found a pebble with her shoe and rolled it beneath her sole. Then she kicked it into the darkness, betting that the cultists had. The rock clicked and clattered along the edge of the cavern.

"What was that?" asked Lammeët, her pupils wide and her features bathed in purple light.

Kuolma didn't have a chance to answer before the cavern filled with the sound of stones tumbling, proving that the cultists *had* understood. Lammeët squeezed Kuolma's hand.

Then the bodies stood. It wasn't a smooth transition. Like pouring out a sack of dice, they clicked and clacked against each other until they were fully upright. They held their swords before them in an effective, if undisciplined, manner.

"Bone animates," said Lammeët, her words bright with excitement. She glanced sidelong at Kuolma. "But why did these become animates and not the ones above?"

"Magic seeps." Kuolma freed her club, its familiar weight centering and reassuring. "Plus, it looks like this was intentional. Those above died because they decided they had no other choice. These died to protect something. That will alone is as strong as any magic."

"What are they protecting?"

Kuolma shot a grin at Lammeët. "Why don't we find out?"

"There's five of them and only two of us."

The dead slowly surrounded them, their eye sockets mere dark pits that nonetheless blazed with undisguised antagonism. They wore their skin in scraps across yellowed bone, barely distinguishable from their clothes' disintegrating fabric, but their blades were as sharp as the day they'd died.

"What do you want to do?"

Lammeët twisted her cane until it collapsed into itself and slid it back into its case. When she spoke, there was a smile in her voice. "Fight."

Warmth spread in Kuolma's chest, burning through any lingering doubt. That was *her* Lammeët. A woman who was as fierce as she was quiet, as kind as she was stubborn, as wild as she was beautiful.

Lammeët drew her sword, a glint in her eyes like a wolf's midwinter, hungry but sure of her strength. Lammeët took her place at Kuolma's side.

The dead attacked. Kuolma got the first one, sending its skull flying with a single hit. But animates obeyed different rules from the living: they had to be fully dismantled before they would stop.

The second one gave Kuolma no time to breathe. Unlike any other animate she'd encountered, it knew how to use its weapon. Its sword came for her as soon as she committed to her club's swing.

But Lammeët was there, meeting its sword with her own in a clash of sparks and metal. She drove hard and fast, no time between her defensive strike and her offensive one, which took the animate's leg. Magic or not, it tumbled to the ground, bones scattering in a cacophony of clattering.

Even as the animate fell, Kuolma beat back another, her club breaking off bones piece by piece, giving Lammeët time for her own fight. When she'd relieved the animate of its skull and arms, she smashed through its ribs and the whole thing fell apart, bones scattering beneath their feet.

Behind her, more bones met the floor with a clatter. That left two animates: one each.

Despite the cold of the cave, Kuolma's gloves were damp with sweat. She clutched the club tightly and met her last animate's rictus grin with her own. She swung at its leg, eager to finish it off and join Lammeët in taking down the last one. It fell, as she'd expected. What she hadn't expected, though, was the chicken.

A bundle of bones barely shin-high careened out of the darkness and shot between her feet. She toppled beside the fallen-yet-still-whole animate, whose boney hands found her shoulders and searched for her throat. Kuolma tried to pry the hands off, but the chicken was back, its beak just as sharp in death as it had been in life. When Kuolma shielded her eyes from that relentless beak, the animate wrapped its fingers around her neck.

The raw magic in its bones met her bare skin. Pain sizzled across her neck like a thousand tiny, stabbing needles. Kuolma grunted, cold sweat breaking out on her forehead. She tried to protect herself from both the chicken animate and the warrior, but every time she kicked, her foot only glanced off bone.

"Kuolma!"

The air parted near her hands, followed by the sound of a hundred tiny bones clattering across stone. The next peck never came. Kuolma lowered her hand in time to see Lammeët swing again, gaze focused, face flushed, stray hairs plastered to her forehead with sweat. Her sword took off the warrior's head, but it wasn't enough to diminish the magical load and stop the animate. Pain blurred Kuolma's vision. Now all those thousand needles felt as if they were slicing *through* her neck. She couldn't breathe.

But Lammeët wasn't done. More bones flew. A ribcage smashed. The weight on Kuolma lifted, bit by bit. Finally, its grip weakened. Failed. The hands fell from her neck.

"Are you all right?"

Kuolma breathed in short, sharp gasps, the pain thudding around her neck like cursed jewelry, which was not far off from reality. When raw magic met living flesh, it left behind fractal scars that never fully healed.

Lammeët's eyes widened, a mirror Kuolma didn't need. She reached for Kuolma's neck, her fingers stopping just short. "Does it hurt?"

"A lot," admitted Kuolma.

Guilt flashed across those eyes. "I'm sorry I wasn't faster—"

Kuolma took Lammeët's hand. Then, because words failed her, she stood and closed the space between them and took Lammeët's lips between hers. They tasted like sweat and rain, like a summer day spent watching the clouds gather, then burst, like running to feel the drops, not avoid getting wet.

They lingered together in that downpour for moments and weeks, hands tracing each other's sides, mouths exchanging each other's breaths.

Finally, reluctantly, they parted. The cold was bearing down on them, sapping away their strength and time. They still had a cave to finish exploring, an exit to find, and—

"Do you want to look in the pool?" asked Kuolma. Anxiety flew through her on razor-sharp wings, a fluttering of fight or flight in her chest stronger than when she'd faced the animates moments before.

Lammeët traced a finger down Kuolma's neck, gaze full of hunger. "In a bit."

But Kuolma had brought up the pool and now she couldn't shake the cold churning in her stomach. While trying to hide the trembling in her hands, she took Lammeët's and started for the pool.

Lammeët let her, but asked, "Why are you in such a hurry?"

Kuolma's throat squeezed shut with anticipation and nerves. All she could do was gesture wordlessly at the pool and croak out, "We should look in the pool. They had to be guarding it for a reason."

Now Lammeët glanced at her with wry suspicion. But she did as she was told, kneeling next to the glowing circle of water. Kuolma brought the purple-edged torch close, but it wasn't necessary. The pool provided its own light.

The water was clear, the pool deep. It descended like another path, this one to another room, another cave, another system that could keep them occupied with exploration for months. Its sides were lined with a soft growth that glowed a pale blue—the source of light and probably the source of worship. And on a ridge of stone, just within reach, a piece of metal glinted in the light.

Lammeët pulled it out. Water spilled off the metal, soaked her gloves. Lammeët turned the piece slowly, eyebrows first furrowed with confusion, then lifting in surprise.

"I didn't know the ancients used marriage bracelets," she said.

"They didn't."

Kuolma plucked the bracelet from Lammeët's fingers and knelt next to her, fingers and hands and arms trembling with the weight of what she had to say. She fumbled with the words she'd practiced until they slipped from her mouth, as awkward as fledglings.

"I haven't always liked you," said Kuolma, already regretting her words, regretting *this*. But the moment had started and it wouldn't pass until she got out every word that had been bottled up within her for months. "But I've always respected you. You have astonished me again and again with your intelligence and kindness. I don't know when I started to like you, but I do know when I started to love you. And I know I can never stop. I could live without you, but I don't want to. I know"—she held up her hand to stop whatever Lammeët had parted her lips to say—"that as principal-elect, you won't be allowed a wife. But you can take a consort. I have guarded you for as long as I have known you. Let me continue to guard you."

Kuolma, eyes prickling with tears, took the biggest breath of her life. "Lammeët doulo Lassaofei—will you let me be your consort?"

Lammeët's lips stayed parted, but no answer came. Her eyes glittered and her hand moved to cover her mouth, but she didn't take the bracelet and the bottom of Kuolma's world dropped away.

"I—I know you said you didn't want a consort—" she began, lowering the bracelet, which had become very heavy all of a sudden. All those weeks away, all that distance growing between them—she should've taken the hint, should've *known*—

Lammeët shook her head and fumbled at the pouch at her waist. After a heartbreaking moment, she found what she was looking for and pulled out something rounded. Metal. She held it out to Kuolma, tears now streaming freely down her cheeks and sobbed a laugh.

"You idiot," she choked out. "You're not going to be my consort. You're going to be my *wife*."

She plucked the silver bracelet from Kuolma's unresisting hands, replacing it with hers. Lammeët slid the bracelet over her hand and onto her wrist, where it fit as if it had been made for her. Of course, it had. Kuolma was still kneeling, reeling from the reversal. She held the new bracelet and rubbed the silver with her thumb. Stylized wolves chased each other around it, their coats made out of snowflakes. Then tears blurred her vision and she couldn't see anything else.

Lammeët pulled her close and met her startled gaze, her smile so wide it could fill the room. "Yes, yes, a hundred times *yes*, Kuolma. I will marry you and only you."

"But—the principal-elect—"

"I'm not going to run," stated Lammeët. She kissed the corner of Kuolma's mouth.

"But it's been your dream."

Another kiss. "Dreams change. I'll be able to do more if I stay in the Council."

"But… these last few months… then where did you go?"

Lammeët kissed Kuolma's top lip. "To your village."

Kuolma pulled back. "What?"

"To ask your family for your hand."

"An elect doesn't need to ask—"

"Not in the past," said Lammeët. "But today? Things are changing. Things *should* be changing. And I wanted to start with respect. Besides," she added, "your family's lovely. I can't wait to see them again."

"How long have you been planning this?"

"How long have *you*?" returned Lammeët. "How long did it take you to find this cave? To get the approval to explore it? And then again, to bring me along? I have to admit, you had me convinced for a while that this was the first time you'd been down here."

"What tipped you off?"

"The marks," said Lammeët. "Kids don't think ahead like that. Which meant someone else had been here recently. Someone like *you*."

"Months," admitted Kuolma. This time she kissed Lammeët.

"Thank you," said Lammeët, against Kuolma's lips. "That was the most fun I've had in years."

"I'm so glad you liked it."

"You know me."

"I do."

A pause, the world forgotten for another few moments as they shared each other instead.

Then,

"Can we do it again?"

The Sweet Tooth
of Angwar Bec
by Ellen Kushner

When Angwar Bec grew too old to fight blood duels, she was still in great demand. She took every gig that came along, from ritual guard at nobles' weddings to demonstration bouts at their coming-of-age parties; the money was good, and it kept her in steel and sweets, her two great passions.

Angwar Bec had a collection of blades that anyone would envy. Her love of cakes and pastries was so well known that her noble patrons would vie for the chance to amaze her with something new at the wedding feast after the ceremony, to which she was nearly always invited. One enterprising city baker had even named a cake after her: the "Angwar Bec" was a startling concoction of anise-scented sponge cake and burnt-sugar icing, filled with chestnut cream.

She did prefer chestnut to chocolate, which made the resident Kinwiinik cacao traders say that, whatever Angwar Bec's mysterious parentage, she certainly wasn't one of *theirs*.

All her life, people had asked her, *What are you?*

She knew what they meant: Who are your parents? And your parents' parents? Did her tawny skin come from Danbar stock? Was her iron-straight, shiny raven hair a gift of some Chartili merchant prince, or his freed bondwoman, or perhaps a refugee from the wars of distant Seren? Had her Riverside whore of a mother found a Kinwiinik trick who actually didn't like chocolate?

She knew what they meant. But she would answer:

I am Angwar Bec.

It wasn't her real name. When she was a kid hanging around the docks below Riverside, she saw *Angwar* painted on the side of a ship from who-knows-where. She had no idea what it meant, but so far no one had come sidling up to her to tell her it was Serenish or something for *Big Ass* or *Sea Snot* or something. It had, to her, the feel of *Victory*.

Bec, she had just made up because it sounded good.

The truth was, she had no idea where she was "from."

"One of my many lovers" was the way her mother had airily expressed it. Her mother enjoyed the phrase, used it a lot. It drove her crazy.

Her real name was Sophie Snell. Her mother—she of the many lovers—had been a singer in a Riverside tavern, who also helped out with cleaning when the boss needed it. Sophie had grown up playing under the tables of the Maiden's Fancy and observing the clientele.

Night after night they came in: the students in their black robes from across the river; the true Riversiders stopping in at their local; the Middle City's aspiring apprentices; slumming nobles from the Hill, all seeking the thrill of rubbing elbows and maybe more with each other.

The ones with the swagger, though, the ones everyone else made way for, those were the swordsmen. No one rubbed up against them without invitation, though everyone stared.

She decided she would be one of those.

Angwar Bec had trained long and hard to get where she was. She wasn't too proud of what she'd had to do to pay for her earliest lessons, down in Riverside, but that was behind her now.

Now she had a snug little berth above a celebrated baker's in the Middle City. She'd wake in the dark to the smell of baking bread, inhale deeply, roll over, and sleep until the bells of the shop's first customers sounded over the door. Then she would rise, stretch, and begin her drill. She knew she need never go hungry again.

What had set her on the road to this comfort was her notorious and unquestionably ill-advised duel with Katherine, Duchess Tremontaine.

It was her very first paid gig, and it began as a joke: Angwar Bec the unknown swordswhatever, lucky to be invited to run practice bouts with some of the more experienced blades in the courtyard of the famous tavern the Sword and Cup, where they showed off their moves to draw the attention of possible patrons. For her, of course, it was always just the drills, never a genuine duel to get her name up on the betting boards, like the men.

And then some drunken young nobles, country mud still stuck to their boots, new to town and looking to make their mark, saw her and decided it would be hilarious to have this fiery dark girl challenge the young duchess at her own midwinter party.

So it was there, in the great courtyard of Tremontaine House, at the highest and most gracious point of the Hill, with the midwinter torches flaming and flaring, the nobles of the city glittering with jewels amid their floating furs, the smells of hot wine and bonfires on the air, the crackling wood eating up everyone's wishes and regrets as fast as the duchess's guests could throw the scraps of paper into the fire, that Angwar Bec bade farewell to her old life once and for all.

The first thing she noticed after she'd passed through the high, iron gates of Tremontaine House, spiked with gilded, wrought-iron flowers, was the cakes: tables of pastries, beautifully arranged on platters everywhere you looked. The nobles were ignoring them in favor of flirtation, conversation, and alcohol. What was *wrong* with these people? She lusted after those confections the way she'd lusted after the sword she bore, a perfectly balanced rapier of folded steel. She had spent her money on that, and not on the other, and so she had a blade to be proud of, but not much to eat lately.

Her mark, Katherine, Duchess Tremontaine, stood in a ring of flambeaux, receiving her guests. Most were coddled against the night cold in furs the colors of forest creatures, but the Duchess Katherine wore layers of brocade in bright jewel colors, laced with ribbons, fringed with bullion—her costume looked as if it would stand up by itself if the duchess stepped out of it. Impossible to fight in such a get-up.

The duchess didn't look old enough to be the holder of so much money and power. She was so young!

Twenty-five, if she was even that, the age when a working swordsman would still be at the height of their powers. She was not homely by any means, with a fine-drawn face and pointy chin; an intelligent face, set in an expression of cautious benignity; but the Duchess Tremontaine did not rank among the great beauties present. Her light brown hair was bound up on her head in an elaborate confection of ribbons and gold cord laced with jewels. It spoke of rank, not of availability.

Angwar Bec squared her shoulders, settled her cloak on them, and stepped forward into the circle of light around the duchess. This was it: her first paid challenge. There was an immediate hush, as everyone waited to hear what she would say.

"My name is Angwar Bec," she announced, and oh, that sounded good. "I bear challenge to the Lady Katherine Tr—er, Talbert." She'd practiced and practiced, but she *knew* she was going to screw that up! "To the Lady Katherine Talbert, Duchess Tremontaine of this City."

The young duchess looked at her, long and evenly. She was shorter than Angwar Bec, but that did not seem to trouble her. "Upon what charge?" Katherine asked.

Here it comes, thought Angwar Bec. It was going to sound so stupid, especially now that she'd seen the lady so splendidly clad out here in the open among the glittering bonfire sparks, the glittering noble guests. She steeled herself to speak clearly and loudly.

"That she is really a man in a dress."

There were gasps, and hoots, and chuckles. At least no one would think she'd come up with that herself. It was clear provocation from one noble to another, with a hired sword to deliver it properly.

The Duchess Tremontaine laughed with genuine merriment, throwing back her head so the light from the jewels danced. "That's a new one," she said. Without moving, she addressed the crowd: "Is anyone going to own it?"

Nobody was. Either the boys who'd hired her weren't there, or they were chicken. It didn't matter to Angwar Bec. This was her fight. She had the contract, and the Court of Honor would uphold it.

The duchess nodded. The entire courtyard was still. A few people were muttering amongst themselves, but nobody moved.

Angwar Bec had a sudden, horrible thought: What if the duchess did not take her challenge? Tremontaine surely had house swordsmen, men of skill and experience, one of whom would be happy to step up, claim the fight, and dispatch the intruder. She wouldn't stand a chance. She would depart this life with her name unknown, never having tasted those little filled pastries with the red and white squiggles on top.

But the young Duchess Tremontaine spoke the formal words herself: "The accusation is false as air, false as the tongues that spoke it. I accept the challenge."

Someone screamed. Her guests had come for a pleasant evening of music, nibbles, and conversation, not to see their hostess covered in gore. But there was also an undercurrent of excitement on the air. Angwar Bec felt it like lightning, like power: the men all ready for a fight, eager to see two women attack each other, already weighing up the odds and passing their bets; the women, some of them very knowledgeable followers of the city's duelists, thrilled at the novelty of this.

"What are the terms?" the duchess asked.

"To first blood," said Angwar Bec.

"Very well." The duchess unpinned the capelet that covered her shoulders, letting it fall to the ground. She called for a maid to divest her of the rest of the brocade infrastructure, to unlace her skirt and her gilded bodice, and finally stood glowing in the firelight, strong and compact, in enough fine linen under-things still to keep her from the cold. Only her long brown hair remained up in its elaborate twists and bindings.

An attendant came running from the house with a sturdy leather vest and gloves, while another brought the Duchess Katherine's own rapier.

Angwar Bec was impressed to see that the weapon was heavy and serviceable, not just a noble's jewel. Until this moment, she hadn't truly believed the stories of the lady who had fought real challenges against her peers on the Hill, and even studied, it was said, with the great St Vier. But when

Katherine, Duchess Tremontaine, took sword in hand and assumed the stance, it was clear that it was all true.

Angwar Bec was pleased to see that the duchess did not bother beginning with the little fiddle-faddles that some people did, twirling and swirling the tip of their blade as though they were trying to draw flowers in the air, or follow the flight of a bumble bee. Such tricks were just for show; no serious opponent ever fell for them. In return she showed her respect for the duchess's swordsmanship by not trying them out on her, either, even though Angwar Bec's wrist and fine point control were some of her best skills. They'd do their work for her later.

But when, she wondered as they circled the courtyard, was *later*?

On the streets of Riverside, Angwar Bec had fought serious and sudden duels, the kind where speed mattered more than style, and the goal was to put your opponent out of commission before they could do the same to you.

That was not her purpose here. She had an audience here. Half the nobles of the city were now evaluating her technique, commenting on her style as they watched her circle the courtyard with just a couple of lengths of razor-sharp steel between herself and Katherine, Duchess Tremontaine. These were not practice blades. She knew how sharp her own was, and while the duchess's had probably not been honed that very afternoon, neither was it likely to be dull.

So when she had her opponent's measure, would Angwar Bec really lunge at the flesh under the white sleeve or the unprotected calf, penetrating the outer layer of cloth and skin to draw noble blood? The thought made her clench her jaw, so that her shoulder tightened and her arm lost its flex.

Oh, why in the Green God's name had she been such a fool as to accept a gig like this for her very first paid and public fight? There was no way that it was going to end without her looking like either an incompetent blade or a Johnny-Go-Mad. If she lost, it was the end of her not-quite-started career as a sword for hire. If she won....

If she won, she knew where it would place her. She'd be typecast as a duelist assassin from the beginning, her only gigs coming from nobles seeking to draw other nobles' blood.

No well-paid, elegant show duels against other fine blades for her, just revenge jobs to the death until a better sword put an end to her.

Angwar Bec was not going to put a scratch on the noble Katherine, Duchess Tremontaine, not if she could help it.

The noble Katherine came in right past her guard in a beautifully fluid motion, which Angwar Bec's stiff arm was slow to parry. She had to fall back, giving ground like a tyro. And the duchess let her. Katherine could have followed up immediately, could have won the bout then and there, but she did not, and it was clear that she did not. Clear to Angwar Bec, anyway, alert to the nuance of the tiniest fraction of speed, of breath, things invisible to the onlookers, who believed they saw two experienced fighters dueling at the top of their bent, fighting to win.

As Katherine let her regain her stance, it came to Angwar Bec in a flash that it did not matter to the duchess whether she won or lost. There was, after all, nothing really at stake for her. Her losing the fight would give the noble boys, Angwar Bec's silly patrons, some notoriety if they chose to boast about it, which they surely would. But it would not affect the Duchess Tremontaine. Everyone knew she was not really a man. Even above the padded fighting vest that hid her figure, her face was smooth, her taut, elegant jawline gently rounded, as a man's would never be. As her breath came more and more quickly, her lips parted to release the occasional grunt of effort in a woman's unmistakable treble.

What was her game? Angwar Bec wondered. Was she just trying to show her guests a good time, not to end the entertaining bout too quickly? The duchess pressed her advantage, pushing Angwar Bec back across the yard. Was Katherine, in fact, simply the better fighter?

Fuck that, Angwar Bec thought. The Duchess Katherine knew the basics. She was skilled at the slow game, the careful and deliberate work of the practice studio. She had technique. What she didn't have was fire. She had probably never fought to the death, never in her life.

Angwar Bec had fire. She had the will to win, and a skill born of more than mere technique. It was time to show the Duchess Tremontaine what she was up against.

The flurry of Angwar Bec's attack was a glory to behold. The guests cheered as Katherine met her thrusts with parries, ripostes that Angwar Bec returned in kind, in a blur of movement. She decided to show off with a twist around her back, a flashy move that still kept herself guarded. And she heard the duchess laugh with delight.

They made their way around the bonfire, to the calls and screams of Tremontaine's guests. The duchess's breath was coming shorter now, her steps a little slower.

A trickle of sweat rolled down Katherine's cheek. Angwar Bec gave her the tiny moment she needed to brush at it with one wrist while the other held off her opponent. The duchess grinned her thanks. Her parted lips were a very becoming rose.

The duelists went around a particularly weird and annoying cornice by the stairs into the house. Not knowing the terrain left the young blade at a disadvantage. She stumbled badly against the plinth along the foot of the wall, but never dropped her guard. And the Duchess Katherine patiently played her out, running through a very basic thrust for her to parry and riposte, while she got her feet back under her and was able once more to advance out of the shadows.

With no idea what had just happened, the guests were hooting their approbation of their hostess's presumed triumph.

But Angwar Bec was beginning to have some idea of the Duchess Katherine's game.

There, in the shadows, she spiraled her blade around the other woman's, sliding them both up until their faces nearly touched.

"Hello," Katherine said softly. "Have you noticed my weakness at defending from high right yet?"

And Angwar Bec understood that the Duchess Tremontaine was not planning to defeat an unknown young sword in her own courtyard, here in front of her noble friends. The lady was unwilling to throw the fight, but she was patiently waiting for Angwar Bec to defeat her.

"I'm about to," Angwar Bec replied, which was really all she could do, given the brightness of the other woman's eye, the exceptional flush of her cheek, and the sharp aroma of her breath.

"Let's make your reputation now, shall we?"

And that, the young sword thought as she moved in for the definitive touch and disarm that later became her trademark, is what made a true noble. Knowing that you'd eat tomorrow, whether you won or lost your next bout. And that your opponent might not.

That night, in bed with the Duchess Tremontaine, Angwar Bec began her discovery of what it meant to be a success.

Katherine fed her cake after sweet cake. Bec ever after associated the taste of anise with the taste of Katherine's skin, the chocolate crushed in her fragrant armpit, the raspberry dipped in her navel. The tang of her hard kisses had a flavor of their own.

But she found she liked the chestnut best.

Danger Noodle
by S.K. Terentiev

"Earth to Jane...?" Sophia held out a bloody chunk of goat, squatting with her purple galoshes bright in the mud. "Liver."

She waved the gobbet of goat at me impatiently and I extended the specimen bag. I waited until after she'd turned back to eviscerating—pardon me, autopsying—her goat of choice before sticking my tongue out at her. "Earth to Jane" my ass.

Goats. Why did it have to be goats?

It's not that I'm afraid—I'm an insurance adjuster working non-standard insurance. I'd been on this rodeo too long to be freaked out by a few goats. It's just their eyes are so creepy, rectangle pupils like tiny mail slots into their brains. The fact that the whole herd was wide-eyed dead around us in the pasture didn't exactly help.

"So what do we think?" I dropped the bag into the cooler at my feet and snagged another one from the kit.

"*We* don't think anything. *We* are still investigating."

I took a deep breath instead of snapping back at her. I'd brought this on myself with the whole anniversary thing; I couldn't exactly blame her for being upset.

"Babes, can we talk about this?"

"It's fine." She shoved another bit of goat into the bag I held out.

Yeah, pretty sure it wasn't fine.

"Today's not over—"

"Can we just focus on the job, please?"

"Okay... sure." I handed her a swab. "So what do you think happened?"

"I don't want to speculate."

"Since when?"

She sighed. "I have a few hypotheses but no theories. There's not much to go on."

That was putting it mildly. We were in the bottom corner of the pasture, nestled up against the fence. The whole herd was sprawled around us without a mark on them, like a caprine sleepover gone wrong. Clouds rumbled overhead but so far the rain had held off, and everything was the muddy gray and green of a Texas February. The only real spots of color were orange construction cones along the road and our SOTCO Insurance van, which was currently Neon Frog's Ass green.

Sophia wasn't a mage with a capital M, but she had enough juice that the van had developed an affinity for her, which manifested in its being a giant mood ring on wheels. From the color, she was at DEFCON Three.

Which meant I'd annoyed her enough to knock her off her game. Knowing her, she was going round and round in her head over what I'd done—or hadn't done. Completely distracted and more frustrated by the minute.

"The fact that the scene's pretty clean means we can rule out things like run of the mill cult sacrifices or a werewolf on a bender, right?" I prompted, stripping off my gloves.

"True…"

She was definitely stuck. Time for a hard reset.

"What about a botched fertility rite?" I mused as I crouched down and snagged a sprig of tiny yellow flowers from a weed, idly tucking it behind my ear. "*Pan's Pastures* is a small dairy, but that kind of thing is right up the satyrs' alley."

I knew a podunk operation like this one didn't have the juice to funnel a whole herd's life force—it'd be like trying to lasso a tornado with a wet noodle. If the satyrs crashed and burned on a fertility thing the whole area would look like Willy Wonka's wet dream of a spring, instead of a handful of weeds in the brown grass. I also knew Sophia wouldn't be able to resist.

She snapped out of it, and I let her explanation of energy waves and quantum gravity wash over me as she went back to running the usual tests. We'd been together long enough that I'd heard it all before, but this was her jam, so I made the appropriate interested noises as I handed her swabs, a handful of dried jackalope kidneys, and various solutions in droppers.

"Some kind of chemical residue here, but not a summoning," Sophia sighed as the Fanta-orange liquid she was swirling with a bit of goat hair remained orange, instead of flashing to black like it should have if there were rift particles.

Probably for the best. The paperwork on a minor god summoning would take hours, and I had plans for tonight.

She capped the jar and stood, stretching the kinks out of her back. A head taller than me and willowy with a love of Pilates bordering on religion, her stretch was a work of art. Beauty and brains, she was the whole package.

She caught me looking and gave me a Not Happening Today Look. The whole package with just enough snappiness to make life interesting.

Her phone rang and she dropped an F-bomb before picking up.

"Hello, Chad."

I winced. Chad was our new direct report and he'd been all up in our business since he came on board. Between that and Sophia's mood it was going to be a fun conversation.

I stifled a yawn. Good time for a coffee refill. Jane, exit stage left.

Grabbing the kit, I headed to the van. I'd tossed and turned all night, too excited about this weekend to sleep. My first cold brew hadn't stood a chance. Through the gate I leapt over the ditch, passing the cones marking the end of the storm-drain construction. They stood like orange sentinels below a *Horny Toad Preserve 0.5 Mile* sign, its cartoon lizard in a red cowboy hat pointing down the road.

The sky rumbled again, and I dropped the kit in the front seat and grabbed my backup latte from the console. I downed half of it as the weather started misting and the wind picked up, blowing the smell of the poultry farm across the street into my face. Ah the country—mud, rain, and chicken shit.

Snagging our ponchos from the glove compartment, I shut the door just as the van broke out into puce polka dots.

Fuck.

DEFCON Two.

Sophia's little chat with Chad must be going swimmingly, and she was well and truly pitching a fit. Which meant *my* ass was grass if I didn't do something pretty damn quick.

She was a professional, but with the van at Toad Ass she might nuke Chad through the phone and it'd be all my fault. Plus, if she blew a gasket the van would too, and we'd be stuck in nowheresville with a bunch of dead goats. Not exactly how I wanted to spend our anniversary.

She hung up as I jogged back through the gate. I shook her poncho out like a low-rent matador as she bulled toward me, muttering under her breath. I caught something about Chad's mom and sheep, but mostly it was unintelligible except for the occasional f-bomb.

"Having fun, love?" I asked as she snatched the poncho from me and shoved it over her head.

"He called me 'babe' and asked if we needed help. Twerp."

Yeah, I'd call that desk jockey for help when the next apocalypse was triggered and not a second before. I reached up and tugged her hood forward, tucking in her dark curls before holding her cheek in my palm.

"You want I should kill him?"

She glowered at me, brown eyes almost black in the stormy light.

"I will! Just say the word, I'm your huckleberry. I mean, sure, there's the whole prison thing. And it's Texas, so I'll probably get the needle, but for *you*…"

She snorted and leaned down to shut me up with a kiss.

"Why Sophia Miller, what will Human Resources think?"

"That you're ridiculous and I need my head examined for agreeing to marry you."

"Technically, it was *me* who agreed to marry *you*."

She rolled her eyes but grinned as she took my coffee. "You're still ridiculous."

"True."

"And I'm still mad at you."

I froze in the middle of pulling on my poncho, and she tugged it down off my face and met my eyes.

I sighed. "Soph, you said you didn't want to do anniversary presents. You said it *multiple times*."

"I know… but…"

"You said, 'We're saving for the Galapagos trip in June, that's enough of a present for me.'"

She sipped the coffee and avoided my eyes.

"I thought you meant it. I messed up and I'm so sorry, love."

"Oh, it's okay." She sighed. "You're right, I did say we weren't doing presents, so it's not exactly fair to be mad at you for believing me."

"Note to self, stop believing Sophia. Got it." I smiled at her. "Stick with me, 'babe,' the day's still young. Who knows what could happen?"

She made a face at me, then grinned. She could never stay mad for long... 'cause I got jokes.

"Okay so what do we have?" I asked, taking my coffee back before she could hog it all.

"Dead goats, chemical residue..."

"What about the Goatman? Isn't he local?"

"The Lake Worth Monster?" Sophia scrolled in her phone. "His Instagram has him skiing in Colorado."

"I know there isn't a mark on the herd but I gotta ask." I held up my cup, the stylized chupacabra barista smiling from the *Vintage Coffee* logo. "Do you think it's weird there's a blood-drinking barista with a taste for goat only a couple miles away?"

"Weird? I don't know, there are hipsters everywhere these days." She shook her head. "And the goats weren't exsanguinated, so that rules him out."

She was probably right. Plus, any man rocking a wig with an epic bun like that was probably into kale and fancy heirloom goats. Dollars to donuts he'd turn up his snout at this herd.

"Maybe we should do a divination," Sophia said, and I made a face. "I know, I know, they're messy. But—"

She stopped, staring at me.

"What? Do I have a bug on me?"

"Jane, what's this?" Sophia reached up and pulled the little yellow flowers out from behind my ear.

"Oh, just one of the weeds." I gestured around at the random spots of green in the grass and trailed off at the look on her face.

Sophia in full Sherlock mode was one of my favorite things on earth. Perfectly sculpted eyebrows frowning in concentration, she muttered under her breath as she made tiny gestures with her fingers, sketching things out in her head. I could practically see the gears in her brain turning, then *bam*! She'd make this amazing leap to the answer. It was the best magic trick I knew.

"Rue," she said, breaking into a smile like the sun and grabbing my arm. "Not weeds, Jane, it's rue."

She tugged me toward the van. "I didn't make the connection. Rue's not native to this region. But the chemical residue all over the bodies... and the chicken farm across the street..."

"What?"

"Basilisk. It's a basilisk. Rue has a natural immunity to their fumes, but I bet the rest of the flora and fauna in the area are dead. Not just dormant for the winter." She halted at the gate. "No, that can't be right. They prefer caves, but the geology is all wrong..."

I looked at the construction cones. "What about storm drains?"

She followed my gaze. "Jane, you're a genius."

The van blossomed lemon yellow as I yanked the back doors open. Inside, it looked like someone had cut the vans of two very different serial killers in half and stitched them together with duct tape. Sophia's domain was all computers and stainless-steel countertops, plexiglass drawers up to the ceiling, carefully labeled with color-coded tags. Everything perfectly organized and Instagram-ready.

Meanwhile, across the divide from the shining lab on wheels was my territory. Kept safe from Sophia's encroachment with the magic of duct tape, my stainless countertops might have been dented and scratched, but the tools of my trade were easy to hand and ready to rumble. Shields and pikes strapped to the ceiling, Kevlar vest hanging next to Dad's old twelve gauge, my favorite machete in its sheath.

Sophia had climbed up behind me and was scrolling through the company wiki on her workstation touchscreen.

"Hey babes, how big a Danger Noodle are we talking here? Huge like the movies?" I asked as I pulled open the middle drawer below my worktop and my new double-bladed battle axe gleamed up at me, *To My Pocket-Sized Warrior* engraved on the handle. Best first anniversary present ever, even with the short joke. Especially with the short joke.

"Danger Noodle." I could practically hear her roll her eyes behind me, and I grinned. "It's not a snake. Picture a rooster-headed snake-bodied reptile. Maybe three to five feet long, not huge. Hollywood always exaggerates."

Not the axe then. Bummer. I slid the drawer closed.

"So what's the rundown?" I asked. Pulling my kukri off the wall, I slid the curved knife out of its sheath to inspect it.

"You're not going to like it." Sophia wrapped her arms around my waist from behind, laying her cheek on my head.

"I never do. That's why they pay me the big bucks." I laced my fingers through hers as I debated my machete before deciding against it—too big for a sewer.

"Poisonous fire breather. Relatively fast, but with a chicken brain, so not exactly Einstein."

"Wait, isn't this one of those things I have to fight with a mirror? Like that bro Perseus?" I rummaged in a drawer. "I have a compact in here somewhere..."

"No, the death glare is an old wives' tale. You don't have to go all Medusa murderer on it." Sophia had Opinions on men who hunt women down in their own homes. "The fumes are the problem, odorless but lethal."

I dropped a kiss on her hand before moving to the large cabinet at the front of the van, just behind the seats.

"So PPE then, what are we talking here, like C?" I pulled open the cabinet door just enough to snake a hand inside and reach for my mid-level respirator.

"Probably more like A."

That stopped me in my tracks and I gave her a Look.

"Yeah, no. You expect me to kill a fire-breathing rooster snake in full hazmat gear?" I closed the cabinet door and stepped over to her touchscreen, scrolling through the wiki entry. She always exaggerated the need for protective gear when my ass was on the line.

"No, of course not, I expect you to *catch* a basilisk in full gear." I snorted.

"One, this says the fumes are not absorbed by the skin but have to be breathed or ingested. Since I'm not gonna eat the thing, a respirator is fine. I'll even do full-face SCBA if it'll make you feel better. If *someone* remembered to refill the air tanks." I narrowed my eyes at her. "And two, why in the name of all that is holy do I need to *catch* a Level Six Hazard instead of killing it?"

"Oh, I'm sure they're protected somewhere." She avoided looking at me and stepped toward the PPE cabinet. "I mean, they're beyond endangered since, most of the time, they're extinct."

Just dropping that illogical comment about extinction as if she was saying the sky was blue.

"Uh-huh." I blocked the cabinet and crossed my arms. "You're not distracting me with the extinct thing, and we're not wearing plastic suits to dance with a fire breather. That's how you end up in a burn unit coated in melted plastic versus just having to draw your eyebrows on for a few weeks. Answer the question. Why should I catch this poisonous Danger Noodle instead of putting it down?"

"Okay fine." She huffed. "Basilisk hardly ever occur in the wild. They hatch from chicken eggs that are brooded over by a toad. Do you know how hard it is to convince a toad to sit on an egg? They're not exactly maternal."

She ran her hands through her hair, making her curls stand up in a halo. "Los Alamos is the only successful research program in the country and they never let any of them into the private sector. It's ridiculous. Who knows what advancements we could make if they'd open it up to the scientific community? They don't even share their findings!"

To Sophia, not sharing research was a crime against every sentient being on the planet and beyond. She ran out of breath and gave me the Look.

Here it came.

"This would be the best first anniversary present ever."

I leaned back against the cabinet doors. Well, fuck. I'd screwed myself on that one by letting her think I hadn't gotten her a present. I'd dropped a ton of hints that I had plans for later when she gave me the axe, but she'd still gotten mad. If I fessed up now it would have all been for nothing.

"You want a Fire Noodle for an anniversary present." I shook my head but turned and reached into the cabinet to pull out our full-face masks, careful to keep my body between her and the suitcase hidden inside.

First anniversary was paper, and our passes to the Weird Archive in Austin were in an envelope on top of the bag.

I'd had to call in some major favors, but we had full access the entire weekend, including a breakfast meeting with the Archivist themself tomorrow. Sophia was going to be a kid in a candy store. After how snappy she'd been all day, no way was I missing the look on her face when we pulled up to the gates tonight.

"This is the last critter we're bringing home for a while." Thunking the face masks down on my work table, I rummaged in a cabinet for air tanks. "Also, new house rule. If it's scaly and more than moderately poisonous, venomous, whatever, it has to stay off the furniture."

In addition to the kukri on my hip, I hooked snake tongs to my belt and reached up for my round shield, but Sophia handed me a small white umbrella instead.

"Welding cloth umbrella. Just push the button, and instant fire shield. Push it again and it contracts."

"You just happen to have a fire-proof umbrella?" I asked.

"Flame-resistant. And after what happened with the dragon? You bet your ass I do."

"That wasn't my fault—he had the flu."

"Yeah but you're not the one who ended up with bangs, are you?"

She had a point there, and I added it to the gear on my belt and stepped out of the van.

Once I'd hit thirty my body had given me an ultimatum. Stretching, warm-ups, and drinking actual water—or else. It was a debate if coffee counted as water, but I began loosening up while Sophia talked quietly to our Backpack of Holding.

It made a loud burping sound and I leaned around the door to watch as she pulled out a squirt bottle of yellow liquid.

The Backpack was a grumpy old man spirit who lived in a yuppie commuter bag in exchange for free wifi and pizza on Saturday nights. The deal was one necessary item a day, so if he felt we might need a bottle of pee, who was I to argue?

He'd never admit it, but he liked us, 'cause we sprang for mozzarella sticks with the pizza. So I wasn't surprised when he burped again and Sophia pulled out a pair of bluetooth speakers on pink harnesses and a plastic containment box. I made a mental note to order him a Dr Pepper and some breadsticks this weekend for going above and beyond.

She handed a harness to me and pulled the other one on, settling the speaker in the middle of her chest.

I eyed my harness. The Backpack knows I hate pink with a passion. You beat a guy at Mario Kart one too many times...

"Don't be a baby." Sophia was linking the speakers to her phone, each one making electronic happy noises as they connected. "We have to be able to hear each other but still drown out the basilisk crows, what with the insanity thing."

I decided to ignore the fact she'd failed to mention there was an "insanity thing."

We headed out after putting on our face masks and checking each other's tanks and gauges. Sophia snagged a fire extinguisher as we left, and I tried not to take that as a comment on my flame-dodging abilities.

The mist let up as we followed the construction around a bend in the road to the entrance of the preserve. Clambering over the gate with its *Horny Toad Haven* sign, we rounded another curve to find a concrete pipe emerging from the side of the hill. The sun broke through the clouds to shimmer off a dingy waterfall, illuminating the culvert like the entrance to a final boss dungeon in a video game.

Lovely.

"I guess it was too much to hope for manhole access, huh?"

"It'll widen out." Sophia smiled as she reached up and switched my headlamp on. "I don't know why you're complaining, shorty. You'll be fine."

Sure, I can't reach the top shelf at the grocery store, but the bright side was I'd be fine crawling through a sewer hunting a fire-breathing bird snake. Thanks, genetics.

"Wait one sec," she said, and flipped through her phone. I had to smile as the opening strains of *Bohemian Rhapsody* started playing from our speakers. Sophia was of the opinion that Freddy Mercury's voice was antiphase to most audible threats, and her *Sound Shield* playlist was three hours of *Bohemian Rhapsody* on continuous repeat.

Freddy Mercury, our last line of defense against siren songs and poisonous Poultry Danger Noodles.

Climbing up into the pipe, I was able to move in a squat, one gloved hand braced on the tunnel wall and the other holding the fire umbrella in front of me like a religious icon against the gloom.

Sophia wasn't so lucky, and cursed as she crawled on all fours, her jeans immediately soaked in storm runoff and the gods knew what else. Yeah, basilisk or no basilisk, she was first in the decon when we got back.

Glancing around, my headlamp danced over "Devon loves Stephanie" spray painted romantically in red on the wall above what looked like rat shit at the water line. I decided we were both taking bleach baths with steel wool loofahs before going anywhere near the van.

The tunnel widened out into the first junction and we stood, Sophia rubbing her knees as she did so.

"I don't like it," I said over my shoulder.

"What?" she yelled back, holding a hand up to her ear.

"I don't like it!" I shouted over Freddy's falsetto and gestured to the smaller tunnel openings emptying into the junction. "With the water level, it's probably in the big one with the access ledge, but it could flank us."

"I got this." She pulled the spray bottle of pee from her belt and began misting the edges of the smaller tunnels.

As I watched her sprinkle pee in a sewer, I marveled again at how lucky I was to have found her. She was truly special.

"Babes… what the hell?"

"Weasel pee," she shouted happily. "Poisonous to basilisks, it won't go near this, so we're golden."

Possibly the wrong word to use to describe our situation, but apt considering she was showering pee all over the place.

She finished and I led the way into the access tunnel, this one tall enough that we could walk upright.

In the distance, something moved just beyond the edge of the light, and we froze as Queen's choir of voices swelled from our speakers. A pair of eyes reflected our headlamps back at us for a moment, then blinked out with a small snort of flame.

Hello Chicken Noodle.

I checked that Sophia was ready with her fire extinguisher and gave her a V for victory when I saw she was recording on her smartphone. She rolled her eyes dramatically behind her mask and I grinned. Then, snake tongs in one hand and umbrella in the other, I sang along with Freddy as we moved into the dark.

At the next junction, I eased the closed umbrella out into the larger open space.

Flames hit it from the right and I pulled back. I counted to ten and stuck the umbrella back out. More flames, maybe a little less intense. Counting to five, I tried again and a comparative trickle washed over the umbrella.

As it faded, I stepped into the room and met the silver gaze of the basilisk. A black comb mohawk on his head, midnight feathers iridescent in my headlamp melding into scales coiled below mantled wings, he swayed like a cobra at waist height.

Oh mama... Sophia had failed to mention fucking wings.

As *Rhapsody* broke into the guitar solo, the basilisk took a deep breath. I threw myself at him and he sprang into the air with a startled look, beak open wide enough that I was grateful to Freddy for the insanity protection.

The next few moments were a strobing nightmare fight. Headlamp swinging wildly, I dodged his tail as it whipped for my face, then struck out with the tongs. I missed, but caught a couple feathers as he darted into the dark.

Leaping across the channel running down the center of the junction, I planted my feet on the ledge with my back against the wall.

A flash of scales and feathers from the right. I flicked the umbrella up to protect my face against a burst of blinding flame.

Chicken Noodle flew around for another pass and I lunged blind around the umbrella as the fire struck. I connected, but couldn't hold as a wing got me in the face. The thing hit like a prize fighter. I dropped the tongs to save my mask and he flapped back into the shadows.

Right. Now I was mad.

"Light me up!" I yelled to Sophia as I scooped up the tongs.

From the tunnel mouth she shouted something guttural like a German heavy metal singer and tossed a glittering handful at the roof above the channel. A fist-sized, black-light firework burst from the ceiling, reflecting off the basilisk's iridescence like a dayglow rave girl against the graffitied walls.

Chicken Noodle puffed up like hell's feather duster in challenge and strafed the Blue 'Shroom firework with flames, lashing out at me with his tail as he went by.

Sophia couldn't hold the 'Shroom for long, and she had to maintain focus the whole time. I needed to end this fast.

I looked around for something to pen the damn thing in with, but other than mounds of trash at the edges of the room, there was nothing. Just Chicken Noodle, me, and Sophia.

Sophia, who was waving the bottle of pee at me as she stared at the 'Shroom and chanted.

Any harbor in a storm, I guess. Jumping the channel, I snatched the bottle and squinted through my face mask, trying to read the words on the nozzle. Bless her, she'd already set it to *Mist*.

Scooping up an empty beer can, I chunked it at Chicken Noodle as I ran toward the far corner. Come and get me, bird brain.

I dropped to huddle under the umbrella as he swooped past overhead, raining down fire. Jumping up, I misted the air like a department store perfume girl, forming a wall of weasel pee in front of me. He'd turned around for another pass and back-winged out of the way, tumbling in the air before righting himself.

Got you now.

I misted for all I was worth, blocking with the umbrella as he darted in and out, trying to blast a hole in the mist as I backed him into a corner. After a weaker gout of flame, I dropped the umbrella and yanked the snake tongs up from my belt, snatching for his neck.

"Jane—*down!*" Sophia screamed, and the 'Shroom went out just as something rose from the trash to my left. I hit the ground as fire tore through the air where my head had been.

Half blind in the light of my headlamp, I scrambled back as a snow-white basilisk rose like a ghost in the dark.

Two. Two fucking Chicken Noodles.

I'd lost the weasel pee, but bashed the thing in the side of the head with the tongs as it dove for me, sending it careening into the wall. Scrambling after it, I pinned its neck with my hand, then yanked my knife from my belt and whipped around to fend off the Black Noodle.

The pee mist had settled and he reared above me, taking a deep breath, fury in his silver eyes. I threw my arm over my head and braced to be barbecued.

"Errrt-uh-errr-uh-errrrrrrrr!" boomed out from the speaker on my chest.

Ash rained down on me as the White Noodle crumbled under my hand.

Dazed, I peeked out from under my arm to see Sophia standing over me, her phone in her hand.

"What…" I said dazedly into the sudden silence.

"I set a rooster crow as my panic button, just in case." She gestured to the pile of ashes under my hand. "Lethal."

"I thought you wanted him alive…"

She pulled me to my feet, pressing her face mask against mine.

"I'd rather have *you* alive, thank you very much." She looked down at me and made a face. "Even if you are a walking biohazard at the moment."

I looked down at myself, covered in ash and weasel pee and gods knew what else from rolling around in a sewer, and a slightly mad giggle escaped my lips.

"Besides, how rare can they be around here if we found two in one afternoon?" She squeezed my hand and stooped to scoop up the fallen umbrella. "It has to be the horny toads, which is crazy. They're not even amphibians! Think what that means. What if it's the word 'toad' that's important and not the actual toad? And who ever heard of American Basilisks with wings? The Archive is going to freak out. I bet they'll fund a study once they see the video. I can't wait to write the proposal!"

She smiled at me as we ducked into the tunnel mouth. "This is the best anniversary present ever."

Given she was having bacon and eggs with the Archivist in person tomorrow, I bet she'd have her funding before the weekend was out.

My life stretched out in front of me, a hiatus from insurance for a series of horny-toad wranglings, punctuated by weasel pee covered moments of terror deep in the sewers of Texas. I looked at her face, dimly lit by my headlamp but shining with nerdy excitement, and grinned.

I wouldn't have it any other way.

Chicago Iron
by Chris Wolfgang

The Model A had a false floor in the back. Three small crates of hooch just fit from one door across to the other. Jean slid into the driver's seat while two of MacMurrough's boys tossed cases of root beer on the bench, their official delivery to Club Sidhe. Usually she rode shotgun, but the last boy had clipped a limestone curb and blown a tire. The jalopy wasn't exactly a Chrysler, but still. She'd be driving from now on.

It was nine at night, and the neon fairy above Club Sidhe's front doors batted her green wings at a clientele that sure as hell wasn't lining up for root beer. Jean drove around back, parked at the kitchen entrance, and rapped on the door.

She pulled her scarf up the back of her neck till it touched the brim of her fedora—she'd given herself razor burn again, and the cold really bit at it. She'd thought the wind on the prairie was bitter in winter, hurtling across the open miles, but here it seemed to take the ice off Lake Michigan and shove it pressurized through the brick canyons of the city.

A bouncer poked his head out, then grunted when he saw her. "Bring 'em in," he said, swinging the door wide.

"You know how this works." She jerked her thumb at the car. "You bring in your stuff while I talk to the money man."

Every delivery, this particular bouncer tried to get out of the heavy lifting and seemed to think he'd manage it each time. He pouted. Again.

She patted him on the shoulder and stepped past into the dimness of the Sidhe. "Where's Alan?"

"In his office," came the grumble, but he obediently shuffled out to the Model A, cussing under his breath. Every goddamn week.

Jean threaded her way through the small kitchen toward the office. A jazzy trumpet was playing a solo in the club proper. Jean still didn't know most of the popular tunes. Maybe she'd get a record player in a couple months.

Wild to think about things like that. Broken Bow's barren fields were still buried in dust, the banks were nest-egg graveyards, and here was Jean Fletcher with more money than she'd ever seen in her life.

Jean pushed open the door without knocking. "New trumpeter out there?" she asked.

Alan Quinelly looked up as she walked in. The thin strawberry-blond was perpetually surrounded by ledgers, slide rules, gnawed-on pencils, and legal pads. "Paid extra for a hot-shot from New York," he said, expressionless as ever behind his gold-wire glasses.

She pulled out a chair across from him. "Oh? Trying to impress someone coming in tonight?"

"Mmm." He went back to his ledger. "Shipment come in all right?"

"Three gallons at nine," she said promptly. "Plus a dollar for the short notice."

"Nine?"

"You wanted the triple-refined gin, right?" Jean smiled and crossed a knee over the other thigh. She brushed the hem of her slacks. "Who's this bigshot you're trying to sweet-talk tonight, anyway?"

"Jean," Alan warned.

She laughed as he reached for his cashbox. "All right, let me guess. Ah… McErlane?"

It was Alan's turn to laugh. "You just fall off a truck? He never leaves his own place, you know that."

"That right?" Alan would let down his guard a little if he thought he was smarter than you. "Gosh, it's gotta be someone just as huge for the trouble you're going to, though. Fancy music, extra booze… Captain Winston?"

It was meant to be another toss-up, something for Alan to scoff at. Jean figured two, maybe three more wild guesses, and the pencil-pusher would be vibrating to tell her what she couldn't add up herself.

Instead, his hand froze on the cashbox. "What have you heard."

Jean gawked at him. "Really? You've got a fucking *cop* coming in for a good time?"

Alan went back to counting out her fee, his jaw tight.

She raised an eyebrow. "Not just a good time?"

Silence.

"Quinelly. He's not trying to tell you how to run your racket. Right?"

"Knock it off, Jean."

"Look, if he's getting bored with taking bribes, I goddamn wanna know about it—"

Alan slid a thin stack of bills toward her. "Make sure the quarts get in all right, then you'll want to leave quick."

Jean put a hand on the cash. "Hey," she said. "What are you up against?"

The gold-wire glasses stayed trained on the desk as Alan locked up the cashbox, set it in the safe underneath his desk, and returned to his ledgers.

"Alan."

"Have a good night, Jean."

If the chief of police had the Sidhe by the balls, it was only a matter of time before MacMurrough's liquor business felt the squeeze. Possibly from a rope around the neck. "Quinelly, buddy, pal, how long have we known each other?"

Alan shot her an unamused glance. "Six months."

"Old friends tell each other things."

He clapped his ledger closed and made a shooing motion toward the door. "Now that we've established the longevity of your average friendship..."

"Alan, I'm serious—"

He leaned forward over the desk. "You think I'm not?" he hissed. "This is way over your head, Jean. Leave. Now."

She studied him for half a moment, then finally stood, tucking MacMurrough's fee into the inside pocket of her suit jacket.

"Thanks for dropping by on short notice, Fletcher," Alan said rather more normally. "We'll take our regular order all the same on Wednesday."

Jean took her time rewrapping her scarf, adjusted her hat. "MacMurrough didn't hire me for show," she said, low enough only Alan should be able to hear. "When I feel in over my head, I'll say uncle, how's that?"

Alan snorted without humor. "You have no idea what you're offering to help with." He glanced at her above the rim of his glasses. They caught the light of his desk lamp oddly. "But if you really have no sense of self-preservation…"

"You let me worry about that."

His mouth thinned. "The Sidhe gets going after midnight. Come back if you're a fool."

She grinned. "Been called worse."

Jean pulled the Model A into the alley behind MacMurrough's diner. Cut the engine and sat there. Laughed at herself a little. She'd just run a delivery by herself, no one to watch her back, and this was when the nerves kicked in?

She thought about a cigarette. But that would only delay the inevitable.

Jean entered the diner through the kitchen, as per usual, and as per usual, Clara Townsend was sitting at one of the three tables. She looked like a female Alan, in her sweater and long plaid skirt, paperwork spread all around her. A low-watt bulb cast light on loose black curls and glinted off the cheap gold bracelet on her right hand. Graceful brown fingers slid over figures on a legal pad.

She didn't actually look anything like Alan.

There was an empty rocks glass on the table, precariously near a corner, shoved there by the stacks of bookwork.

Jean crossed the floor and picked up the glass. "What are you drinking?"

Clara's head snapped up, a pair of thin wire frames slipping down her nose. "Goddamn, you're silent as a cat." She blew out a breath and slapped her pencil on top of her paperwork. "Do you eat owl feathers for breakfast?"

"Mmm, I wear a dandelion-fluff crown to bed, too. Keeps my shoe leather from creaking." Jean waggled the empty tumbler. "What do you want to drink?"

"Don't make fun of things you don't understand." Clara glared up at her, then adjusted her glasses primly on her foxy face.

"I understand you're as superstitious as my dear granny, may she rest in peace. It's more charming on you, though."

Clara clicked her tongue. "I know you keep a fifth of rye somewhere in here. That'll do."

Jean smirked as she went to the distillery closet, a false door in the diner's little storeroom. The bottle was on a high shelf, far back enough no one would see it if they weren't looking. Jean, all of six feet since she was sixteen, grabbed it easily. "What were you drinking before I got here, Townsend?" she called out. She heard an exasperated sigh, and her grin got wider.

"I wasn't drinking your rye!" Clara protested.

"Know you weren't." Jean tossed her hat on the diner counter, gave her hair a quick smooth—the Brylcreem toned down the ginger color at least—and grabbed an extra glass. She poured a couple fingers, one for Clara and one for herself, and came back to the table. "You couldn't reach the bottle with a ladder."

Clara took her glass. "Who's saying I'd use a ladder?"

"What, you climb up the shelves when no one's looking?"

"Maybe I fly."

Jean paused, drink in hand. "I knew it."

Clara went still. "Knew what?"

Jean grinned. "You're an angel."

Clara stared, then blew out a huff. "And you can't see what's right in front of your own face. I was just drinking water, relax."

Jean pretended to choke on her whiskey. "What? Why? You work for a bootlegger."

"Oh, that reminds me." Clara held out her hand, palm up. "Alan's fee?"

Jean took a swallow of her drink, reached into her coat, and pulled out the bills, holding Clara's gaze. Clara dropped her eyes immediately and flicked through the stack. Busied herself making a notation in her ledger.

It had taken Jean months to be able to hold that steady brown gaze, but she could do it now. Mostly because she'd discovered that if she didn't look away, Clara inevitably did. It felt like winning.

Jean sat and idly drank, watching.

"Don't you have a home?" Clara asked at last.

"Kicking me out, Townsend?" There wasn't much appeal in killing time in Jean's postage-stamp apartment before going back to the Sidhe. She'd had enough solitude in Broken Bow.

Clara took a sip of rye and didn't respond. Didn't even look up. Jean grinned. That meant no.

"By the way," Jean said suddenly, "I found out who the bigshot is that Alan's wooing with MacMurrough's fancy gin tonight."

The No. 2 pencil scratched to a halt. Clara's full red lips swept into a sly smile. She folded her arms on top of her books. "Do tell," she murmured.

Jean forgot to swallow until the rye burned the back of her throat. She tried to lessen the inevitable cough. "He's keeping a cop happy."

Clara frowned. "That's not so unusual."

Jean hummed in agreement. "But I'm getting a whiff it might be something a little bigger. More than just a bribe and some free booze here and there."

A brow went up, black as a crow's wing. "Someone wants in on Alan's business?"

Jean shrugged and sipped her drink. "Quinelly wouldn't say much about it."

Clara tapped her pencil on her arm. "Well, who is it?"

"Would you believe Captain Thaddeus Winston?"

Clara went perfectly still. Jean wasn't confident she was breathing, couldn't even see a pulse in her smooth throat. After a long moment, Clara's fingers curled on top of her notepad, red nails scratching against the paper.

Jean raised an eyebrow. "That name mean something to you?"

Clara's throat worked before she spoke. "Doesn't every bootlegger in Chicago know the chief of police?" Too light, too flippant.

"Which does not explain that reaction."

Clara leaned back in her chair, her slouch creating new curves in her rust-colored sweater. "Winston's proud of his reputation as a hardass when it comes to Prohibition. He cracks down on business that's rather relevant to me being able to eat. Should I wish him well?"

Jean was good at knowing when someone was lying. Or not telling the whole truth, which often amounted to the same thing. "Maybe he thinks you should have other business?"

Something sharp darted across Clara's face, gone before Jean could be sure what she saw. "I'm more aware than you of what business the good captain would have me take up."

Jean leaned forward. "You have personal experience with Winston?"

A closemouthed smile, and Clara took a long sip of her rye. She stood with Alan's fee and walked over to the safe hidden in the floor behind the diner counter. She disappeared from view as she knelt to deposit the cash.

Usually, Jean could tell if an idea was bad. Usually she avoided them. However... "Feel like going out tonight, Townsend?"

The safe door clanged shut. A beat of silence, then Clara came back into view. She rested both elbows on the counter and held Jean's gaze. "What was that?"

Jean tossed her a grin that was more confident than she felt. "Alan told me to come back to Club Sidhe at 1:00 a.m. I'm thinking of taking him up on the invitation. You should come, let me take you out. Show you what a gentleman I am."

Clara tilted her head but didn't look away. "Alan wouldn't tell you to come back tonight. Not if Winston's involved."

"He pretty much told me."

"So he didn't."

"Wanna find out with me if I'm wrong?"

Clara pressed her lips together, and Jean grinned. She knew when Clara was trying not to laugh.

A roll of the eyes. "What's your plan, Fletcher?"

"Me?" Jean adjusted her necktie. "I'm going to Club Sidhe to have a quiet drink, listen to some good jazz, and watch you verbally eviscerate every man who tries to talk to you."

"I don't do that."

"Right. That's why MacMurrough's boys always tip their hats to you. That or stare in silent awe. None of 'em have ever seen you castrate someone with your vocabulary."

"*Why* does Alan want you back at the Sidhe tonight?"

Clara was too damn smart. MacMurrough had pulled a lucky card when he lured her away from New York City to be his accountant.

"Because he knows I'm a gifted problem solver?" Jean tried for a charming tilt of the head.

"Not this kind of problem."

"You sound awfully sure." When Clara didn't say anything, Jean added, "Look, I know it's dope, right? Greedy police chief wants to run heroin through a speakeasy, and he thinks Quinelly can't tell him no." That was the only thing she could think of that matched Alan's warning about Jean being in over her head. True enough, she'd never gotten close to that game. But if MacMurrough's crew could help nip it in the bud, they could keep Irish territory from devolving into a bigger blood-bath than it was already.

Clara's jaw clenched. She glanced at her paperwork strewn over the table. "Clean up for me. I'll meet you back here at half past midnight."

Jean's chest went hot. "You got it." Too fast? "You need me to walk you home?" Yes, too fast. Slow down, Fletcher.

Clara's red lips curved sweetly. "See you at 12:30, baby."

Jean nodded and stayed in her seat as Clara shrugged into her coat and stepped out the back door into the night. Only then did she lean forward, elbows on knees, and wipe a hand over her face.

Baby.

Clara didn't have her glasses on at 12:30.

She walked into the diner wearing a shin-length wool coat Jean had never seen before. A sparkly black headband wrapped around her forehead and got lost in a wonderland of short, loose black curls, highlighting big round eyes and thick black lashes. Shiny blue heels clacked across the filthy floorboards until they came to a stop at Jean's table.

Jean slowly put down the novel she'd gone home and grabbed to pass the time. She made a show of scanning Clara up and down.

Clara tilted her chin up, the sparkles in her headband winking, and didn't look away once.

"Well." Jean had to say something. Something cool, some-thing teasing, something cocky to hide behind. "Not what we're used to around here, Townsend."

Clara cocked one hip. "Just because I don't go out all the time doesn't mean I can't play the part."

Jean stood and picked up her hat off the counter. "If this is you playing a part, warn us before you make the stage your living. Give us time to take our heart pills."

She risked a look at Clara. She was adjusting her navy silk scarf, patting her curls. Fidgeting. Maybe she wasn't so immune to outrageous flirting....

Jean's ears went hot, and she hastily put on her hat. "The car's just in back."

Ten minutes to pull up to Club Sidhe. Snow was beginning to fall. It would be rough getting home if they stayed late. Jean glanced at Clara in the passenger seat out of the corner of her eye.

Clara's hand, one sparkling costume ring glittering in the dim light, clutched the scarf at her throat. She was staring at the flickering neon fairy above the club's entrance as if it were a snake. If Jean was very still and listened close, she could hear tiny, sharp breaths. Like a panicking mouse.

"Hey." Jean put a hand on Clara's coat sleeve. "You don't have to go in."

Dark lashes narrowed at the neon sign. "No. I rather think I do." Clara inhaled deeply, and her expression smoothed like glass. "Open my door like a gentleman."

Jean was out of the car before she realized she'd moved.

Clara took her arm, light and graceful. Jean may as well have been escorting a queen to her throne as they walked up to the bouncer.

The man was twice as wide across the shoulders as Jean, and a few inches shorter. His eyes widened at Clara's approach, and he opened the darkened glass doors with a grand sweep. "Ma'am," he said with reverence.

Clara smiled sweetly at him and stepped inside.

"Keep up the elegance, Steve, it's a good look," Jean murmured as she moved past him.

The bouncer straightened with a glare. "Cover is twenty cents."

Jean gawked at him. "You let her in!"

"Yeah, ain't she lucky she don't look like you. Twenty cents, Fletcher."

Grumbling, Jean fished in her pockets and pulled out a couple dimes, then hurried in before Clara got too far away.

A hostess in a short fringed dress was already greeting Clara and looked up with an appreciative smile at Jean. She was used to it. Also used to the moment of adjustment that smile went through once it came out she was Jean and not John. But tonight, she returned it with a brilliant grin. "Table for two, please. A bit away from the stage and the lights, if you can." She winked.

"Well, if the lady doesn't mind?" The hostess raised an eyebrow at Clara.

Nice. Good on Alan to train his staff not to let a woman get put in a tough spot.

"As long as the hands stay where I can see them," Clara purred, and batted her lashes just once at Jean.

When Jean raised her hands in surrender, it wasn't entirely a joke.

At a small table with a single lit candle, Clara undid the buttons of her coat and paused. Jean belatedly realized she, too, was playing a part and stepped behind her to slip the coat off her shoulders.

The thing about Clara *was...* she was petite all over. To the point you almost wouldn't notice how short her skirt was tonight. The beaded tassels on the hem barely covered her garters. Neat little hips, shapely calves, and a high chest—

Jean snapped her eyes up to the stage where a trumpeter was soloing. Safer.

"I can take that for you," the hostess murmured. Jean felt the coat slide out of her nerveless fingers. She barely got herself together enough to hand over her own hat and overcoat, then clumsily pulled out Clara's seat for her.

She smelled like tea roses when she moved, skin warm from the wool.

Jean closed her eyes, just enough to tell herself to *focus, Fletcher*, then reached for the small menu as she sat next to Clara. "You drinking?" she asked, pretending to look at the coded piece of pasteboard.

"No."

Jean glanced up at the stiff tone. Clara was ramrod straight in her chair, trying and failing to scan the room without being obvious.

Jean leaned forward and tapped Clara's wrist with the menu. "Hey," she said quietly. "Look like you belong. Relax." She smiled, her best one she saved for... well, no one, actually. But not the smirk she gave the boys.

Clara made an odd half-gasping, half-laughing noise. "Look like I belong?"

"Okay, that was vague. Pretend you like being with me, that's a start."

Her shoulders did lose some rigidity then. "But I'm a terrible liar."

"*That* is a lie, and a bad one, because I saw you cover for the kid who was stupid enough to try drinking from MacMurrough's stock last month."

She sniffed. "That? MacMurrough didn't need to worry. And it won't happen again." There was something dark and satisfied in her smile.

Jean chose to ignore it. "Come on." She risked it and set a hand on Clara's wrist, keeping up the wattage of her charm. "Act like you're having a good time, and you can look around to your heart's content. I'll watch your back, you watch mine, what do you say?"

She expected a roll of those big brown eyes, putting Jean at her proper distance. Instead, Clara faced her fully, even leaned a little close. "You mean that?" she asked.

She sounded damned serious. Jean avoided serious, unless it was about the business. But sometimes you felt a tipping point, recognized you were on the edge of this or that. You had to go some way, and the other would cease to be an option.

Jean knew which way needed to stay open forever.

"Always," she said. It was easy, in the end, to say.

Clara held her gaze for a long moment. Then smiled, so relieved, so breathtaking. Jean wasn't used to instant valida-tion for life decisions, but it was there, behind her red lips, in the flash of her white teeth.

Clara opened her mouth, smile still welcoming as heaven, then her gaze lifted to a point past Jean's shoulder. Brown eyes iced over.

Jean knew better than to turn around. "Hey. Hey." She tapped Clara's wrist again. "Look at me."

Clara's breath came fast. But she focused on Jean, eyes too wide, bones too tense.

"Winston?" Jean asked.

"He just came out of the hall next to the stage," Clara managed. "He's talking to Alan."

"How does Alan look?"

"He, um, he's tense. But smiling."

Jean huffed. "I just bet he is." *Easier than taking a gat to the head.*

"Oh, they're moving."

"Honey, you need to be less obvious. Look at me. And I hate to say this, but… smile?"

Clara shot her an arch look.

Jean grinned. "There we go."

"Alan got him to take a table close to the stage… He's order-ing from a girl." Clara's jaw clenched. "He's trying to get her to sit down."

Jean fisted her hand on her trouser leg. "Is it bad?"

"Alan sent her away." Clara's voice was barely a whisper. "Winston doesn't look happy."

"Glad Alan's got a spine somewhere in there," Jean muttered.

"Jean. He's—"

Voices rose behind her, but Clara grabbed Jean's hand. "Don't look." She stood from her seat.

"Clara?" Jean said, startled.

"Meet me in the alley in twenty minutes." Clara took a step toward the stage, eyes like a deer in headlights. A tight whisper: "Please don't be late." Then she was striding away from their table. No, sashaying. Jean whipped around in her chair and watched that fringed gold dress sparkle under the club's low lights. The dark curls gleamed. Smooth brown shoulders moved with supple grace. Jean could almost swear she was glowing.

Accountant? Where?

Clara's blue heels stopped just at the police chief's table. He was big and muscled, and his hair was a thick, wiry gray. No uniform tonight; he wore a quality suit, well tailored. Captain Thaddeus Winston, having come out of his chair to argue with Alan, paused to smile for Clara.

Jean didn't care for that at all, but she stayed put. They definitely should have at least *talked* about a plan for digging into the captain's business, but there was fuck-all she could do about it now.

Clara almost seemed to ignore Winston, instead chatting with Alan, teasing, giggling. He stared down at her, gold-wire frames obscuring any expression in his eyes. Winston didn't stand idle for long. He leaned forward, teeth bared in the charming way of things deep under the sea, his hand extended to Clara. Jean was relieved she wasn't close enough to hear anything. This was difficult enough to stomach.

She flipped open her pocket watch. It was an old-fashioned clunky trinket, the only thing of any value she'd taken when she left the farm.

1:16 a.m.

Twenty minutes. She bit her lip.

"Your girl is playing with goddamn fire, honey."

Jean turned around slowly in her seat, putting her back to the stage. A blonde cocktail waitress stood at the table, a tray in one hand, the other resting on an angular hip. Helen had been serving at the Sidhe longer than Jean had been working with MacMurrough. Tonight, she wore a satiny red dress and a tense expression.

"Nothing wrong with making conversation." Jean leaned back.

Helen eyed her. "You don't know who he is."

"Chief of police, last I heard. And not the first one who leaves work at the office, by a long shot."

Red lips thinned, and Helen looked tired. And somehow old... like a stone carved by years of rain into a new kind of beauty. "Bootlegging wasn't enough for you?" she asked quietly. "You had to find something worse?"

"What's worse?" Jean whispered. *Tell me I'm right, tell me it's dope, and then I can—*

Helen straightened enough that the circle of candlelight from the table no longer cast on her face, and it was as if her cheeks hollowed and her mouth widened and her teeth....

Jean stared.

"I'm only saying this because you seem like a good kid." The voice was thin and rasped over Jean's ears like a brick across knuckles. It *seemed* to be coming from Helen, but it damn sure wasn't her usual sultry timbre. "Take us off your list. You don't see Alan's orders anymore. Never come back to the Sidhe."

"What the hell," Jean breathed.

Helen sighed, a rather human sound, then shifted in her heels, and her face came back into the dim light. Young and blonde and pretty once again. "But for tonight, what'll you have?"

Jean's brain was a stuck record of *what. what. what.* At last, she managed, "A Barry's tea. No milk." Translation: Mac-Murrough's gin, neat. "Please," she added, because she felt she'd better.

Helen tucked her bob behind one ear. "Sure." Her eyes darted to where Clara was conversing with Winston and Alan. "Anything for the... lady?"

Jean cleared her throat. "Nope."

Helen grinned, perfectly normal. "Knew you were a smart boy."

Jean watched her walk to the bar. There was the usual sway of her skirt, the low laughter. Jean had probably imagined the face and the voice. And the teeth. No one had teeth like that. Like little needles all in a row....

She glanced over her shoulder to check on Clara. She was laughing at something Winston said, her fingertips brushing his barrel chest. Alan caught Jean's eyes, and she read subtle worry behind those glasses.

She gave him a bare tilt of the chin across the oblivious crowd between them. He could move on; Jean was watching.

The captain handed Clara his own drink. She hesitated before accepting it, but Jean only noticed because she was looking for it.

Jean glanced down at her watch. *1:20 a.m.*

Helen brought her gin, set it down with a smile. "Made you this one myself. On the house." She left without another word.

Jean eyed the rocks glass. What was Helen playing at? Jean took a long sip. She was jumping at shadows. She scowled across the crowded club toward Winston's table. And nearly dropped her glass.

Two men stood nearby, clearly Winston's boys, casual and watchful. One had a wreath of glowing green leaves above his slicked-back hair. The other had bony spikes tearing through the padded shoulders of his suit. They curved up and back, and when he turned just a little, the suggestion of a wing shifted in the light.

Jesus, Mary, and Joseph. Jean's heart slammed against her ribs. Her eyes shot back to Winston and Clara.

He was enormous. Bigger than a man could possibly be. Where his suit couldn't stretch, it was stitched together with scaled skins that nearly matched his pinstripes. A fiery green crown, its spires woody thorns, turned a slow circle around his gray head as it nearly touched the club's low tin ceiling.

And Clara—little Clara Townsend—floated several feet off the floor with a pair of sparkling, green-gold wings. They dripped like melting icicles all the way down to her satin heels.

She smiled sweetly up at the beast in front of her and drained the glass in her hand.

1:29 a.m.

Winston leaned forward, rough and huge next to the fragile china of her bones. Whispered in her ear, right under her headband. His nose brushed her curls.

Jean felt the tightness of the holster snug under her left arm. Was a gat even worth anything here? And she'd been worried about a new dope game in the neighborhood... What the hell did anyone call this?

Clara handed Winston her empty glass. She swirled in mid-air, her wings tracing a warm, glittery arc that dusted her skin with its shimmer. He didn't even pretend not to watch. Bastard all but tilted his head to one side as she floated down to earth and strolled into the dim hall running alongside the stage and out of sight.

1:30 a.m.

Winston didn't wait a full minute before he followed. Impatient. Sure sign of someone confident in his own safety. Well, if you were seven feet tall and three times as wide as a Barnum strongman with your own goddamn magical crown....

Jean's breath picked up the pace, never mind her attempts to keep it even. Maybe the gin had some new drug in it after all. Damn Helen anyway. Did Alan know what his people were shilling here?

The man with the bony wings tearing through his suit threw a whole dollar onto Winston's table and followed his boss into the hall by the stage. He paused halfway down, spread his feet, and folded his hands patiently. No exit through the stage door, it would seem.

Jean clenched her glass. *1:32.*

The second flunky, the one with the glowing wreath above his head, left to stand by the bouncer at the front door. Steve looked uncomfortable but didn't tell him to piss off.

Nobody in or out, then.

1:33.

Close enough.

Jean tossed some change on her table and headed for the restroom. Alan had a bolt-hole in the gents' that let you slip into the kitchen and then, if your luck held, out the back door to the alley. You just had to know where to tap on the cinder block wall.

A drunk was trying to fix his necktie in the mirror above the one sink. He had two tiny goat's horns sticking out of his forehead. Jean shoved him out the door and flipped the deadbolt. No sense making it easy for anyone—any*thing*—interested in following.

The cinder block wall took longer to open than she remembered. *1:34.*

Damn, damn, hurry.

It spilled her out into the club's little kitchen next to a box of onions. She swept her eyes around the counters and shelves. Only one cook tonight? His back was to her, evidently focused on…an empty skillet on the stove. She had just enough time to note how his chef's coat stretched badly over wide shoulders before he turned around, his hands loose at his sides.

His fingers were too long. He had nails like rooster talons. Gray eyes pale as ice glinted in a rough face, and the man smiled. "Going somewhere, pretty boy?" He had the faintest brogue, but it was trapped in a high, raspy voice. Like Helen's.

"Told a girl I'd take her home," Jean said, all pleasantness. "She's waiting for me, so—"

"Ah. The sparkly dish you came in with?" He was in front of her suddenly. She hadn't seen him move. "She found someone more her type." His grin widened. "Why don't you go back inside, listen to some music?"

Jean wondered if he knew she could see the unreality of his hands, the otherworldly color of his eyes. "I said I'd take her home." She took a slow step toward the door but didn't look away from him, whatever he was.

"Now don't be like that. You're gonna get your nose broke, poking it in places it don't belong. End up looking like me. Nobody wants that." A heavy boot took a step forward with far too little sound.

She was wasting time.

She yanked her pistol from under her jacket and had it leveled at his nose before she blinked.

Icy eyes stared, but only with surprise. When he laughed, her gut rose in her throat. There was a difference between a bluff and someone who really wasn't worried at all.

"You should try," he encouraged. A talon tapped against his wide chest. "One of my hearts is somewhere around here, maybe."

She pulled the trigger. The gun barked in her hand, and the bullet may as well have hit a wall of cotton in front of him. She saw it hang in midair, as if it was confused about not going forward, and then it dropped to the kitchen floor with a ping. Her pistol followed.

She'd never heard anything like his laugh before. Eyes grew larger, neck stretched long, and joints popped as limbs lengthened like cottonwood branches. And she remembered, vaguely, the horseshoes over the barn doors at home....

She lunged to the left, ripped the skillet from the stove, and brought the iron down on his right wrist. The bone cracked loud.

The man roared, and he grabbed the front of her nicest shirt with his left hand. "The hell'd you do to me!" he screamed.

"Fae shouldn't fight in a kitchen!" She stiff-armed a counter to keep from falling into him. He brought his head down low and fast, and she just barely missed the headbutt, taking the brunt of the blow to her shoulder. "Mother*fucker*!" she yelled.

She raised the skillet again, couldn't get it up past the tree-branch arm that fisted her shirt, and settled for slamming it into his knee. He screamed and collapsed, still yanking at her shirt. She switched the skillet to her left hand and caught the counter with her right to keep from being dragged to the floor. The buttons gave way and scattered all over, under the counters and into crates of cabbage and onions.

"God*dammit*, I'm never gonna find all those again." She brought the skillet down hard on his face.

He went still. His hand slowly dropped from her shirt, fell to his chest with a thud. His right wrist lay at his side, swollen purple and at an odd angle.

Breathing hard, she pushed against the counter to stand upright. The skillet dropped from her hand to the floor. He looked like a tree had seen a man from a distance once and thought it'd give the shape a try. Something silvery poured from his nostrils. Maybe a couple broken front teeth, too.

"Shit." Jean scooped up her gun from the floor and stumbled toward the kitchen's back door. "Clara." She put her shoulder to it and tried to quiet her breath as she stepped out into the cold.

Distant traffic. The band, a little louder inside—had someone told them to turn up the volume? The wind, always the wind in Chicago. And something that smelled of tin in the air.

"I said *no!*"

And Jean moved on silent feet.

"Pretty bird, what did you think you were agreeing to in there?" Winston was amused and cruel. His voice rolled deep, a river filled with gravel.

"You come any closer..." Clara sounded like a trembling little bell "...I'm...I'll—"

"You'll what? Please tell me." A crackling, staticky sound, and a clatter, and then a high-pitched gasp that had Jean running toward the corner of the club's building. "I gotta tell you, little bird, I love to laugh."

Jean flattened herself against the brick wall and peered around.

Clara was leaning against a trash bin, one hand to her face, the other arm keeping her propped up. She had to be freezing, in her slinky dress. Her shiny satin heels were stained with winter slush. Her stockings were soaked from her knees to her shins. Only one of her green-gold wings fluttered; the other lay limp on the cold metal of the bin.

Winston loomed over her, his back to Jean, his green crown ablaze with new thorns. His hands, huge bear paws, held no weapon. But did he need one, really?

Something glinted in the snow on the alley floor as Winston's shadow moved away. A pearl-handled knife Jean had never seen before. Tiny gold lightning bolts skittered over the shaft, up and down. Mesmerizing.

"Wait," Winston said softly.

Jean tore her eyes off the knife. He was reaching for Clara's face. Jean's gun was tucked firm in her hand. It was the first time its weight felt useless.

"I know you," Winston said, so smooth and quiet.

Clara scoffed, but some fear leaked out. "I've never met you in my life."

"No, no." Winston waved her comment away. "Your eyes..." His hand darted out, snagged her sparkly headband, and ripped it from her hair. Clara hissed through her teeth, and Jean tasted copper.

Winston laughed. "I didn't see it before. But when those eyes glare... You're what? That kid's mother? No, too young. His sister?"

Clara's face sharpened, and she bared needle teeth. "His name," she bit out, "is Jamie."

Winston threw his head back and roared his delight. "He's a senseless battery in a mound under Queens now, sweetheart." He stood up straight, threw her headband into the slush at his polished wingtip shoes. "Jamie. Right. Smart little bird. Asked all kinds of clever questions about where my den's power comes from. But look... now he knows."

He took a step closer and leaned a palm on the trash can lid Clara huddled against. "Do you know how much gold fae will give to buy magic siphoned off creatures they never have to meet?" he whispered, too close to her neck.

Clara's voice had razor blades in it. "I'll kill you."

Winston loved that. Laughing like a kid at the movies, he reached for her throat. "You don't even have a weapon anymore, sugar."

Jean shoved away from the brick wall and ran for him. She could barely see Clara's brown eyes, wide and shining, turn toward her.

"Who says?" Clara choked out.

Winston whirled just in time to take Jean's .38 whipped across his face. Blood splattered the slush in the alley, and he howled, hands over his face. Results were in—two out of two fae susceptible to getting their noses broken.

Jean got her toe under the pearl-handled knife. A smooth kick, and it was in her hand, and then in his throat down to the hilt.

She'd never knifed a man before. She narrowed her eyes as he grabbed at his neck, then slipped and fell to his knees. The ground shook under her feet. His bones must have been as dense as the Rockies. He slumped onto his face, gagging. The crown flickered above his head, once, twice, then winked out entirely.

Gunshots were prettier deaths, that was sure.

She glanced at Clara, still half sitting, half lying on top of a trash can. Her hand shook at her throat, and she was coughing a little, tears on her lashes and down her cheeks.

Jean shrugged out of her suit coat and threw it over her, mindful of the limp wing.

Clara's laugh was raspy. "Finally see what's in front of you, Fletcher?" The laugh turned into a small choking fit.

"You're very funny. We can chat about all our secrets later. For now…" Jean knelt to pick up the headband from the slush. She held out the sparkling ribbon. "Here I am, right on time. Your weapon."

Clara took a shaky breath and slid off the trash can onto her feet. Pretty heels staining in the snow. She lifted Jean's chin. "No," she whispered. "My baby."

The kiss was somewhat different from the ones in Jean's daydreams. She hadn't pictured a seven-foot corpse at her feet, for one thing, and there had been fewer wings involved. But here in reality, her knee turning cold in the snow and ice, her neck arched, eyes closed, savoring the softness of Clara's lips against hers, tasting the salt of a fairy's tears….

Jean decided it was still an excellent beginning.

In the Salt Crypts
of Ghiarelle
by Jennifer Mace

The captain looms behind his salt-carved desk, his craggy face gone distant with horror. His lips move, but Élan's not really listening. There's a sinking feeling in her throat, like a plum stone swallowed by mistake.

"—and that," he continues, the tap of his thick fingers breaking through her haze, "is why you arrested Her Royal Highness, Princess Nikolia of Myrne, heir to the amalgamate crown of our late king-consort's foster brother, Archduke Nikolaus, and our closest ally against the depths? For standing in a corridor?!"

Fuck.

Élan has approximately a half-dozen things to worry about right now, but... sink it, did the princess have to be from Myrne? She *likes* Myrne; their olives and candied citrus are delicious, and their traders know the bawdiest songs.

The princess, whose posture transforms the hard-backed guardroom chair into a throne, coughs delicately into her jewel-ringed fist. "Actually, my title translates to 'crown duchess'," she corrects, exquisitely polite. "Myrne has no princesses." One triple-layered violet sleeve—so exquisitely and fashionably slashed Élan had mistaken them for rags in the crypts' dim light—falls away from her wrist, which is already blooming into a bruise from Élan's ungentle grasp.

"My apologies, Your Highness," the captain says, and bows—bows!—from his seat. "Rest assured, Gendarme Sentienne's actions do not represent Piegny's, or His Highness's, broader view of Myrne."

"Of course, of course," the crown duchess murmurs with a wafting gesture of fabric. The scent of foreign flowers momentarily fills the room, and Élan valiantly exerts herself not to cough. "The gendarme was just doing her job, I'm sure. I imagine tensions are running high."

It has been twenty-three days since Queen Marielle and her consort were laid to rest in the salt caves beneath clifftop

Ghiarelle Palace. Their sole heir, Prince Arin, hides in his tower, wincing at the slightest noise. The few surviving gendarmes divide their off-duty hours between hammering dents out of plate armor and scrubbing blood from uniform tunics, now most of the funerals are done with.

You could probably say things were a *little fucking tense*.

Élan wants to protest, but there's no point; the captain won't take it well. Sweat beads on his forehead, catching on angry new scar tissue across his brow. It's not *that* warm. This woman scares him.

"If Your Highness is not offended..." he says, cautiously.

"How could I be?" Now she's gotten her apology, the crown duchess is as sweet as honey. Her accent droops and swirls the words into a soothing music, if you ignore what she's actually saying. "It's as you say: Piegny, Myrne—are we not the best of friends?"

"Absolutely." He's nodding like a pigeon, but his eyes, when they cut to Élan, are mean as a leashed hawk's. "I'll make sure of it."

Élan swallows. She's sure he will.

Once the crown duchess leaves, in a flourish of beautiful dark curls and billowing robes, the captain turns beady eyes on Élan.

"It wasn't just any corridor, Captain," she blurts, breaking painfully free of parade rest now the enemy's left the room. "She was kneeling *right outside* the queen's crypt, sir; she wouldn't leave, wouldn't say anything except some magewaffle about plants, and if she was after their blood—"

"I don't give a single foundering fuck where you caught her, Gendarme, or what you *thought* she wanted." His face is as tight as the seal on a tomb. "Anything short of wrist deep in His Highness's ribcage, you bow and scrape and make nice, understand? We're drowning in titled outlanders, and I won't trust a tidesborn one of them till there's a head under that crown again. Yes, this one wants a wedding, not a war, but if you piss off royalty too much that might *change*, Gendarme. Do you want that to *change*, Gendarme?"

"No, sir!" Élan barks.

"Then get out!"

"Yes, sir!"

As she turns to go, she hears, quietly, "Endless oceans, let's hope our boy's head will hold the weight."

Like the crown duchess's arrival was a signal, salt-wreathed Ghiarelle goes from fortress to circus overnight. Carriage after carriage, shorecraft after riverboat, by dirigible and even by dromedary train, dignitaries stream through Ghiarelle's crystal gates and up her cliffs from the perilously hungry sea. There are dukes and marquesses and clan heads, two tussling mage schools from opposite corners of the Saiqur wastes, and a Prince of Flame from clear across the Sundering Ocean, all bound for His Highness's coronation.

Not that Élan's seen so much as a glimpse. For her catastrophic fuckup with the Crown Duchess of Myrne, the captain has bolted her to the most depressingly static station upon which he can justify wasting two fully armored gendarmes. She's pulling double shifts, barely time to stuff bread and cheese into her face before falling into a fitful sleep; the other gendarmes avoid her gaze, like her new station's the catching kind of curse.

It didn't used to be this way.

Guarding Prince Arin's door in the lead-up to the coronation should have been an honor and a joy. It isn't. Since the funeral, grief has burned their laughing moon-bright prince away to a husk.

Oh, he does the minimum required for the revelry: he sits at high table during dinner, and opens the dances, and welcomes the diplomats before running back to the dark silence of his rooms. But he does so wound tight with clothing, collars pulled high enough to hide half his face, eyes bruised-looking and hands flinching from contact. Even the sound of silverware makes him wince; he eats his meals in private.

It isn't Élan's place to worry.

She's just a guard.

Then again, she's not sure there's anyone left whose place it would be. Her partner-at-guard certainly doesn't seem to.

Mind you, it's entirely plausible Guilhan had all fellow-feeling bleached out of him as a child; if not, then losing his partner to the depth-spawn has certainly finished the job.

"Food's late," she says, because it's true, and because if she stands here much longer she's going to scream. "I'm going to check."

She makes it three strides before Guilhan whisper-yells, "Come back here!" after her.

Élan pauses. "We're to keep him safe," she says, and keeps it simple, like he's a child. "Starved isn't safe. Nor's poisoned, if someone intercepted it."

"But—"

"Sundering seas, Guilhan, leave off. I'll be back before any-one knows it." Frankly, she could stay away long enough to cook His Highness's dinner herself and still expect that to be true—and she's a godsawful chef. "Surely you can hold your piss for half an hour?"

She leaves him there, gaping like a fish, and tries to squash the spiteful flash of pleasure at knocking him off his dignity before she gets tempted to do it again.

Reaching the kitchens kills what's left of that petty joy faster than snuffing a candle. They're quiet. The kitchens are *never* quiet.

Cooks and pages and wood-bearers alike have clotted around a wound in the middle of the floor: a fallen boy, a tray spilled, and a dark-haired kneeling figure in layer upon layer of thin-spun robes.

"What happened?" Élan demands, grabbing a page girl near the back of the pack.

"Simo just—fell," the girl answers, jaw slack. She can't be more than thirteen, fourteen; barely as high as Élan's shoulder. "Cook yelled he wasn't breathing, and then—the lady, she…" Simo. That's the prince's page, isn't it?

"Air mage," another woman says, hair braided back and netted like a baker. She nods grimly. "Pulling the breath back, most likely. Lucky she was passing. Poor kid. Run ragged, must be, to collapse like that."

Élan carefully pushes through the crowd, nudging people apart with her spear butt. It's the Crown Duchess of Myrne at the center of the circle, dark lashes fanned across those high-boned cheeks, motionless as if she's posing for a coinsmith. Because that's precisely Élan's luck.

Air mage. Huh. All right. Not just a froth of fabric and jewels, after all.

The crown duchess hovers one hand over the fallen boy's still face, the other over his chest. If Élan listens closely, she can hear a thin, musical hum, wavering like light on waves. The kitchen staff's whispers easily drown it.

Ah, fuck. If that chef's to be believed, then the noble arrived only after the boy fell. She can't have caused it. She's trying to help.

Élan passes a hand over her face, and turns, putting her back to the pair. Captain's going to have her head for getting within a spear's length of the woman, but there's a child at risk. Élan braces her feet, plants her spear, and lifts her chin.

"Make space!" she says, pulling parade-ground pitch and posture around her like a surcoat. "Step back!"

With the grumbling noise of thwarted gossip, the crowd disperses. Élan glares the last few stragglers into submission, makes sure someone has sent for a physician, and circles to kneel cacophonously on the other side of the fallen child.

It's undeniably the prince's page: not only does the royal blue uniform mark his rank, the boy's a fosterling noble from one of the southern kingdoms, with skin a brown almost as dark as his close-curled hair. She's seen him frequently, this past week.

His chest moves, though barely. The crown duchess is frowning.

"What do you need?" Élan asks, and the woman's face tilts towards her.

"I thought I recognized that voice," she says without opening her eyes. Her smile is thin. "Do you sing, Gendarme? You've the lungs for it."

"Well enough," Élan replies, bemused.

"Give me five notes, then, ascending and descending. Slowly." It's a voice used to unquestioning obedience; if she resents past indignities at Élan's hands, the feeling has been buried in impeccable etiquette. So Élan sings.

The crown duchess does something complicated with her hand, then her eyes blink open. Simo's chest continues to rise and fall, tied to the rhythm of Élan's voice.

"There's something…" she murmurs, leaning over the boy's face. She peels his lips back and runs her fingers over his teeth before Élan can say a word—not that she would, trapped as she is humming Simo's lungs full and then empty again.

It's a queer sensation. Magic doesn't run in her family, and Élan has never so much as stirred the brine in an offering dish. Does the crown duchess feel this powerful all the time?

It would explain the way she holds herself. Even kneeling on the grubby-tiled kitchen floor, the line of her shoulders is as straight as a sword. Her sleeves are rumpled and she's getting spit on her fingers and she still looks like a statue sprung to life.

Élan yanks her attention back where it belongs. While she's allowed herself to become distracted, said distraction has stuck half her hand down the page boy's throat.

"What are you—" Élan says, forgetting, and the boy's ribs stutter.

"Keep singing!" the noble snaps, though Élan has already realized her mistake and is grasping frantically for lost notes. She goes too fast, too high, loses control, and the boy gasps, back arching off the tiled floor, jaw clenching. The noble swears, or possibly casts—Élan barely knows enough Myrnish to not get swindled—and yanks her hand free, skin scraping against teeth.

There's a long strand of something sickly greenish-white clutched between her fingers, emerging from the boy's mouth.

The crown duchess keeps pulling, muttering under her breath. Élan can't look away, song trailing uselessly off. It's impossible, it's nauseating, and it's clearly hurting the boy.

Eventually, the crown duchess sits back on her heels, hands tangled with a red-flecked mass of strands, and the boy gasps on his own, ragged and out of sync. His eyes shoot open. His previously limp hand clutches at his chest. A look of bewildered shock crosses his face. And then, the tears.

As a cook bundles the child away towards hot drinks and soothing words, Élan leans in. "Is that—" she asks quietly, staring.

The mage doesn't even glance up from examining the mass of plantlife. "Oh, no, no," she says, voice sweet. "Of course it couldn't be anything to do with the strange growths I was investigating when a gendarme so diligently took it upon herself to escort me from the back corridors without so much as a sample."

The flower has thorns, it seems. Flustered, Élan swallows a strange burst of guilt. "I—" she starts. And stops.

The crown duchess has dropped her pointedly vacant smile and is carefully pinching a segment near the vine's tip. The fibrous mass from inside Simo's lungs is largely without leaves, but near the top, where it would have reached the open space of the boy's mouth and nestled in behind his teeth, several sharp green teardrops unfurl.

Damn it. Élan recognizes those leaves. The forsaken woman had been holding a plant with identical ones down in the crypts. A plant Élan had knocked to the ground, and presumably trampled, when she'd seized, cuffed, and dragged her prisoner before the captain. A plant Élan had assumed the woman smuggled in to use as a pretext for her infiltration.

"Is it... a curse?" Élan asks. Her voice isn't quite low enough, and a prep chef fumbles a chop on a nearby bench, knocks an onion to the floor. They're being watched.

If something evil is taking root in Ghiarelle, gossip and panic will only spread it faster. Élan shifts closer to the noble.

"Maybe." The crown duchess frowns over her sample. Up close, Élan notes golden flecks in her brown eyes, like the speckled feathers of a falcon. Her olive skin is very smooth. "I don't know yet. But either way, it's bad."

Élan is a professional. She is a highly trained, highly *disciplined* member of an elite armed force of guardsmen and women who have protected salt-wreathed Ghiarelle for *generations*, against enemies foreign and domestic and suboceanic alike. She needs to report this. Immediately. It's beyond suspicious— why would a foreign mage, unfamiliar with the palace, be the one to catch a disharmony this severe? There's an undeniable chance Nikolia's behind it, or at least familiar with its origins.

But how would the home-grown priests and secular brine mages have noticed? Those who survived the attack which took Their Majesties have exhausted themselves on the repairs;

Élan can't say she's seen robe nor scepter inside the palace for a week or more. All their fears are turned out to the sea, to the things which lurk beneath the waves. There's no attention left for trouble within salt-carved Ghiarelle.

The crown duchess's robes are speckled with blood—she's ruined them to save a servant boy. And even now, with Élan kneeling before her in full armor, spear close at hand, her attention is on the vine, not the threat.

Élan's struggling to keep her gendarmerie-trained paranoia pointed where it should be.

Besides, if she takes this to the captain, like she should, he's going to think she's holding a grudge. He's more likely to take back her tunic and put her out to pasture, no matter how little he can afford to lose another spear these days.

No. She's alone in this. She needs to figure it out herself.

The first rule stabbed crudely into the lintel over the gendarmerie's barracks is very simple: if there's a threat in the palace, odds are it's aimed at the royals.

So Élan watches every step of the preparation for the prince's lunch, then carries it up herself instead of appointing a replacement for Simo. It's as clean as can be hoped. Even so, as the door creaks open beneath her cautious knuckles, Guilhan glaring from the side, Élan's palms sweat.

"Your Highness?" she calls into the dim, silent chambers.

There's a slithering rustle of cloth on cloth. "Simo?" It's a little hoarse.

"No, Your Highness," Élan says softly, and, praying she hasn't caught him crying, crosses to the table by what once had been crystal-clear salt-paned windows facing out across the depths. The paysans had been called to crosshatch them first thing, and when that had proved insufficient for her prince, the staff had depleted half the wing of carpets to keep away the light. It's cursed effective: the room's sepulchral. She can see shapes, but nothing small or detailed.

"Simo had a bit of an... accident, but I've brought your lunch, Highness. I'm Gendarme Sentienne."

"Ah." There's no recognition in his voice as the prince shuffles out from behind the bed curtains. "Thank you, Gendarme."

It's a dismissal.

Sink it, she still can't see. She *will not* leave without confirming he's safe.

Clumsy, Élan bows, and contrives to knock the window hangings askew. A blade of light slices through groggy darkness, and Élan scans the chairs, the floor, even the carpets, looking for any sign of the curse. White vines against milk-white salt—there's nothing, and nothing, and nothing.

"Drowning depths, Gendarme," the prince swears, one hand thrown up to shield his eyes, and Élan, guilty, flicks the curtain closed.

"Sorry, sir," she says, unthinking and terrified, and backs away, because:

There's a tiny twist of teardrop leaves curling amongst the lace of her prince's embroidered cuff.

"Well?"

All in all, the crown duchess has dealt gracefully with getting dragged wrist-first out of a lazy afternoon cocktail reception. She'd smiled and bowed and made excuses; she'd left her wine and her circle of enraptured fellow diplomats with a flutter of cloth and perfume. She'd let Élan pull her through servants' passages and narrow archways until they'd emerged in the chill dim crypts beneath. Even now, her question is composed as much of worry as irritation.

The effort of keeping upright and silent through the rest of her interminable shift has turned Élan's voice to salt. Her neck muscles feel like iron from clenching her teeth. She can barely swallow, let alone answer.

Even in the heart of the palace, despite the brinecraft purifications and the rituals of cleansing after death, her prince is under attack.

She should have gone to her captain, but this isn't his kind of battle. A half-seen glimpse of a leaf clinging to her grief-stricken liege? The captain would never impose on His Highness's privacy at such slight evidence from a currently disgraced junior guardswoman. A servant child afflicted by some strange infection? All too common, this close to the malevolent deep. He'd think her saltstruck, afflicted with battlefear. Jumping at shadows.

Which is why she has to cast her lot here. With the only other person who has noticed the trouble. And known enough to cure the page boy, besides.

"This one wants a wedding, not a war." The captain's words hadn't been meant as an endorsement, but they will have to be approval enough.

Élan licks her lips. Draws a breath. Tries again.

"I saw..." No. Not that. "My prince, he had..." Or that. Sink it, where are the *words*? Her heart is pounding, palms sweating.

"You came down here," she manages. To the crypts. "Before. Is it...?"

The crown duchess looks around, lips firming as she registers where Élan has brought them. "The origin? Possibly. There's only one way to find out."

Élan swallows again. "This isn't your duty, Your Highness," she says, staring fixedly at the noble's left ear. "I'd understand if you didn't—that is, I can't ask you to—"

"Oh, stop that," the crown duchess says, and grasps Élan's arm until she's forced to meet the noble's eyes. They're deadly serious. "There'll be time enough for diplomacy later. I don't want to see this spread any more than you do." She waits until Élan nods, then pushes away and starts down into the darkness. "And don't call me 'Your Highness'," she says, voice echoing against the naked stone. "Surely by this point, you can use my name."

Élan's not sure she dares.

It's odd how much she wants to.

There's no chance to dwell on it. In the days since Élan last patrolled here, the vines have grown past hiding.

The deeper the pair of them walk, the less inclined they are to speak, stepping carefully around the spots where falling light has coaxed leaves from the embedded growth.

Nikolia crouches by the largest patch, tracing her fingers along the walls. "Here," she says, and hums. The tips of her fingers glow, and the rock turns just translucent enough to follow the bundle of vines down into the floor. It vanishes beneath the carved lintel of a locked crypt entrance.

"This matches what I pulled from the boy." She grimaces like a child reminded they had to eat the hated seagrass they'd prayed the parent had forgotten, and says, "So much for hoping I was wrong."

It's wry and inclusive and utterly human. All at once, Élan is struck by how much she *likes* the woman. She laughs, unintended, and it feels a little like choking.

Nikolia stands, concerned, and Élan waves her off. "Nothing, nothing," Élan tells her. "Are you certain?"

The mage clicks her tongue. "I've forgotten more about horticulture than your entire salt-blighted nation has ever conceived of," she says, drier than Piegny's admittedly drought-prone soil, "and this is no kind of gods-given plantlife, to grow so fiercely here without the sun. Who knows what it's feeding on."

"I… might have some idea," Élan says, much as she hates to give her morbid suspicions a voice. She busies herself with the keys at her belt, unhooking them and fumbling through the ring. "This is where I caught you, last time." Her fingers are clumsy in her armor, and it takes three tries to recover the key for the door in front of them. "That's Queen Marielle's crypt."

This is almost definitely treason. No foreigner should so much as breathe into the royal tombs, let alone set foot there.

But a choice between honoring the dead and preserving the living is no real choice at all, or so Élan tells herself, leading them down towards the light.

Salt-pale vegetation dips in and out of the walls as they walk. It means one of two things: either the barrier spell didn't take, and the crypt's been open to sky and sea for a month, allowing this thing entry, or the curse was seeded when the depth-spawn ripped Queen Marielle's head from her body and tore the king consort's chest open from navel to neck. She's honestly not sure which option's worse.

The stink of rot rises with the sunlight as they round the last corner into the open burial cavern.

Élan has never seen one in person. They're sacred, secret places, meant for priests and family. It's smaller than she'd imagined. Calmer. More picturesque, with the twin crystal biers and the blue of sky and sea not ten yards from their feet.

Chill afternoon air blows in through a silver-flecked filtering barrier, carrying the cries of sea birds and the crash of waves. Beautiful it might be, but one step too far, and it's a long, tumbling death onto the rocks below.

Nikolia trails her fingers over the encasing crystal as she walks, vines crunching under her sandals. "Ugh," she says, one sleeve pressed over her face. "Should it smell like that?"

The vines underfoot flinch from Élan's armored feet as she reaches the crown duchess's side. Élan draws a breath, as shallowly as she knows how.

The smell nearly chokes her. Boiling swamps and tide pools long abandoned by the sea; something like iron, but sweeter. It clogs her throat like crematory smoke.

"No," she manages, swallowing against a sudden rush of nausea. "The salt, it... preserves. It's meant to, anyway." Seal a body in a chunk of salt three times its size, and very little disintegrates.

Nikolia rounds the end of the biers and drops to a crouch, one sleeve held as a mask. Her fingers trace the strange, brown-flecked symbols painted onto the smooth chalk floor.

"Gendarme..."

"Élan," she corrects. She's either coming out of this one a hero or unemployed; hearing the title right now is a little too pointed a reminder.

That earns her a quick, bright glance back over Nikolia's shoulder. "Élan, then. Can you clear these?"

"These" meaning the vines covering the floor. Élan turns her spear blade-down, gets it under the matted plantlife and starts flipping clumps of vines towards the heaped mass of the things piled near the open edge of the cliff. She turns her head back towards the biers whenever her burning lungs force her to inhale. She's taking no chances of picking up a parasite; Simo's blood-flecked tangle is prominent in her memory.

Is the cliff the answer? Did some creature of the depths manage to send its tendrils up the rockface? The way the vines flinch and shrivel from her blade's salt-blessed metal suggests something otherworldly. The smell grows worse.

The uncovered symbols Nikolia is tracing are too detailed to be depth-spawn work. She makes a low, worried noise.

"Well?" Élan asks, planting the butt of her spear. "*Is* it a curse?"

"Not... quite." Her voice is tight. "Dear gendarme, perhaps you could... step towards me. Slowly."

She's looking past Élan.

Élan turns.

At first, she can't tell what the crown duchess is staring at. There's nothing standing or moving behind her; no threat that she can see. The floor below her feet is mostly clear of vegetation, and flaking glyphs spread in a circle no wider than the haft of her spear. She's a foot from the biggest lump of plant matter, and her scraping has nudged up the edge of it. Long white strands are writhing slowly back towards the drop, unveiling even thicker roots below.

Sundering seas, this smell. It crawls down the back of her throat, meaty and sweet. Like something's died and been abandoned to rot.

"Gendarme. *Élan.*"

Élan bends, creaking, at the knees. Twitches back one more knot of weed from the pile.

Ah. Not roots. Not roots at all.

Fingers.

Hadn't she just seen this lace cuff, those rings? The hands have swollen in death; the flesh is distended with weeks of rot, soft to bursting, wrapped and wreathed in vines.

Élan stumbles back, gorge rising, as the shape becomes clear—there a leg, a foot, here the torso, vines dipping in and out of flesh like a needle through cloth.

"Be careful!" Nikolia cries, but Élan can't; her feet scuff against the floor and something in the air comes suddenly taut.

There's an unheard noise, a plucked string so deep she feels it in her bones, and the shapes below her feet turn as hot as coals.

"*Élan!*" There's a burst of sound—a song?—and a gust of air flings her back. Élan loses grip on her spear, on the floor; she hits Her Majesty's bier with a sound like a horse kicking over a smithy and clatters to a heap on the ground.

Get up. She has to get up. Her head is ringing.

The vines are moving.

Where is Nikolia?

One hand to the floor. Roll onto her side. The stone is shuddering. Glowing red, too, which is deeply fucking problematic, but if she stretches—Élan gets her fingers against the butt of her spear, grabs, fails. Curses as it clatters away. Scrabbles a little farther. Succeeds. Gets the spear in her hand, plants it against the floor. Shoves. Makes it upright.

Across the crypt, the silver-thin glinting barrier shudders once, twice, then shatters into a thousand sharp-edged fragments. Tendrils of green-leafed vine appear around the cliff-edge, weaving like snakes tasting the air.

Nikolia's by her side, safe, steadying Élan when she stumbles. "What..." Élan tries to ask, but there's blood in her mouth. She spits. "What is it?"

"A resurrection array, as far as I can tell," the mage says, stepping in close against Élan's non-dominant side as the vines surge closer. She's gained a lightness to her tone again, but it's clearly taking her some effort. "An attempt, anyway. It never works." Her eyes are more whites than iris. "That's your prince? He's a few weeks dead, I'd say. He must have really loved them to try."

It hits like a stave to the ribs, the sixth or seventh in a day, when your body is burning and it takes a second to even realize you've been hit.

He's dead.

Prince Arin is dead.

That pile of flesh and torn-apart fabric, the smell, the black smears on the floor—it's her prince. Her liege. Her duty.

"Stay close," Nikolia says, low-voiced and sharp. The trickle of vines has become a wave, a waterfall of sharp-leafed greenery cascading in from the ledge. Élan puts her back to the mage's, raises her spear. Adjusts her grip. Braces herself, as Nikolia begins to hum, eerie and double-layered.

Air whips in from the sky beyond, tearing through the vines and making them writhe. Élan narrows her eyes against the gale as the mage wraps them in loop after loop of wind. Nikolia's silks billow and surge like edged weapons themselves, and the rush of vines hesitates, slows, and coils to a stop.

It can't get to them, is Élan's first thought.

And then:

It doesn't want to.

The vines have stopped in the center of the circle, coiling in and in. The sun-warmed greenery is joined by white tunneling vines from the walls and floor, by brown flesh-stained strands which tug free of Prince Arin's remains with wet, slurping noises. The mass presses together like baby rats in a nest, pushing into and somehow *through* one another, growing fatter and taller inch by inch.

Élan swallows. The sigils' red glow is rising.

"Nikolia..." she says slowly. "I think maybe we should. Leave. Now. Quickly."

The mage's shoulders shift against Élan's armor when Nikolia pauses to draw breath. The ribbons of air slow, but don't stop.

It's too late, though. Much too late.

Prince Arin steps from the circle, pale and nude and flawlessly human from crown to sole. He brushes a leaf from the corner of his mouth, and it flutters to the ground.

"Ah," he says, tilting his head. His voice is hoarse. "The guard. How unfortunate." On the ground behind him, unearthed by the transformation, the corpse's distended face lolls. Its cheek, pressed against the ground, has darkened with pooling blood. The crypts' preservative barrier has kept insects from her prince, at least. His eyes are whole, grey-filmed and blank as they stare into hers across the magic he wasted his life to buy.

"Your Highness," Nikolia says behind her, exquisitely polite, and Élan shudders.

The *thing* inhabiting Prince Arin's form barely looks her way. "Inconvenient," he says, stepping daintily over the painted lines. "But not insurmountable." He moves almost correctly, but there's something off about his skin. It's writhing strangely, pulse pressing up from underneath in ways no heartbeat ever would. Wherever light touches flesh, green wells up and is quickly suppressed.

Do something! Élan shouts at herself in horror. *You have to—*

The prince reaches out. His hand is, as ever, delicate, and his wrist curves as elegantly as a dancer's. The tip of his finger bulges.

"Lift," Nikolia's voice, a thread of a whisper, "your gods-damned *spear*."

And Élan does.

She gets it between them like a barrier, and the prince's eyes narrow at its engravings, even as vines burst from beneath his skin. They're fast, but Élan's faster. Two hands on the haft, and *block*, and *twist*—the plant-prince-monster hisses with pain, vines withering against the blessings, but that won't last for long; the haft is only wood. Élan steps back, gets her blade between them, and slashes. The monster flinches.

"That's it," she says, barely hearing herself. "You can't beat—"

The flesh of his back begins to writhe.

Ah, fuck.

"Run!" Élan shouts, raising her spear as the prince-thing's flesh bursts like rotten fruit. She's answered only by the sound of song and wind, the hiss and tear of steel against vine—and *slice*, and *parry*, and *lunge*—and the sound of a monster laughing.

Nikolia's not backing off. Élan can't protect them both. The vines are fast, and agile, and their master is clearly enraged by the singed ash a holy weapon makes of its tendrils. Élan can't spare more than glances.

They're enough. She catches moments: the crown duchess by the royal biers, ferocious, her robes a seething whirlwind of silks slicing vines to shreds. Ducking towards the wall, the melisma of her voice tearing away strands from Élan's spear-haft, cutting it free when Élan'd thought she'd have to lose it. Catching Élan's eyes over the thing's shoulder, determined, blood on her cheek, drawing breath for another attack as Élan pulls the monster's focus.

"Hey!" Élan yells. Nikolia creeps along the smooth-carved wall. The monster's face is Élan's prince's, even now. Scorch marks pucker down its chest, left arm gone and the right a sea of writhing vines, whipping out to fend her off. Its naked feet are smeared with her prince's blood and rot. "What'd you think was gonna happen, tidescum? You think we wouldn't catch you? You think you were gonna get to rule?!"

This thing, it's foul and it's cursed but it's impatient, bad at pacing itself; it doesn't understand the ebb and flow of combat. If the mage can bind it long enough, if Élan can get blessed steel through its heart....

It opens its mouth, and the tongue is as pale as clam flesh. "I like crowns," it says, and smiles, boyish and aloof, turning its head like an owl. "I like killing people who wear them."

And in a burst of plant-flesh, it knocks Nikolia back into the wall so hard that the dull thunk of her head against stone echoes louder than the sudden absence of her song.

The monster says several things after that. About loyalty and rewards. The contract between knight and monarch. It tries to bribe her. Steps in close, like it thinks her silence is defeat, is acceptance. Lowers its guard.

Élan's not really listening. There's a heavy rushing noise drowning out its words, like she's stuck in a tidal cave and the ocean's roaring in, tugging at her knees, her waist, her shoulders.

All she can see is Nikolia's body, crumpled and silent. A statue of a different kind. An effigy.

It's not even her kingdom.

She'd sensed something wrong, and Élan hadn't *listened*, and now—

Élan raises her spear.

Gets the blade up against its gut while it's busy tempting.

Shoves.

There's some yelling, at first. Once it realizes. Screaming. Thrashing.

Vines burst from its trunk and scrabble up her gauntlets, her spaulders. One gets into the gap beneath her left armpit and makes it through the gambeson, then two, stabbing; another gets into the hinge at her side, weaves deep beneath her skin. She crushes her left arm down before the tendrils can reach her lungs, grits her teeth against the burning, and holds.

The pain hovers somewhere out of reach, sickly and searing. She's going to pay for this.

But she's gotten the broad blade of her weapon up deep into its guts, and she's pierced the green, underwater glow hiding beneath its mockery of a ribcage. Light spills out, cascading down along the etched blessings like blood down a butcher's runnels.

The noise fades down to a crackling desiccation. The flesh blackens, then crumbles, then falls to dust.

Élan falls too. She goes to her knees before her prince, whose poor corpse has been knocked back across the floor. It's much the worse for wear, trampled and broken by the fighting. Not suitable for clear salt, anymore. Better, perhaps, for burning.

He'll never be her king. Not now.

Maybe he never wanted to, to try something like this.

It's not his fault, she tells herself, and mostly manages to believe it. He thought there was a chance. He must have been desperate.

Her eyes sting. She's weeping.

A breeze from the open sky beyond blows dust up off the floor. Light as ash, it dances back towards the salt-rock biers, staining Their Majesties' tombs with grit.

It's time to get up. Time to stand, and turn, and climb the stairs; find a priest. Turn herself in. Let the wheels start turning. There'll be council votes and pledges of allegiance, royal cousins fighting cousins for what's left of the throne. War, if that goes badly. Death.

In a moment. Everything hurts.

It seems distant. Insignificant, somehow, against the weight of what's been lost.

Nikolia.

Élan staggers upright. She uses her monster-killing weapon as a crutch with every step. There's no one to see. Nikolia's eyes are closed.

Élan lowers herself to the floor, free hand pressing her gambeson up against the ooze of blood she'll have to deal with eventually. Up close, she can tell the woman's breathing.

Something hot and burning rushes up her throat: relief, or hysteria, or maybe anger, who the fuck knows. "Wake up," Élan says, and if her voice is shaky, she's earned it. "Come on, princess, there's no drowning way I'm carrying you." She puts her hand on one limp shoulder. Squeezes.

"'M not a princess," Nikolia says, eyelids twitching, and bats Élan's hand away. "By the mountain, my head feels like I tried to outdrink Niko." She blinks, and shifts farther up the wall, pain creasing deep valleys into her face.

Her pupils are lopsided, but she seems aware. "Not... quite," Élan says, not sure how to explain what'd *actually* taken place, but the crown duchess's gaze catches on the dead prince, the ash-strewn floor, the blackened scorch where the beast had burned away.

"Ah," she says, straightening with a wince, and retrieves a smile from some hidden reserve. "Really, now. You couldn't wake me for the fun part?"

Her hair is a bird's nest and there's blood smeared down the side of her face and those gold-brown eyes are still struggling to focus and her robes really do look like rags, now, and—

Oh, Élan thinks, quiet as a stone dropped in a pool. She's beautiful.

"I, uh," Élan says. "Maybe overreacted. A little. When you fell."

Nikolia laughs, briefly, then flinches, pressing one hand to her forehead. "Oh, you know," she says, and waves airily. "Under the circumstances I might be inclined to forgive your presumption. Just this once." Her eyes dip. "I might even admit to being... impressed. Gendarme."

"Élan," Élan whispers.

"Élan," she repeats, solemnly. "You're far too tall, you know. Kneeling like that."

"What?"

She laughs again, nose crinkling, and says, "Come down here, sink it. I can't *reach*."

So Élan does.

When they kiss, it's with the taste of blood and salt hot between them. Despite the fear and desperate horror, Nikolia is soft and warm against her. The scent of flowers clings beneath the char.

But, "Wait," Élan says, pulling back. "I thought... Prince Arin."

"This one wants a wedding," her captain had said. She glances back across the room and winces. There will be no weddings here. Not for quite some time.

When she looks back, Nikolia's watching her, centuries and kingdoms heavy behind her eyes. "It could have been, in another life," she says slowly. "What's happened here will kill more futures than that one."

Élan swallows. The sea behind and beneath them is very loud.

Over time, even the tallest cliff might fall to the relentless bite of waves.

Piegny will fall far faster than that.

"Will you... stay?" she asks, words dying on her tongue. "Will Myrne...?" It's not her place to ask this; it's a question for councilors and regents and bishops, not soldiers bleeding in the crypt of those they failed to defend, wreathed in rot and ruin. But she's here. And they aren't.

Nikolia's eyes are wide. "I—" she starts, and falters. "I can't promise that."

Élan looks away. "Of course," she manages, and fumbles back, gets a hand underneath herself. Starts to stand. "Of course. I shouldn't have— We should—"

"I'll try, though."

Élan pauses.

Nikolia is looking up at her, chin raised, jaw set. "I can't make promises for my brother," she repeats, and lifts her hands, imperious.

Élan raises her gingerly to her feet. She's unsteady, her bare fingers slipping against Élan's gauntlets. But she makes it.

"But I want that," she says, firm as the mountains. "And I don't know if you've noticed, my dear gendarme"—she lifts her hand, presses her thumb against the ridge of Élan's cheekbone, wipes away the salt that's dried there, and smiles—"I tend to get what I want."

The City Unbreachable
by Yoon Ha Lee

The City Unbreachable was not, technically, a city. Veiled from the senses of other ships, powered by the rituals of matter-antimatter particles kissing, it fled from the shadow of the great and growing empire called the heptarchate. The people of the city-that-was-a-ship told stories of that home of old, and honored its traditions even as they scorned its rituals of torture.

Anjen had been born in the City Unbreachable in Year 319 of its flight. Years ago she had served as the head duelist of Azalea House, not only expert in the arts of sword and gun, but master of etiquette and prize of her family. Now, though, Azalea House had fallen upon hard times. Where once its members numbered one hundred, only Anjen and her two cousins remained. The last bell-stroke of their doom came when the far-duelists of the heptarchate almost caught the City Unbreachable eight years ago, when its veil faltered. Anjen fought bravely in that battle. The City's denizens still sang songs of her bladework, and of the far-duelists she had cut down. But one of them had injured both legs so that she could no longer walk.

Today Anjen prepared for a summons from the head duelist of Luna House. Despite Azalea's diminishment, Anjen had saved the finest of her dresses, and the fiercest of her jewels, that she might be fit company for those high of rank. Her cousin Rohaz, their expression anxious, brought out the finery for her inspection.

The dress's rich magenta, in honor of their House flower, pleased Anjen, and its white-and-gold embroidery was in the pattern known as *fractal cunning*. In better times she would have worn a coronet of azaleas, of silk if not the flesh of flowers, but the House no longer owned the former, and no one grew azaleas anymore in the City's treasured gardens.

"He's not to be trusted," Rohaz said. "The only reason Luna House wants anything to do with us is because we're expendable."

"Ah," Anjen said, leaning back in her floater chair, "but we're expendable and *very competent*. This is an opportunity."

"Cousin," Rohaz said, turning the dress around at a gesture from Anjen, "it's just us and little Kihaz. Let it go."

"Nonsense," Anjen said briskly. Her keen eyes had spotted a frayed thread near the collar, but she owned a scarf of blushing silk and pale quantum lace that would cover the blemish. "It's worth hearing him out."

She'd heard many things about Khev of Luna House, the one head duelist who had not dueled these past eight years. Most of the rumors made her uneasy. But she couldn't afford to be picky about her allies, and she was confident of her ability to navigate the situation.

"I don't like the suddenness of this summons," Rohaz said, still stubborn. "It's not proper."

Anjen laughed wryly. "As if we're in a position to stand on propriety."

Nevertheless, Rohaz made a good point. Khev of Luna House should have given her time to make her preparations, scant as they were. Even if he didn't care about her convenience, his reputation for courtesy should matter to him. A stickler for procedure, was Khev. That he deviated from it spoke of no small desperation. The question was, could she turn it to her House's advantage?

She slept in the ice-vaults, but the City Unbreachable had not forgotten her. Lio of the Catastrophe Hand, they called her, Lio of the Wayward Bullet. She had lost her House twice: first when the City's mayor-commander swore her to his service, as head duelist of the City entire; and second five years ago, when the same mayor-commander repudiated her because she failed to stop his sibling's assassination.

Lio of No House, known also as Lio of the Ashen Sword: In her vault her dark hair remained in its familiar crown of braids, with a pin of gold on the left and a pin of black on the right. Before her freezing she had removed all ornamentation from her jacket and trousers, also black. A keen eye would have spotted the constellations of holes where both had been adorned by gold embroidery and the fretwork of the beads. At her side rested her sword of old, which the engineer-smiths of the City had worked their wizardry upon, transmuting the once-bright metal to the tepid color of ash.

Lio slept in the ice-vaults, but she would not sleep much longer. Already the ice receded from her skin.

Rohaz escorted Anjen to the section of the City that Luna House ruled. Even if she hadn't memorized the City's layout to the smallest detail, she would have known it as Luna's territory. Immense plaques upon the walls depicted luna moths at rest, carved in subtle facets upon alabaster quarried from worlds whose names no one remembered. In the background, in an implied inverse sky of milky white and translucent cream, inlay of gold and silver depicted the constellations of bygone skies.

Anjen's chair conveyed her in comfort while Rohaz paced her. The folds of her dress covered one ruined leg, while the artful slit revealed the other. She had done nothing to conceal the livid scars, which stood out against her dark skin. In her hands she held her sword of office, demurely sheathed in black leather; a magenta tassel hung from the weapon's hilt.

Luna House's guards stopped her at the checkpoint, itself marked by a banner of gray and white. The guards would have impressed a less-astute observer, given their uniforms: silk-of-stars and velvet in House gray and white, and sword hilts gleaming at their backs. But their postures betrayed a telltale sloppiness. In her prime Anjen would have been able to take them easily, and even now, if she'd come with an assassin's intent, she could have caused them no small trouble.

"Your sword," said the one on the left with an air of apology that Anjen was all too used to.

"It stays with me," Anjen said, deceptively soft.

A shadow fell across her feet, lengthened, stopped. It led to a broad-shouldered man, his costume as elaborate as the guards', but no more. He had contemplative eyes in a brutish face. Unlike the guards, he stepped with a duelist's exquisite command of measure; he stood just outside the range of her sword, had she drawn it.

239

"It stays," the man agreed. He pivoted on one heel, as neat as a dancer, and bowed to her a fraction more than courtesy required.

Anjen knew him: Khev of Luna House. If she wasn't mistaken, he had manufactured the incident for her benefit. The guards took his orders; he could have them recycled, and replacements ordered from the birthing chambers or ice-vaults, if he judged their conduct unfitting.

She allowed her eyes to widen, feigning gratitude. "Master Khev," she said, and dipped her head with an apologetic gesture. "I can't do you the honor you are owed—"

"As if I would stand on ceremony," he said, when she knew he would do exactly that if it gained him an advantage. They were alike in that way. "You may depart," he added to Rohaz.

Anjen smiled with her eyes so that Rohaz knew that she wished them to go, even if it wasn't, strictly speaking, *safe*.

After Rohaz had left, Khev led the way into the labyrinthine halls of Luna House. The two of them passed brittle, gleaming curtains composed of preserved moths' wings and beads of brilliant gunmetal, racks of swords with their blades broken in battles ancient, and—the most blatant display of Luna's influence—copies of the master star-charts, of lapis lazuli inlaid with abalone and gold. At the end of these wonders, Khev spoke a word in a language that survived only in Luna, and a door opened in an unassuming expanse of wall, wide enough to accommodate Anjen's chair—a courtesy she had not asked for, but which she noted.

The room thus revealed had little of splendor to recommend it. Within rested a plain desk of metal, and a chair of the same. A weapons rack against the wall showcased two spare swords and a rifle. She had seen the excellence of his swordplay and his marksmanship eight years gone.

"I'm honored by your attention, Master Khev," Anjen said with a calculated touch of breathlessness.

Khev sat behind the desk, frowning, and ignored the overture. "Forgive the precipitous summons," he said. "The mayor-commander is dead."

Anjen grasped the significance immediately, unexpected though the news was. The mayor-commander had designated no heir despite the pleadings of his advisers, in an effort not to favor one House over another. While the mayor-commander formally cut their ties upon ascension, the ideal was better honored in theory than in practice.

"Was there any warning?" she asked. She'd never heard that the mayor-commander was ill, but such knowledge would have been suppressed. What she really wanted to know was whether or not the man had been assassinated. After all, he had declined to appoint a new head duelist to serve as his body-guard after he dismissed Lio the Catastrophe Hand.

"I was one of six people called in to witness the autopsy," Khev said. "Ship surveillance caught the whole thing on camera. He slipped on a wet bath tile and cracked his head."

"What an ignominious death," Anjen murmured. "And my part in this is—?"

"Your maneuvers have not escaped my notice," Khev said. "Azalea may be much diminished, but every time I treat with the Common Houses, they defer to your opinion. You govern them in all but name, in the way of shadow. They may not rule the ship's high positions, but there is power yet in numbers. When I put myself forward for the mayor-commander's seat, I want the Common Houses' support. You are the one who can deliver it."

Pretending ignorance would have insulted him. Anjen tipped her head up, meeting his eyes. "No Supreme Tournament?"

"The other five High Houses will not oppose me," Khev said.

She believed him. "Make your offer, then."

"Your pride is not dead, I see. That's good."

She ignored his condescension. She'd endured worse.

"I will adopt Azalea," Khev said, "as a cadet branch of Luna, should everything go as planned. A generous offer, I'm sure you'll agree."

He was right, as much as it rankled. She would have to give up her independence and be explicitly subject to Luna. But herself, Rohaz, and little Kihaz, the youngest—the three of them could not afford to be choosy. It was unlikely that any of the other head duelists would offer Anjen better.

"And if you fail?" Anjen inquired. If Khev had judged poorly, and even one of the eligible duelists insisted on a Supreme Tournament—if Khev lost a duel—

Khev lifted a shoulder, let it fall. "Then I don't see that I owe you anything."

This came as a relief, although she was careful not to let him spot it. After all, she didn't want Azalea beholden to a failed candidate. She nodded, biting her lip in pretended dismay. "When will the mayor-commander's death be announced?"

"Tomorrow morning," Khev said. "The mayor-commander's seat will be determined four days after that."

Eight years ago, Khev had been one of the City's finest duelists. Anjen herself would have hesitated to face him. But here he was, going out of his way to avoid the Supreme Tournament. She was certain none of the eligible Houses had a duelist his equal. What was he afraid of?

On the morning after the High Houses announced the mayor-commander's death, the woman named Lio walked out of the ice-vaults, newly awake, and toward the shadow-turbulent Seven-Sided Stage.

People parted for her, not because they held her in any regard, but because they recognized her. They remembered how she had failed the mayor-commander. Through the crowds she walked, and murmurs rose around her.

Six-and-one head duelists already stood before the City's wolf-priest, Khev of Luna House foremost among them. Lio didn't fear him; didn't fear anyone who stood in that great and grim company. The Common Houses were entitled to a representative, and that seventh duelist had already been determined. Lio saw them in their ceremonial white-and-gold, a spider brooch gleaming upon their breast.

The crowds parted again, this time for a woman in a floater chair. Lio did not slow. The woman, magnificently garbed in magenta silk and pearls the color of scalped stars, her face half hidden behind a mask of unliving petals, accelerated to plant her chair in Lio's path. A sword of office rested in her lap.

"You of all people cannot claim ignorance of the City's traditions," said the woman in a voice that was as deferential as satin, and just as deceptive.

"I do not recognize you," Lio said, "or your authority." A dangerous thing to admit: her years in the ice-vaults had fractured her memory. For all she knew, she had once supped with this woman, or tested her blade, or dealt her the injuries that required her to use the chair.

The woman met Lio's gaze squarely, although she had to raise her chin to do so. Then Lio knew that she had, indeed, been a duelist; that the sword in her lap was not for show. "There are six-and-one duelists," the woman said. "Six for the High Houses and one for the Common Houses. I speak for the seventh, Peris. There is no place for you here. There will be no Supreme Tournament; it has been agreed."

"Who are you," Lio said, as direct as a sword-thrust, "that you answer for Peris?" Indeed, the person known as Peris, the one with the spider brooch, stood fidgeting, watching the confrontation sidewise.

"I am Anjen of House Azalea," the woman replied, "and no blade is drawn by the Common Houses but that I will it so. No word is spoken in the Common Houses but that I know its purpose. And I know of your long exile in the ice, and I say to you now: turn back."

Lio admired Anjen's forthrightness. She had a fencer's excellent posture even seated; her voice rang with the clarity of glass on glass. Lio would have liked to duel her, once upon an injury. "You have spent the past years well hidden, Anjen of Azalea," Lio said.

The wolf-priest gestured impatiently. "Is this a substitute for Peris of the Common Houses?" he asked. "We are ready to declare Khev of Luna the new mayor-commander by unanimous acclamation."

"I am better than a substitute," Lio said, raising her voice. "I represent the interests of a party on whom we all depend, and who has heretofore been shut out of the Houses' decisions. I represent the silicate mind of the City itself."

The shadows upon the Stage shifted and stirred, taking on the shapes of the Houses' emblems, from Anjen's own Azalea in its full-skirted splendor to Luna's extravagant Moth, and more besides. There were birds of shadow, their wings primly folded, and trees of shadow with poetically curved limbs, and an entire array of shadow ornaments, some more abstract than others. Even the unfortunate Peris's seven-limbed spider could be seen, in honor of the Common Houses. Each shadow represented the soul of its House.

But a greater shadow yet swallowed the throng, sparked through with filaments of silver light. Everyone recognized its silhouette, born as they had been upon the City Unbreachable: the shape of the ship itself. The lights above and the lights below turned silver, brightening and dimming four times, and a light rose up around Lio herself.

"A bold gambit indeed," Anjen said, inclining her head, and Lio fancied she glimpsed admiration, however reluctant, in her eyes. "If we do not permit a Supreme Tournament, then the ship itself will turn against us. Is that the threat?"

"It is," Lio said. Moved by impulse, she reached out for Anjen's hand, and Anjen allowed her to take it. "Wish me the flowers' own fortune," she said, "whether I rise or fall."

"I will do better than that," Anjen replied cryptically, her eyes smiling like a new-kindled star.

"Then that is good enough for me," said Lio, who had never relied on any luck but her sword-arm, and pressed forward for the wolf-priest's blessing.

Anjen receded into the crowd, deliberately avoiding Khev's glower.

"He's frowning," Rohaz commented, as if she couldn't tell. "He will have words for you, cousin."

"It's not important," Anjen said. Either Khev would win, in which case it was the same as if he had won the seat by acclamation, or he would not. She had rallied the Common Houses to his cause, and now that the Supreme Tournament was going to take place after all, the duelists would face Lio upon a terrain of the Common Houses' hopes and fears.

Peris was young, and hotheaded, and easily seduced by whispers of glory. But they would not win; Anjen had not selected them for their ability to win. They would duel flamboyantly, and please the Common Houses—Anjen knew well their love of spectacle, and just as importantly, she knew that Khev would not be able to resist prolonging the match by toying with Peris.

Lio—Lio was another matter. Anjen had never faced Lio's sword, back in her dueling days, and counted herself lucky even as she mourned the lost opportunity of challenge. To face a duelist of such consummate skill—she missed those days. Her skills were other, now.

"She's going to win," Anjen breathed.

Rohaz blanched. "You can't let her," they said. "That's as good as backstabbing Khev. If he thinks you've backed someone else—"

"*Look at her,*" Anjen said. "Look at the way she walks. The way she's stopped calculating distances because it's gone instinctual. She's the better fencer. If I had only known she'd walk out of the ice-vaults—"

"She's the *Catastrophe Hand*," Rohaz said, still disbelieving. "She failed at her job. She's bad luck all the way down."

Anjen smiled at them, her heart merry. "Then we have something in common."

Three hundred forty-nine years ago, when the City Unbreachable had another name, the tyrants of the heptarchate upgraded their starships. "Upgrade" was the preferred euphemism. The new starships were space-faring aliens, unparalleled in their fleetness, cyborged and slaved for the convenience of their human passengers.

The City's original crew discovered the truth of the upgrades and fled in protest—a long, slow flight, using outdated stardrive technology. It would take them generations to reach a world beyond the heptarchate's shadow, there to settle. By Anjen's time, most of the crew's descendants had forgotten this original purpose, or dismissed it as irrelevant.

The late mayor-commander had not had any intention of continuing the original mission, and his would-be successor, as represented by the six-and-one duelists, were of like mind.

But the ship itself—the silicate webs that formed its mind had gained at first sentience, and then cunning. The ship had other ideas.

Lio the Catastrophe Hand faced a gauntlet of six-and-one duelists, but she faced them not alone. Her shadow stretched out behind her, in the shape of the City itself, and its jeweled circuitries.

The dueling arena was thick with shadows, forming a dark terrain. Some of the shadows came from the Common Houses. Hostile elements, unpersuaded by Anjen's influence, swarmed Lio like hornets. She did not cut them down—couldn't have, even had she desired it. But the light of her sword, ashen, drove them back.

This was an art peculiar to the fencers of the heptarchate and preserved in the City, however much its people would have preferred to deny their heritage. *Slay a shadow, stay a shadow,* went the old sere chant: the idea that the soul could only properly be viewed in darkness, and from darkness roused.

Not for nothing had Lio been head duelist of the City entire. With scorn she met her first human opponent, and the second, and the third. She could read entire volumes of intention in a flick of the gaze; gave away nothing of her own, except in feint. Her opponents were skilled; she was better.

The fourth and fifth opponents fell as easily as the first three had. It was over so quickly that only an expert eye could have traced the parries and counter-parries, the clever angulations of the blade. Lio did not toy with them, out of respect.

Then Khev of Luna fell back, so that she faced Peris next, and out of sequence.

Peris fenced bravely. With another five, ten years of experience, their aggression would have been backed by an equal measure of cunning, and they might have had a chance. Not for nothing had they become a favorite of the Common

Houses. Their shadow was an agile, seven-limbed spider, and the onlookers cheered to see it rear up.

But bravery was not enough. Lio invited Peris to attack too deep, and this they did, believing that the subtle opening was an opportunity. Lio's answering counterattack took off their hand at the wrist. It was her idea of mercy, for she didn't want to kill such an earnest fighter.

At the last Lio stood before Khev of Luna, her blade marrow-pale and blood-dark. He had not yet unsheathed his own sword of office, although the gray jewel in its pommel shone the color of rain and regret, and his moth-shadow fluttered its wings in warning. "You could have slept in the ice-vaults," Khev said, "and lived until the journey's end. It's a shame I will have to cut down such a master of the blade."

"I will not kill an unarmed man," Lio replied. "Not here of all places. Draw your weapon."

"I had hoped to do this peacefully," he said, "but very well."

Khev drew into parry prime, and then a perfect en garde, and the duel began. His moth-shadow wavered, but the man himself was unmoved.

Lio feinted at his blade, to which he replied with cunningly timed disengagement; his blade made a tight circle about hers, without making contact. She invited attack, as she had with Peris, which he disdained. Her next feints met with similar patience, and he refused to be drawn out.

Khev lowered his blade then. Lio wasn't fooled. His arm remained in perfect alignment, and she had noted the uncanny speed of his responses. If she attacked him carelessly, his blade would whip up and pierce her arm. Cautiously, she tested his defenses, and indeed, only her own reflexive parries, as fast as his, kept him from running her through. Each time, he returned his blade to that lowered position, an open taunt.

They remained at impasse for some time. Lio not edthe strange wavering of his shadow, and wondered at its significance. But she had been in the ice-vaults for too long, and she did not know what internal conflicts Luna House might hide, that might challenge the legitimacy of Khev's position.

Then the fragrance of azaleas swirled through the air, and Lio knew that Anjen had kept her promise, whatever her reasons. Khev's face darkened, the first emotion he'd betrayed since entering the Tournament Supreme. Suddenly his shadow changed shape, and a murmur of dismay went around the arena. Here he was able to disguise his true allegiance no longer: instead of Luna's Moth, his shadow took on the form of the heptarchate's seven-spoked wheel.

Now Lio understood why the City's silicate mind had intervened. She was its instrument; she could not suffer the traitor to live, even if he had the support of the City's Houses. If the terrain-of-shadows remained favorable to him—

Lio had not reckoned on aid from that quarter, but the hostile elements among the Common Houses' shadows, which had previously buzzed around her and threatened to foul her blade, instead drew back, allowing her an unimpeded view of Khev. The smell of azaleas ghosted through the air.

Khev, who must have sensed that the terrain of shadows was turning against him, lifted his blade and advanced. Lio gave way again and again, forcing him to sweat over every centimeter. Her blade bobbed up and down, making a moving target of her arm. She circled his point, feinted, circled again. *Am I going to riposte yet?* she asked him in the language of the sword.

Again and again she feinted until his attention slipped toward the City-shadow at her back. It was only for a second; a second was all she needed. Lio lunged with a whipcord swiftness that drew gasps, had she been listening. Khev brought his sword up in a belated circular parry. She saw it coming, disengaged neatly, and slipped past to pierce him through.

Lio pulled her blade out, and he fell. "Why?" she asked him in the rustling silence. "Why betray the City, which once you served so well?"

"It is a long journey to the nameless world we seek to colonize," Khev replied, "and I wanted its end." He smiled faintly. "I have found it after all, if not in the way I expected." Then his grip slackened, and the sword with the gray jewel fell out of his hand, and the heptarchate's wheel dwindled until it was an ordinary man's shadow again.

Lio stood unseeing as the shadows everywhere in the arena resumed the ordinary laws of light and geometry.

The wolf-priest approached her, cautious of her blade. "It's done," he said, and repeated himself when she looked at him blankly. "You've won the Supreme Tournament. You're the new mayor-commander."

It took a moment for the words to penetrate the adrenaline haze. Then she shook her head, impatient, and scanned the crowd until she saw the floater chair and Anjen splendid in her dress of bright magenta. "No," Lio said, beckoning with her off hand until Anjen approached.

Anjen's eyes met hers, intent and smiling.

Lio smiled back and saluted her with her sword, still stained with Khev's blood. "I didn't win. *We* did." She bowed then, with all the elegance of her station. "*She* is your new mayor-commander. After all, she knows the ways of the City and its Houses, and how to govern. I am but her blade."

"You do me too much credit," Anjen murmured as she maneuvered her chair up to Lio.

Lio wiped her sword clean and sheathed it. She leaned over, perfectly balanced all the while, and pressed a kiss to Anjen's lips. Their eyes met. Anjen's eyes were bright as stars and dark as shadows, and Lio knew they would partner each other perfectly in the days to come.

The Commander
and the Mirage Master's Mate
by Elaine McIonyn

The shoreline's jagged edge surrounded the little fleet. Gannets wheeled around grassy cliffs as fishing vessels put out from a series of harbors. It was no ordinary shore, however, but a carefully crafted illusion.

An image of an island had been mathematically configured, transformed through vertical and horizontal planes, flipped across multiple axes. The results were projected by light-warping lenses into the aether at precise distances from the Hardweather —a recent and now indispensable addition to naval warfare: a mirage ship—to create the shield of false shore. Its aim was to confuse the enemy, adding a crucial layer of protection to both the island and the fleet that guarded it, which consisted of two first-class frigates, five brigs, and the fourth-rate frigate *Hardweather*.

Commander Sora Larking stood tall in her blue uniform jacket on the *Hardweather*'s quarterdeck. Her cocked hat was tucked under her arm, and the wind tousled her short sweep of dark hair.

"And how are the top-hands getting on with their new spyglasses?" she asked her officers.

"I can't say we've had much progress," the first lieutenant said. "Truth be told I had no idea that aether-spyglasses were quite so... puzzling to use."

"I once looked though one out of curiosity," Sora said. "All I could see was the back of my own head." She broke into a smile and swelled with pride. "No, I suppose it takes a certain variety of genius to use such equipment..."

Several officers rolled their eyes. It was no secret that the commander's lover was Lirren Harter, the mirage-master's mate, who had joined the crew the preceding winter. Lirren had passed the Mathematickers' Guild examinations with distinction, and was skilled in the use of aether-spyglasses and other aether-paraphernalia.

"With luck," the lieutenant said, "we may find geniuses among the top-hands who can be trained in their use."

"Indeed. And then we'll have plenty of eyes to see through any aether-trickery the Elarans use to get at our miragers," Sora said. "Continue with the training. Now!" She clapped her hands together and turned to the purser. "On to the matter of victuals! Do we have enough to keep us going until we next put into port?"

As they discussed provisions, raised voices were heard from up on the poop deck. The words disappeared on the breeze, but the ill-tempered tone was clear.

Sora sighed. "My apologies for cutting short such an agreeable subject," she said, "but I suppose I ought to see what's going on up there."

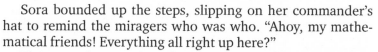

Sora bounded up the steps, slipping on her commander's hat to remind the miragers who was who. "Ahoy, my mathematical friends! Everything all right up here?"

The two miragers pivoted to face her. Hadden Darlett, the mirage-master and architect of the false shore, was poised at the aetherscope, a tall brass device that turned calculation into illusion. It was covered in lenses, gyroscopes, switches, and levers, and was bolted to the deck beside the stern rail. Darlett himself was a stocky man of middle years with a sagging face that seemed all the heavier when he frowned.

"All under control, Commander, it's simply a... divergence of views."

Sora's glance shot towards Lirren, who was brushing away strands of her fair hair from her spectacles with one hand. Her other clutched an aether-spyglass, its shaft bristling with little brass switches. Behind her stood a calculation engine, a device that (as far as Sora understood it) was a large and complicated abacus with cogs and levers.

Lirren did not look pleased, and Sora fancied she knew why.

"Harter?" Sora addressed her directly.

Lirren resumed her customary composure. She held up the aether-spyglass. "I have seen something worrisome three points off the starboard quarter, Commander, and I believe we ought to take action. I can't identify what it is yet, but I ran the parameters through the calculation engine, and the results aren't consistent with the aether fluctuations from our own mirage alone."

"I see," Sora lied. "And Darlett—you presumably disagree?"

He sniffed. "I take Harter's conclusions with the usual pinch of salt, Commander." Sora frowned at Darlett's insult towards Lirren, but did not reprove him. She and Lirren both needed his goodwill.

"I wished to verify her findings before reporting them to you," he continued, "but she took umbrage at the suggestion."

"If the anomalies are an Elaran trick," Lirren said, "then we don't have time to recalculate it all over again. They're less than a mile from our stern."

Sora saw nothing amiss out to sea. But she trusted that Lirren's concerns were founded.

"Then perhaps I should raise the alert flag to warn the fleet immediately. Better safe than sorry."

Darlett stepped up between Sora and Lirren.

"Commander, with all due respect, it would cause unnecessary panic to raise the flags prematurely. It is my professional duty to verify Harter's findings, given her... previous record of competence, along with her wild theories about what an aetherscope is capable of."

Lirren flushed and looked away. Sora swallowed an urge to rebuke Darlett. An aetherscope experiment Lirren had conducted aboard her previous ship, the *Scallop*, had led to a senior officer losing both legs and an arm. It had cost Sora several long-standing favors to keep Lirren in the navy, and only on condition that the "rogue mirager's" discipline improved. Sora's career fate and Lirren's continuing service aboard the *Hardweather*—their future together—now hung on Lirren receiving a good report. As her immediate superior and a respected mathematicker, only Darlett could issue such a report. It would not do for Sora to fall out with him, even if he was a puffed-up old basket.

Sora nodded. "If you must. Get on with it."

Lirren did not look Darlett in the eye as she handed him the aether-spyglass. While he took up position beside the calculation engine to check Lirren's observations, Sora beckoned Lirren to her side.

"Sorry, darling," she whispered. "Much as it pains me—"

"I know." Lirren's lips were clenched tight, but her grimace turned to a smile as she looked at Sora. "I want him on our side, despite everything. But at this particular moment, I'm concerned about whatever's out there." She gestured across the stern rail. "If my calculations hold, then it's almost the size of the *Hardweather*. Perhaps a fifth-rated frigate, or a large sloop-of-war—"

Sora jerked back in alarm. "*What?* I thought you meant something small and obscure—how could something that size get so close without our noticing?!"

"The Elarans have been getting very good since they started kidnapping our miragers."

Sora surveyed the surroundings. The other ships in the fleet were some distance away; the closest was a brig, the *Cormorant*, too far away to be of much use.

"Commander?" Darlett's voice had a strained note to it. "Commander! My preliminary observations are incomplete... but I advise we raise the flag!"

"In fact," Lirren continued, "they're so good, they've just snuck up beside us."

The mirage of empty sea and sky fell away from the enemy frigate just as the vessel came abreast of the *Hardweather*. Two gangplanks slammed down upon the *Hardweather*'s starboard gunwale, and Elaran sailors swung lines with grappling hooks into her rigging, lashing both ships together. A boarding party in green breeches and jackets poured across.

At more than three hundred strong, Sora's crew likely outnumbered the boarders—but they were nowhere near ready for action. Top-hands scrambled down the rigging to join the fight; those off watch had to be roused from their hammocks; and officers rushed to distribute guns and powder.

From below came the first volley of enemy cannon-fire, puncturing the *Hardweather*'s hull.

After ordering the alert flag to be raised, Sora rushed the miragers down to their assigned hiding places. The navy had few miragers, and they were invaluable. Protecting them was a mirage ship's duty. Darlett and Lirren were to be concealed in different spots to lessen the risk that both the *Hardweather*'s miragers would be lost in a single attack.

Darlett launched into a tirade as soon as they were below decks.

"Damn it all, Harter! If you'd worked faster, I could have checked your numbers and raised the alarm sooner! What's *wrong* with you?"

Sora glanced sharply at Lirren, warning her not to rise to his words. Lirren simply scowled and rolled her eyes when she knew Darlett couldn't see.

Sora marched them to the officers' cabins at the rear of the gun deck, where a dozen or so officers were hastily arming themselves.

"That's the way to do it, lads and lasses!" Sora cried. She gestured to the ceiling with her hat. "Get above and give ''em what for! Except you four—" She waved at a group of warrant officers' mates. "I want two of you down here at all times to guard the mirage-master's hiding place. The other two will follow me."

Darlett was still spouting off about Lirren's supposed inadequacies as Sora unlocked the bosun's cabin with her master key. She promptly stuffed him inside.

"Stop blustering, man, and pull out that panel under the bed. Curl yourself up and get inside. You'll find a pistol, powder, and shot down there—be prepared to use them if you're found."

Darlett huffed. "I'm a scholar, Commander, not a fighter, I—"

Sora grabbed his jacket and yanked him towards her to remind him of her physical strength. They were almost nose to nose. Darlett simply gaped.

"All that time you spent arguing with Miss Harter instead of listening to her—that's going to cost *lives*, Darlett. The lives of ordinary crew who don't have a designated place to hide. The least you can do is show some dignity."

Sora shut the door, glad to see the back of him. If Lirren hadn't needed his favor, Sora would have had him flogged for insubordination long ago. She ushered Lirren away and beckoned to the other two mates she had called upon.

"To the sick bay. We'll hide Miss Harter there, and you will guard her with your lives. Understood?"

They nodded, though both wore grim expressions. Sora followed them out onto the cramped gun deck. A ragged contingent of crew members was making a belated start on loading the *Hardweather*'s nineteen starboard guns. Their iron wheels rumbled like a coming storm while shouts of combat came down through the hatchways from the top deck. As Sora stooped to avoid cracking her skull on the low ceiling beams, Lirren spoke into her ear.

"I have a cherished daydream about filling his bed with mirages of eels while he's in it. Perhaps even real eels. But more pertinently right now, I think there's a way to turn the odds in our favor."

Sora glanced at her. "Is there? If you have some miracle idea, I'm all ears."

"It's simple—with Darlett out of the way, I could—"

The report of enemy cannon issued from their right-hand side: a great boom followed by a sickening crunch as another volley of eight-pound shot burst through the hull. Sora grabbed Lirren and hurled them to the floor to avoid the wood splinters slashing through the air.

The dust cleared, and Sora sprang up. Even through the thick smoke, it was clear the hull was badly damaged. One gun had been knocked on its side, and crew members lay groaning about the deck.

Sora helped Lirren to her feet.

"Are you all right?"

Lirren dusted down her uniform and adjusted her spectacles. "Bruised, but unharmed."

"Very well." Sora turned to the gun deck at large. "Bring the injured to the sick bay, then return to loading. Let's put a few holes in their ship. Hop to it!" She took Lirren by the hand.

"We can't hang about here. Come on. And tell me this miracle idea." She gestured to the guards she had commandeered and marched along behind them. Lirren spoke rapidly.

"With Darlett gone, I could displace the boarders with the aetherscope. Just pick them off one by one."

Sora's stomach, usually dauntless, turned to ice.

"What?"

"You know very well what. Displacement! Moving matter with the aetherscope, not just light."

"Ah." It was not what Sora wanted to hear. "You mean picking someone up and flinging them somewhere else?"

Lirren huffed. "If you want to put it like that, yes. Pick them off our ship and fling them back to their own. They wouldn't know what was happening. They have no counter-strategy."

Sora winced. "Like you did on the *Scallop*?" Much as she cared for Lirren, she didn't know what to make of her arcane aether-theories. But she did know that a repeat of the *Scallop* incident would go down poorly with the admiralty.

Lirren pulled Sora behind a thick support post by the center stairwell, where there was a little shelter from the chaos of deckhands hauling guns and running for powder.

"I wasn't at fault! If that damned lieutenant had followed my instructions, he'd still be in one piece. It *can* be done. And what of it if a few Elarans lose the occasional limb?"

The two guards had stopped and were now peering back with impatience. Around them, gun crews worked ropes and ramrods while their lives hung in the balance. Their vigor and courage made Sora hungry for action.

"If that plan backfired, you'd be out of the navy, not just off the *Hardweather*." Despite her mounting impatience, Sora's heart sank at the thought. The two seasons they had spent together on this ship had been the happiest of her life. If they had to return to seeing each other only during shore leave, she might wither.

"I used all the influence I have to keep you in your post," she said. "I can't do it again."

A pained look crossed Lirren's face as she gestured to the deckhands around them. "So you won't save your crew from the boarders?"

Sora opened her mouth to retort, but Lirren cut her off.

"And you don't trust me any more than Darlett does?" Her brows drew together as she looked Sora dead in the eye.

Sora's whole body tensed, and she spoke through clenched teeth. "Damn it all, Lirren, I have every confidence in you—which is why I can't send you up top. We can ill-afford to lose our miragers." She took a deep breath, softening her stance. "And I can ill-afford to lose you myself—"

There was a loud thud beside them. A young man in a blue jacket had tumbled down the stairs from the top deck. The hilt of a cutlass projected from his chest, blood spreading across his white shirt. His eyes were wide open in disbelief.

A deckhand in Elaran uniform leapt down after him and curled his hand around the hilt to pull it out. More Elaran boots tramped down the stairs, and Sora grabbed Lirren to run the few remaining yards. Just as they reached the bulkhead between the gun deck and the sick bay, another round of cannon-fire smashed through the *Hardweather*, scattering more fixtures and crew. One of their guards pitched forward, landing heavily on the boards. The other opened the door in the bulkhead and shunted Sora and Lirren inside before joining them.

The sick bay was cramped. Its three hammocks were already occupied and stained with blood. The heavy air stank of the stuff. At least a dozen wounded sat on the floor waiting for the surgeon. They saluted Sora when she entered, and the sight of them filled her with a prodigious urge to go up top and fight side by side with her crew.

The surgeon was at his operating table stitching a deep, gory cut that an older top-hand had taken to the belly. The man winced, but saluted Sora all the same. The surgeon glanced up at the newcomers before returning his gaze to his work.

"Commander!" he said, with a cheerfulness out of place in the circumstances. "I've been expecting you. I see our plans to hide Miss Harter are bearing fruit?"

Sora's fingers swept the hilt of her cutlass; her impatience to join the action was rising.

"Indeed they are. Lirren!" She gestured to a wooden chest behind the operating table. A scatter of nasty-looking

257

medical instruments lay on the floor beside it; the surgeon had evidently emptied it in haste to accommodate Lirren. "Climb in there."

Lirren turned to face her again.

"If you allow me," she whispered, "I can put a stop to all of this." She gestured to the wounded, who peered inquisitively at them. "I can get rid of the Elarans in no time flat, and we can save our lot from getting maimed and worse."

Sora sighed. Her patience was running low.

"This is a mirage ship. Our duty is to support mirage work. The crew are here to protect you—it would be a poor reward for their hardship if you put yourself in the way of enemy bullets and blades." She brushed Lirren's cheek with her knuckles. "Let me get rid of the Elarans the old-fashioned way. It's what I'm trained to do."

Lirren's lips were parted and ready for further protest. "But—"

Sora placed a hand on her shoulder. "Please don't make me order you. If it comes down to it, my duty has to come first."

Lirren's posture slumped. "Then there's no more I can say." She turned towards the hiding place with a resigned expression. Sora had no time to dwell on the disagreement. She took out her loaded pistol and drew her cutlass, calling on her reserve of impatient energy. The remaining guard stood beside the door.

"Stay here and defend Miss Harter at all costs," Sora said.

"Aye, ma'am."

Then the guard opened the door, and Sora charged out into the fray.

The gun deck was thick with the sour, sulphurous odor of gun smoke. On the wooden planks, fighters stumbled over the bodies of at least twenty crewmates, either killed or blacked out, but the Elarans were losing vigor, while Sora was still fresh.

She expended her single pistol shot almost straight away, right into the chest of a cutlass-bearing woman barreling towards her. Sora made for the nearest stairwell, where two Elarans blocked her path.

She was no stranger to close combat. She slashed away the first man's cutlass with her own and followed by smashing his nose with the heavy pistol-butt in her left hand. She kicked the other fellow back onto the deck, dashing his head against a powder chest.

Up she fought, slashing at and grappling with boarders who were descending the steps. At last, she ducked through the hatchway and emerged into the open air. The top deck was a mess of combat: the clash of cutlasses, the snapping and smoke of pistols, linen shirts streaked with red. It was hard to be certain, but those remaining of the *Hardweather*'s crew seemed outnumbered by the boarding party. In spite of the odds, Sora threw herself into the fight, belting the nearest Elaran across the head with the pommel of her cutlass and knocking him to the deck.

Her uniform marked her as the commander, and sure enough, half a dozen boarders split from their fellows to round upon her. She dispatched the first few in a whirl of cutlass, pistol-butt and vicious kicks. A stocky man with a stubby blade lunged at her like a pit dog. Sora dodged his attempt to run her through, but stumbled over a fallen comrade. The man kicked her square in the chest, pitching her to the deck. Her pistol clattered to the boards.

A sinewy older woman in an officer's hat shoved her boot-heel into Sora's ribs, knocking the wind out of her. The woman cocked a pistol and pointed its barrel right at Sora's wheezing face.

A bosun's whistle shrieked across the deck. Sora did not recognise the signal, but the woman with the pistol glanced in its direction, hesitating for just a moment. Sora knocked the pistol from her grasp and grabbed her arm, pulling her down. She rolled away from the woman and sprang up, panting to regain her breath.

The group of Elarans turned away from Sora and dashed back to their gangplanks. The woman in the officer's uniform clambered back upright. Sora raised her cutlass, ready to parry, but the officer had lost all interest and was now hurrying after her crew.

Sora's guts froze—were they retreating because they had succeeded?

Had they taken Lirren?

She called out to the crew members who remained standing on the top deck.

"Shoot them with all you've got left! Don't let them away unscathed!"

A few pistol shots rang out, but only a couple hit home. The enemy vessel had already caught wind in its sails and was peeling away from the battered *Hardweather*. As the Elarans drew in the gangplanks, the ship disappeared once more behind a mirage of empty air. The encircling mirage of shoreline was broken and fractured on the horizon, lost without the care and attention of the miragers. Some way off the starboard quarter, the brig *Cormorant* scudded across the waves with full-bellied sails, too late to be of any help.

Sora begrudgingly acknowledged her Elaran counterpart's skill in organizing the whole escapade as she floundered back down the stairs to check on Lirren. Her boots had scarcely touched the gun deck when a voice called out for her.

"Commander! Commander!"

She turned to see a warrant officer's mate dashing up from the stern cabins, red in the face, swerving around fallen crew members and debris. He was one of the guards she had stationed at Darlett's hiding place.

"The mirage-master!" he cried. "He's been taken!"

Time froze for a moment as Sora absorbed this news. She hadn't given Darlett the slightest consideration since she left him in the bosun's cabin, assuming him safe.

"What happened?"

The young fellow panted as he relayed his report. "They came... through the stern windows... They used their own ship's boat... and paddled up behind us... They used hooks and all sorts to climb up..."

Sora leaned against a wooden post. "Cunning scoundrels!"

The young man stopped to take a deep breath. "I heard a commotion in the cabin, so I turned to see what it was... There were two Elarans, pulling him out from under the bed. He had a pistol, but he just waved it around... One of the Elarans challenged us with a blade, we couldn't save him... They bundled him out the window, and I looked out and saw their boat. I made to fire my pistol, but the boat vanished..."

Sora thumped the wooden post with her fist. "More damned mirages. Using our own people against us, no doubt." And now Darlett would become yet another mirager pressed into Elaran service. A precious naval asset that Sora had been entrusted with, now lost. She rested her forehead against the post and closed her eyes. This would shatter her reputation, already tainted because of—

Sora jerked out of her slump. Was Lirren safe? Had the Elarans devised some trickery to get at her as well? Her heart lurched with foreboding as she turned back around toward the sick bay.

There, striding towards her, was Lirren herself, with no more ill-effects than a creased uniform and crooked spectacles. Sora rushed forward and threw her arms around her.

"You're safe! Goodness, there's one thing to be glad about, at least..."

Lirren returned the gesture before standing back.

"I heard enough of that report to know what happened. But there *is* a chance."

Sora didn't have to ask where this line of thought was leading. She turned it around in her mind. It was still fraught with danger, but her prior caution had not averted catastrophe. And they both still needed Darlett and his good word.

"Whatever the punishment for this will be, it can't be worse than whatever they'll do to me for losing Darlett... Very well. Let's try it your way. Are you going to fling Darlett back here through the aether?"

"That would be impossible. He'll be below decks where I can't see him, and neither can the aetherscope." Lirren grinned. "No, Commander—I'm going to fling *you* over *there* through the aether."

The ship's cook ascended the steps to the poop deck bearing a bottle of brandy and a crystal goblet.

"From my personal stores," he said. "Pre-war vintage."

He filled the goblet, handed it to Sora and saluted. "An honor to serve you, Commander." Sora pretended not to notice the note of farewell in his words. She swallowed a large mouthful of the brandy.

"Thank you." She leaned against the starboard gunwale, stomach tumbling with apprehension. She glanced across her shoulder. The swift little *Cormorant* was heading in the likeliest direction of the Elaran ship, having received instructions to do so from the *Hardweather*'s flag signals. Sora had given the orders for form's sake, though the plan was all Lirren's.

The cook stood aside for a petty officer bearing a boarding axe. She bowed as she presented it to Sora.

"As you requested, Commander." Sora drained her goblet and returned it to the cook, taking up the axe. She weighed it in her hand; it was top-heavy, with a solid blade.

Lirren was behind the aetherscope, its lenses glinting like an array of watchful eyes. She popped her head out from behind the device, peering out to sea through her aether-spyglass.

"The Elaran ship is two points off the starboard bow, a mile and a half out. More or less dead ahead of the *Cormorant*." She patted the aetherscope. "I've arranged it so the Elarans will see several false replicas of the *Cormorant* approaching them from various angles. The more confusion the better. Don't forget, once you've completed the first stage, stand up straight on the stern rail so that I can see all of you. Tuck in your limbs and stay absolutely still." Her finger described a rough outline of Sora's body in the air. "I have to capture a section of aether, and if you stick an arm or leg outside of the section, you'll lose it—like that twit on the *Scallop*. Now!" There was an unnerving air of finality to Lirren's tone. "Ready?"

Absolutely not, Sora thought. "I—yes?"

One corner of Lirren's mouth lifted into half a grin, which Sora always found charming.

"Reluctant?"

Sora hesitated a moment. "Well... I'll do anything I can for one of my crew."

If Lirren was smiling—even half-smiling—then she couldn't be all that upset with Sora's trepidation.

"But you're here all the same," she said. "Waiting for me to experiment on you. If I can't have outright enthusiasm, I'll take that." She moved back behind the aetherscope and began operating the device once more. The realization hit Sora that if this did not go to plan, she and Lirren might never see each other again. Panic washed through her—is this how she wanted them to part?

"Darling," she said, "don't ever doubt that I lo—"

When an aetherscope casts a mirage, there is always a moment's lag (or so Lirren explained it). The operator presses down on the final switch, and then—a pause—as the illusion travels through the aether before landing in its intended place.

Sora knew she was in the pause. She knew by the indistinct streak of grey sky overhead and dark sea below. She also knew by the sensation of bilious sickness in her throat, something she had not felt since her first storms at sea.

There was just time to realize this when she found herself on the poop deck of the Elaran ship.

"—Vvv?"

She almost toppled over with disorientation, but had the sea legs to right herself and get on with it. The rival aetherscope was beside the stern rail to her right. Out to sea, six identical brigs were branching away in all directions from a single point—there was no way to tell which was the real *Cormorant*. A gangly young man in an Elaran uniform operated the aetherscope. He must have heard Sora's heavy landing, for he turned to face her with a puzzled expression.

Sora shoved him aside and lunged at the aetherscope. She swung the boarding axe and tore straight through the device's workings. Lenses shattered, brass fittings flew over the stern rail. The first stage of the plan was complete: the frigate could no longer hide behind a mirage.

"You're one of ours, I assume?" Sora asked the man. He nodded, looking incredulous. "Sorry about that. Had to be done. I'm going to rescue my mirager, you see."

"By yourself?!" His gaze darted past her and his expression turned grim: three Elaran officers tramped up the steps from the quarterdeck.

Sora climbed onto the stern rail and stood erect and compact. "Of course not!" She gestured quickly to the many *Cormorants*, whipping her hand back to keep it within Lirren's outline. "I'll be bringing one of those."

Two Elaran officers unsheathed their cutlasses, while a third raised his pistol.

The pistol issued a crack—but the sound was cut off.

Sora landed on the *Cormorant*'s quarterdeck, right on top of the steers-hand. The brig lurched to starboard as the combined weight of two people pushed on the wheel. Sora regained her feet, helping the bewildered steers-hand back to his post at the wheel.

She addressed the brig's astonished commander, a young first lieutenant.

"Apologies for my inelegant arrival. And apologies for commandeering your ship. You will have noticed a frigate appear from thin air about a mile off your port bow? I'm taking your crew to board it. Is that clear?"

The lieutenant stood to attention and saluted. "Absolutely, Commander."

The *Cormorant*'s crew did not match the enemy frigate's in numbers, but they were fresh and eager, their guns were loaded and ready, and they had the element of surprise in their favor. While the *Cormorant*'s crew slid up on the frigate's starboard, Lirren had arranged one of the mirages to mirror it, bearing the threat of boarding on the port side as well. The Elaran crew were in confused disarray as they began their defense. Sora left the main action to the *Cormorant*'s first lieutenant and wove through the chaos, using the axe to both deal out blows and parry them.

Sora hurried below decks to the ship's hold. With the axe, she tore at the locked doors of storage compartments, checking each in turn. The first five held provisions and tools. As she smashed a hole in the sixth door, she spotted a blue jacket.

"Darlett! Is that you?" She peered in. The blue-jacketed figure was sitting up in the corner.

"C-Commander?" One final blow and a hearty kick, and the hole was big enough to walk through. Darlett all but leapt into her arms. "H-how did you…"

"We can't hang about—the Elarans will be coming down here for powder and shot. Follow me."

Sora led him up to the gun deck, where she had to fight her way from one stairwell to the next, pushing through the blades and smoke in the cramped space. Darlett was an utter encumbrance. He clutched at her jacket and treated her as a shield, tugging her in front of him in panic when he perceived danger. Her smooth dodges became unwieldy lurches, and she took several heavy cuts to her arms, face, trunk. The axe was an unrefined weapon, but had a certain brute authority in these close quarters, knocking aside thin cutlasses and biting into incautious flesh.

She emerged onto the top deck bruised and bloodied, her uniform in shreds. There was a ferocious fight to starboard where the *Cormorant* was lashed as its crew battled the Elarans for control of the ship. Sora stuck to the port side, where the fighting was thin and the top-deck cannons stood idle, and dragged Darlett astern.

"Commander!" Darlett gestured to the *Cormorant*, its sails visible above the frigate's gunwale. "Is that one of our brigs? Surely we ought to board it?"

"No, Darlett, we're taking another way—step lively!"

The Elarans were putting up a fervent struggle against the Cormorant's crew. Sora nudged Darlett to the ship's side so she could put herself between him and the rest of the fighting. She held her boarding axe ready.

"Has the *Hardweather*'s boat come for us?" he asked.

"Not the boat. Too slow, too dangerous. There's no time to explain it, just follow my—"

"Commander, I don't appreciate being left in the dark—I *must* know where you're taking me!"

Sora ground her teeth. "Your commander has come to rescue you in person—do as I order! We're going where Miss Harter can see us and use the aetherscope to—"

Someone yelled in the Elarans' language above her head— Sora looked up, and only just dodged an Elaran top-hand dropping down from the rigging in an attempt to land on them. She took advantage of his fumbled landing to swing the axe straight into the back of his knee, cutting his tendons to bits.

Darlett crouched and cowered beside one of the unmanned guns. "Good *blazes*! Commander, you can't be serious— Harter's theory is lethal!"

"It works, Darlett! How do you think I got here? Get up on that gunwale. Avoid the rigging—there's a clear spot."

Darlett shook his head and clung to the frame of the gun.

"I'll be cut up like that fellow on the *Scallop*! I might as well stay here and be cut up by the Elarans!"

Sora paused. Did Lirren really need a good report from him anymore? The *Hardweather* was now full of witnesses who could attest that her method worked safely.

She bent down and, for the second time that day, grabbed him by the jacket, holding the axe's blade perilously close to his face.

"This isn't a polite invitation—do as you're told, or I'll have you flogged and report you to the admiralty for wanton insubordination and inferior mathematical skills. Climb up there!"

Darlett opened his mouth to retort, then seemed to think better of it. He was far from nimble, but he used the gun as a foothold to climb up as best he could. Escape was finally at hand.

Sora's glance darted between him and the fighting on the starboard side. The Elarans' energies were focused on the quarterdeck, mercifully. As she watched, a woman in a blue jacket broke off from the fight and dashed towards her.

"What news?" Sora cried. "Have we taken the ship?"

As if by way of reply, the woman drew two cutlasses—one from each hip. Sora barely had time to register that her breeches weren't white—they were green. The jacket was stolen. This was the lean Elaran who had nearly shot her aboard the *Hardweather*.

Sora had no time to draw her own cutlass. The Elaran came at her with both blades at once. The boarding axe could only parry one of them. The other bit into her shoulder, breaching her already ragged sleeves and slicing straight into flesh. The woman wielded both cutlasses while dodging Sora's attempted blows with a dancer's coordination. Injured and drained from acting as Darlett's shield, Sora raised the axe to parry one blade—and failed to evade the other. The Elaran brought a cutlass down upon the back of Sora's right hand, severing the tendons. She cried out in horror as the axe fell from her grasp. Her opponent pushed her up against the gunwale and pulled back one of the cutlasses, ready to thrust it into Sora's chest.

There was a blur of blue jacket at the edge of Sora's vision. An almighty snap rang out, and the woman was enveloped in a puff of smoke. As she fell backwards to the deck, Sora saw Darlett had fired a pistol straight into her side where he couldn't possibly miss. He promptly dropped it and flinched.

"I didn't use it when they took me!" he said, his voice high and strained. "I'm a scholar, not a—"

"That's abundantly clear, Darlett." She held up her blood-soaked right hand and winced in pain as she tried to flex it. None of her fingers moved. "Agh! I want to get off this damned ship *now*. Darlett, climb up and hold onto the mast-stay as best you can."

Darlett obeyed. With much huffing, he clambered into position on the gunwale and clung to the bundle of thick ropes that held the mainmast steady.

"You say Harter's method works, Commander?" Darlett's voice was still strained.

"Perfectly!" Sora climbed up after him, wheezing for breath. Darlett helped her up, and she leaned on him.

"How does this work?" he asked.

"Just stand compact and keep bloody still. She'll bring us over when she sees us. And don't forget, Darlett, I get no credit for this rescue. All the planning was down to Miss—"

"—Haaaugh!"

Sora landed back on the *Hardweather* in an uncontrolled fall. Around her, a gaggle of officers who were gathered on the poop deck applauded and whooped in delight. Sora struggled into a sitting position. She rested her injured hand on her leg, staining her white breeches red. It was dawning on her that she may never use it again, and would become another of those officers with a lifelong disablement and a corresponding nickname among the crew. She felt ill with pain, exhaustion and loss of blood, but also thrilled at Lirren's success—and at this ready batch of witnesses whose word could restore her reputation. Elevate it, indeed. Even an injury like this was a price she was willing to pay for such an outcome.

Darlett was next to her, examining each of his limbs in turn. They were all present and correct. He was clutching a bundle of severed rope from the Elaran ship—the mast-stays had evidently been caught in the outline.

Lirren shouldered her way through the assembled officers, grinning with triumph.

Sora looked up at her. "It worked!" she panted. "You mad genius!"

"That is the finest compliment I've ever—" Her face fell. "Your hand!" She hunkered next to Sora and whipped out her handkerchief to wrap the wound. Sora smiled at her.

"It was viciously attacked by an Elaran. Nothing to do with your wonderfully useful methods and theories. As I was saying, Darlett, all credit for your rescue goes to Miss Harter, who has now successfully flung people through the aether three times. Which is bound to change naval warfare forever, wouldn't you think?"

The assembled officers murmured in agreement. Lirren glared meaningfully at Darlett across her spectacles as she tied off the makeshift bandage. He cleared his throat.

"I suppose... I suppose the commander has something of a point."

Still panting, Sora clapped him on the back with her good hand, harder than was strictly necessary. "That's the spirit! The sort of point one might put in a report to the admiralty, I dare say?"

Darlett looked to Lirren again. "I... Well. I suppose, one occasionally underestimates... yes, and something of an apology is, as it were, perhaps—"

A raucous cheer from the ship's waist cut his words short. It spread in an instant to the officers, who turned to regard the Elaran ship. Sora followed their gazes —their own navy's flag was being hoisted by the *Cormorant's* crew.

"*Huzzah!* Another mirage ship for our side!" Sora made to stand, with Lirren's assistance. Lirren helped Darlett up as well, and they cheered together as they watched the flag reach the top.

When the jubilation subsided, Sora clapped Darlett's back again.

"Someone get this poor man a drop of grog. He's had a trying day. In fact—double grog rations for everyone, and triple for our miragers!"

The officers cheered their commander, then drifted into excited, chattering groups. Darlett was pulled aside to give his account of the story, and Sora and Lirren had a brief moment to themselves.

Lirren lifted Sora's newly bandaged hand to her lips and kissed it ever so delicately.

"If Darlett can bring himself to express his gushing gratitude on paper, I'll be able to stay in the navy after all. And aboard the *Hardweather*."

Sora smiled. "She's a good old tub, if you can put up with her commander."

Lirren looked her up and down. "I do wonder if a commander who can't keep her uniform intact can keep a ship afloat. But I'm open to persuasion."

Sora cocked an eyebrow. "Then may I begin persuading you over a drink in the mess?"

Lirren linked Sora's good arm and saluted, adding her charming half-grin as she made to rejoin the rest of the crew. "Aye aye, Commander!"

The Epic Fifth Wedding Anniversary of Zaynne the Barbarian and Tikka the Accountant

by *Elizabeth Davis*

Zaynne, daughter of glades and man, ferocious warrior blessed by the stormworn menhirs, who slew Urghal the Ghoul King, cradled a skull made out of rainbow petrified wood in her hands. The skull was carved from the heart of a world tree that had held up a long-forgotten cosmology. This heart was taken by the archmage Yipath, who then carved the skull and shaped the enchantments for his lover, carried in death into the Tomb of the Stone Pharaoh. It contained enough raw power to make any wizard worth his staff drool.

Zaynne knew it would be the perfect paperweight for Tikka, her ever-patient wife. She imagined it sitting proudly on the endless stacks of papers, drawing the jealousy of every other accountant in the office. Maybe even the jealousy of the lawyers and magistrates.

The years weighed lightly on Zaynne's shoulders, and she was still able to recount how she met Tikka with the same freshness that most people could remember yesterday. Actually, Zaynne couldn't remember yesterday that well. What with the multi-day bender from a drinking contest with giants, a concussion from a cave-in, and with the mummified guardian's mind-warping magic, the whole past week was pretty much shot.

Zaynne and Tikka's auspicious beginning had started with Zaynne's first dragon. Or more specifically, her first dragon hoard. Zaynne drove her wagon into town, the severed dragon head riding shotgun, and a mound of gold nearly falling out with each bump on the poorly paved road.... Among the cheering villagers and the awestruck children, there was Tikka. Standing calmly, quill pen swishing in her ledger, the only sign of excitement her fingers pushing her pince-nez up.

Looking at Tikka's carefully pressed purple robes and conical hat, Zaynne thought she was like the other officials: soft, easily startled, and unwilling to be late for lunch. When Tikka made her declaration of the Seven Queens' Windfall Tax—which could be paid in standard coin, equivalently appraised treasure, or through service to the clockwork crowns—Zaynne tried boasting, arguing, and even a few threats. Tikka did not waver, her face impassive as she patiently tapped her feather quill against her ledger until Zaynne ran out of steam. Only then did she speak up, simply stating that Zaynne should step away from the wagon until she finished her counting. Never had Zaynne—who had faced down the dragon Zathargyaxs the Wrathful Flame and the Cult of the Spiraled Squid—been so utterly defeated.

That was how Zaynne—with her armor all shined and furs all brushed—came to stand in front of Tikka's desk as her coworkers gaped. Which led to Zaynne carrying Tikka—clad in white and bright summer flowers—over a broom to a clapping and singing crowd. Still, this wasn't the time for reminiscing, Zaynne reminded herself as she picked up her feet.

This was the time for washing up and changing into her rarely used formal gown for an evening at the finest restaurant in the city of the Clay-Armed God. (Restaurants, Zaynne was led to believe, were just like taverns, meadhalls, and food stalls, but fancier because a restaurant was Elvish. Zaynne didn't really worry as long as there was wine.) More important than wine, for the first time in their five years of marriage, Zaynne would be on time. She was going to celebrate her anniversary right.

Zaynne began her ablutions by climbing the steep hill to the Tenebrae family's ancestral home, only a temperamental pegasus ride from the City of the Clay-Armed God or the Great City of the Sleeping Tortoise. It was a home she shared with Tikka's brother Tallin, Tikka's parents, and a whole host of children. (Nobody was sure where the children had come from, but everybody agreed that they belonged.) Not to forget the army of servants and field hands who made sure that rumors from the farthest farm made it to the Tenebrae House and that old covenants were upheld.

The sprawling stone and wood manor overlooked fields of waving grain, pegasusi pens, and shadow groves, and Zaynne felt short-lived relief to have returned. (Among other emotions. Zaynne still found it weird to call a house with four walls and a roof "home." Before marrying Tikka, the closest thing Zaynne had to a house was a mammoth-skin yurt. However, the Tenebrae Manor didn't smell when it rained, and the lawn was big enough that she could set up her yurt when she felt too confined—nights that Tikka would join her, light-footed and giggling like a girl escaping from her parents' watchful gaze.) Her relief was short-lived due to the smoke rising from the lawn of the Tenebrae House. The smoke was too voluminous to be a mere trash fire; its blackness was stained by bright sparks and it stank of magic.

No longer joy but fear and anger brought Zaynne to the porch of the Tenebrae House. Under the awnings, Tallin worked at his outside desk while Rosie practiced her chang harp. Tallin looked up from the thick stack of papers with a relieved smile and ink-stained face. "Thank the gods, big and small, that you arrived before I sent my letter off to the Adventurers' Guild. I still need to send off these letters to the Mage Guild and the Royal Guard. Really, the sort of things they let happen to non-adventurers these days..."

Zaynne got on with Tallin, who was something called a "gentleman scholar," boasting that his work had been published in both the *Royal Journal of Discovery* and *Mage Quarterly*. She appreciated that he didn't talk down to her and occasionally sent her on quests to help find something called a "thesis," but she did think that he should leave the family library more often.

He gave a deep sigh. "We haven't even been able to put the fire out. With the Druidic Garden Competition only a few weeks away, Mother has already begun composing her laments. Father is off trying to calm the pegasusi."

"What happened?"

Rosie broke her pained concentration and jumped up eagerly from the chang harp. With her clear voice, light fingers, and strong running legs, Rosie was considered a future Candidate for the Royal Bardic College. "It was a wizard. An actual wizard." She raised her hands, fingers open wide to show the extent of her excitement.

"I suspect he was actually a sorcerer, since he didn't have a staff." Tallin bent over, his quill scratching away.

"He appeared in a puff of blue smoke and set the lawn on fire! Then he stood there, in his dark cloak." Rosie drew her arms across her face, hiding herself behind an imaginary cloak. "And then... he called for Tikka!" She twisted her face into an imitation of Tikka's sternest expression. "So, Tikka came marching down, ready to do battle. And they argued. And argued, and their argument was actually really boring despite him being a wizard. But then, he wrapped his cloak around her and flew off like a giant bat—"

"Bats don't fly like that, they flap more. It was more like a flying manta ray."

This critique did little to abate Rosie's enthusiastic flapping before she pointed to the west, into the seawind. "He flew off that way!"

Zaynne already knew who it had been, glancing down at the still-burning mark—a three-eyed cobra. "Severus Severyn the Serpetine." Only one mage used the mark—mages take intellectual property theft very seriously.

"Wasn't he responsible for that zombie army earlier this year?" Tallin asked.

"Didn't he create the imp plague?" Rosie asked. "They were cute."

"Yes, and more! That snake in human skin has been a thorn in my side ever since I started adventuring. This must be his way of getting revenge for all the times I have upset his plans, wrecked his lair, and stolen his fine silverware. He's too much of a coward to face me directly!"

"Do you know where he might be?" Tallin asked.

"His lair is on the cursed Isle of Aha'Hal in the Fang Archipelago." With that, Zaynne tossed the anniversary skull onto Tallin's desk.

"Wait!" he called out before Zaynne could finish storming off. "The pegasusi are still too startled to be flown. Take the boat instead."

The *Octopus Bride* was a retired fishing boat, snuggled against the docks. The only voyages she had been on for years were nominal fishing trips with overstuffed sandwiches, flagons of ale, and the occasional caught fish. She woke with surprise when Zaynne jumped in and struck the tow rope, not even unfurling the sail or setting the rudder. The *Octopus Bride* was still blinking sleep away when Zaynne unshipped the oars and started rowing with all her might.

(It's a well-known fact that the greatest single source of non-magical energy is the rage of a barbarian. The Seven Queens and their clockwork crowns once tried to harness this energy for the good of the kingdom, not just for the despair of monsters and evil overlords. However, the queens and their crowns quickly learned that the vast quantities of ale needed, and the frequency of quarrels when barbarians gathered together, made the project impractical.)

The *Octopus Bride* was finally fully awake as she sailed at speeds undreamed of in her saltwater dreams. She sped past fishing boats that had been tall cedars back when the *Octopus Bride* was a working ship, their fisherman gasping, unsure if they saw an illusion or an actual boat. For the first time in her life, the *Octopus Bride* left behind her secluded blue bay for the greater sea's rollicking gray waters.

Zaynne brushed off the *Octopus Bride's* wide-eyed worry as they crossed into the whale's road, where even the seagulls refuse to fly and beg for food. Zaynne was oblivious to the sea-serpent coils that rolled under them, the hooves of the hippocampus, and even the steady, silent stare of a giant black umibōzu. Zaynne only had scorn as they rowed directly into the ocean-boiling showdown between Leviathan and Kraken, even as the *Octopus Bride* desperately tried to steer away. Zaynne paid no heed to the tentacles and tail crashing down.

The *Octopus Bride* despaired, closing her eyes, foreseeing a new life as driftwood. Instead of hearing the rending of wood and canvas, there were the two sharp thuds of Zaynne's oars hitting flesh, and the whiffing of air. The *Octopus Bride* hesitantly cracked open her eyes, only seeing the suddenly empty sea where Leviathan and Kraken had disappeared over the horizon. Zaynne, still rowing, didn't notice.

Zaynne was too busy ranting about Severus Severyn the Serpentine.

"That weaselly sack of bones! Any respectable sorcerer would've kidnapped me. Kidnapping my wife is an underhanded scheme befitting the lowest of the lowest of the rat empires, not even the most cruel lich would break the adventurers' code—"

Zaynne took no notice of the heralding rocky reef that encircled the cursed Isle of Aha'Hal. Three sirens—woman-headed and bird-bodied—stirred on their rocky perches, chirping as they warmed up their vocal cords while the *Octopus Bride* came closer.

"Come to us and listen," the black-haired oldest sang. "Come and learn the language of the birds, and the writing in the stars. Come to us and listen!"

"Come to us and listen," the brown-haired middle one sang. "Come and learn of where the gods hid diamonds before time, and where the gold flows like water. Come to us and listen!"

"Come to us and listen," the blonde-haired youngest sang. "Come, for we have men whose pecs are the size of your head and women who are even bigger. Come and listen to us!"

The eldest and the middle exchanged side glances while the youngest fluffed her feathers, filled with pride at her new lyrics.

Zaynne's boat came closer, and the sirens grew excited before the boat sailed on by, splashing them as Zaynne's words clouded the air. "When I get my hands on him, I will feed him his own pancreas tied with his own appendix—" Zaynne had a remarkable grasp of anatomy from years of killing—and being eaten by—monsters.

"Some people have no appreciation for our hard work," the eldest sniffed as she shook off the salt-water spray.

"My mermaid penpal talks about pirate ships and merchant vessels that pass by Shark Reef. We should move down there," said the youngest, with all the authority of years she did not have.

"We have sung at these rocks for generations—we will not give them up for some tropical fad," the oldest spoke, ruffling her feathers.

"Maybe we could move down there for the winter," the middle one suggested as they nestled into a familiar argument.

Hours later, Zaynne's boat beached itself upon the cursed Isle of Aha'Hal. The *Octopus Bride* warily watched the hooting swamp as Zaynne threw down the anchor. Zaynne gave no hesitation as she left the sandy beach behind, marching right into the dark depths of the swamp, her footsteps sploshing.

Giant crocodiles swam toward her, mosquito-spites sharpened their proboscis, and fanged birds of paradise swooped down, all eager for adventurer flesh. Even a napping basilisk awoke, watching the scene through its third eyelids.

Zaynne jumped on the convenient crocodiles, hopscotching from nose to nose so their surprised jaws snapped only on damp air. She swatted carelessly at mosquito-spites and fanged birds of paradise who dove too close, sending them careening into each other. And the whole time she continued her rant.

"He's the son of a toad and a she-dog. And not even a nice dog. A dog that has mange, rabies, and leprosy. So did the toad! And his grandfather wasn't just a leprous lamprey—"

The basilisk decided that this was a very nice patch of sunlight and there was no reason to leave it to deal with Zaynne over there.

As the wildlife scattered, monsters fled, and even the plants shrank back, Zaynne made her way to uplifted land: the Black Fortress that was the lair of Severus Severyn the Serpentine. A fortress surrounded by sheer walls of black volcanic glass, with only one gate. A gate with seven locks, which could only be unlocked by the seven keys of Grossd'mn, the Blasphemous Plaguewalker. Were that not formidable enough, the wall was guarded by an army of skeleton warriors, all shapes and sizes, from the diminutive dwarves to the hulking carapace of a kappa titan.

As Zaynne marched out of the swamp, the skeletons stopped lollygagging and straightened into intimidating force. A smaller —human-sized—one stepped forward, their prized helm shining in the weak sunlight. They held up one hand in the air. "Halt, trespasser!"

Zaynne stopped, both in foot and mouth, as concentration creased her forehead.

"These are the lands of the great and magnificent Severus Severyn the Serpentine. As you see, we are many and you are only one. Turn back—"

Zaynne charged. The skeleton herald drew their sword, ready to meet hers, but she jumped and landed on his head. The skeleton herald dropped their sword, flailing for a skull now stuck in their ribcage, as Zaynne flew through the air to catch the arm of an ogre skeleton. As it raised its limb to squish her with its other hand, she swung from the arm bone, landing on the upper thigh of the kappa titan. She quickly climbed over a massive hip, ducking safely inside the carapace. A look of discomfort—somehow—passed over its bony face. Giant hands dropped a house-sized battle fan, and slapped around the carapace, trying to dislodge the climbing barbarian. Zaynne steadily held on as the carapace shook, nimbly jumping from spine vertebrae to rib between earthquake strikes, before diving off the cervical bones to the other side of the wall.

The skeletons watched her, then gave a collective shrug. It was just their job to guard the wall, not what lay inside the wall. She wasn't their problem anymore. "She just jumped on Thorin," a skeletal warrior decked in rusted green laminar armor remarked. "Just jumped on him like he was a mushroom."

"My spine feels a bit funny," the kappa titan—Aku— complained, his hands soothing his mishandled carapace.

"Adventurers," the ogre skeleton snarled. Thorin mumbled something deep within his ribcage.

Zaynne swept crushed vegetative matter from her armor. Thankfully, a roll through the garden of belladonna, foxglove, larkspur, oleander, wolf's bane, and amanita mushrooms had broken her fall.

In front of her stood a twisting tower, its black spire piercing the heavens. Standing at the single metal door, a gargoyle made up of spiny skin, horned heads, and clawed feet tucked away a small paperback with a lurid cover. He reared to his full height as Zaynne marched forward, then boomed, "Those who wish to disturb the studies of the great and magnificent Severus Severyn the Serpentine must prove their strength in mind as well as brawn. In order to pass, you must answer all my riddles and find a riddle I cannot answer."

"Fine," Zaynne growled. "What's metal, two feet long, and hurts more going in than going out?"

The gargoyle nervously eyed the sword at Zaynne's side before giving a long sigh. "Look—me, Arthaxas the many-eyed, Lytle the squid, and Bob the lurker-in-the-darkness, we meet up for cards every week, and I got this thing going on with Cubie the Gelatinous Rhombus... We don't need to make things difficult for any of the others, which would happen if we don't have a fourth for euchre, or Cubie decides to go full digestive on whoever is left. Why don't you do us all a favor and take the back stairs up to the big guy?" With a single wave of his claw, a smaller door appeared on the side of the tower, expertly disguised with signs advertising that it was not a door.

Zaynne gave him a stern nod before climbing the stairs.

Climbing the stairs, even the back stairs, of a magic tower is an incredible experience. Magic energy sparked over Zaynne's head; the stairs rumbled and shook. Books, scrolls, and eldritch abominations flew up and down, carried by the wails of apprentices. Vistas to other worlds opened, showing desolate landscapes and luscious courts. At some landings reality grew weak, abstract, squamous, cubist, or sometimes just fuzzy. Zaynne marched through all of this—also past ancient libraries, abominable laboratories, and abundant store rooms—with nary a glance. She only stopped long enough to kick open the door at the top, the one marked "private—do not enter."

Severus Severyn the Serpentine's inner sanctum was a vast room, covered in layers of plush carpets, walls hosting elaborate tapestries, and carefully placed sculptured lamps meant to serve as conversation pieces—all of it dominated by Severus Severyn the Serpentine, now transformed into a giant snake with Tikka in his coils. (Turning into a giant snake never helps, but Severus Severyn the Serpentine was a traditionalist.)

"You—a mere mortal—think that you can command me, a powerful immortal sssorcerer?" Severus Severyn the Serpentine ominously hissed down at Tikka.

Tikka's expression was that of implacable patience, but Zaynne could tell she was irritated. Her pince-nez had slid down from its normal spot.

"You get your hands-limbs-tail off my wife!" Zaynne interrupted.

Severus Severyn the Serpentine jerked his head to look at the intruder. "What foolish sssimpleton intrudesss upon usss?"

Zaynne raised a fist in the air and squared her shoulders while shouting, "I'm Zaynne the Barbarian, who defeated your army summoned from Mitra's meteor, who stopped your Grand Ritual of the Two Moons—"

"Oh, one of you," he hissed dismissively. "I will deal with your inconsequential grievancesss in turn."

"She is also my wife," Tikka added, "since you weren't listening the first time."

"Wife? People ssstill do sssuch thingsss?" He glanced at the sword at Zaynne's side.

"Wait, if you didn't kidnap Tikka to get revenge on me, then why did you kidnap her?" Confusion broke through her anger.

"For possessing the temerity to audit my taxesss!" he roared.

"We wouldn't have audited them if you had done them correctly," Tikka primly remarked.

"According to you sssssluggard gnashnabsss, how did I mishandle my taxesss?" He lifted Tikka closer to his giant mouth.

"First of all, you claimed your minions as dependents when they should be listed as employees—"

"Balderdash! I don't pay them. I give them ssshelter, sssubstance, and sssalutory ssservice, I well-nigh rear them!" His hood flared up, fangs dripping.

"All that can be listed as pay using the Employment Law tome—"

"Sssilence! You diminutive zounderkitesss should be jubilant that I bothered to sssend you wherewithal at all! Your infuriating and labyrinthine sssystem ssserves a kingdom I owe naught!"

"Actually, you used the kingdom's highways during your zombie invasion, you use the services of the kingdom's coast guard to keep this island safe from pirates and marauders, and the kingdom's mail service comes out every week—which you used to send in your faulty tax filing." Tikka freed an arm from the coils to push up her pince-nez.

"Enough!" he spat.

"I would suggest listening to the accountant," Zaynne threatened.

Severus Severyn the Serpentine's head drooped. His hood folded and fangs retracted. "You ponderousss cumberworldsss impetrate too much—how is any vainglorousss sssorcerer expected to persist in this eon?"

"My firm helps clients with filing taxes, and specializes in saving them money on their tax returns." Tikka's hand twitched, trying to hold a quill that wasn't there.

"Your firm could assist me?" He unraveled his tail from around Tikka.

"Yes. I have several suggestions for you." Tikka didn't pause her spiel as she regained her footing. "How long have you been a wizard?"

"I was begat before your mewling ancestors even mastered the sssparks of magic." He rose to the height of the roof, scales turning from black to vibrant purple.

"So, more than one hundred years?" From under her robe, Tikka pulled a few thin sheets of parchment and her back-up quill, then used Severus Severyn the Serpentine's scaly body as a writing surface.

"Thousandsss!" he hissed, posing for all to admire his grandeur.

"That means you are old enough to file for the heritage tax credit for places, objects, or people of significant cultural value." Tikka's quill swished as she continued to talk. "Are you planning on building any more structures on this island?

"I fail to fathom, sssspindly flibbertigibbet." His scales dulled, and he tried unsuccessfully to pull his tail away from Tikka, finding nowhere to escape.

"I see that this island is part of the Fang Archipelago. Would I be correct in assuming that it contains basilisks?"

"Most assuredly it's ssswarming with those lepidote lususss naturaesss," he boasted. Zaynne wondered if some of those squawks in the swamp were her stepping on one.

"If you aren't planning to expand your fortress, you could turn the rest of the island into an environmental haven for basilisks, and thus receive a refund on your property taxes."

"I remember when Sssaint Ulric championed hisss crusade against the Basilisk Kingsss," he hissed wistfully, eyes staring off into the distance.

"I suspect those annual celebrations of his victory are the reason they are now endangered," Tikka said dryly, dragging Severus Severyn the Serpentine back to reality. "That woman who scryed on your crystal ball earlier—Enchantress of Amar?"

"Why do you inquire, you insensate gobermouch?"

"If your relationship with her is long-term, you may want to consider marriage to get the family tax credit."

"Our amalgamation is rife with treachery, carnality, and acrimony. No cleric would enslave our ssstygian hearts in pietistic matrimony." He flared his hood again, scales bright red.

"You don't need a cleric ceremony—just a civil one for the tax credits. As long as you are both of age and willing, the state will marry you."

"What? The world has transfigured immeasurably..." His hood folded again, and his scales faded to a light pink.

"Of course, these are only my initial suggestions." For the first time, Tikka broke eye contact. She rummaged around in her pockets and produced a small parchment card. "For a full consultation, please contact the address below to schedule. Note that we will be billing at our standard rate."

"Ssstandard rate! You presumptuousss—"

There was a *shwink* as Zaynne drew her sword.

Severus Severyn the Serpentine looked at her nervously. "Ssstandard rate accepted. Our adjudication is sssatisfactory." With that, he turned his scaly back, letting Zaynne and Tikka know that the meeting was over.

They were halfway down the stairs before Zaynne's fuming started to idle, and Tikka was able to relax her face enough to form normal expressions.

"Thanks for coming for me," Tikka softly said, taking Zaynne's arm while stepping over a family of yellow tarantulas. "I may have been stuck listening to him for days before he calmed down enough to see reason."

"I will always come for you," Zaynne reassured, squeezing Tikka's arm. "I'm just sad that you won't be getting to go to the restaurant tonight."

"Oh, it's fine," Tikka said dismissively, waving with her free hand. "The reservation is for two days from now."

"What? But you told me it was today." Zaynne searched her holey memory, felt at least somewhat sure that what she said was true.

"Yes, because you've never been on time for our anniversary, dearest. Last year, you got carried away by the wind demons, and the year before that, you were recruited by the Seven Queens and their clockwork crowns to fight against the Northern giants. The year before that—"

"Hey! I made it on time our first year."

"You were literally dropped on our roof by a roc." Tikka gave her a gentle smile, easing Zaynne's wounded pride. "After all these years, I'm still learning how to accommodate your occupation. I do it because I love you." Tikka gave a contented sigh.

Zaynne looked forward to the evening: berating a gargoyle into giving them a ride to the boat, Tikka soothing the boat as Zaynne pulled up the anchor, and watching the stars as the *Octopus Bride* took them home. Not that bad of an anniversary, all things considered.

The Parnassian Courante
by Claire Bartlett

The tournament began on the first day of high summer. Sunlight trickled like honey through the long windows of the Vane Hall, leaving long, glowing strips on the bonewood floor. Shadows merged in greeting, and court shoes clicked and shuffled. The hall was filling fast, and murmured voices swelled into a river of speculation: who would be the first to try for the princess's hand, and did he have a lesser or greater chance of winning than the man who came after?

People were calling it the succession tournament, the marriage game, the princess duels. Astrid called it horrible. And she got a front-row seat.

Her stomach clenched like a fist and her nerves jumped whenever she looked over to the stage. It was a low, wooden platform, with a raised dais for the king's throne at one end. At the other, a young man rolled his arms, breezily unconcerned. Agmund, the oldest—and largest—of the Birk family. He was one-sixteenth giant and it showed in his eight-foot frame, his colorless hair and jutting cheekbones, the hands that held a fencing sword the size of an actual fencepost. Astrid compared her missing fingers with his whole left hand and felt a pang of envy. Perhaps they shared common ancestors, but there was a man who never had to choose between selling himself and freezing to death in one of Jotunheim's snowstorms.

King Olve beckoned his daughter to him and she reluctantly came. He clapped her on the back and whatever he said made her roll her cornflower-blue eyes and smile a grim, hard smile. The feud between King Olve and his daughter was infamous. She'd broken an engagement with the Aska family when she was twelve, and she'd refused to reconsider or take another suitor. She'd told her father in private that she wanted girls, not boys, but while the law of the land did not forbid two women to marry, Olve seemed disinclined to allow it. Heirs, he complained. Alliances. Suitable matches. Their arguments became more heated, until Nik made the challenge: anyone who could defeat her in single combat could marry her. They'd shaken hands, arranged the tournament, and now people flooded in from all areas of Jotunheim and beyond, ready to try their skill.

Astrid forced herself to stop looking at Nik and focus on the court around her. She'd been selected as a student scribe for the tournament, and she had to keep her professors impressed if she wanted to keep the assignment... and her scholarship. It was a two-tiered task: aloud, most people talked of petty nothings like the weather or the evening's festivities, but their bodies spoke a different language. They wore flowers and colors to support their preferred candidates, and fans fluttered in argument over who had what kind of chance. Astrid's pen flowed over her paper, documenting all she saw with broad sweeps and comforting rasps, until a short trumpet blast made her start and squiggle ink across the page. She stifled an urge to curse like Nik would have done and looked up as King Olve took his throne.

The throne was a bonewood chair carved intricately with a scene of Jotunheim's giants of old locked in battle with a brigade of men. Olve sat just over a giant's back in a courtly assertion of dominance. He and his daughter shared red-gold hair, copper skin, and sharp noses. But his eyes were dark and calculating, while hers had always been warm and ready to smile. And when he spoke, his voice scratched, not at all like her melodious tone.

"Anyone who knows my daughter Nikhilde has seen her strong will," the king said. Astrid bit her lip. *Strong will* was an understatement. "She exercises it in all she does, and so it would be foolish to make an exception for her marriage, no?" He laughed. The court followed. In his corner, Agmund smirked, but Nik said nothing. Her fingers fluttered as though exercising an invisible flute. "And so, the game! Any man who can defeat my daughter in combat may claim the right to marry her. He need not be of royal blood or high standing, or even of the first five families. He may be as rich or as poor as any other man in the kingdom. But the losers pay—a thousand daler per match."

Thus ensuring that nobody poor could enter, Astrid thought bitterly. Olve's steward announced Agmund as the first challenger, and he and Nik bowed to each other. "Your weapon of choice?" the steward said, though everyone already knew the answer.

"Fencing foil." Agmund was a celebrated champion.

Nik nodded curtly. She wouldn't have expected anything else. She took her foil from the fencing master, and they faced off.

"First to draw blood," the king pronounced, and brought his hand down in a decisive chop. Astrid's own right hand clenched around her skirt.

Agmund leapt forward, all grace and speed and unbelievable reach. Nik ducked easily under his arm and slashed up in a move that made the assembly catch their collective breath. He parried, stepped within her guard, forced her back. Their foils flashed like silver whips.

Nik bared her teeth as she turned his blows aside, and Astrid could see how her arm trembled each time their foils met. He was far stronger than she. All the same, she managed to swipe at him again and he only avoided her by leaping back to the edge of the stage. He blew a kiss at her, then lunged.

He has some trick up his sleeve, Astrid thought.

But if he did, he didn't have the chance to use it. His puckered lips widened in a snarl of pain, and Nik skipped nimbly backward, bringing her foil up. The tip glistened darkly.

Slightly disappointed applause broke out around the hall. Astrid bit her lip again to keep from smiling.

For the first time, Nik's eyes slid to hers. The corner of her mouth twitched. *See?* she seemed to be saying. But when she opened her mouth, she said, "Who's next?"

Astrid first met Nik three years prior, in the basement of the Elfin Crown. It had been a classic autumn day in Jotunheim, all howling winds and sleet that would turn the night streets to ice, and both her clothes and her research notes were soaked. Contrary to popular belief, part-giants were not immune to Jotunheim's weather, so she set up at the circular table in the corner with a glass of wine and a couple of extra candles to try to dry everything out a little.

She was working on a paper for a student conference. *From War to Seduction: the Evolution of Courtly Dance.* She didn't notice Nik until she heard a sharp, "Oh." Nik stood in front of her, peeling off soaking layers to reveal a loose black shirt and leather trousers. Despite the gloom of the basement, her skin glowed from long hours of exercise in the sun. Her eyes were as bright as the sky, her nose crooked from some fight she lost long ago. Back then she had long hair, and it hung in a copper braid over one shoulder. She'd never been good at schooling her expression, and her full mouth was twisted in amusement or annoyance. Behind her stood her manservant, who was most definitely on the *annoyance* side. "We were told this table was free."

Astrid resisted the urge to jerk her partially amputated hand under the table. "I—my apologies," she stammered. She knew how to address the princess of Jotunheim in court—and her manservant—but the princess was clearly trying not to be recognized, and her eyes were so blue, and she looked so puzzled that Astrid didn't know which manners were best. Her eyes lingered on the hollow at Nik's throat.

Nik stared. Astrid stared. Behind those blue eyes, suspicion kindled. Finally Nik said, "If you pretend you don't know me, I'll buy you the most expensive wine you'll ever taste in your life."

Astrid scooted over and let Nik drop onto the bench beside her. Warmth flushed over that side, as though Nik carried a sun in her belt pouch. Nik nodded to the manservant, who shot Astrid a black look and disappeared upstairs. Astrid pretended to look through her notes, though they seemed slick and uncooperative in her hands. Nik smelled like wildflowers and sweat. And she was looking at her.

"I've seen you before," Nik said.

Astrid's tongue stuck to the top of her mouth and nothing she did could unstick it. The Princess Nikhilde had always seemed so far away at court, so bright and charming and ready to laugh with her friends and acquaintances—the sort of people Astrid could never hope to stand among as equal. And now Nik was here, turning that bright look on her, turning her mouth up like she was ready to be charmed. Her hair looked burnished in the candlelight, the sort of color Astrid longed to see on a bolt of silk. "You've been at court," Nik guessed.

Astrid nodded. At court she would have curtsied and presented herself, as though she had any names or titles worth offering. But if Nik wanted to be at court, she'd be there, so Astrid said thickly, "I study. Courtly etiquette. And, um. Non-verbal court language." Her tongue fumbled on *nonverbal*. Those blue eyes were wide, amused, brimming with some kind of mischief, and entirely focused on *her*. How was she supposed to think about anything else?

"You're not one of the first five families?" Nik said.

Astrid was tempted to laugh, but she'd have to force it and it'd come out bitter and uncomfortable. "Just a student," she replied.

The manservant reappeared with a black glass bottle and poured bright orange wine into two glasses. As he slid them across the table, Astrid did not miss the warning look he gave his mistress, slightly aggrieved with his head tilted toward Astrid. Nik only smiled, showing off lovely, even teeth.

"And you study… court language."

"Nonverbal court language," Astrid corrected before she could stop herself. Heat flushed her cheeks, but Nik didn't seem to mind the contradiction. "Mostly fan language. And flower language."

Nik took a sip of wine. "Fan language is mostly gossip, isn't it?"

Astrid felt a small sting at the words. They always came with an unspoken question: *why?* Why study something so unabashedly feminine, so synonymous with frivolity and pointlessness? Why not study something useful, like which kingdoms went to war five hundred years ago because two kings couldn't settle who had the larger prick in a more civilized manner?

But she wasn't about to lecture Jotunheim's princess on women's standing in the world. The princess already knew. She was famous for picking up every martial art for which she could find a tutor, and she'd risen to the rank of captain in the Jotun high guard. She wore her ceremonial uniform at court and had dueled more than one nobleman over a lady's honor. So Astrid said, "It's quite intricate, actually."

"Oh?" Nik raised an eyebrow.

Astrid took the invitation for what it was. "Fan language acts more like a living language than almost any other kind of nonverbal communication. It has grammar, clauses, loan phrases—" She stopped. Nik looked baffled. She tried changing tactics. "Ladies used to put bronze edges on their fans, you know? As a defense against anyone who got too intimate."

"Ha!" Nik took a sip of wine. "I know a few ladies who could have used that." She gave Astrid a sidelong look. "But I suppose we're more civilized now." She glanced at Astrid's belongings, scattered across the table. "You don't have a fan."

"Do I need one?" Astrid said.

Nik smiled. "That entirely depends on your definition of *too intimate*."

She should be studying. She should be finishing her paper, or sketching her dress design for court approval, or practicing a particularly complicated courante. Instead she cupped her face with one hand, writing a new paper in her mind: *Courtly Flirtation Outside of the Court.* She was, after all, being handed a delightful research opportunity.

Nik defeated six men on the tournament's first day, though not every one was as quick a fight as Agmund Birk. After each one, her eyes met Astrid's and she smiled as if to say, *easy*. The fan language whipped around the room, almost too fast for Astrid's hand to copy it down. The court was divided—the five families had each put forth a contestant, to no avail. It irritated them that their power, influence, and nobility would win them nothing. On the other hand, they greatly enjoyed seeing their rivals' sons brought low. The spectacle entertained them. And when Nik faced off against an outsider—some foreign count who came to try his luck—everyone took pride in the way she disarmed him and nicked him on his solid chin.

Olve was more pleased than any of them. He'd just seen his treasury grow by six thousand daler, and Astrid wondered whether he wanted his daughter to lose at all.

When the tournament adjourned for the day, Astrid handed her notes to the sour-faced steward and began to circulate. This was the second part of her job: observe the court, and make a further report at the end of the night. Her university scholarship required that she spend twenty hours at court per week and maintain appropriate scholarly and courtly conduct.

She'd never found it difficult to do her job before. But as she moved among the crowd, her head filled with bitterness and her heart with ache. She recorded each argument and wager and tried to push down her feelings of hopelessness. A half-wild idea had formed in her mind when Nik first announced the competition: to pick up a sword and try her own hand. But Astrid had never been one for combat, and it would be obvious if Nik threw the match. And Astrid had no money to pay the thousand-daler loser's fee—at least, not unless she sold something. She ran her fingers over the scar on her left hand. She'd gone down that road once, and she'd vowed never again.

The musicians struck up a Parnassian courante, and her feet drew her towards the floor. Dancing had always been easy for her, and she never lacked for partners. Now she agreed to the first Aska cousin who asked.

The courante was a little like a competition itself—he tried to "capture" her by taking her hand or elbow or waist to draw her into the dance, and she tried to evade him. Her fan felt like an extension of her arm and she snapped it open just as he reached for her fingers. She twirled one direction when he swept in toward her waist from the other, used her fan as a shield and closed it in time to push his wrist up so she could turn under. The dance was fast, but Astrid didn't falter. She knew the steps like she knew her own name.

They ended the dance pink-faced and smiling. The Aska cousin conceded with grace, and Astrid was back in the real world. Back with the fine wines and confections and endless speculation of the party.

She retreated to the back of the hall and opened the door to the library. She just needed a moment. She could collect herself, steel her heart to the endless gossip, and prepare to do her job. But as soon as she pulled the door closed, fingers wrapped around her wrist.

She recognized the suntanned hand, and she let Nik turn her gently around. "I knew you'd come in here," Nik said. She'd lit just enough candles to see by, enough to set her hair dancing with gold. A tongue of light flicked over one cheekbone, and her blue eyes seemed like dark ocean pools.

"Maybe I came to get a quote," Astrid said. Nik was still dressed in her tournament clothes, and the smell of her set Astrid's head spinning. "To hear what the great princess has to say of her victories."

"They were nothing. As long as you were sitting in the front row." Nik cupped her cheek. Her voice was low and rich and tinged with sadness.

Their lips met gently at first, but Astrid could taste Nik's desperation, and she had a fair share of her own. She let Nik press her against the door.

"You had the punch." Nik smiled against her mouth.

"Two cups." Strawberry was her favorite, though Nik hated it.

"Good." Nik planted a string of kisses from the edge of her jaw down her neck. "I ordered it for you."

Astrid choked on her laugh. The wife she wanted made sure Astrid got strawberry punch at *her* parties. "What did you drink, then?"

"Water. I can't be hungover tomorrow." She drew back, considering Astrid's mouth. "It's bad for the concentration."

Astrid put a hand on her chest as she tried to lean in again. Nik had always been determined, single-minded, stubborn. It had been endearing when she tried to teach Astrid to fence; funny when Astrid tried to teach her to dance. Now the inch of air between them was thick with named longing and unnamed despair. Nik couldn't stubborn her way out of this predicament, not forever. "Don't you think we should talk?" Astrid whispered.

Nik swallowed. She looked so soft, from the down on her cheek to her wounded expression. "Come up to me. When you're finished working. Then we'll talk."

They wouldn't talk, Astrid knew that, but she said, "Okay," against Nik's mouth as she leaned in for one last hard kiss. She'd never been able to refuse Nik anything.

Nik's rooms grew cold as the fire died down, and they snuggled together under her quilt. Outside, the classic Jotun winds howled, sweeping away the warmth of the day and turning dew to ice on the grass. Astrid fought off drowsiness, skimming her fingers over the crest of Nik's bare hip and down her thigh. She wanted to bury her head in Nik's shoulder and sleep, wake up famished in the middle of the night and let Nik order them a grand feast while she finished her notes or sewed. But tomorrow brought more competition, and if Nik lost then this was their last chance together. Astrid took a deep breath and forced her words out from around the lump in her throat. "We can't do this once you're married."

"Why not?" Nik's fingers ran gently along the seam of Astrid's left hand, where her last three fingers had been severed by a white-hot mage knife. Nik's voice turned bitter. "I'm sure my husband will have his share of indiscretions. Though I suppose I wouldn't blame him."

Astrid felt a slice through her heart. The lump in her throat grew. It was so hard to talk. "*I* can't do this after you're married." Because the thought of dancing around some man, of being the dirty secret and never the proudly displayed wife—she'd rather cut it all short now, finish her education and get a court placement somewhere else. Nurse her broken heart and start over.

Nik stilled, and the silence was heavy and stifling and horrible. Only her fingers still moved, back and forth across the line of Astrid's scar. "I meant what I said," she whispered at last.

They'd fought before the contest was announced. Nik had offered to renounce everything and run away. To stop being royalty and just be Nik. She thought Astrid was worth giving it all up.

Except she didn't know what it was like to be penniless. She'd never had hunger pangs so fierce she thought she'd vomit. She'd never gotten a meal only because her mother had given up her own. She'd never gone to the mages and asked to be tested, to see how thick her giant blood was, to see if she could sell off pieces of herself. But Astrid had. She'd watched her mother go back again and again—giving up her foot, then her shin, then her thigh. Her bones had been turned into beads and her blood lent potency to elixirs. Her muscles went to animal feed, and every time Astrid saw the ten-foot oxen or the king's giant warhounds, she wondered. She wondered if she'd recognize her mother in the animals that ate her.

Astrid's mother had put her little girl's future above everything. She'd sold off almost half her body before the procedure went wrong and she died of gangrene, and she spent that money on as nice an education as she could buy—nice enough that Astrid won a scholarship to the university and a sure place at court. All Astrid had had to do was dry her tears and sell the last three fingers on her left hand to buy passage and a room. And if she ran away with Nik, it would be for nothing. Her mother's sacrifices and her own accomplishments. Perhaps she could get a job assisting some town scribe, but without a letter of reference she'd be working for pennies, lucky to get more money than she used in a month.

"Everyone wants mercenaries," Nik said, as if she'd read Astrid's mind.

"And mercenaries don't get breaks and hot baths, or fights to first blood."

"I'd provide for you—" Nik said.

Astrid's bitter laugh was far too loud in the silent room. "My father was a mercenary. Look how well he provided for us. Died mercenarying somewhere far away, and we never even got his last month's wages."

"Well, what do you want?" Nik pushed herself halfway up. Her red fringe fell over her eyes and Astrid resisted the urge to brush it back. She didn't want to see the anger and hurt there. "I don't want to give up on you. Is that so bad? Is that so foolish?"

Yes, Astrid wanted to cry. Because she'd known from that night in the Elfin Crown, she'd known from the moment Nik's lips first touched hers: all this was doomed to fail. She'd never expected her warrior princess to love her. And now the invisible knife twisted in her heart whenever she thought of Nik, smelling of sweat and leather, with a crown on her head and a consort that wasn't Astrid.

Her face was wet, and her throat was choked off. She didn't dare breathe, because if she breathed she'd sniffle, and then Nik would know she was crying. "I didn't bring you here to fight," Nik said into the long silence. "I wanted…" She flopped back on the bed. "I don't know what I wanted."

She wanted everything to be different.

Me too, Astrid thought.

Astrid slipped out of bed as summer light threaded gold and pink across the sky. She gave a sleeping Nik one regretful kiss, then hurried back to her university rooms before anyone could catch her sneaking out in yesterday's dress. She couldn't do much about the puffiness under her eyes except hope that the cold morning air would reduce it a bit. All the same, she got an affronted look from the king's steward as he greeted her and sent her to her station at the front of the temporary stage. She resisted the urge to check the front of her dress for stains as she set out her materials.

A pin fell out of her hair and into the inkwell. She'd forgotten to rebraid it. No wonder the steward had sneered. Professionals looked like their servants had spent hours on their appearance, not like they'd barely had time to wash and dress.

The second round of the tournament was announced, and the whispers began almost immediately. Six members of the five families were eager to try their hand for the kingship today. As the first candidate was announced Nik caught Astrid's eye and twisted her mouth in derision. *Don't be cocky*, Astrid pleaded silently. But she'd never known Nik to be anything else. Nik ran a hand through her hair and selected her opponent's weapon of choice, knives.

He'd obviously hoped to catch her off guard. As soon as the match began he flung a knife with sharp precision. Nik dodged it easily and slid within his range, almost lazily slashing her own knife across his arm. He left the stage sulking.

The next, who had the paleness but not the stature of a giant, wanted to duel with quarterstaves. They sprang back and forth like dancers, staves clacking against each other in an agitated beat. Nik had more training with pointy things, as Astrid liked to call them, but her feet moved swift and sure. He gave her a good jab in the ribs that elicited gasps from the crowd and nearly stopped the match—but Nik grimaced and swept her staff around, knocking him off his feet and letting him crack his head painfully on the floor. She jabbed his nose with the end of her staff and he got up, blood trickling.

After Nik's third victory the tournament was paused for punch and refreshments. Astrid slipped into the library and rebraided her crown, sticking in her hair pins like vengeful little swords of their own. She ran last night's conversation through her head, over and over, trying to turn it to a different outcome.

Nik couldn't possibly want to abandon the throne. She didn't know what it meant. She was just making a grand gesture—and now she felt rebuffed that Astrid wouldn't return it. Maybe she feared that Astrid only loved her *because* she was a princess. In which case, the best way to prove Nik wrong would be with a grand gesture of her own. But what?

Astrid winced as she stuck a pin too vigorously and too close to her scalp. Maybe she could duel Nik with hairpins. Or ink-wells. If she got in a lucky shot, she could hit Nik's beautiful nose and bloody it the way Nik had bloodied the suitor with the quarterstaff. Or maybe she could sneak red ink into the ink-well, and make it *look* like blood—

She sighed. Her fantasies were running away with her, and fantasies wouldn't provide solutions. Perhaps what she should really do was appeal to Nik's father, use the rhetoric her professors had praised to convince him to stop the tournament. He'd never let her marry Nik, but at least Nik could marry for love. But he'd never been inclined to entertain Nik's impassioned pleas to choose a woman before. *It's a phase. You need children. Don't be absurd.* Words she'd hurled against the walls of her room while Astrid tried to comfort her.

He could be tricked, perhaps. Kings didn't like to lose face, and if she could win the public to her side... but how? Short of drawing a sword and leaping into the ring herself, anything she did would be seen as an undermining tactic.

She thought about it as she recorded the matches and the audience, noting down who was most disappointed—and who most relieved—when a candidate traipsed off the stage, sweating and swearing under his breath. She stopped looking at Nik, even though she could feel Nik's gaze, like a brand, every time she won a fight. *I'm doing this for you.* Postponing marriage because every extra night was one they could spend together. A grand gesture Astrid wanted to repay but didn't know how.

As the five families quieted their rage, the festivities were announced and the court moved to the Merchants' Hall, where refreshments had been laid on fine bonewood tables. Nik waited until the most eminent lords and ladies had been served, then slipped into line in front of Astrid.

"Last chance," she murmured as she took a piece of cheese with a lump of jam on it.

"I beg your pardon, Your Highness. Last chance for what?" Astrid asked, carefully polite in case anyone was listening.

"You know what." Nik moved away, and Astrid followed. She kept her face composed, opening her scribe's book as though she were still working. Nik pressed gingerly on the side that had taken the quarterstaff blow. Her red-gold hair stuck sweaty to her forehead. "I can't win forever. Every day risks... everything." Her blue eyes filled with pain.

She wasn't looking for a grand gesture. She was looking for a way out. A way to escape forced marriage and everything that came with it.

"I want to," Astrid whispered, worrying her lower lip between her teeth and looking down at the scribe's book in her hands. "I'm thinking."

"About what?" Nik asked.

She never got her answer. The music began and Felag Eik asked Astrid for a dance. As she allowed him to lead her to the floor, she glanced back at Nik. Nik's mouth was a thin slash, her eyes going hollow. As if her faith was being sapped from her. Perhaps it was no more than Astrid deserved. But she remembered the constant ache of hunger, and she looked at the space where her sold fingers once sat, and she tried to ignore the stab in her chest.

In addition to being piqued that he'd lost his axe-fight earlier that day, Felag Eik was utterly talentless at dancing. He had the size of Agmund Birk, but lacked the grace. He stepped on her toes with a muttered apology as the roundel started up, then turned in the wrong direction and nearly hit Lady Embla in the chest. Astrid had never been plagued by so incompetent a dance partner. *Except Nik,* she thought with a bitter twist of her heart. *And at least she had the grace to look embarrassed—*

Astrid stumbled into Felag. She knew what she wanted to do. And perhaps it would get her fined a thousand daler she didn't have, but it was a grand enough gesture. And maybe, *maybe* it could get them what they wanted.

On the third day of the tournament, Astrid dressed in the best dress she owned, a wine-red thing with capped sleeves and fine lace across the bodice. Her skirt was full but fluid and her fan was of a rich, red, heavy silk, tipped with bronze. She put her hair not in the semi-practical braid crown, but piled upon her head in the tradition of grander ladies. When she looked at herself in her speckled mirror, she saw a fraud. The sort of woman who dressed wealthier than she was to catch a rich man's eye. *But isn't that what you're after?* she thought. *Minus the man, of course.* Besides, if she succeeded, she'd be facing this feeling every day. She might as well get used to it.

She received a few surprised looks for her appearance, though not as many as she'd feared. Plenty of court women were dressed more opulently and no one had time to look at a scribe with no family name. The king's steward frowned, but it was less severe than the look he'd given her yesterday. She willed the knot in her stomach to loosen as she took her place and set out her materials. She couldn't afford to be sick all over her gown.

In the light of day this felt like a much more foolish proposition than it had last night.

She glanced at Nik, who was pulling on leather gloves, her face resolute. Nik didn't look to her. She stifled a pang. *Just don't give up today.*

Nik's first suitor was a third or fourth Embla cousin, who'd chosen the broad sword as his weapon. His well-muscled stature caused a flurry around the room as people assessed his chances. He was surprisingly swift, too, darting forward almost before Nik got her guard up and forcing her to make an awkward pirouette to avoid getting impaled in the arm. When she tried to retaliate he batted her sword aside with lazy confidence. He was much stronger than Nik, and he knew it. Astrid smoothed one hand over her dress as she tried to keep her other from shaking against her pen. Around the room, fans slid open and shut in appreciation. He pressed his attack in a series of swings that made Nik's arm shake and Astrid's ears ring. Nik kept conceding ground, backing up until she reached the edge of the stage. Her teeth were bared, though in anger or in concentration Astrid couldn't say.

Embla smiled wide. But his lazy arrogance was his undoing. Nik feinted left, right, then dodged left. His sloppy footwork caused him to stumble, and Nik's sword flashed across his wrist. He shouted a curse and his sword fell to the ground. A few fat drops of blood spattered around it.

Nik pinned her hair out of her eyes and took her weapons master's handkerchief. "Next?" She smiled, a sun of a smile, a smile that said no one could touch her. But she would still not look at Astrid.

Her victory seemed to dishearten the next two young men, who were nervous from the start and easily defeated. Her anger was radiant. As though she'd given up on Astrid and now all she had left to fight for was herself. She didn't hold back as she crossed knives with the cardinal's nephew and she kicked Lady la Yr's third son in the stomach when he tried to seize her around the waist. And maybe, Astrid thought, it was too late to make her grand play.

After the sixth victory, Nik peeled off her gloves. "That's it," she said.

"There is one more name on the list…" the king's steward said, frowning at it.

Nik turned to her father, narrowing her eyes. "We agreed six per day." Accusation colored her voice.

Her father put up a conciliatory hand. "We did. I have condoned nothing."

Astrid swallowed. She'd snuck to the steward's book while he was arranging the mid-afternoon refreshments, and added her name in the standard court script.

"Who is Astrid Garwe?" the steward demanded.

Nik's head whipped around. Astrid stood, smoothing the front of her dress. "I am she," she said in her practiced court lilt. She tried to ignore the way the fans lashed into complicated judgments around the room. She flipped open her own fan and took a deep breath. "I am Astrid Garwe, of no family, of no land, of no tithe. I wish to compete."

Nik's eyes widened in panic. The steward, on the other hand, gave a short, ugly laugh. "With what weapon?"

Astrid tilted her chin. "If I win, I take the princess's hand. If I lose, I pay the full fine of a thousand daler." She'd have to sell the rest of her left hand to get it, but, well—grand gestures and all that. "Are we agreed?"

The steward glanced to his king.

"There is no restriction upon age or standing. Anyone who can defeat Her Highness in combat may claim the right to wed her," Astrid pushed.

There was a rustling around the hall. The king could hardly refute her after claiming that the contest was so egalitarian.

"Any *man*," the king said. He smiled tightly, but Astrid could see the anger behind that smile. Perhaps he guessed who Astrid was—or perhaps he just didn't like the reminder that Nik didn't want to marry a man. "I'm afraid, my dear, that any *man* who defeats my daughter in combat may have the right to marry her. You don't qualify."

Astrid straightened and took a deep breath. She wanted to be queen, and queens didn't bow. "If I may beg clarification on a matter of law: in year thirty-four of the reign of your esteemed father, the Giant Inheritance Laws established that any individual who was, at most, one-sixteenth giant, was to be considered a man." She folded her right hand around her left. "And as I am one thirty-second giant, am I not legally of the race of man?"

Around the room, the murmurs were more appraising than damning. It was a classic play—the humble woman of the people against her monarch. And it was support Astrid would need.

Nik's mouth twitched. "The law is the law, Father dear." She spoke as though she did not particularly care, but Olve narrowed his eyes, suspicious. She slid her gloves back on. "I'll accept the challenge. Name your weapon."

The only sign she was nervous was the slight bob in her throat. Astrid smiled and said, "I challenge you to the Parnassian courante."

The conversation that flowed around the room was much less friendly this time. It was one thing to bend the rules, another to make up new ones.

The king snorted. "We haven't offered anyone else art contests or poetry readings."

"Yet many dances have come from a form of combat. Weaponless martial arts have been accepted under the terms of the contest. And the Parnassian courante is directly developed from Jotun war dances." She fluttered her fan. "I'll even dance you to first blood," she offered sweetly.

They were silent for a moment. Then Nik threw back her head and laughed. It was a loud laugh, a triumphant laugh, a laugh that promised Astrid everything and set her on fire from her toes to the top of her head. "Are you sure you don't approve, Father? She'll make an excellent politician." Around the room, fans swayed—many in disapproval, many in approval. Nik raised her voice. "I accept your challenge. After all, it should be my choice, shouldn't it? And I have not yet turned a candidate away."

"We will need music," Astrid said, waving to the king's chamber musicians who waited to start the evening's music.

Astrid didn't look to the king for permission. She kept her eyes on Nik, who was still laughing like Astrid had told a joke that had just changed her life. As the music began Astrid skipped back, forward, back again, turning into Nik's outstretched hands as she fumbled half-forgotten steps. Her fan snapped and sliced across Nik's arm. Nik gasped and stopped, gaping at her hand.

"Papercut?" Astrid said.

A red stain flushed the cuff of her cream shirt. Nik laughed louder than ever.

"Don't go yet," Nik grumbled, pulling Astrid closer. She buried her nose in Astrid's shoulder.

"We're getting married in five hours. I have to prepare." Astrid tried to wiggle from beneath the coverlet, only to find Nik's arm wrapped solidly around her waist. "I'm not even supposed to be in here," she giggled as she kissed Nik's forehead.

"As if you ever cared before," Nik said.

"I've never gotten married before," Astrid pointed out.

"But as soon as you go out there, you'll be set on by everyone. I won't have you to myself anymore."

"Look on the bright side," Astrid said. "Your father's come round." Perhaps it was because most everyone else had, or perhaps it was because she'd danced several ambassadors into a corner and pledged them to agreeable trade deals. Six months later and he even greeted her with a kiss on the cheek.

Nik only snorted at that.

Astrid cupped her cheek. "Let's go," she said. Warmth pulsed inside her. "Tomorrow will be even better than today."

Nik rolled on top of her, pressing skin to skin, pinning Astrid's wrists to the bed. "I don't know about that," she murmured, dipping down to brush Astrid's lips with her own. "I intend to make today a *very* good day."

And that was a challenge Astrid was willing to suffer.

The Scholar
of the Bamboo Flute
by Aliette de Bodard

Liên's first duel at the Phụng Academy was bewildering, and almost unfair in its simplicity.

She let Mei—the fey, mercurial schoolmate half the academy seemed to avoid—take her to the arena. They paused at iron-wrought gates with a huge lock and a clear sight of what lay beyond: a crumbling platform by the river, overgrown by banyan roots. On the lock were characters that slowly morphed into letters. Liên bent, and her seal—Mother's seal, the one she'd carried on a chain around her neck for more than nine years—touched the lock, and the letters shivered and rearranged themselves to match Mother's style name on the seal.

The Hermit of the Bamboo Grove.

The doors creaked open. Leaves rustled, the ceaseless sound of a monsoon wind whipping tree branches in the forest.

"I must ask," Mei said. "Are you sure?" She was so oddly formal. Her tone and the pronouns she used for herself and for Liên sounded like something from a scholar's chronicle.

"Why?" Liên asked. She readjusted the hairpins in her top-knot: they'd slipped sideways while she was walking to the arena. She hadn't been told much, merely rumors: that the arena was where the best scholar students went to prove themselves; that Mei was the key; that Mei's revered teacher, the chair of the Academy, held power beyond Liên's wildest dreams, and it all flowed through Mei.

Liên didn't much care about dreams, or power, but she wanted to *excel*. She needed to *excel*, because she was the scholarship kid, the one on sufferance from the poorest family, the orphan everyone looked at with naked pity in their eyes.

Liên wanted to be seen for who she truly was.

Mei's face was utterly still. Her skin shone with the translucence of the finest jade, as if she were nothing more than a mask over light incarnate. "Why? Because it's dangerous."

Liên frowned. "You mean, it might get me expelled?"

Mei laughed. As she did so, Liên finally realized the sound that had been bothering her since the gates opened wasn't the background noises of the forest, but a slow and plaintive noise, the first bars of a poem set to music. "No. It might get you killed."

Inside, on the platform, someone was waiting for Liên. They were nothing but a dark silhouette at first—and then, as light slowly flooded the arena, seeping from Mei's body into the stone, and from the stone into the banyan roots and the neighboring river, Liên saw who they were. Dinh, another of her classmates, an arrogant and borderline abusive woman who thought the world belonged to her.

She was holding a flute. It wasn't yet to her mouth, but her fingers were on the holes already, and everything in her suggested impatience to play. "Younger aunt," she said, to Liên. "What a pleasure. Let's get on with it."

It might get you killed. "Wait. This is a *music* competition?" Liên said. "I don't understand."

But Mei's hands were already on her chest—an odd flutter as they connected, then they did something that Liên didn't fully see or understand, and a sharp, stabbing pain ran through her, as something that seemed to have become stuck between her ribs came out one small, excruciating bit at a time—and it hurt as it came out, and Liên couldn't breathe anymore, and it felt like the time she'd knelt by her parents' coffins, hoping against all hope they'd come back. "Mei," she tried to say, but it tasted like fire and blood in her mouth.

"It's all right," Mei said. "Take it."

"Take what?" But Liên's hand closed on the thing protruding from her chest, and she drew it out with the same ease as she'd draw a brush from its holder.

It was a flute. A plain bamboo one, unlike the bone-white one Dinh was holding, with three simple holes and a shadowy, ghostly fourth one. It was so achingly familiar, so achingly comforting, and Liên let out a breath she hadn't even been aware of holding. Her fingers fit easily onto the first three holes, and the flute was at her mouth, the smooth and warm touch of bamboo on her lips.

"Elder aunt," she said to Mei. "What's—"

Mei's face was grave. "Your instrument."

Liên lowered the flute away from her mouth. It cost her. "People just don't grow flutes!" Not even the famed scholars, whose ranks Liên so desperately ached to join.

Mei's hand swept the arena. It was awash with light, the banyan's roots receding into shadow, and in the luminous mass of the river Liên saw a flash of large and iridescent scales. Dragons? No one had seen dragons in the world for centuries. Surely.... "Many things are possible, here," Mei said.

"The power—" Liên started, and then stopped, because she didn't know what to say. She didn't know what was being offered here beyond myths and legends. "You said it could change the world."

Mei's smile was dazzling. "It can do everything you could ever need or want, elder aunt. If you follow the rules. If you reach the end of the duels."

"What are the rules?"

Another smile. "Play. Be ranked. Advance."

Liên's hands tightened on the flute. A chance to be the brightest scholar in the world, to advise emperors and sages. To leave her mark at the heart of things. "Power," she whispered. And, to her dead, revered parents, "Watch over me, Father and Mother."

"Begin," Mei said. She was standing in the middle of the platform, on one of the banyan roots.

She didn't know how! But then Dinh started playing, and Liên's words of protest froze on her lips. It was haunting and beautiful: a slow-rising melody about solitude and the need for strength, and the beauty of geese flying in the sky, and the banyan's roots seen from the moon. As she played, the light flickered in the banyan roots and in the river, and Liên could see how the flute in Dinh's hands beat the same rhythm as the heart in her chest.

And then it was over, and Mei turned to Liên. "You," she said.

"I can't—" Liên began, but her hands were already moving.

When she breathed into the flute, she felt, not music, but words come out—all the poems she'd written in her room at the

Academy, trying to capture the beauty of rivers as dark as smoke, of willow leaves scattered in empty rooms—all the essays and the memorials and the pleas she'd trained herself to write for the good of the empire—and the other things, too, the courtship songs she'd burnt before they ever reached the courtesan she had a crush on, the ones about lips like moths' wings and skin the color of jade. Her fingers moved on the holes of the flute, towards that shadowy fourth hole at the end—finally touching it with a stretch that felt as natural as breathing. When her last finger slid over it she remembered Mother's poems and songs, the ones about dragons in the river and cockerels whose song could destroy citadels, and pearls of blood at the bottom of wells—she was playing and speaking and it all felt like one long breath that burnt in her lungs forever and ever, and then....

Then it stopped.

Shivering, shaking, Liên lowered the instrument from her mouth. The banyan's roots were alight. Overhead in the canopy, pinpoints of light shone like wayward stars—no, not stars, but a flock of luminous birds—and in the river something large and sinuous shimmered in and out of existence. She felt light-headed and empty, as if she'd just run from one end of the Academy to another. And Mei's face... Mei looked not distant or fey, but like someone whose hunger had finally been sated.

Dinh was pale, but it wasn't the pallor of light, just exhaustion and fear. She looked from Mei to Liên, and then back again. Mei said, simply, "Liên wins."

"She—" Dinh opened her mouth as though she was going to argue, but Mei was by her side, gently closing her hand around the flute, which was slowly vanishing. Back to her own body? What were the flutes, exactly? Where were they coming from?

"Go home," Mei said, and her voice wasn't unkind. "There are other arenas to prove yourself in." Mei watched, thoughtfully, as Dinh staggered through the door.

The light in the banyan tree was fading. So was the creature in the river, and Liên's own flute. It did nothing to diminish the terrible emptiness inside.

"You'll feel better after you eat," Mei said, turning to Liên. Her gaze was dazzling and luminous. "Come on."

"I—" Liên's voice felt all used up. "Where?" She walked behind Mei because she didn't have any willpower of her own left, and she might as well. They went through the gates and the deserted gardens of the Academy—how was already night, where had the time gone?

A single path with a few lanterns led to a building a little apart from the other buildings. The path wove through a garden that had once been rich, but was now in a state of disrepair: the ponds had become masses of churned mud choked by lotus flowers, and the pavilions were dilapidated ruins with missing roofs, the rain dripping on chipped stone. As they walked up to the lone building that reminded Liên vaguely of a pagoda or a watchtower, the rain became a slow, warm drizzle that plastered Liên's topknot to her skull.

The tower's gates were closed. Mei threw them open, spattering water on the slats of the rich parquet. Inside, someone sat at a low table, sipping from a cup of tea: a man of indeterminate age, wearing the clothes of a scholar-official, his topknot impeccable.

"Child," he said, rising with a smile towards Mei. When he moved, the same light as the one Liên had seen in the arena limned him for the briefest of moments. "Younger aunt." His smile was dizzying and magnetic. Liên felt at the center of the world, held in the web of his attention, and sagged when his gaze moved from her to Mei. She hadn't eaten anything, and it was only sheer stubbornness that had kept her moving.

"This is Liên," Mei said. "She just won her first duel. Elder aunt, this is Hiểu Sinh, my Revered Teacher."

"Liên." Sinh turned back to her and smiled, and again that flash of warmth swept through Liên, making her feel larger and worthier. "Welcome home, Liên."

There were rules, ones Mei hadn't mentioned. Odd ones like not eating garlic or onions, which made this seem like an offshoot of a monastery. And odder ones still, un-monastery-like: that the winner of the duel would move into the house and share a room with Mei. Sinh said it with a meaningful glance at Liên, which Liên chose to ignore. It wasn't that Mei was unattractive, but being set up together like that was just too weird, and at no point had Sinh asked for Mei's opinion or permission. Besides, Liên wanted to climb through merit, not marriage.

The duels she'd expected. They were irregular, huge occasions that required intense and feverish preparations. Sinh hinted there would not be many to fight, but would never share more details. "You will know when you're ready for the power," he said, and never would budge from that frustrating statement.

There were classes, too. In between Liên's usual regimen of Statehood and Classics and Poetry at the Academy, Sinh would invite Liên to his study and pour tea for both of them, and talk about... Liên was never too sure what they talked about, only of Sinh's eyes shining like jet, and of Mei, sitting behind Sinh the entire time, occasionally moving to replenish tea or dumplings or dipping sauces.

"I don't understand why the flutes," Liên said.

Sinh had spread a chess board between them, though he made no move to play. "The flute is the scholar."

Liên opened her mouth to protest it was not, that the Four Arts of the gentleman scholar included music but on the zither, and then Sinh flipped the board, and all words fled.

It was an old, old board, so old it was engraved with the characters of the Chinese colonizers rather than the letters of the Việt alphabet. Pasted on it, carefully held behind a pane of what looked like glass—but no glass was so fine, or shone with such pulsing, warm light—was a painting.

Whoever had drawn it had skills worthy of the old masters. The brushstrokes were flowing and sure, and they suggested details with economy. The painting depicted a single scholar, standing before a rocky spur, fingers on a flute of deep green jade with complex carvings. And in front of him... in front of him rose a great dragon, antlers gleaming, pearls scattered in her mane, and maw at the level of his flute.

"Scholar Vương," Sinh said. Behind him, Mei had risen. She laid a hand on the painting for a brief moment, closing her eyes as if some memory were painful. "His music was so powerful it could change the world." His hand nudged Mei's aside, touched on the details of the scholar's clothes. "Summon dragons from the river and speak to the Dragon Princess herself."

"Power," Liên said. Her breath caught in her throat. She'd seen the banyan tree, but she hadn't realized....

Sinh laughed. "You want to be adviser to *emperors*, child. Don't give me that shocked look, your dreams are written large on your face." He laid his tea cup on the floor, stared Liên in the eye until she had to lower her gaze or be openly disrespectful. "You dream too small."

"I don't!" Liên said. She—she wanted to make her parents proud of her, whatever heavens they were watching her from.

"Mei told you this power could remake the world." A gentle snort. "Adviser. You will never summon dragons if you keep yourself so contained."

How could he dismiss her so easily? Liên opened her mouth to protest, and found a touch on her arm: Mei, gently holding her and shaking her head. *Apologize*, Mei mouthed.

She had done nothing wrong, but Sinh was her teacher now. "I'm sorry," she said. The words tasted like ash on her tongue.

"Good," Sinh said, nodding briskly, as if the whole matter weren't even worthy of mention. As if he hadn't called all her dreams small and worthless. "You have another duel in a week's time, child."

After the lesson was over, Liên exhaled. The breath hurt.

Mei walked with her as she steered away from the corridors, and towards the door of the house—and the waiting gardens. They were unlike the ones in the Academy, where everything was staid and named: here trees grew wild, and lotus flowers choked the ponds.

"He means well," Mei said. "He's seen a lot of students."

"And how many have gotten as good as Scholar Vương?" Liên couldn't help the sharpness in her voice.

Mei smiled. "A few. Younger aunt..." She smoothed out the folds of her tunic, and Liên realized Mei was nervous and scared. And no wonder, with Sinh being so overbearing.

"I'm sorry. You shouldn't have to run peacemaker between the two of us."

"It's what I do."

What did *she* do? "You don't duel," Liên said, before she could stop herself.

Another smile, but this time it was more relaxed. "No. I don't have that talent. I'm not a scholar." It was said easily and matter-of-factly. She didn't care.

"You make the flutes."

A laugh, crystalline and careless, and Liên heard the hurt beneath.

She laid a hand on Mei's arm, felt the warm tautness of her—felt something shift within her, her heart becoming too large. "Big'sis." The intimate pronoun—the one reserved for an older, close friend of one's generation—rose to her lips as easily as breathing.

"I don't make the flutes," Mei said. "I just…" She spread her hands. "I just make it easier for you to manifest them. They're *yours*."

"You don't approve."

Mei jumped. "What makes you think that?"

"The way you speak." They'd reached a dilapidated pavilion on a spur that looked like someone had tried, badly, to evoke Scholar Vương summoning the Dragon Princess.

"I think he shouldn't push you so hard," Mei said. "You're sixteen? You remind of a child I once knew."

"Seventeen," Liên said, stung. "I'm an adult."

Mei's face was unreadable. She leant on the chipped railing of the pavilion, looking at the river. "So you are. And an…" She stopped, then, looked at Liên. "A driven person."

"You were going to say orphan," Liên said, bristling. But Mei didn't sound like the other students, the ones who had mocked her for having no family or connections.

"Yes," Mei said. "Having no parents can be hard."

Liên shrugged, though she missed them. "I lost them when I was young. I don't remember much about them." It wasn't quite true. She had dreams with Father's perfume and Mother's voice singing her to sleep. But what was true was that she remembered the coffins and the vigil in the temple more than she remembered them living—the way the air had been heavy and breathless, as if before a monsoon that would never come, the smell of incense curdling in the air, the rough feel of the mourning band on her forehead, the way it kept falling down into her eyes—her eldest aunt's hand, bringing it back time and time again, her grim frustration that she was a child and everyone expected her to keep silent and out of the way.

"Sinh would say you could bring them back to life with the power," Mei said.

"And is that true?" She'd said Sinh, not herself.

Again, that unreadable look. Mei's hand rested by Liên's on the railing. Liên's fingers ached to draw her close. "I don't know," Mei said, finally, and there was clearly something that she wasn't saying.

"I don't want to bring my parents back because there's an order to things," Liên said. "Rules in heaven and on earth. Why should I be breaking them?"

"You're dueling."

She was—and it wasn't just about being like Scholar Vương—but also the way that the music of her flute flowed through her—the way that it seemed one long, slow breath, finally released—the way that her anger and her grief and her ambition finally merged together and became something beautiful and pleasurable. The way it made her feel alive. "Is that breaking the world? Mei, what is this power? Why is Sinh so evasive?"

"Do you trust me?"

And wasn't that a barbed question? "I don't know," Liên said.

"Fair." Mei sighed. "I can tell you this: the power breaks no rules. It's merely an ascension, like the sages of old." But again there was something she wasn't saying.

"You asked if I trust you. Should I be trusting Sinh?"

"He's my Revered Teacher and I love him," Mei said. "Come on, let's go back to the house."

They walked back a hand's width from each other, Liên acutely aware of the way Mei moved—of the sway of her hips, how her lips opened slightly when she walked too fast, barely revealing the nacre of her teeth—what would it feel like, her lips on Mei's lips? But she was acutely aware of another thing, too.

Mei hadn't answered her question about Sinh.

Liên's opponent for this duel—her seventh at the Academy —was a much older girl, Thụ Kiếng. Everyone in the Academy had heard of Thụ Kiếng. She routinely organized poetry contests and won all of them, and her calligraphy was so good it was exhibited in the Academy's classrooms and corridors.

Liên didn't want to fight Thụ Kiếng, because she was going to lose.

"You won't lose," Mei said. They stood on the arena platform, between the banyan roots. Liên held her flute to her mouth: plain, unadorned bamboo with that fourth hole—four for death and all that had brought her so far. It felt so flimsy and inadequate.

It wouldn't be enough.

"She's a *scholar*. A proper one. The bright one. I don't even know why I'm here, big'sis!" Liên's hands clenched on her flute. She was an orphan from a poor family, a girl from the country playing at being a scholar. Who was she, to think she could attain the power of legends?

Mei wrapped one hand around Liên's—gently reached with her other, to touch the flute—and Liên shivered, as if it were her lips Mei was touching. "You're here because you're worthy." Her gaze, wide and luminous, held Liên's—Liên's throat was suddenly dry. "Because you are seen."

Liên drew in a deep, shaking breath. "Big'sis." Mei's hand moved from the flute, rested on Liên's lips for a bare moment, and warmth spread from Liên's face down her spine. She ached to reach out—dared not reach out. "*I* see you, lil'sis. Vương's heir. I see you. You will do this, because you can no more fail this than stop breathing." Mei withdrew her hands, leaving Liên shaking. "Big'sis."

"Ssh," Mei said, but her gaze lingered on Liên's face a little too long, and her eyes were half-lidded with hunger and desire. "I have Thụ Kiếng to fetch."

Liên waited. She lowered her flute, and laid a hand on the banyan tree. It was cold and dark now, only brought to life by flute music. The river was lifeless, too. No, that wasn't true. It teemed with those silver flashes she'd already seen. She knelt and trailed her hand in the water, heedless of the cold. The flashes came closer, nipping at her fingers. Fish. Small silvery carps, weaving in and out of her hand, gently tickling her— and for a moment she wasn't Liên or the current champion of the duel, but simply the girl she'd been in a faraway past, the one who'd played in the river while her parents were in their study.

"It's been a while, hasn't it?"

Liên scrambled to her feet. Thụ Kiếng was standing next to her, holding a flute of glass. Mei leaned against the banyan tree, waiting for them to start. "What do you mean?"

Thụ Kiếng was tall, her hair brought back in an impeccable topknot, her face classically beautiful: smart and chiseled, her hands long and elegant. She made Liên feel like a country bumpkin. "The river." She smiled. It was bitter and fragile. "We all splash into it as children, coming home muddy-handed with only a memory of fishes to show for ourselves. Until our parents remind us that it's time to put aside childhood and study hard."

Liên flushed. "I didn't have that." She wasn't sure what to say.

"I know," Thụ Kiếng said, and it wasn't unkind. "You want to summon the Dragon Princess?"

Liên said nothing, but she thought of the painting she'd seen in Sinh's study—of the dragon rearing up. What would that kind of power feel like? "Maybe."

"Mmm." Thụ Kiếng sighed. "The Dragon Princess vanished from the world at the same time as Scholar Vương."

"Vanished?"

"No one knows what happened." Thụ Kiếng's voice was wistful. "I think they just reached a point where they couldn't outrun the laws of nature anymore. Heaven doesn't bestow blessings without some kind of expected behavior." A sigh. "I don't know what's in the river, but I don't think it's the princess anymore. I don't think anyone can reach her."

Liên said, finally, "Does it matter?"

A long, measuring look from Thụ Kiếng. "To you? No, I think not. Come on. I think she's waiting for us."

"I don't—" Liên stopped. She wasn't about to tell Thụ Kiếng she was afraid, but Thụ Kiếng saw it anyway.

"You can concede," she said. "But you won't, will you?"

Liên clutched the flute. "I'd be shaming my parents if I lost."

Thụ Kiếng cocked her head. "Would you?"

"What do you mean?" But Thụ Kiếng had already turned away from her, towards Mei.

It was Liên's turn first, because she held the title. She raised the flute to her hands, still feeling the fish dart between her fingers—and when she played, the river came out. It was the fish and the mud and the sound of the water, and their barely remembered house—and Mother's measured voice, composing poetry; and Father's, laughing and answering her, his own voice weaving between verses. And as she remembered her parents her finger stretched, found the fourth hole of the flute, and the music poured out of her in a rush that lifted her and drained her at the same time.

She came out of the song with her heart hammering in her chest. The platform was awash with light. In the canopy of the banyan, the flock of luminous birds was larger, and the branches supported the looming moon. Something was climbing from the depths of the river, a dark shadow about to break the surface of the water, and Mei wasn't leaning against the tree anymore, but looking at the river with tears in her eyes.

"My love…" she whispered, softly, slowly.

Thụ Kiếng was staring at her, and at Mei. "That's hard to follow." She lifted her own flute, slowly and ironically, and brought it to her lips. The music that came out of it was small and slow: a dirge for a girl who had refused Thụ Kiếng, and a boy she'd loved, but who fell ill and had left the Academy, never to come back. It all sounded… tinny, as if from a great distance, and when Thụ Kiếng lowered her flute, the tree had barely lit up. In the river, there was hardly anything, a shadow of a shadow, diving almost immediately out of sight again.

"I concede," Thụ Kiếng said, bowing to Mei. And, to Liên, "Think of what I've said."

And she left.

Liên wrapped both hands around her fading flute, trying to stem the shivering of her whole body.

What she'd said.

Would you? Would you be shaming your parents?

And she knew what she'd already known before playing: that she wasn't scared of shaming her parents. She was scared of losing. Of losing her place in the house and Sinh's cryptic lessons.

Scared of losing Mei.

Mei was leaning against the banyan tree, her eyes on the river. "Let's go home," Liên said, slowly, tentatively. "Big'sis?"

"It's your second to last duel," Mei said, and her voice was tight. "Did you see the river?"

The dragon rising from the heart of it, close enough that she could see their head about to break through the water. Close enough that she could touch them. The Dragon Princess, Sinh had said, but Thụ Kiếng thought that the princess was long dead. What was below the surface of the water?

Her second to last duel. That felt unreal. Unearned. "Surely—"

"Sinh will tell you. It's almost over, lil'sis." Mei turned towards her—and in that one moment as she started moving, in that one unguarded moment, Liên saw her face, and her bearing. It wasn't tears of joy or nostalgia in her eyes, but rather of her entire being wracked by a pain so great it made her cry.

"Big'sis!"

"Lil'sis?" Mei's voice was puzzled.

"You're in pain."

"I'm not," Mei said, but it was as if the song had granted Liên double vision, overlaying Mei's graceful demeanor with a deeper truth. "You're lying. What's wrong, Mei?"

"There's nothing wrong." A grimace, utterly inadequate against the way her entire body was braced against the pain. "Nothing's *changed*, lil'sis. Come on, let's go home."

That last rang with a sincerity like nothing else, but the implications were horrific. Nothing had changed? Liên followed Mei back to their quarters, watching her, watching the way she held herself: that small pouting with her lips she always did when she walked, that quiver. But it wasn't pouting, was it? Merely a scream, held back, and the way she moved was elegant and graceful, a mask that slipped here and there—hips jutting out a bit too far when a thigh spasmed; lips closing a fraction, thinning; fingers clenching for a mere breath, pupils dilated just a bit too much.

Had she... had she always been like this, since the start? Had Liên been blind, the entire time? What did it mean?

What was wrong?

In their room, Mei busied herself, brightly—a little too much, a little too brashly—making dumplings and noodle soup. "You need food, lil'sis."

Liên waited until Mei was done. "It's Sinh, isn't it?"

"I don't understand what you mean."

"He wants something from you, and you're in pain because of that."

"I already told you I'm not in pain."

Liên drew in a deep, shaking breath. "Big'sis." She put into her voice all the things that usually went into the flute song. "I can see it. I can see you. Ever since the duel. The last one."

"You can't possibly—"

Liên said nothing. She didn't touch her chopsticks, either. She just stared until Mei gave up busying herself and sat cross-legged on the floor with her head cocked—and every so often she'd flicker, and Liên would see her bent backwards, her chest pierced with shadowy swords. Not just a few, either. There were so many impaling her, hilts and blades and crosspieces all jumbled together. How could she—how could she even breathe or talk or move?

"That's not possible," Mei said. Her voice was filled with dawning, fragile wonder. "No one has ever—"

"No one. How many times have you done this, Mei?"

A weary sigh. "Too many." Mei flickered again—arched backwards, face tense and slick with sweat, the swords' blades glinting in the lantern light—they flexed as she moved, with the clear sound of metal on metal.

"You said it was the last duel. You said it was almost over. What's happening, Mei?"

Mei said, finally, "I don't want to see you hurt."

"You held me. You touched my lips. Was that part of the plan, too?"

"No!" Mei's voice was full of panic. "I would never. Big'sis. Please. I would never—"

"Sleep with me? Sinh hinted, didn't he? Putting us in the same room is kind of unsubtle."

Mei's face was drawn with pain, haggard. The blades in her chest glinted with blood and sweat. Liên fought the urge to hug her. "I would never lie to you by faking feelings. And you didn't."

"Didn't what."

"Sleep with me. That... that mattered." She made it sound like an extraordinary feat.

"That's basic human decency," Liên said. "Wait." Her voice was flat. "You said this had happened too many times. There were others."

Mei didn't deny this, which was as good as an admission.

"They slept with you."

"It's... it's nothing more than I deserved, for what I've done."

"No one deserves—" Liên stopped, because she didn't know how to say it. What kind of twisted universe did Mei live in? And—more pressingly and importantly—how long had it all been going on? "He's thrown you at duelists, and they've taken advantage."

"Not always."

"Often enough." Liên's fists clenched. "Big'sis—" She did reach out then, not to kiss Mei like she desperately wanted, but simply to squeeze Mei's shoulder, gently and slowly and watching warily for any signs Mei didn't want it. But all she could see was the pain: the swords impaling Mei, their weight bending her backward. "I can see swords, Mei. They're going through your chest. What are they?"

Again, no answer. "You can't tell me. It's Sinh, isn't it? What hold does he have over you? Is it the swords?"

A silence. Then, "The swords are my fault. My pain to bear. Because I was the one who suggested it all, you see. The arena. The duels."

Liên stared at Mei, suddenly chilled. "You—what does he want, Mei?"

"The music." Mei's voice was flat. She ran a hand through her own topknot, catching on the golden hairpins. "He lost it, and he was so desperately unhappy. He—" She breathed out, her face filling with that same wonder she'd shown, back at the river. "He was so *young*, once. So full of light and striding across the land as if he understood all of it, from the carps to the stars in the sky. He held my hand and *saw* me. Truly saw me, just the way I was."

Somehow Liên didn't think Sinh's desperate hunger was going to be filled by simply listening to Liên play. "My flute. He wants my flute."

"The flute of the player strong enough to summon the dragons in the river. Perhaps even calling the Dragon Princess Scholar Vương summoned. He won't be able to play it for long. Playing a flute not your own burns it." Mei's voice was mirthless. "But he'll have it. Sinh always gets what he wants."

Including Mei. "Because you give it to him, don't you?" Liên didn't have words for how much it hurt her. Sinh's betrayal was nothing unexpected, but to know that Mei would stand by him no matter what. "Always and always."

A shadow of that same wonder in Mei's eyes, brittle and dark. "He smiles, and I see it again. The heart he had when he was younger…"

And was that enough reason for what she was doing? "And what happens afterwards? When he's walked away with the thing inside my chest? He just steals people's lives and you let him?"

Bitter laughter from Mei. "It won't kill you. Just—" She spread her hands. "It will hurt. Every day, it will hurt."

"Like swords in your chest?"

"It's not the same thing!"

"Is it not? Because it sounds like he's just leaving a trail of broken people behind him. Including you."

"You don't understand." Mei pulled away, stood up. The swords flexed as she did, driving deeper into her flesh—a clink of metal against metal, and Mei stopping, gasping, her eyes closing for a brief moment, sweat running down her forehead. "There's nothing you can do, lil'sis. Nothing you can change. Just—just go. Find Sinh. He'll know you're ready."

As if she wanted to find Sinh and offer herself for the slaughter. "You don't trust me." That hurt, a lot.

"You're a *child*." Mei's voice was cold. "Playing with flutes and with songs and not understanding what's happening."

"You're not helping me understand, are you?"

"Because you can't!"

"That's pointless!" Liên rose, too, scattering chopsticks and bits of herbs. "Help me, Mei."

But Mei had turned away from her, and wouldn't speak anymore.

Liên ran. She didn't know where she was going and didn't care—her feet pounded the shriveled grass of Sinh's gardens, and the hills, and the road leading to the arena, and back to the buildings of the Academy—the classrooms where teachers waited to impart wisdom from the sages, where her classmates would be waiting for her to take her place—until she finally reached a knoll of grass. She sat, sheltered by the branches of a willow tree whose dense jade foliage cut off her view of the world.

You're a child.

If she closed her eyes she would see, again and again, Mei's drawn face, the careful way in which she moved.

Every day, it will hurt.

Sinh would take everything from her, just as he had taken everything from Mei, and she didn't know enough to stop him. And Mei... Mei would stand by him, and that was the worst.

How many times have you done this, Mei?

Too many.

And yet... Liên remembered the hand in hers, Mei's fingers on her lips for an all too brief moment. *You are seen.* That conversation in the gardens, Mei telling Liên that Sinh shouldn't push her so hard. Mei cared, didn't she?

And did Liên care?

"You look like a whole turmoil of thoughts," an amused voice said.

Mei's gaze jerked up. It was Thụ Kiếng.

The former duelist wore scholar's robes and an impeccable topknot. Her seal—a match to the one that had allowed her access to the dueling arena—swung on her chest as she sat down next to Liên. It was a smaller and newer thing. Her personal one?

"Steamed bun?" Thụ Kiếng asked.

Liên took it, because she didn't quite know what to do. They nibbled together in almost companionable silence. It was pork and cat's ear mushroom, and a small but perfect quail's egg in the center, the yolk dissolving into sharp, salty powder in Liên's mouth.

"Feeling better now?"

Liên couldn't see the point of diplomacy. "I don't know what you're trying to achieve."

Thụ Kiếng laughed. "Not everyone has hidden agendas within hidden agendas. I'm out of the dueling game. I lost. But for someone who won everything, you look decidedly unenthused." Her expression was distant, almost serene.

Liên stared at the swaying willow branches. She thought of Sinh and flutes and music and stealing the work of his students. Of Mei and swords and kindness. "It's the last duel," she said. And it would be against Sinh. "Why?" she asked, finally.

"Why do I duel? Because in spite of myself, I believe in miracles. There was a girl, you see." Thụ Kiếng's voice was wistful.

"You want someone to love you?"

"No," Thụ Kiếng said. "You know that can't be forced. But I wanted to show her that... stories could be real. That there could be happiness ever after."

Liên remembered the song in the arena, the one Thụ Kiếng had played. "The boy. The one who loved you back."

"He's dead. Or out there in the world, which is perhaps the same thing. This is his seal," Thụ Kiếng said, lifting the seal around her neck. "The last thing he gave me before he left. Why do you duel, younger aunt? And don't tell me your parents. That's what granted you access to the arena in the first place—your mother's seal and all it symbolized—but that's no longer true."

Liên said nothing, for a while. "She's in pain."

"Mei? Nothing that she didn't bring on herself." Thụ Kiếng's voice was almost gentle.

The swords are my fault. "How long has it been going on?"

A shrug, from Thụ Kiếng. "Who knows? They've always been there, insofar as I know. You hear about the chairmen of the school, but I think there's only ever been one, wearing different faces and different names."

"Always." It was vertiginous and unwelcome. "All that time." All that time in pain and denying it. "It shouldn't be that way." And she had something Sinh wanted. Her flute. Her music. All that had shaped her as a scholar. She could bargain, if she wanted it badly enough.

Did she?

What kind of person would it make her, if she walked away from Mei?

"You want to help Mei?" Thụ Kiếng stared at her for a while. "Oh, I see. That's the way it is."

"No," Liên said, before she could think. "I don't—"

"Care for her? Of course you do." Thụ Kiếng laughed. "This doesn't have to be a love that echoes down lifetimes, lil'sis. It just has to be enough. But you know that she'll stand by Sinh. They've stood by each other all that time. Asking her to step away, no matter how well-intentioned..."

"She loves him." It shouldn't have hurt so much, when Liên said it. Because how could Mei possibly love Sinh?

"Sinh? Yes." Thụ Kiếng played with the jade seal at her neck—the dead boy's. "She will not thank you, you know."

"For rescuing her."

"You're assuming she will view it as a rescue." Thụ Kiếng sighed. "You're a real scholar. Never standing for injustice or unfairness." She used an uncommon word for "real," one that meant "bright" and "real" all at once, like a miniature jewel. "Because I wouldn't walk into that arena, myself."

Liên sighed. She thought of Mei and of—not love, but a connection, and care for each other. "I guess it's all up to me, then."

Mei was waiting for Liên at the arena's entrance. She was wearing the long, flowing, five-panel robes of the imperial court, red silk with golden embroidery of flowers and mythical animals. She'd unbound her hair, and it hung loose on her shoulders, with the golden hairpins scattered in their strands like stars.

She looked like someone out of myths, out of fairy tales—someone Liên would watch dance and later share celestial peaches with—someone breathtakingly, fragilely beautiful, like cracked celadon.

"Lil'sis?"

Liên just stood and gaped. "Big'sis."

Mei walked to her. Linh breathed in a smell that was cut grass and the sharpness of a storm. And then Mei bent forward, and kissed her, and she tasted like steel and salt.

"Big'sis," she said, gasping, when Mei stopped, and still stood close, close enough to touch.

For a moment, there was the same slow wonder in Mei's eyes there had been in their room, when she'd understood Liên could see her pain. "I wanted…" Mei said.

"It's all right," Liên said. And slowly, gently, kissed her back until her mouth was full of Mei's sharpness. "It's all right to want." She was everything to Liên, and they both knew it would not last.

"Not here, not now." Mei's voice was bitter. She pulled away. "But thank you. For the kindness." She flickered again, and Liên saw the swords, sprouting from her chest as if she'd grown a tree of thorns from within, a tangled mass of gleaming sharpness and bloodied blades.

Liên said, finally—because Thụ Kiếng was right, because she couldn't rescue Mei against her will—"you said I was a child. You said you didn't trust me. I need you to—" She stopped, then, because she didn't know what she said that wouldn't be platitudes, or a rerun of an argument they had already had. Instead, she reached out, and wrapped her finger around the hilt of a sword in Mei's chest. She hadn't expected to make contact—she'd thought they'd be as ghostly visions without power to wound—but what she grabbed was cold and slick and *hungry*.

Old sins and blood and punishment and the will of heaven and the order of things and love cannot should not triumph because nothing is eternally unchanging....

She let go, gasping. "This has to end. It's not fair. It's not equitable."

Mei's face hadn't changed. "I told you—"

"I know what you said," Liên said. She raised her hand—slowly laid two fingers on Mei's mouth, in the curve of those lips drawn back in a pain Liên couldn't alleviate. "That it's your fault. That it's all for him. That it's worth it. That I'm a child."

"Do you think I kiss children?" Mei's voice was stiff, barely audible. Liên didn't move her fingers. She pressed, gently, against Mei's lips.

"No. But still... things end," Liên said, gently, and with more confidence than she felt. "And you matter. I'm not asking you to trust me, but will you stand by me?"

"I don't know," Mei said, and Liên knew then that she wouldn't. That she couldn't, because Sinh was her whole world and her whole being.

A chance. That was all she wanted. A chance for Mei to change. To cut the cord that bound her to Sinh, the chain of complicities and bargains Liên wasn't privy to. A chance. *Give me this, please, Mother and Father. Let me matter. This is how I want to leave my mark on the world. Please.*

"Watch me," she said, instead, and withdrew her fingers from Mei's mouth, reluctantly. She wanted to kiss Mei again, but it was no longer time.

"Always," Mei said, and her voice was sad.

The doors were closed, but this time they opened at Liên's touch. The characters on the lock contracting to display, not the name on the seal around Liên's neck, but a single archaic word in Việt.

Nhân.

Humaneness. Altruism. A fundamental virtue of the scholar. Liên would have laughed, if she felt in the mood to laugh.

As they walked, Mei laid a hand on Liên's chest, and this time there was no splitting of the world, no difficulty to breathe—and Liên was still walking but she was also holding her own flute. "Why is it so easy?"

Mei smiled, and it was a shadow of the expression that had endeared Liên to her. "You're so close to ascension. Didn't you realize? You barely need me anymore. You could manifest this with just a thought."

Liên didn't feel close. She felt small and scared and powerless. How old was the thing she'd stepped into, and how presumptuous was she for thinking she could change even a fraction of it?

The arena was dark, but someone was sitting at the center. "Child," Sinh said, and as he rose, the banyan lit up, and she saw that he'd brought the chessboard, the one with the painting of Scholar Vương summoning the dragon—except that he'd laid the pieces on the painting's side as though for the beginning of a game.

Sinh had changed his clothes, too. He wore long, loose azure robes and a large sash adorned with peach-tree branches; his hair was tied in an elaborate topknot, held in place by silver pins. In fact—

Liên looked to the board for confirmation. He was dressed exactly as Scholar Vương in the painting. "Modeling what you're trying to steal?" She hadn't meant to be wounding, but she was acutely aware of Mei at her side.

Sinh raised an eyebrow. "I see you are not ignorant. You are wrong, however."

Liên raised her flute, an inadequate shield. By her side, Mei had fallen to her knees, and this time the swords going through her weren't ghostly. They were real, and Mei was bleeding on the floor, curled and gasping and struggling to breathe.

Mei. No no no no.

Mei!!!

"Wrong?" Liên knelt by Mei's side, trying to grab a sword, any sword—to pull it out of the mass of sharpness and blood, but Mei kept writhing, and the swords moved with her, dragging across the floor, their hilts and blades clinking against the stones, the entire mass opening up with Mei's ragged breathing and convulsions, like an obscene flower. Mei. No. No no no. "You've used her. You've used all of us to steal power. How wrong am I?"

An amused laugh. Sinh knelt on the other side of Mei, making no move to help her. "Almost. I'm not stealing. I *made* this power: I'm only taking back what is owed to me."

Owed to him? "I don't understand—" Liên said, and then she looked at him—really looked. Mei's swords were now real, but so was another thing: the hole in Sinh's chest, through which jutted a tip of a broken flute of deep, gleaming jade.

I made this power.

Sinh laughed. "Yes. I'm not a thief, child."

"You're Vương. Scholar Vương. You—"

"What became of him. What's left of him."

And Mei—Mei who was contorting and bleeding on the floor of the arena—Mei, who wore the dress of a princess of the imperial court....

"The Dragon Princess," Liên said. The words didn't feel real. They couldn't be. "You. You cannot be alive."

"Hunger will do odd things to time," Sinh said. "Stretch and thin it, so that nothing is quite right—tea with dregs of ashes, a lover's touch dragging bone fingers across my skin, the river shimmering with corpses. She was right: I only feel alive when I play."

Her flute. Liên's hands tightened on it. "And you broke your flute."

A shrug. "Power can be used for many things, but I used mine wrongly. Too many worldly things: a palace and serving girls, and jade and silver, and the kingdoms of the world at my feet. I won't make that mistake again."

No, now he just enjoyed having one person utterly devoted to him. Liên had to stop herself looking at Mei. "So just the music, then."

"You've felt it," Sinh said. "You *know*."

A heady rush of pleasure unlike anything she'd ever felt, the sensation that she could be anything and do anything, the wonders of the birds and the dragon in the river…. "Yes," Liên said, because she wasn't him and didn't lie.

"This is why I need your flute."

"Are you asking?"

Sinh shrugged. "Usually, I'm the Revered Teacher, and the students will do what I ask because they trust me. But you—" He frowned, staring at her as if he didn't quite know what to make of her.

Liên said, "Free her. And I'll give you the flute." She kept her voice low and emotionless, but it was hard, because Mei was screaming.

"Her?" He looked at her, and at Mei. He laughed, softly. "I'm not holding her prisoner."

But some cages didn't have overt jailers. Liên's mouth clamped on pointless words. "Walk away."

Again, laughter. "Give me the flute, and I won't interfere."

Of course, because he didn't need her. His face said it all. He thought Liên was throwing herself headlong at useless hopes. Liên… didn't know if she disagreed, but she had to do something. "Deal," she said. "Now go."

When she passed the flute to Sinh, she felt as if she was handing him the heart in her chest.

"Finally." He laughed softly, gently, and seemed to grow taller—and as his hair came loose and fluttered in the rising wind, and as his skin glowed alabaster, she finally saw what Mei had: the young scholar flush with dreams and glory, the man whose music transcended this world, strong enough to summon from the heavens and the river's depths.

"Mei. Mei." Liên tried to grab the swords, but she couldn't. They kept flickering out of reach, and the hilt was oddly shaped and always shifting out of her reach. "Mei, please."

Sinh walked to the river, stood in the banyan's shadow. When his fingers slid into the hollows she felt them, one by one, as if they were resting on her skin, above the collarbone—and a sibilant whisper rose from the tree.

Trespasser thief taker of songs.

A note like a plucked string, and there was a sword, hanging in the air—the same swords sticking from Mei's chest, the ones Liên was desperately trying to pull out. Its voice echoed like thunder across the arena.

The will of heaven cannot be flouted punishment must be meted out the order of things cannot be violated.

Sinh barely glanced at the sword. He gestured, fluidly and carelessly, towards Mei. "Take her."

The sword shifted towards Mei, the strength of its presence—sharp and slick and hating—sending Liên to her knees.

Do you consent?

Mei's gaze rested, for a brief moment, on Liên. She smiled, with tears in her eyes. "You're so young," she whispered. "Playing with objects of power as if they were toys. There is no respite."

"Big'sis, no!"

But Mei's lips had already parted again. "I consent."

The sword dove for her, just as Sinh started playing. "No!!!"

Each note felt drawn from the veins in her chest, and it was discordant and tentative—and Liên was on her knees, struggling to breathe, struggling to see anything through the tears in her eyes—her hands bloodied and cramped from trying to hold swords. The new sword joined the others, one more addition to a tangled mass—one sword for each stolen flute, one more nail in a coffin of everlasting pain. The banyan's lights were flickering, and she couldn't think anymore, she couldn't—

Mei's voice, a memory of that time they'd fought over the dumpling soup.

He held my hand and saw me. Truly saw me, just the way I was.

He'd seen her. What had he seen?

Sinh was still playing, and the lights were slowly filling the tree and the river. The huge and dark being in the river finally broke free—and it was the wizened and algae-encrusted shadow of a dragon, emaciated and infested with crawling, dark shapes like insect parasites, antlers broken and oozing dark liquid.

Seen.

How dare he? A wave of nausea and anger wracked Liên.

Seen.

"Princess," Liên whispered. She pulled herself up, crawled to Mei, each gesture sending a fresh wave of pain down her chest. "Dragon Princess." Her voice stumbled—she couldn't remember the archaic words anymore. "Dragon." She lifted a hand—drew, slowly and haltingly, the old characters. "I see you."

Dragon.

Princess.

Mei.

The characters hung in the air for a brief moment, shifting to seal script, the same cursive shape on the seal around Liên's neck. Mei's face, drawn in pain, turned towards her, and Liên saw scales scattered across her cheek, iridescent patches that shone with a breathtaking light. "Mei," Liên whispered, and Mei's lips thinned on her name, and in her eyes shone the same slow wonder she'd shown before, and a shadow of her desire as she'd kissed Liên.

And abruptly Liên could breathe again—could, for a moment only, see Mei, curled around the shape of the swords transfixing her. One of them was less fuzzy and less shadowy than the rest. The last one, the one that had come from Liên's flute: its hilt was the same color and opacity as the fourth hole in the flute had been.

Liên closed her eyes, and tried to remember what it had been like to play. All her poems and all her songs, and all of Mother's old stories, and dragons in the river, and citadels brought down by theft, and people turning to stone by the seashore—and swords with jewel-encrusted hilts—and her finger, reaching out, slid and connected with hard metal and old, everlasting hunger.

The will of heaven is punishments there should not be mercy she consented....

"I do not," Liên whispered, and felt the sword pause in its ceaseless litany. "It was my flute, and I do not consent!"

The blade came free. The weight of it sent Liên to the floor, before she pulled herself up, gasping. She held nothing but smoke and shadows, the vague shape of a sword. She—she could kill Sinh while he was still engrossed in the music. An eye for an eye, blood for blood. She could feel the sword's quiescent hunger, its anger, its rage at the way student after student had lost their hearts to Sinh. It was not right. It had to be made right. She wanted—

She wanted to help Mei, not a bloodbath.

Help me. Father, Mother, help me do the right thing. The needful thing.

She drove the sword in the earth, feeling the shock of it in her bones; the shape of the hilt in her hand, what it had felt like when she'd connected, when she'd taken the weight of the blade in her hand.

Then, slowly and grimly, she went for the rest of them.

As when she'd played the flute, it was a matter of putting her fingers in the proper space—of reaching out across the length of metal or bamboo and finding a hole that shouldn't have been there. She didn't feel flush with words or poems, simply struggling to keep the emptiness in her chest from consuming her whole.

The flute in Sinh's hand was burning now—slowly starting to fade, a dull, distant pain compared with the effort of grabbing one sword after another—to hold hilt after hilt, planting blade after blade in the floor of the arena. Her hands were slick with blood and sweat, and her legs shook and locked into painful spasms.

Sword after sword after sword, and there was no end to them, the countless students whose flutes Sinh had used up. *It's my fault*, Mei had said, and yes, she had not stopped him, but an eternity of pain while he walked free... how was that fair punishment?

Liên reached out, again and again, and finally her hand closed on empty air. Surely she'd missed one... But when she looked, she stood in a field of swords, and Mei lay beneath her, gasping.

Traitor coward thief. The swords' combined voices made the earth shake. Heedless, Liên knelt by Mei's side. "Big'sis. Come on come on. It's over."

Mei's lips were blue. "Lil'sis." Her smile was weak. "It's... never... over."

A noise, behind her. It was Sinh. He held burnt bamboo fragments in his hands: the remnants of Liên's flute. He looked, curiously, at the swords scattered around them. "A fine effort," he said. "But in the end, it will avail you nothing."

"Shut up," Liên said. And, to Mei, "Look. *Look*." And, gently cradling Mei's head, turned her towards the river, towards the skeletal and almost unrecognizable dragon, slowly sinking back beneath the waves. "That's what he sees, big'sis. Do you truly think that's who you are?"

Mei's face was drawn in pain. The swords were quivering, thirsting for blood. She'd earned nothing but a reprieve. "Lil'sis."

"Look," Liên said, and then everything she'd done—the swords, the burning of her flute—hit her like a hammer, and she flopped downwards, as the swords rumbled and started tearing themselves away from the ground. "*Look!*"

Mei was crying. It was slow and noisy and heart-wrenching.

"Come, child," Sinh said to Mei. He was halfway to the gates of the arena, one hand on the wrought iron. He tossed, carelessly, the fragments of Liên's flute on the floor, and Liên felt as if she'd been stabbed as each one hit the stones. "Nothing ever changes. Come home."

"Big'sis. Walk away from him, please."

Mei didn't say anything. Sinh waited, arrogant and sure of himself: for everything to start again, for the old games to resume. For other duels and other thefts.

"Please..." Liên's words tasted like blood. "There's no time left. Please."

A final rumble, and the swords tore themselves free, and dove, again, towards Mei.

Liên screamed before she could think. "Take me, not her. I consent!"

In the frozen instant before the swords dove for her, she saw Mei's shocked face—the same shock on Sinh's face—rising, shaking and heavily breathing, stretching and changing, and saying a single word ringing like a peal of thunder.

"No."

"You can't—" Sinh said.

Mei's voice was cold. "I do not consent." The swarm of swords shivered and shook, turning from Liên to Mei and from

Mei to Sinh. "She will not take my pain, and I will not take his anymore."

"Child, please," Sinh said. And another, older word. "Beloved…"

"No," Mei said. She was long and halfway to serpentine, with the shadow of antlers around her snouted face, her hand gripping Liên's shoulder like iron—and she was so beautiful, so heartbreakingly beautiful, brittle mane streaming in the wind, antlers shining with weak and flickering iridescence. "Find someone else to bear your guilt."

The swords shivered from Mei to Sinh to Liên—the weight of their presence oscillating as they shook and shook and shook—and then they finally dived for Sinh.

His mouth moved. He tried to say something: words that were drowned by the rush of air, by the angry whispers of the swords as they came for him. They faded to a faint shadow, a shard of darkness lodging itself into his chest. He fell, gasping, to his knees, breathing hard—and finally got up, shaking. His face was slick with sweat, but his voice was assured and smooth.

"Nothing has changed," he said. "I'm still the chairman of the Academy."

He'd find someone else, wouldn't he? He no longer had Mei, but it would just start all over again—the duels and the flutes and the abuse, sheltered by the Academy the way it had always been sheltered.

Nothing had changed.

"Come on," Mei said. She pulled Liên up, slowly.

"Big'sis." Liên was a mass of sore and unhealed wounds and fatigue. She'd freed Mei. That mattered. It had to. One person at a time, and yet how much it had all cost…. "Big'sis…"

"Ssh." Mei laid a shaking hand on Liên's lips—two fingers, pressing against her flesh, and then the rest of her face, bending towards Liên: a brief, exhausted kiss that resonated in Liên's chest, setting her entire being alight. "Let's go, my love."

"Where—"

A short, exhausted laugh. "Out there. The world isn't the Academy, and it holds more than his games. Let's go. Anywhere. Come."

They walked supporting each other. They didn't spare a glance for Sinh, who still stood over the shards of Liên's flute, whispering "nothing has changed" over and over.

Slowly and carefully, they picked their way out of the arena, holding each other's hands—walking measure by agonizing measure towards the iron-wrought gates—out of the arena, out of the Academy, and out into the world that awaited them both.

With thanks to @mainvocaljiu for help with naming Sinh.

About the Authors

Claire Bartlett

Claire Bartlett is an author of YA and adult speculative fiction. Her critically acclaimed debut, *We Rule the Night*, was called one of the best books of 2019 by Publishers Weekly, and her novel *The Winter Duke* features more sapphic romance between soft scientists and cheerful warrior women. She grew up in Colorado, but studied history and archaeology around Europe before settling in Denmark for good. You can find her full bibliography at www.authorclaire.com.

Elizabeth Davis

Elizabeth Davis is a second-generation writer living in Dayton, Ohio. She lives there with her spouse and two cats—neither of which has been lost to ravenous corn mazes or sleeping serpent gods. She can be found at deadfishbooks.com when she isn't busy creating beautiful nightmares and bizarre adventures. Her work can be found in *Eerie River Publishing: Patreon July 2020; Eternal Haunted Summer: Summer Solstice 2020;* and *No Safe Distance: Stories from Quarantine.*

Aliette de Bodard

Aliette de Bodard lives and works in Paris. She has won three Nebula Awards, a Locus Award, a British Fantasy Award, and four British Science Fiction Association Awards. She was a double Hugo finalist for 2019 (Best Series and Best Novella). Her most recent book is *Of Dragons, Feasts and Murders*, a fantasy of manners and murders set in an alternate 19th Century Vietnamese court (released by JABberwocky Literary Agency, Inc.). Her space opera books include *The Tea Master and the Detective* (2018 Nebula Award winner, 2018 British Fantasy Award winner, 2019 Hugo Award finalist), and the upcoming *Seven of Infinities*, in which a poor principled scholar and a disillusioned sentient spaceship must solve a murder, but find themselves falling for each other. Her short-story collection *Of Wars, and Memories, and Starlight* is out from Subterranean Press.

K.A. Doore

K.A. Doore is a writer and shouter of queer sci-fi and fantasy who lives in mid-Michigan with her coffee, cats, children, and wife. The Chronicles of Ghadid is her debut fantasy trilogy, starting with The Perfect Assassin. While she enjoys writing about stabbing and stabbing implements, she's actually terrified of blood, but she'll be fine as long as no one learns about that. Find her at kadoore.com or follow her @KA_Doore.

Ellen Kushner

Ellen Kushner's *Riverside* series begins with the cult classic *Swordspoint*, followed by *The Privilege of the Sword, The Fall of the Kings* (written with Delia Sherman); and, most recently, the collaborative prequel *Tremontaine* for SerialBox.com and Saga Press. The author herself recorded all three novels in audiobook form for Neil Gaiman Presents/Audible.com, winning an Audie Award for *Swordspoint*. Her mythic fantasy novel *Thomas the Rhymer* won the World Fantasy and Mythopoeic Awards, and is a Gollancz "Fantasy Masterwork." She has taught writing at the Clarion Workshop, the Odyssey Writing Workshop, and Hollins University. She lives in New York City with her wife, author and educator Delia Sherman, and a great many theater and airplane ticket stubs they just don't have the heart to throw away, especially not now. "The Sweet Tooth of Angwar Bec," while written as a standalone story for this volume, does happen to take place about five years after the events of *The Privilege of the Sword*. She currently is finishing a fourth novel in the series. She's on Twitter as @EllenKushner. Her website is www.EllenKushner.com, where you can also sign up for her SubStack newsletter.

Ann LeBlanc

Ann LeBlanc lives in Massachusetts with her wife, where she writes about queer yearning, culinary adventures, and death. Her fiction can be read in *sub-Q Magazine*, *If There's Anyone Left*, and the Spring 2021 issue of *Fireside Magazine*. She edits for *The Spectacles Blog* and can be found on Twitter at @ RobotLeBlanc.

Yoon Ha Lee

Yoon Ha Lee's debut novel, *Ninefox Gambit*, won the Locus Award for best first novel, and was a finalist for the Hugo, Nebula, and Clarke awards; its sequels, *Raven Stratagem* and *Revenant Gun*, were also Hugo finalists. His middle-grade space opera, *Dragon Pearl*, was a New York Times bestseller and won the Locus Award for best YA novel. His next novel, the standalone fantasy *Phoenix Extravagant*, will be out from Solaris Books in October 2020. Lee's fiction has appeared in venues such as Tor. com, *The Magazine of Fantasy & Science Fiction*, *Clarkesworld Magazine*, *Lightspeed*, and *Beneath Ceaseless Skies*. Lee is a lapsed épée fencer. He lives in Louisiana with his family and an extremely lazy cat, and has not yet been eaten by gators. You can find him online at yoonhalee.com and patreon.com/yhlee.

Jennifer Mace

Jennifer Mace is a queer Brit who roams the Pacific Northwest in search of tea and interesting plant life. A two-time Hugo finalist podcaster for her work with *Be The Serpent*, she writes about strange magic and the cracks that form in society. Her short fiction may be found in *Cast of Wonders*, *Syntax & Salt*, and *GlitterShip*, and her poetry has appeared in *Uncanny Magazine*. While *Silk & Steel* is far from the first anthology she has pitched to the internet, this is the first time the internet has called her bluff. If you want to keep track of her future hijinks, you can find her online at www.englishmace.com.

Freya Marske

Freya Marske lives in Australia, where she is yet to be killed by any form of wildlife. She writes stories full of magic, blood, and as much kissing as she can get away with, and she co-hosts the Hugo Award–nominated podcast *Be the Serpent*. Her hobbies include figure skating and discovering new art galleries, and she is on a quest to try all the gin in the world. Her debut novel, the queer historical fantasy *A Marvellous Light*, is forthcoming from Tor.Com Publishing in 2021. Find her on Twitter at @freyamarske, or at freyamarske.com.

Elaine McIonyn

Elaine McIonyn spent her wayward youth jaunting around Europe, teaching English, and translating. She lived in Austria, Germany, and the UK before returning to her native Ireland just in time to join the staff of Dublin 2019 – An Irish Worldcon. She is a graduate of the Odyssey Writing Workshop, class of 2018. She is also, perhaps unwisely, licensed to sail dinghies and small catamarans. She co-runs a sci-fi and fantasy writing group in Dublin and lives with her partner (and a selection of loose-leaf teas).

Cara Patterson

Cara Patterson is a Scottish writer who dabbles in any genre that takes her fancy, sprinkling in generous helpings of diversity, puns, and sarcasm. Between the *Out of Time* time-travel series, published under the pen name C.B. Lewis, and a range of short stories in award-winning anthologies, she's starting to get a handle on this writing lark.

Alison Tam

Alison Tam is a queer Taiwanese-American writer and occasional game developer. Her short story "Beauty, Glory, Thrift" was part of the Book Smugglers' Gods and Monsters series, and her personal essay "The Drag Kings of Taipei" was featured in *Autostraddle*. To her knowledge, she has never fought a duel.

Alison likes writing about complicated diaspora emotions, women who love and appreciate each other, and non-Western worlds. She's lived in Taipei, Shanghai, and California, but her home will always be online. You can find her on her website at alisontam.github.io or on Twitter @TheTamSlam.

S.K. Terentiev

S.K. Terentiev lives in the wilds of North Texas, where she's on the hunt for the perfect latte or tacos al pastor. A member of the DFW Writers' Workshop, she writes speculative short stories and is currently working on her first fantasy novel. She's never seen a chupacabra or a werewolf, as far as she knows. She can be found on Twitter at @SKTerentiev or her website SKTerentiev.com.

Django Wexler

Django Wexler is the author of flintlock fantasy series *The Shadow Campaigns*, middle-grade fantasy *The Forbidden Library*, and YA fantasy *The Wells of Sorcery*. His latest is the epic fantasy *Ashes of the Sun*. In his former life as a software engineer, he worked on AI research and programming languages. He currently lives near Seattle with his wife, two cats, and a teetering mountain of books. When not writing, he wrangles computers, paints tiny soldiers, and plays games of all sorts.

Chris Wolfgang

Chris Wolfgang writes and edits sci-fi and fantasy fiction in Omaha, Nebraska. She changes her hair color frequently, attempts to study foreign languages outside of a classroom, and occasionally reads tarot. Follow her on Twitter at @chriswolfgang for queer feminist yelling, often about things she finds exciting, but sometimes not. She's a delight.

Neon Yang

Neon Yang (they/them) is queer, non-binary, and the author of the *Tensorate* series of novellas from Tor.Com Publishing (*The Black Tides of Heaven, The Red Threads of Fortune, The Descent of Monsters, The Ascent to Godhood*). Their work has been shortlisted for the Hugo, Nebula, World Fantasy, and Lambda awards. A Clarion West alum, they graduated from the University of East Anglia with an MA in Creative Writing and currently live in Singapore.

Kaitlyn Zivanovich

Kaitlyn Zivanovich is a former Marine Corps intelligence officer and current speculative fiction writer who pens short stories to avoid editing her novels. She's lived a good chunk of her adult life in the Middle East, and speaks enough Arabic to get around Egypt but not enough to impress anyone in Morocco. She is a graduate of the Viable Paradise Workshop and an associate editor at *PodCastle*. Kaitlyn grew up as a Third Culture Kid, and she and her husband are inflicting the same lifestyle on their four loud children. Currently they all live in a small farming village in Okinawa, Japan. Pre-coronavirus she spent her free time hiking, traveling, and learning new languages. Now she stress-bakes and binge-watches Turkish TV shows.

Acknowledgements

We owe so many thanks for making this book everything it could be. We (Django, Janine, and Macey, that is) would be especially lost without our Kickstarter backers. Thank you for believing in this anthology!

These wonderful people made this book possible (so that we could pay our artists, our cover designer, and all the other people whose work went into making this a high-quality product). In particular, we'd like to thank the following backers for their contributions (in alphabetical order by first name because you have to order things somehow):

9th Level Games
A. Charis Goldflam
A. Fourtet
A. Hancock
A. Jade
A. Miura
A. Rachel Haddix
A.Okuonghae
A.Y. Chao
Abigail
Accolade Aula
Acolet
Adam Duke
Adam Pilfold-Bagwell
Adam Puckette
Adam S. Gravano
ADC
Adri Joy
AdriAnne Strickland
Adrien Barnes
Adron Buske
Aemil K.
Aerylaance
Afik "Ninja" Blitz
AG.91

AH
Aidan Doyle
Aidan Miller
Aily & Mimi
Aimee Benson
Aimee Ogden
AingealWroth
Aisling nic Lynne
Aiyesha
AJ Ryan
AK Turza
Akhila Sriram
Al Clay
Al Julian
Alaina
Alan Wu
Alana M T
Alanna Noel Solomon
Alastor
Aleida
Alena Cicholewski
Alessandra Cristallini
Alex "Fox" Dell
Alex Caligiuri
Alex Claman

Alex Hardison
Alex Jackson
Alex Leitch
Alex Leuthold
Alex McKenzie
Alex Miller
Alex Roscura Guerrero
Alexa Donley
Alexander Belford
Alexandra Martin
Alexandra Rowland
Alexandre Muñiz
Alexis Eaton
Alexis Lockwell
Ali Fisher
Alice Kroutikova
Alice Lemieux
Alice Reininger
Alice Southey
Alicia Z
Alison C
Alison Lam
Alison Mann
Alison N
Alleyne Dickens
Allie B.
Allison Drinnon
Allison Hewett
Allison Hinds
Allison Liem
Alyssa Carter
Alyssa Hull
Alyssa Marie
Alyssa Ziegenhorn
AM Meca
Amaelalin
Amalia Nanciu

Amalie N Ingham
Amalija Vitezović
Amanda Besch
Amanda C. Davis
Amanda Cook
Amanda Davidson
Amanda Pester
Amanda Sumner
Amaryllis Jeanne Quilliou
Amber Dawn Loranger
Amber Marie Goss
Amber R Lewis
Amber Yust
Amberle Browne
Ambrai
Amelia Facchin
Amy Boggs
Amy Hirst
Amy Huang
Amy Schaefer
Amy Zhou
Amy Zuverink
An Especially Belligerent
    Magpie
Ana Maria Curtis
Andi DiSpirito
Andi Kent
Andie Krutsch
Andie Larson
Andrea L
Andrea Mitchell
Andrea Salt
Andrea Tatjana
Andrea Viemeister
Andrew C
Andrew Lyons
Andrew Taylor

Andromeda Taylor-Wallace
Andy Kinzler
Angela Banks
Angela Song
Anita "Neeters" Twitchell
Ann Zhu
Anna Cook
Anna Goldberg
Anna Kat
Anna Lynch
Anna NW
Anna S
Anna Smith
Anna-Rose Kirchner
Anne Gwin
Annie Blitzen
Annie Fitzgerald
Anonymous (10)
Anonymous H.
Anrea Jones
Antha Ann Adkins
Anthony Chanza
Antoine Dailly
April Herms
April Ouimet
April Walsh
Apurva Desai
Aria Stewart
Arnela Bektas
Artemis
Ash B
Ash Brown
Ash Hawrychuk
Ash Humphreys
Ash J
Ash Walker
Ashe

Ashe Azrak
Asher Holy
Ashleigh B.
Ashley Hedden
Ashley Kelly
Ashryn Brynmore
Ashtin Johnson
Astrid & John
Atthis Arts
Aunt Dena for Tia
Aura ❀ V
Auri Wang
Ava Dickerson
Ayla Ounce
Aynjel Kaye
B. A. Hencher
B. Chugg
B. K. Neville
B. Woodchuck
B.C. Kinney
B.T.Halko
Beatrice
Beatrice Waterhouse
Belle McQuattie
Benjamin Hausman
Benjamin Jaeger
Bernd Linke
Beryl Egerter
Beth Culp
Beth Morris Tanner
beth ⁺✦
Bethany L. Sherwood
Betsy Hanes Perry
Betsy Hanes Perry
Betty
Bhavya Tanguturu
Bill Frerking

Black Lives Matter
blackcoat
blatanville
Blazej Szpakowicz
Blue
blue wisteria
Bob/Sally Milne
Bobbie Crane
bonnie blossom
Bonnie Warford
BookGeekGrrl
Bookwyrm
Brad Ackerman
Brad Gardner
Bradamante Smith
Brandi
Brandon Eaker
Brandon Long
Breanna Teintze
Brendan
Brenna Noonan
Brett Bennett
Brian A Liberge
Brian Quirt
BRITTANY AND LAURA
    MOELLER
Brittany Buell
Brooks Moses
Bruce Baugh
Bry Shuter
Brynn R.
C Ferguson
C. Corbin Talley
C. L. Polk
C. Lynn Reimer
c.billadeau
C.E. Huddleston

C.N. Rowen
Cait Greer
Caitlin and Emmelie Pinz
Caitlin Colbert
Caitlin Ellerbe & Elizabeth
    Vandermolen
Caitlin McDonald
Caitlin Starling
Caitlyn Modaff
Calamity's Child
Cali Martin
Calista Melano
Calley Oresick
CalypsoTea
Camilla Boslev
Camille Lucas
Cara Murray
Carah Helwig
Care Ryan-Smith
Carina S.
carisa Bjorngaard
Carl A Carter
Carl M.
Carl Rigney
Carla H.
Carla M. Lee
Carlin Wednesday
Carly
Carmen Fernandes
Carol Fujimoto
Carol J. Guess
Carol Mammano
Caroline R.
Caroline Wong, Hayley Bhola
Carolyn Elizabeth
Carolyn M
Carolyn Saber

Carolyn V.
Carrie Anderson
Carrie Hausman
Caryn Cameron
Caryn Ojemann
Casey Andrew
Casper Miller
Cass Holiday
Cassandra May
Cassandra Panek
Cassie A Stearns
Cassie H.
Cassie Katarn
Castella Semaphore
Cat
Cat Bascle
Cat Langford
Cate Crowley
Catherine Baker
Cathin Yang
Cathy Green
Cécile Taquet
Ceillie Simkiss
Celeste J
Cena Ringwald
Chaitan Bandela
Charles Bailey
Charles T
Charlie N
Charlie Rodgers
Charlix W.
Charlotte G.
Charlotte Wight
Chel
Chell
Chelle Parker
Chelsea Buchler

Chelsea Fay Baumgartner
ChelseaJahaliel
Cheryl Morgan
Chigbo Ikejiani
Chloe Isla
Chloe R.
Chloe Smith Lopez
Choco
Chris C.
Chris Joseph
Chris Mangum
Christina Bell
Christina Kjellstrand
Christina Koller
Christine Hanolsy
Christine L
Christine S
Christine Welman
Christopher Hwang
Christopher K. Davis
Cían Lupiani
CJ Gibson
CL Biles
Claire Farron
Claire Keeney
Claire Mead
Claire Reynolds-Peterson
Claire Rojstaczer
Clare Janke
Clarissa C. S. Ryan
Clarissa Stefek
Claudia Drobel
Claudia Fontana Santoyo
Clayton Culwell
Cliona Shakespeare
Cody Woodson
Cole F.

Cole Lopez
Colleen O
Colleen W.
Coral Moore
Corey Thatcher
Corinna Cornett
Cos
Court
Courtney S
Courtney Willis
cozyhades
Cristin Heart
Crystal
Crystal Lynn
Curtis Mitchell
Cynthia Gonsalves
Cynthia Harper
Cynthia Phillips
D A
D Franklin
D. Daly
D. J. R. Allkins
D. Kleymeyer
D. Moonfire
D.A. Straith
Daenyx
Dalia R
Dan
Dan Lyke
Dana Musser
Dana Swithenbank
Dani Dee
Dani L
Dani Stull
Daniel Lin
Daniel McConville
Daniel Schwartz

Daniel Silvermint
Danielle B.
Danielle Costello
Danielle Pegan
Danté!
Darcey W.
Darcy van de Rijt
Dave "What Rough Beast"
    Bretton
Dave Dubin
dave ring
David Anderson
David Farnell
David Holden
David Mackie
Dawn Carlos
DCD Khandro
Deanna Bushman
Deanna Moore
Deb Block-Schwenk
Debbie Benson
Deborah Hooker
Dee Bosa
Deike Pintat
Des
Desireé Thatcher
Destiny Andrews
Devin Helmgren
Devin Miller
Diana Fox
Diana LW
Dice Disasters
Dina Quaas
DiscovertheStars
Dodie Sullivan
Dr Janelle Cooper
Dr. Serenity Serseción

Drea Delariyala
DresdenQ
Duskwind
Dusty
e
E M Potter
E. Blackburn
E. Ellis-Neenan
E. Russell
E.L. Winberry
E.V. Moebius
Earl Scott Nicholson
Edward H. Carlisle
Edward MacGregor
Eileen L
Eimear B
Eimear Ellis
El Faith
Elaina Martineau
Eleanor Ferron
Eleanor Grey
Eleanor Talley
Elena Pereira
Eleonor Lagercrantz
Elf M. Sternberg
Eli Kilgore
Eli Palmer
Eliana Dimopoulos
Elijah Gill
Eliot Parks
Elisabeth Banks
Elisabeth R Moore
Eliza Darrow
Elizabeth Ayme
Elizabeth B.
Elizabeth Elliott
Elizabeth Fitzgerald

Elizabeth Goldgar
Elizabeth Lauderdale
Elizabeth Sargent
Elizabeth Selby
Elizabeth Sullivan
Elizabeth Twitchell
Elizabeth Weir
Ellen Declairing
Ellen Green
Ellen McCammon
Ellie Franklund
Ellie Whitfort
Eloise Darrow
Elysandra
Ember
Emery Redman
Emilia Lee
Emily
Emily Cain
Emily Collins
Emily Cromwell
Emily Lomax
Emily Roycraft
Emily W.
Emily Wall-Winkel
Emily Williams
Emma Brown
Emma Holt
Emma J. Sweeney
Emma Johnson
Emma Olson
Emma Roy
Emma Simovic
Emma We
Emmaline Conover
Emmanuel Colvin
Ephie

Ereka Regan
Eri M. Rasmussen
Eric
Eric Karoulla
Eric Willey
Erica "Vulpinfox" Schmitt
Erica L Frank
Erica S.
Erik Dutton
Erika L.
Erika Peterson
Erin B
Erin Barbeau
Erin Forte
Erin Himrod
Erin Middleton
Erin Page
Erin Peterson
Erin Subramanian
Ernesto Pavan
ESC
Esther N
Esther O. Lee
Ethan Pantel
Ev Starshine
Eva Johanna Hartel
Eva Müller
Evan Schmid
Eve
Eve Smith
Eve Swan
Everett Worth
Eversong
Evil
Fabienne Schwizer
Farah Ismail
faustine

Felice Hunter
Felicity Fisher
Felix Simonson
Filip Hajdar Drnovšek Zorko
"filkertom" Tom Smith
Fin Byrne
Finley
Fiona M
Fiona Nowling
Fish
Florencia Herra-Vega
FLSocialworker
Fran Dare
Francesca G.
Francis Waltz
François Thibault
Fred Yost
Friday Afternoon Tea
Friday N
G Antonas
Gabe Krabbe
Gabi, Cei & Emi
Gabrielle Lianne
Gabrielle Tyson
Gabylc
Galia Godel
Gargareth
Garonenur
GeekFeminist
Genevieve Cogman
Genevieve Iseult Eldredge
Geneviève Paquin-Saïkali
Genie Tan
Geoffrey Jacoby
George A. Nemanic
Georgia Morgan
Georgia Taylor

Georgie Stroud
Gerald Gaiser
Geralynn Martinez
Gesina A. Phillips
Gessika Rovario-Cole
Gillian Dawson
Ginny Lurcock
Gio Faughnan
Giselle Grenade
GlassesOfJustice
Glyn Reid
Gotherella Biovenom
Grace Ashton
Grace Niu
Grayson Pickard
Greg Jayson
Gretal McCurdy
Griff Green
Griflet Rose
Guin Kelly
Gwen Stacy Bard
H Lynnea Johnson
H. Lee Dunn
Hadas Sloin
Haley Nixon
Hallie Tibbetts
Hanako Games
Hanna Taylor
Hannah Davis
Hannah Elspeth Catterall
Hannah Hunter
hannah kierspel
Hannah R. Holmberg
Hannah Verdonk
Hans Chun
Harper Cottingham
Hart D.

Haviva Avirom
Hayden Fuller
hdp
Heather Devine
Heather Eccles
Heather Holt
Heather Mong
Heather R. Valli
Heather Rose Jones
Heather Valentine
Helen
Helen Eastwind
Helen Lambert
Henrik
Hilary Bisenieks Brenum
Hillary Jeffrey
Historia Reiss
Hobbes LeGault
Holly "Jamie" Jamerson
Holly J
Holly Roberts
Ian Thomas
IB
ilana gallardo
Indiana T
Iris Jong
Iris Z
Irish Harvey
Isa T.
Isabeau J. Belisle Dempsey
Isabel Palomares
Isabel Wilson
Ishtarre
Isis C.
Ivy A.
Ivy Aku Allotey
Izzy Wasserstein

J Lin
J MacLeod
J. Aelwood
J. Kusluch
J. van Bleisem
j.3. bearden
J.E. Zarnofsky
J.J. Irwin
J.M. Coster
Jac♥Jes
Jack Clark
Jack Gulick
Jack Hazard
Jack Welter
Jackamanda Jones
Jaclyn Wright
Jacob P. Torres
Jade Barr
Jade Robeck
Jadin
Jae Steinbacher
Jaime M Garmendia III
Jaime Mayer
Jaime O'Brien
James Lucas
James Mallek
Jamie Perrault
Jamie Sands
Jaminx
Jana C.
Janora Curtis
Jasmin Bonilla
jasmine Jaffarian
Jasmine Stairs
Jason Miller
Jaunita Landéesse
Jay Fernandez

Jay Lofstead
Jayla N.
Jaymie Wagner
Jazmin Quezada
jazzcatte
JC Hay
JC Hoskins
JC Kang
JD
Jean-François Héon
Jeannette Ng
Jeff Eppenbach
Jeff Reynolds
Jeffrey Shiau
Jemima Warne
Jen Gheller
Jen R. Albert
Jen S
Jenelle Clark
Jenn & Aly Wise
Jenn Lyons
Jenn Watson
Jenna W
Jennayra
Jenni Bravo
Jennifer "Kiriana" Barndt
Jennifer Bee
Jennifer Doherty
Jennifer M-S
Jenny Graham-Jones
Jenny Yau
Jeremy Brett
Jeremy Nelson
Jeremy Reppy
Jess Ambrose
Jess Belmont
Jess Caruana

Jess H
Jess Muskin-Pierret
Jess Turner
Jessa M
Jessa Willson
Jessica Eleri Jones
Jessica Fainges
Jessica Gilson
Jessica Grady
Jessica Hammer
Jessica Jo
Jessica Oxton
Jessica Peterson
Jessie Hall
Jessyca "Jess" Taborsmith
Jill Seidenstein
Jim DelRosso
Jin Joo Wilk
Jo Miles
Joann M Koch
Joanna B
Joe Frizzell
Joe Kitchen
Joel
Joel Short
Joelle Parrott
Joelle Vitzikam
Johanna Solomon
John "The Gneech" Robey
John Appel
John Bankert
John Menninger
Jonah Segovia
Jonathan Cohn
Jonathan J Leggo
Jonathan Lee
Jonathan Narvaez

Jordan Buller
Jordan McAdam
Jordan S
Jordan Shiveley
Jordyn Burke
Josefin W.
Joseph Hoopman
Josh Lowry
Josh Medin
Josh Quick
Joshua Pevner
JS Groves
JT
Juanita Albro
Judith Solomon
Jules Bouzigues
Julia Blackwood
Julia McKinney
Julia Milliken
Julia Truman
Julian C. Sy
Julie Holderman
Juliet Kemp
JullesT
Juniper
Justin and Quinn
Justine Atkins
Justyna
K Everett
K. Kovarik
K.A. Lynch
K.C. Ahia
Ka Fortner
Kaden Burkhardt
Kaden M
Kae Petrin
Kai Mills

Kait Johnson
Kaitie Ensor
Kaitlyn Ferguson
Kaleigh Cara-Donna
Kam
Kamryn Rene
Kara Snow
Karen DeWysockie
Karen Healey
Karen Hesse
Karen Kincy
Karen L.
Kari Dayton
Karine R.
Kat S.
Kat White
Kat Yoshida
Katarzyna N.
Kate Cook
Kate Goodheart
Kate Larking
Kate Malloy
Kate Mergener
Kate Pennington
Kath Iwinski
Katharine (thiefofcamorr)
Katherine Long
Katherine McCallum
Katherine Prevost
Katherine S
Kathleen Grigsby
Kathleen Mills-Curran
Kathleen Moyer
Kathryn Heffernan
Kathryn Soderholm
Kathrynne W.
Kathy Schrenk

Kati James
Katie Burke
Katie Hilleke
Katie Lynn Moore
Katie M.
Katie Redderson-Lear
Katie Warren
Katy Broussard
Katy L. Wood
Katy Weisman
Kay
Kayden Persephone Black
Kaye Asplund
Kayla Fontenot
Kayleigh Saum
Kaylene Ruwart
Kaz Q
KC
KC Swan
Kel
Kellan Sparver
Kelle Connolly
Kellie Hultgren
Kelly I
Ken Finlayson
Ken Schneyer
Kerry Seljak-Byrne
Kevin Baijens
Kevin Boyd
Kevin Lemke
Kevin S.
Keyana Sequeira
Khaeta
Kiera Crist
kieranfae
Kim Callan
Kimberley Lam

Kimberly Wallace
Kimmy Curran
Kira
Kira Yeversky
Kirby Bullock
Kirsten Mentzer
Kirstine Sø Dieckmann
Kirun Amiri
Kit Bruce
Kitty McGarry
Kmi
Koma
Kona Goodhart
Konstantin Koptev
Kosmos
Kris Mayer
Kris Millering
Krista Gigone
Kristen Danley
Kristen Flippo
Kristen Muenz
Kristen Phillips
Kristen Simper
Kristi Chadwick
Kristi Wright
Kristiana Josifi
Kristie M.
Kristin Bledsoe
Kristin Calvert
Kristin L. Rollins
Kristin Selzer
Kristina Bennett
Kristine Kearney
Kristjan Wager
Kristjana Vilhjálmsdóttir
Krys Kamieniecki
Krystal Bohannan

Kusheil
KVC
Kylie Stoneking
Kylie Szymesko
L Bright
L McCauslin
L. M. Spielberg
L.C.
Lady of Sparrows
Lainwen
Lana
LandisTheThief
Laura D.
Laura Denham
Laura Fliegel
Laura G.
Laura García Franco
Laura H.C.
Laura Kathryn
Laura McVey
Laura Sales
Laura T.
Laura Warner
Laura Wilkinson
Laurel Vucak
Lauren Edwards
Lauren Hoffman
Lauren Jacobs-Pollock
Lauren Raye Snow
Lauren Ring
Lauren S.
Lauren Wallace
Lauren Wheaton
Lauren Wright
Lea Mara
Leah Groess
Leah Neustadt

Leah Rice
Leife Shallcross
Leila
Lemondropt
Lera Kotsyuba
Leslie Crone
Levi Qışın
Levynite
Lex Obie
Lia Blum
Lilac Llama
Lili Y
Lillian MacKnight
Lilly Davis
Lima McCabe
Lin Simpson
Linda H. Codega
Lindsay Scarpitta
Lindsey Petrucci
Linnea Nilsson
Lisa Bao
Lisa M Richardson
Lisa Padol
Lisa Peachey
Lisette A.
Littlemarimo
Liz "TERFs Can Choke" Hayes
Liz Fisher
Liz Kulka Hetherston
Liz L.
Liz Lutgendorff
Liz M.
Liz Novaski
Liz Warner
Liza
Liza C Kurtz
LM Zoller

Lo
Logan Webster
Lorna Toolis
Lou LaRey
Louise Lowenspets
louisxiv
Louve errante
Lucie Marasco
Lucy Fox
Lucy Hadden
Lukas Feinweber
Luke
Luke Morton
Lyn Murnane
Lyndon Baugh
Lynne
Lynne Sargent
Lyse McToaster
M. Ellis
M. Murakami
M.A.Derr
M.G. Versluis
M.M.
Mab
Mackenzie Plowman
Madeleine Barber-Wilson
Madeline Bernard
Madison Burns
Madison Metricula Roberts
Madison Skwierczynski
Maeghan Roach
Magali Ferare
Maggie Gilligan
Maia Rose
Maja Lund Petersen
Malis Vitterfolk
Malka Rivka

Manda Mc
Mandy Pederson
Mandy Wetherhold
Mango F. J.
Marc Rouleau
Marcia Franklin
Marcus Baseler
Margaret Moser
Margaret Obenza
Margaridha Pereira
Margo MacDonald
Marguerite Kenner and
    Alasdair Stuart
Maria C. Ludwig
Maria Morabe
Maria Nygård
Mariah Griffin
Marian Elizabeth
Marilisa Wall
Marissa Lingen
Marja Erwin
Mark Gerlach Jr
Mark Gerrits
Mark Williams
Marlowe
Mary Alexandria Kelly
Mary Beth Decker
mary crauderueff
Mary Curry
Mary Gardiner
Mary Olivia
Marzie Kaifer
mashedpopoto
Mat S.
Matt Daly
Matt Frazita
Matt Hope

Matthew Orphir Cartier
Matthew Smitheram
Maureen Zahn
Max G
Max Kaehn
Max Whiskeyjack
May
Maz Hedgehog
Mazal Horesh
McKinley Valentine
Meadow R.
Meej Jupin
Meg Bevilacqua
Meg McArthur
Meg Osborn
Meg Wilkes
Megan Daly
Megan E. Daggett
Megan Fauci
Megan Gadd
Megan Green
Megan Hungerford
Megan Miller
Megan Morrison
Megan Prime
Megan Reardon
MegaZone
Meghan Bohn
Meghan McCusket
Meghann Gorney
Mel Choyce-Dwan
Mel Emery
Melia Gibson
Melissa A
Melissa C. Perez
Melissa Caruso
Melissa Cebrian

Melissa DeLucchi
Melissa Goodyer
Melissa Kibler
Melissa Klocke
Melissa Sayen
Melissa Shumake
Melissa Skudra
Melody "The Gay Cousin"
Ellison
Meredith Downs
Meri (@Geek_Manager)
Merry Merry Princess
Meta Raappana
MHalla
Mia Moss
Mia Patton
Michael Smith
Michael V. Colianna
Michał Jakuszewski
Michele Ford
Michele Howarth
Michele Howe
(@neverwhere)
Michele S
Michelle Chilkotowsky
Michelle Labbé
Michelle Moreno
Michelle Oriolo
Michelle Records
Michelle Stelter
Michelle Wierenga
Mikayla Hutchinson
Mike "PsychoticDreamer"
Bentley
Mike Brooks
Mike Mazzacane
Mila Jabs

Milo
Miri Baker
Miriam R.
Mischa Wolfinger
Misha B
Misha Grifka Wander
Misty Lee
Mochi
mojen
Molly C Miller
Molly Franklin
Monica Barner
Monica Hurley
Monica Shum
Morgan and Rob Kostelnik
Morgan Kakuk
Morgan L. Bornstein
Morgan Swim
Morgan Tupper
Morgane Bellon
Morrigan Proude
moss
Murray Sampson
myrialux
MythSigh
N Graham
N. Queen
N.D. Roberts
Nadine
Nancy Unruh Berumen
Narelle Bailey
Narrelle M Harris
Nat S
Natalia Mole
Natalie C.
Natalie Ingram
Natalie Schmidt

Nathan Monson
natsora
Nhu Le
Nia Dalby
Nick M.
Nicole Chase
Nicole Fletcher
Nicole McMichael
Nicole Schuck
Nikhitha Kotha
Niki
Niki Pell
Niki S
Nikki
Nineite
Noel Rivera
Noemi S.L.
Nonnie Grayson
Nora Howard
Nora Mo
Nora Snefer
NorD
Noreen Walsh-Esrey
Nuance V Bryant
Nyssa Whitehead
Oathkeeper
Octavia Atlas
Olivia Howard
Olivia L.
Olivia Link
Olivia Montoya
Olwen Lachowicz
Ophelia
Owen Cook
P. Anderson
Packy
Paige Kimble

pamgaea
Pancha Diaz
Parvinder Kaur Panesar
Patricia M. Brent
Patti Kardia
Patty Kirsch
Paul Jordan
Paul Mirek
Paul Weimer
Paula F-C
Pauline Arsenault
Pauline Zed
Paxtenne Falls
Peter Brichs
Phoebe Barton
Phoebe Seiders
Pierce A. Erickson
Piper Lewis
Poetry
Preston Bannard
Psilence & maus
Queen Katicus
quercus
Quinn Vega
R Harmon
R J Theodore
R Jones
R. Choi
R. T. Quackenbush
R.V. McKee
Rachael M
Rachel AE
Rachel Coleman
Rachel Gollub
Rachel Johnson
Rachel L.C.M.
Rachel 'Rae' Hagen

Rachel Ross
Rachel Smith
Rachel Swan
Rae Alley
Rae Knowler
Raecchi
Raelyn D
Random Yarning
Raquel Arambula
Ravyn Winter
Ray B.
Rebeca Roeland Vergara
Rebecca (ToxicFrog) Kelly
Rebecca Crawford
Rebecca Downard
Rebecca Harbison
Rebecca Herman
Rebecca Romney
Rebecca Slitt
Rebekah Leah Moss
Rebekah Wheadon
Reese Hogan
Regina Wilson
Reid Ashley
Reija P.
Reiko Meyers
Remmik Petra
Renee G
Renée Virginia Cardineau
Rhiannon Newhouse
Rhiannon Raphael
Rhys Benson
Rich Coker
Rich Walker
Rick Cook Jr
Rick Ohnemus
Riikka Puttonen

Riley Kane
Rin Astray
Rin Seilhan
Risa Moreno
Risa Wolf
Risu Alto
River W
RJ Hopkinson
RJ Pedie
RM Ambrose
Rob Wynne & Larissa March
Robb
Robert Dahlen
Robert J R
Roberta Taylor
Robin Hill
Robin K.
Robin Portune
Robyn McGough
Rohrer
Roland Miller III
Roman Kofman
Ronald H. Miller
Roni Gosch
Roo Jones
Rosa Williams
Rose
Rose Hill
Rosie Clarke
Rosie French
Rowan Sage
Roxanna Southern
RP
RS Mason
Ruth & Colleen Dosch
Ruth Crook
Ruth Federico

Ruth P
Ruth Poultney
Ruth Swift-Wood
Ryan (Pug Majere) Anderson
Ryan Giesbrecht
Ryan Holland
Ryan J Smith
Ryan Muther
S. Barnes
S. Felkar
S. Jean
S. Lee
S.M. Beiko
Sabrina Nobile
Sade
Sadie Slater
Sally 'Wishie' Pritchard
Sam Blake
Sam Courtney
Sam Hawke
Sam Hotchkiss
Sam Jacobs
Sam Rose Clements
Sam Schwanak
Sam Squires
Sam Sussman
Samantha Herdman
Samantha Kappes
Samantha Ting
Sammy C.
Sandra Atwood
Sandro Quintana
Saphryel
Sara A. Mueller
Sara Beckman
Sara Cox
Sara Joiner

Sara Norja
Sara Rose
Sara T. Bond
Sarah Bea
Sarah Burns
Sarah Cantu
Sarah Coldheart
Sarah D
Sarah E. Andrews
Sarah Fletcher
Sarah Goslee
Sarah Hendrica Bickerton
Sarah Hester
Sarah K
Sarah Kaiser + Chris
    Granade 💔
Sarah Rivera
Sarah Schultz
Sarah Waites
Sarah Weintraub
Sarah Williams
Sari Veijalainen
Sarika Lambrix
Sariya Melody
Sasam
Sascha
Sashah Li
Scar
Scarlet
Scott King
Scott Schaper
Scylla
Seamus Quigley
Sean Anderson
Seán Byrne
Seana McGuinness
Seann Alexander

Seg&Lune
Seraphe
Serendiipitii
Serenity Dee
Serpent Moon
Seth Alter
Seth Kadath
ShadowTiger
Shana Jean Hausman
Shane VD Levune
Shannon Clark
Shannon Haddock
Shauna Roberts
Sheila Porter
Shelby Dickinson
Shelley Y
Shelly Cerullo
Shelly Tan
Shenwei Chang
Shervyn
Shiri Sondheimer
Sia
Siân Pearce
Sierra Tavasolian
Sima Sprackman
Simon Hardy
Simon L. B. Nielsen
Simone van de Steeg
Siôn
Siti Mariam BAB
SkulleryMaid
Skywings14
Smote
Snugglebutt
Sol Foster
Sophia Grace
Sophie & Bronwyn

Sophie Shufro
Sophie Virrion
Souvraya
spacevalkyries
Spirit Waite
SR Martin
starfetcher
Steph Wetch
Steph Wyeth
Stephanie
Stephanie Adams
Stephanie Burgis
Stephanie Charette
Stephanie Cranford
Stephanie Levasseur
Steve B
Steven D Warble
Steven Danielson
Stuart Chaplin
Sue Armitage
Suko
summervillain
Susan S.
Susan Tarrier
Suss Wilén
SuSu
Suzie L.
Sven Wiese
Sydney Dunstan
Sydney Stutsman
Sylph Valens
T
T. Melito
T.F.D
Taco
Takuma Okada
Talia Hibbert

Taneka Stotts & Christina McKenzie
Tansy Rayner Roberts
Tanya Marie Hern
Tara Hillegeist
Tatyana Araujo
Tayah Blanck
Team Milian Ingram
Tell B
Tempest Bonds
Termina
Terri104
Terry Fairchild
The Professor & The Poet
Thea Flurry
Thea S
Thérèse Elaine
Thimblerig
Thomas Bull
Thomas McManus
Thomas Parker
Thornae
Tia Kalla
Tia N.
Tibicina
Tif Kieft
Tiffany Meuret
Tiffany Wise
Tim B
Timothy Walsh
Tina Gilman
Tina Klassen
Tina Pancho-Bernadett
Tina Yang
TJ Berry
Tobias Wheeler
Tom Foster

Tom Zurkan
Tony Eng
Tori
Torie Catashitz
Torin Wong
Traci Collins
Tracy Adair
Tracy Tanoff
Trina
Tristan Gohring
Tsana Dolichva
Twila Oxley Price
Ty Wildwood
Tyche
Tyler Lyn Sorrow
Unabashedly Rose
Urs S Stewart
Ursula Whitcher
V Vesey
Valerie
Valerie Mores
Vanja Tizi
Veltyr Drake
Vera Vartanian
Veronica Ramshaw
Vesp
Vex Godglove
Vicki S.
Vickie R.
Victoria Camper
Vida Cruz
Viki Van Ness
Violet Moon
Viveka Nylund
Vivienne Jones
Vlad Giulvezan
Wakelyn Stewart

Wendy K Johnson
Wendy Schultz
Werewolf of London
Weronika Mamuna
Wess Wolf
Whiona
Wil Bastion
Will Vesely
Willow B. Rolin
Winnie WK
WJ Gross
Wol (Fantasy Inn)
Wren Alyssa
Xander R. Crowley
YHL
Yin
Z Aung
Zahra Linsky
Zara Petković
Zara R. Smith
Zarina Parpia
Zasabi
ZCH
Zeb Berryman
Zee!
Zen Hance
Zoe Stachel
Zoey Jones
Zupeiza
zvi LikesTV

Made in the USA
Monee, IL
05 December 2020

51039875R00208